THE WAVES TAKE YOU HOME

THE WAVES TAKE YOU HOME

A Novel

MARÍA ALEJANDRA
BARRIOS VÉLEZ

LAKE UNION
PUBLISHING

This is a work of fiction. Names, characters, organizations, places, events, and incidents are either products of the author's imagination or are used fictitiously. Otherwise, any resemblance to actual persons, living or dead, is purely coincidental.

Published by Lake Union Publishing, Seattle

www.apub.com

ISBN-13: 9781662513954 (hardcover)
ISBN-13: 9781662513947 (paperback)
ISBN-13: 9781662513961 (digital)

Cover illustration by Raxenne Maniquiz
Cover design by Adrienne Krogh

Printed in the United States of America

First Edition

To Abuela Juani,
the greatest storyteller I've ever known

CHAPTER ONE: CARACOL

Caminito was the start and the ending of this story. Since I was young, Abuela told me that my place was not in the kitchen, everywhere but in the kitchen. She feared for me the all-consuming flame that she said was life as a restaurant owner. Abuela imagined my hands with rough calluses, my mind busy with interminable thoughts of dishes and of having to cook day in and day out. She feared the idea of me merging with the strong, solid walls that encompassed her prison, a life subdued to family obligation.

But like all things forbidden, that only drew me more.

The night that changed it all, Caminito's floor was vibrating from all the foot traffic—waiters were busy with trays carrying Abuela's Colombian Spanish specialties: paella, tortilla Española, and sizzling steaks. Barranquilleros were dressed elegantly with long, flowy dresses and crisp, freshly ironed shirts. An echo of delight and laughter reverberated throughout the room. I wasn't supposed to be there; Abuela had already kicked me out once when she caught me in the kitchen with Anton, trying to help him cut some vegetables for a broth.

"Te vas a quemar! Anton, no te dije that she shouldn't be in the kitchen?"

Anton had shrugged. "Doña, yo . . ."

"Nada, no exceptions."

Anton had looked at me with those puppy eyes that meant he felt guilty. Anton was Abuela's protégé, and keeper of her culinary knowledge and the family recipes that we served at the restaurant.

But not being able to have a place in the restaurant only made me want it more. I was in love with the broths, sauces, and spices in the kitchen. The frantic rhythm of the dance that was working together on a busy night. I was in love with the sense of possibility, of everything that you could make with simple, good ingredients.

Whenever she would kick me out, I would always say, "Sí, Abuela." And then return in a moment when she was busy greeting customers. I had inherited more than her love for cooking and food—I had also inherited her stubbornness. Mamá had too.

After having been kicked out once that night already, I wasn't returning to the kitchen to cook but to tell Mamá I was going out with Rafa. Mamá didn't like him, either, but she was easier than Abuela because she was often distracted by whatever guy she was seeing.

I entered the restaurant and tried to go straight to the kitchen. Abuela was there, wearing her jet-black hair pinned up and a black skirt suit with buttons that looked like shells. She was smiling at two customers, an old couple who came to the restaurant every Friday to always have the same thing: paella to share and a bottle of rioja.

"I swear, Doña Emilia, this paella is better every time I try it," Don Víctor said, looking at his wife, Ruth, who had her face buried in her plate.

"Mm-hmm." Ruth nodded. "The best one in the city."

Abuela smiled with recognition. "Claro! We just won best paella in the city for the third time in a row—" Abuela's eyes darted to me as I crossed the sea of waiters and people who were dining at the restaurant. My heart was beating fast, and I was walking as briskly as I could, but I knew I couldn't escape her hawklike gaze. "Excuse me, one second please," she said, and I glanced briefly at Don Víctor and his wife, who were looking at each other with the knowing smiles that only those in an old but pleasant marriage can share.

"Violeta! A dónde vas?"

Abuela asked where I was going, following me as I closed the kitchen door. Mamá was there, talking on the phone and smoking a cigarette. Abuela was about to eat her alive; she had just arrived. Mamá wasn't one to linger in the restaurant; she always had plans. It had been that way since I was a kid—Abuela took care of the restaurant and of me. If Mami was a feather, Abuela was a block of cement: heavy and rooted to the ground with nowhere to go.

"What's going on here?" Abuela said, looking at Mamá hiding in a corner. Mamá didn't know whether to drop the cell phone or the cigarette first.

Abuela released a breath that could have unleashed a cyclone. "Paula, throw that away! You're going to burn down this place!"

Mamá did as told and stubbed out the cigarette with her shoe. Abuela closed her eyes and muttered something under her breath, turning her back to her daughter. "What's going on, Vi?"

At my eighteen years of age, I knew better than to say anything.

"What is it, Vi?" Mamá asked, taking a deep breath. It was impossible to relax in Abuela's kitchen.

"I am going out," I said. "I just came here to tell Mamá so you both wouldn't worry."

Abuela shook her head and walked to the sauce station, where Anton was mixing some sauces in different pans. Abuela tried the bubbling béchamel with a small spoon and told him it was good but to add more pepper and salt.

An exhalation of relief; she didn't know it, but she had loved my sauce. In secret, I had prepared that sauce with Anton to use in one of the night's specials: luscious chipotle chicken crepes with a béchamel sauce topped off with avocado. Anton said they were too heavy, but I thought they were perfect: creamy and spicy and comforting.

"Una pizquita," she said and pinched her fingers to indicate how little he needed to put in. Anton nodded, and we looked at each other. We shared that love and reverence for Abuela. When she said something, our first instinct was to obey.

"Are you going to see that plumber's son?" Abuela said, lifting the lid of the red tomato sauce that she'd spiced with paprika and red pepper flakes. The smell traveled into the kitchen. "Didn't I forbid it?"

"A-Abuela," I stammered. "You can't forbid it. I'm eighteen. You can't forbid me from doing anything anymore."

It felt right when I said it. But why was my leg shaking?

Mamá shook her head. She was softer than Abuela, but she agreed with her. "She's right, Vi. Nothing good is going to come out of that. You have the opportunity to make a life for you that's just yours. In less than a month you'll go to college in the States—the opportunity! We didn't have that. We never left this country. Who knows who I'd have been if I had done that?" Mamá tapped her feet, probably anxious for another cigarette.

Abuela set the lid on the pot as if putting a lid on my heart. "No significa no. You're not going. My ears are buzzing from all the talk in the barrio. All I hear about is you and the son of that plumber. You're going to college abroad; focus on that."

I had done all the essays and applications knowing that Abuela wouldn't let me miss this chance. For her, it was *our* chance. My visa had been approved a few months ago, and everything was ready. She had decided that this was what I needed to do. I knew it was a way of keeping me from Rafa and sending me away. Rafa said he was going to wait for me, but I didn't want to go. I loved the restaurant, and I wanted to be here, at home, with him. I could study art at the local university and then focus on my two passions: art and Caminito. I didn't need to go away, but she would never understand that. Abuela always thought she knew better.

Abuela sighed loudly and opened her mouth, ready to yell at me. I knew all the cooks at their stations wanted to look, but they couldn't; they didn't dare. Doña Emilia was as loved as she was feared, even by her own family.

"I am going," I said, pushing my shoulders back and standing tall. I tried to straighten my leg. I lifted my chin up, holding on to the fire I felt in my chest. This was the time to stand up to her; it was now or never. Rafa and I were running out of time. We needed to see each other. To figure out how we were going to stay together. "I'm going. You can tell your friends whatever you want. Lo que quieras." I snatched the keys to the car and went to the back door quickly so Abuela wouldn't have time to grab me by my dress.

"Ay, Vi. We're your mirror, mija," she said with a sadness in her voice that contained all her disappointments in love.

Mamá and I locked eyes for a moment. She was letting me go, but her gaze was telling me to stay. Was this a test?

"Vete pues, no te vas?" Abuela lifted her thin eyebrow. *Weren't you leaving?*

I gripped the keys of the car, my hand shaking. She was challenging me to disobey her. To see if I would even dare.

"You're eighteen, you're right. If you want to be with that bueno-para-nada, I can't stop you. Go! Make your mistakes, like we have."

I remembered Rafa's words from the night before, when I had sneaked out of my house to see him. We had been worrying about so many things: If I had to go to the States, could we do long distance? Could I stay? I was eighteen. If I made that decision, would Mamá and Abuela ever forgive me?

Rafa had taken my hands between his and said, "Just because Abuela and Mamá said no to us, we can't say no to ourselves. We have to fight."

I turned back and walked out of the kitchen, feeling the fire in my step. My family's journey had been cemented by decisions of leaving, staying, and setting paths on fire that might have taken them on kinder, better roads. Abuela said my name one last time, and after that, she raised her voice, not caring if the whole restaurant could hear her.

"Violeta," she yelled from the kitchen. "I just want what's best for you. One day you'll see."

I kept walking, one foot in front of the other, leaving Abuela and Mamá behind.

~

Rafa was the cause of every fight Abuela and I had ever since I was fifteen.

That night, Rafa took me to the beach. Our beaches in Barranquilla didn't have crystalline blue water or white sand, but after dusk, the sky was covered in stars, and the breeze had its own melody. Everything was ready for my departure: the visa, the dorm, the winter clothes. I was going to school in Vermont, an opportunity that very few people in Colombia had. We weren't rich—far from it—and I knew that it was a sacrifice for us. Then why was I so unhappy? I grabbed Rafa's hand; he was the only one who understood why I didn't want to leave. I was in love with him. But not only him: I loved the rhythms of the restaurant, walking the streets of Barrio Prado in the afternoon, being with Abuela. I was happy here; I didn't get why I had to leave. Not even Anton was supportive of my reluctance. "It's a good opportunity. I would love to study abroad," Anton had said, his hands already covered in little cuts by the age of eighteen.

I knew. There were years—no, decades—of sacrifice that Abuela had endured in order to open Caminito and then to have enough to send me to the States. My body was equal parts guilt for not appreciating the opportunity and love for Rafa.

Rafa and I had so much in common. His parents had deposited all their dreams on him. Rafa dreamed of music, but he knew he had to be a doctor. On his broad shoulders, he was carrying dreams inherited from his family.

"Rafa." The word left my lips. Rafa's brown eyes were cloudy, as if he were somewhere else. "What's wrong?"

I pushed his dark, thick hair back and kissed his forehead. I knew what was wrong. Neither of us wanted to part ways. He'd said that he would wait for me—but it wasn't the same. We didn't want to be apart.

Rafa was wearing a white guayabera and formal pants. Why so elegant? I was wearing a thin red flowered dress that flowed in the wind. When I held his hand, I realized it was shaking.

"Nada, I'm just . . ." Rafa opened his deep-brown eyes wide. "Nervous. That's all."

The playa was empty. Nothing was around but the sound of the wind going and returning. Our life together felt like it was stretching, and we were jumping ahead, just to return to this beach, to this moment. My heart jumped.

"Ay!" I covered my mouth with my hands when I saw him on one knee. His legs trembled. I was eighteen, and he was twenty-one, and I had never felt younger than at that moment. "Rafa!" I said, my eyes wide, not believing what I was seeing.

I looked up at the full white moon—the only witness of what was about to happen. My heart was beating fast, and the pressure in my chest was the first sign that something was not right.

"Vi . . ." He looked up as he opened a tiny dark-blue box. "Would you marry me?"

His voice was breaking, and I wasn't sure what to say. I wanted to stay, I did; I didn't want to leave him. But we were so young. Marriage was complicated in my family. A story of men who left, or men who stayed and made life hell. The men in our family had not been kind, and the women in my family had the scars to prove it. Passion and love weren't things that ended well for us.

If I married young, just like Abuela and Mamá had married, would my life be an extension of theirs?

Sí: the word was on the tip of my tongue, and yet I couldn't say it. I knew why he was proposing. If we got married, and we showed everyone that we were serious, Abuela couldn't make me leave. Right? I was sure I loved him, that I wanted a life with him, everything with him. I opened my mouth to speak, but it was as if Abuela had put a spell on my tongue so words would not come out. Only air. Instead, my head was swirling with thoughts. Thoughts of my life in the States, about how he could afford the ring, of Abuela's rage. Her voice at the restaurant, saying, "I just want what's best for you, mija."

Did she know something I didn't? Was life in the States what was right for me?

What if I wasn't old enough to know what was best for me?

I dropped to my knees so I would be at eye level with him. I put his face in between my hands. "Rafa," I said as softly as I could, already regretting the words that I was about to say. At that moment, I let fear wash over me, pushing love aside. "I . . ."

"Sí?" Rafa said, still holding the box.

"How could you afford this ring?" I suddenly said. In my voice, I could hear Abuela's harshness. The tone of voice she used when she spit out her venom when people didn't do what she thought was best.

The ring had a single band with an esmeralda in the middle. He had probably bought it at the city center, where there were thousands of Lebanese jewelers who crafted beautiful pieces and sold them cheaper than at the stores in el Norte. But still, he couldn't afford anything there or anywhere. I wondered if he had used the money for his next semester of med school to pay for it. Rafa and his family had money only for the necessities. I stared at it, trying not to feel too much, knowing deeply that this ring was not mine. Rafa couldn't afford something like that without depriving himself and his family of things they needed. We had to return it.

"I just did, no te preocupes." *Don't worry.* Rafa was still kneeling, sand blowing in the wind and me huddling in front of him. The beach was silent, and it appeared as if we were the only ones on it. A pain burned in my chest, as I knew that this moment was not ours, that the salt in the air and on my eyelashes and on the tip of my tongue was warning me against getting carried away. Rafa was a practical man, and yet his spirit had room for dreams of us getting married, building a life together, despite our age.

Rafa was waiting for the answer he wanted, the only logical answer to him.

"How are you going to pay for med school next semester, ah?" I said, tears welling up.

"No te preocupes." Rafa was unmovable. "I'll figure it out. What do you say, Vi?" Whenever he pronounced my name, my knees trembled. Back then, I'd thought I could never say no to Rafa.

"Ajá, where are we going to live?" I asked, considering my life in the States for the first time without the influence of Mami and Abuela. What if I could make a path that was different for myself?

It didn't feel like a decision I had made on my own, and yet it was a decision that would make my life different from the ones the women in my family had lived. In Barranquilla, the future looked back at me with the faces of Abuela and Mami. The lives that had been shrunk by men and duty. Possibility in their lives was nothing but a word.

"I'll get us a place. No te preocupes." Rafa looked at me, and I knew then, in the glimmer that was diminishing in his dark eyes, that he had realized I wasn't going to say yes.

"Rafa, why don't we get up, and we can talk about this?" There would be many years and sleepless nights where this moment, the memory of Rafa's eyes on the beach that night, would freeze my bones more than any day in the harsh northern winter could.

"I won't move until you give me an answer." Rafa's voice came out trembling. I wondered if he was about to cry.

"We're so young, Rafa," I said, as if I were apologizing, my voice breaking. "We have so much time."

Rafa closed the box as quickly as one closes a book they're done with.

"I'm afraid to think there's no later for us, Vi," Rafa said, getting up. "I don't know, once you move to the States, maybe you won't come back." He extended his hand for me to help me up, and then he walked in the direction of the road.

I was convinced I would be back. Rafa's eyes had welled up with tears, and as I ran behind him, I knew that I couldn't let go. He was an extension of me—I knew his touch, his smell. The way he dreamed harder than anyone I knew and held on to the ones he loved. After his father had died shortly after Rafa turned seventeen, he had known that people weren't eternal. I wondered at that moment, lifting my long dress up to not fall, if we were eternal, as I had believed until then. If we could make it.

"Of course I'll come back. Where are you going?" I said, trying to keep up, running out of breath.

"We could still catch a taxi, if we rush."

"Rafa, look at me."

Rafa turned back. He wiped his eyes with the back of his hand quickly, in one single movement. Ay, his pride. His dad had taught him the importance of hard work and also of pride for the men of Barranquilla. These were something to safeguard because they were the only things people couldn't take away.

"I'll come back; you're my heart. I'll come back for you." My lip was quivering, but I couldn't break down. I wasn't the one being told no.

I pulled him to me and held on tight. Something in the air indicated finality to the night. "I promise," I said to him. "I will." Rafa kissed my hair.

"I will," I kept saying, but deep down I knew.

The same way that the wind never blew twice, not in the same way, I knew that I would never get that ring—that moment—back.

Rafa and I would never be the same.

~

The next few days I spent in my room, blinds shut and with my head under a pillow. Abuela tried to get me out of the room—she even gave me a once-in-a-lifetime opportunity to cook in the kitchen, no need to hide. "Sólo esta vez," *just this once*, she said, standing at the door. When I didn't answer, she knocked even harder. "Violeta, I don't know what happened that night, but you're going to the US. Está decidido."

Rafa wouldn't pick up the phone. I tried again and again, my heart in my throat every time he didn't pick up. Had I messed this up? But how could I say yes? Too young, we were too young.

I even went to his house multiple times. Doña Magdalena, his mother, would open the door. A worried expression on her face: "Mija, qué pasó?" I shrugged, not ready to tell her what happened. Had he even told her he was going to propose? Probably not. She loved me, but even she would have told him that we were too young. He needed to focus on school.

"He doesn't want to talk right now," she said, standing in the doorway. "But I'll tell him you came. I'm sorry, mija . . . he's not talking to me either."

I spoke to friends, and no one had seen him or talked to him.

Every time after going to his house, I would come home defeated. I hadn't showered in days; I just couldn't understand how we had lost it all so fast. Why couldn't we just talk about it? I was about to leave for the US, and we wouldn't even get to say goodbye.

"Mija." Abuela spoke through the door. "I'm worried."

Silence. I wouldn't dare say a word. I knew her—this had been her doing. I didn't trust her.

"Just come out. For a little while." I could hear Abuela's breathing on the other side of the door. Her face pressed to the wood.

I let out a sigh. My pillow was damp, and my eyes were probably small from crying so much.

I tried calling him once more. Nothing. Just the lonely tone of an unanswered phone. "Rafa," I said to the wind, because no one was there with me. "Just pick up."

~

A couple of days after, still not having spoken to Rafa, I left the room. Leaving felt like telling Abuela she was right. Those days, I had a pressure in my chest I couldn't shake. Everything in my life felt decided at that moment. I was only eighteen, and I was so scared of arriving in a different country where I didn't know anyone and no one knew me.

Abuela was outside, pretending to clean, but I knew she was waiting for me.

"Ya?" she asked. What she was really asking was whether I was done crying. She was wearing a cinched-at-the-waist cream dress and her pearl earrings.

I nodded, my head saying yes, but my spirit was still confused. "I can go." I swallowed hard, thinking that there was no way that she wouldn't let me stay. Perhaps being somewhere else would help me forget Rafa. I could start over. It's not like she wanted me in the restaurant, anyway. "If you want me to go, I'll do it," I said softly, looking down.

Abuela lifted my chin slowly. Her dark eyes were looking straight at me. "You're making the right choice, Vi. I promise." Her voice was so assuring and definite. I believed her.

~

Abuela didn't talk about her childhood years much, or her youth. Bisabuela, her mom, had been an elegant woman, with green eyes and silver hair from an early age that she wore pinned up. She was taller than all of us, different from the rest of the family. Her skin was milk white, but her luck with men was also not great.

Bisabuela had been married to an anthropologist, a bitter man who found pleasure only in booze, dominoes, and books. Bisabuela used to say only two things came out of that marriage: Abuela's birth and an invaluable lesson about time.

When I was little, Abuela was not like the other grandmothers. Not a maternal bone in her body, she would sit me down on her lap, on her favorite sofa in the living room, with a glass of scotch in her right hand. Abuela was not one to like kids' stories, but ghosts and family tales—perhaps, I realize now, in our family they were the same thing. As she shook the ice in her whiskey glass, she would tell me about Bisabuelo and Bisabuela.

In the sixties Bisabuelo had spent six months with the Misak indigenous people studying the way they viewed time. This tribe didn't believe in linear time but in circular time, where there is no beginning or end but a loop. Time was not a line but a snail-shaped circle, everything always returning to the center.

"What about months or years?"

Abuela would shake her hand, as if she were dismissing an old part of herself. A person she had shed like old skin.

"Who knows?" She stared at the wall, as if she were seeing something that was no longer there. "Those were just some things your bisabuela believed. After her husband told her that story, she was obsessed with the idea that time repeated itself. We were always returning to the center. Pero sabes, it is true that sometimes you find yourself in the middle of a moment, and you say to yourself, 'Yo he vivido esto antes.'" *I have lived this before.* ". . . No?"

I didn't know. Not yet, so I would shake my head.

That night, under the bright moon of Barranquilla, Rafa had disappeared from my life.

Proving that perhaps my luck with men was no different than that of the rest of the women's in my family who had come before me.

But what I had ignored was that life always had a way of pushing you toward the center of the caracol, where you belonged.

Life always found a way of making you return.

CHAPTER TWO: BROOKLYN

Living in New York was a dream until the days that it felt more like a nightmare. Going down the stairs with five posters and a bag stuffed with other illustrations, my iPad, and a warm sweater, I told myself that another day in the city was another day closer to my dream of being able to sustain myself with my illustrations. I heard Abuela's voice in my head: "Sarna con gusto, no pica . . . ," which translated to something as outrageous as *Scabies with pleasure does not itch*. Abuela would always grin and make me finish the sentence: "Y si pica . . . ," *and if it itches*, and then I would have to say back, "No mortifica."

And if it stings, it doesn't kill.

Abuela had been a cancer patient for two years, and in the last six months it had progressed even more. Abuela no longer joked as much as she used to. Her jokes were replaced by a string of complaints. In New York I was always rushing, but even in the in-between moments I was always thinking about her. How had she spent the night? Was she eating? But those thoughts were always taken over by the next task.

As soon as I tried to open the door to the building with one hand, the five posters ended up on the floor, and I had to kneel to get them, and then my phone started buzzing.

It was Liam. Had he forgotten something when he left the house in a rush that morning? I put all the posters under one arm and picked up the phone between my shoulder and my ear.

"Amor, what's up?" I said, harsher than I intended. "Sorry, I . . . need to take posters to Ollie in Bushwick, and then I need to run to Union Square for another appointment. What is it?"

I should have zipped my coat up. But now it was too late; both of my hands were occupied.

"I just knew you had a big day ahead. I wanted to see if Ollie liked the illustrations."

"I'm just leaving the house."

There was a pause on the phone, which meant Liam was checking his watch. "But Vi, it's ten thirty a.m. I thought you were meeting him at nine thirty. It's going to take you at least half an hour to get there."

"Uh . . . the posters needed some finishing touches. I . . . messed up."

"It's okay, Ollie is nice, he will—"

"Liam, I love you. I need to run down the stairs and get these posters to Ollie, okay?"

"Okay, do you want me to call you an Uber? Might be faster."

I hesitated. I did. But I also did not feel good receiving his help, after he had pointed out I was late. It was my own fault, as it often was. I needed to climb out of this hole myself.

"Sorry, can't talk. It's okay. I'll figure it out." From an early age, Abuela had taught me that the most important thing was to assume consequence. I had made the mistake of lingering in the apartment working on the posters; now I had to figure it out on my own.

This part of my routine was familiar. In Brooklyn, I always felt that I was racing faster than my thoughts. I was never on time for anything.

On the subway, I bit my nails for the whole ten-minute commute, and then I ran from Montrose for ten minutes until I reached Ollie's house and got in the industrial elevator in his building, trying to catch my breath.

That elevator was rustic and old, and it made too much sound for it to be working properly. If I had more time, I would've taken the stairs, but I needed to be at work at twelve. I checked the phone; there was a text from Liam saying to call if I needed anything. It was already eleven.

My heart was racing from running, and when Ollie opened the door, I was still recouping my breath.

"Vi!" he said. "Come in. Are you okay?"

He wasn't wearing a shirt, and his hair was disheveled. He smelled like cigarettes and rum—on a Monday. I was glad to see him, even if I thought I could stop breathing at any moment. I dropped the posters on the wooden table and went to the kitchen and served myself a tall glass of water. I held a finger in the air to tell him I needed a second before I could speak.

Ollie closed the door and walked to the kitchen to greet me. He planted two kisses on my sweaty cheeks. It was a habit he had adopted ever since he came home from a two-week trip to Spain.

When I set the empty glass on the counter, I realized how glad I was to see him. Ollie was my favorite boss I'd ever had in this city and a good friend. When I was working for him, he had told me that I needed to quit his restaurant and work on illustration full time. I had what it took. He was the one who gave me the final push. And now here I was, three years later, still working freelance. Every month I worked harder than the one before, and every month I struggled even more to pay bills.

"Damn." He laughed. "I should've put on a shirt."

I had seen him without a shirt so many times. Once at the restaurant he had taken his shirt off because it was too hot in the summer in the kitchen. It wasn't long until one of the chefs told him to put his stupid shirt on. Ollie laughed. "Of course, of course," he had said, because he was like that.

I liked Ollie; the way he lived life was different from the way I was raised. I was brought up to have my guard up and be vigilant. People didn't always have the best intentions. But Ollie had the luxury of being open, trusting.

"Coffee?"

"Please." I walked to the reclaimed wood table I loved so much and put my hands on the surface, taking in the craftsmanship of the wood. Quick coffee. Show him the posters. Leave.

Although Ollie always looked fresh from the bedcovers, his house was clean and inviting. I took my coat off and left it on a brick-red chair. I counted the posters and was able to breathe when I realized I still had five and I hadn't lost them on my way here.

I unrolled them and put them on the table, one by one. The posters were for the annual fundraising weekend event that Ollie threw at his restaurant, Santuario. Liam and I never missed it. There was a party on Friday night, cinema day on Saturday, followed by a chef's family-style dinner, a small artisans' event on Sunday, and last a chef's barbeque. I had made posters for all the events, which meant that the margin for little errors and changes was big but the timeline was not. In Ollie fashion, he had called me on Friday to do the posters, which meant not a lot of time. All weekend, I had sat on my drawing chair, thinking about each poster that would capture the Mexican American spirit of his restaurant and the artistic community vibe it had.

Ollie paid better than any of my other clients. "Dios," I muttered under my breath. "Let these posters be okay. I need this to be okay." He approached me with a cup of coffee. Ollie was not good at keeping romantic relationships, or at real-life stuff like keeping a shirt on, but he was good at making coffee.

"The first sip of this coffee is the best part of my day so far," I said, taking in a hint of wild berries and caramel.

"Café de la Sierra," he said. "Not too far from Barranquilla, right?"

I felt a pang in my chest when I heard the name of my hometown, thinking about the majestic mountains of the sierra that had inspired the first poster. I closed my eyes, feeling the foam on my feet on a warm beach. The film of sweat that would linger on my skin every day at Barrio Prado—light and airy dresses, a taste for a warm beer after a long sunny afternoon. "Not too far," I said, not letting myself linger in the memory.

"Vi, Vi," he said. "I love this." He was looking at the first poster, picking it up. Ollie did not like computers—he liked paper, and he always insisted on seeing printed versions of everything. He looked at it up close, as if he were looking at a rare painting.

"I love the creatures and the mountains on the back."

I had drawn light-blue abstract figures hiding in the chain of mountains of the sierra, surrounded by the vast red flowers, palm trees, and wild animals. Colombia and Barrio Prado were colors to me. I leaned into the deep oranges and the cerulean blues that made you think of the ocean. The warmth of the smiles, the harshness of the soles of your feet against the warm sand.

"What about the lettering? The date, the details?" I said, already feeling jittery. Ollie's coffee was strong.

He read the poster out loud—"Perfect"—and then examined the others. I favored bright colors in my work, monsters and creatures inspired by legends and family stories. I loved sketching the lush mountains, the flowers I grew up with, and the colors of home. The empty streets of my old neighborhood that I was convinced were plagued by ghosts.

"I can't believe you did all this on the weekend."

I had deep rims under my eyes to prove it, and I thought I was developing a low fever from not sleeping.

"I know." I shook my head, thinking that one day I would have a client that would give me a proper timeline to work in. After art school in Vermont, I'd moved to New York to pursue my illustration dream, working in restaurants to support myself at first. Mamá and Abuela had been so upset about it. "We didn't send you to the States to work at a restaurant." But I had to survive somehow. The rhythms of the restaurant, especially Santuario, had been comforting. They were a tune I recognized.

I had slowly been getting more and more illustration clients, and balancing the different projects was still as hard as it had been at first.

One day it would get easier. "That's why you need to triple-check the dates and the details."

A high-pitched ring sounded on my phone. My watch said 11:30 a.m. "That's my alarm. I need to leave. I have an appointment with the publisher at twelve p.m." I grabbed my coat and gave him a kiss on the cheek. In Colombia, we greeted people with only one kiss.

Ollie checked his phone. "Isn't that the mean woman? Don't you hate that job?" He took another look at the poster, as if it were a treasured possession instead of a piece of paper.

"Yes. But I love paying rent. Sorry, gotta run. You know she hates me. I mean, when I'm late." I zipped up my coat. I was still warm from running all the way to his house.

"Vi, what have I told you? Time is finite. It slips through your fingers. You shouldn't do stuff you hate."

I smiled and walked closer to him. I threw my arms around him and gave him a quick hug. "I also have so many bills, and"—I checked my watch—"half an hour to get to Union Square."

"I'll take you. Let me get my keys."

"Okay," I said, taking one last sip of the coffee. "And a shirt," I reminded him. "Ollie! And a coat."

~

Ollie drove an old olive-green truck that was always full of supplies for the restaurant and paper.

He made room in the truck for me, which meant I was sandwiched between an old computer and documents from the restaurant that he stored in the car. If it was up to Ollie, he would file his taxes on an old typewriter.

We listened to some soft classical music.

"It's Icelandic."

I burst out laughing, glad of the distraction from being late for work but feeling more feverish. "Why does it always have to be like that with you? Why can't it just be classical music; why does it need to be from Iceland or something?"

He looked at me and smiled, and then directed his eyes at the road. "I have good taste, that's all."

We drove in silence as we crossed the Brooklyn Bridge. Whenever I approached the bridge and got closer to this job—freelance work illustrating books for early readers—I would start developing an itch. The job had a crazy quick turnaround. They would send me batches of books to illustrate in a couple of weeks. I had started this job on the side as a way to earn money, but it had consumed me. I knew I wasn't paid fairly, but I was scared of letting the job go. It was steady money, and the competition in New York was ruthless.

My palms started sweating, and my mouth got dry. I wanted to run, but I couldn't get out of the car. I was being driven to my self-imposed sentence. I couldn't tell Ollie what I felt because he was always telling me to freaking quit that job. Quit, quit, quit. Do jobs that you love. He was like Liam, and they had grown up with certain opportunities. They didn't understand that there were things and obligations that tied you to the world when you were an immigrant woman of color. I couldn't just "quit." I needed to make rent, to justify my stay here, to always be proving myself.

"So how are things with Liam?"

My hands froze even though all the windows were closed. How were things with Liam? That was a great question. We had been together for four years, and we loved each other and the life we had built together. It was a quiet life. A good life—respectable.

"Good," I said, realizing that it hadn't come out as convincing as I pictured. "Good, I mean, big talks, you know." Lately Liam had started talking about marriage and kids. It was a natural conversation, after four years together. But our life was full of contrasts. We were both twenty-eight years old, but I was broke; he was not. I was an immigrant, and his parents were two wealthy academics from New York City. Although we were both comfortable in the relationship, I didn't feel ready to head in that direction yet. So much seemed up in the air at the moment, job wise and in my mediocre bank account. I needed to be settled first; I wanted to make my family proud before I got married.

"How are you doing?" I asked, trying to divert attention.

"Oh, Vi, you know me . . . I never stay with anyone for too long." He turned to look at me for a second. "Are you happy?"

"Yes," I said, looking at the landscape, the buildings in Manhattan spreading in front of me. I was happy. Many people wanted this life—New York, fighting for your dreams and knowing that sacrifice often did not come cheap and dreams didn't come true when you were just having a good time. This was part of growing up. I was building a life that belonged to me and no one else, on my terms. Away from family, I could build a life away from their opinions.

"You know what I always tell you?" Ollie said, entering Manhattan and letting out a sigh. "I am twelve years older than you."

"Fourteen," I interrupted. Ollie was forty-two, even if he didn't like to admit it.

"All right, Vi. You don't have to do all the things you think you should do. Finding yourself in a bit of a mess is good sometimes."

I smiled weakly at him. Santuario had gone bankrupt a couple of times; he had been close to losing it all, and yet he had managed to survive and to turn things around. Ollie was no stranger to reinvention. However, there was something worn out in his spirit. He was like a light that was always dim and flickering, despite his endless generosity to his friends and his community. I didn't want that either. I wanted to build a life that I was happy with.

"We're here," he said, as he parked in front of the building.

The bitterness in my mouth came back, the warmth in my forehead.

"You don't have to," Ollie said.

I gave him a quick hug and nodded. "But I do." I got out of the car and closed the door behind me, my legs suddenly made out of cement. Every step was a struggle.

I opened the door to the tall building and looked up, the sight of it making me feel small, and I closed my eyes—telling myself that perhaps I was closer to making my dreams come true and getting paid more for my work. Maybe it was a matter of working harder, right?

"Right?" I said out loud. "Right," I repeated, walking to the door of the building.

The elevator ride was silent; I was the only one there. I pressed the number 20, and as the car went up, an emptiness set up on my stomach that reminded me of that plane from Colombia to the US, ten years ago. How sweaty my palms were, and how utterly alone and scared I felt as the plane landed in the unknown.

The elevator doors opened to the publisher's office. My boss was already waiting for me.

"Vi," Charlie said, a smile planted on her face. She pushed her wavy yellow locks away from her shoulders. "Thrilled you could make it."

Was she being sarcastic? It was hard to tell with Charlie; she always ran on a passive-aggressive—or aggressive aggressive—nervous energy. I should apologize, right? Best to be safe.

I gripped the portfolio. "Sorry," I muttered. "The train—" I started to make an excuse.

"We don't have all day, let's go." She put a hand on my back and started walking with me to her office. I tried to keep the pace, feeling the eyes of the secretary and the rest of the office as I followed Charlie in her impossible high heels.

~

Obedient. That's how I was raised. Mami was always running off, and she often left me with Abuela to take care of me. Abuela raised a daughter with little help from her husband and had built a Spanish Colombian restaurant in Barranquilla, Colombia, with the help of her mother. She didn't have time for me to protest about not wanting to eat something or wanting to go to the park. No es no. *No means no.* I internalized it, so much so that sitting in that office under the white lights, I feared that I still hadn't found my voice to fight back.

Charlie handed me back the iPad and closed her eyes. Her forehead no longer moved, as a product of her Botox appointments every month, but I had known her long enough to know she was upset.

"I thought I said I wanted bright oranges, happy colors." Her voice was calm, reflective, as if she were suggesting something rather than stating it.

"Yes," I said, taking back the iPad and looking at the illustrations myself. This was a book about emotions for kids and how they can resemble the weather and seasons. The author had a vision of doing the book all in shades of blue and lavender, soft colors. I wanted to honor her vision, but Charlie often said that kids deserved happy colors. But did kids deserve only one thing?

"But the author mentioned—"

Charlie sighed as Alma, her secretary, opened the door with a matcha oat milk latte and a work phone in the other.

"Sally is on the line for you."

Charlie rolled her eyes and stared right at me, as if she could smell my fear of not being able to pay rent every month. "Vi, we've worked together for a long time. You're one of the freelancers I hire the most." She stood up and straightened the invisible wrinkles on her structured navy-blue dress. "But this only works if you listen to me. Do you work for me or for the author?"

I looked behind me and exchanged glances with Alma, who shot me a look that said, *Don't answer that.*

"You understand?"

No, I wanted to say. This was the author's vision—not mine, not Charlie's. My job was to support her words and bring them to life.

"But—" I tried to say, but Charlie was already walking.

"Change the colors on this thing and send it to me tonight."

I could not possibly do that. I needed to choose a new color palette; I needed to try different things and change the illustrations to fit the colors. An image of me working late at night on my iPad flashed in my head, a premonition of how that night was going to go. No way. "I can't possibly—"

Charlie shrugged. "I believe in you. You should have listened to me," she said, already through the door.

Alma stood there, holding the door open for me. Her lips mouthed an apology. I walked out of the office, feeling eyes on me again. I probably wasn't the only freelancer leaving the office deflated like that. I took a deep breath, feeling the weight of the olive-green bag I carried around all over New York City with illustrations, my iPad, and my computer. This city had the power of making you feel like everything was possible, and at the same time making you feel invisible.

~

When I got home, it was already dark. The table was full of sketches, notebooks, and pencils from all the work I had been doing these past few days. Even if I illustrated mostly digitally, I liked to start ideas on physical paper. That night I was supposed to be illustrating some food menus for a neighborhood restaurant, and now I needed to rework my illustrations for Charlie—vibrant oranges and yellows mixed with cerulean blue were in my head. I sat on the couch for a minute, my eyes closing and my body drifting softly, as if I were at sea.

Liam didn't like mess. But my body was so tired, oh so tired. I let the warm waves I grew up with carry my tired bones.

"Babe." I heard a familiar voice as Liam entered the apartment. The steps I had memorized in four years of being together. "Brought home takeout from the Thai place down the street you've been wanting to try. I figured you'd be too tired to go out." The sound of keys being dropped on the counter reached my ears.

My eyelids were made out of cement. "You're home." My voice was caught in between being awake and asleep.

"I'm home," Liam said as he approached and kissed me on the lips. "I'm home."

That night, I hugged him a little tighter than I would normally. Liam always smelled the same, like mint soap and aftershave. His cheeks and neck always kept warm, despite the cold. He'd say it was because he was born in a place with seasons; every year his body would wait for the winter. But I knew this was something special about him—some people were not able to hold on to the warmth.

"Hey," he said softly.

I kissed him again, more intensely this time. He got on the couch without taking off his coat and lay on top of me. Even after four years of our being together, his kisses were still intense like the first day. This is why I live here, I told myself. This was part of my dream too.

The passion I had felt for Rafa had the power to blind me, until at times I didn't feel like I was able to think straight. But with Liam I felt clearheaded and safe. Passion, I had been taught, was like walking in a room in the dark—you never knew when you were going to misstep.

"You okay?" Liam stopped for a second. My face felt warm since I'd napped with my winter coat on. "You're so warm. Do you need some Tylenol?"

"I'm okay," I assured him. "Just a little stressed with work, and worried about Abuela." I put a hand on his face. "But I'm okay. If I'm with you, I'm okay."

~

Liam and I had met in Bushwick at 8:00 p.m. in January four years before, when I was twenty-four years old and ready to give up on New York. It was a dark winter night, one of those where the wind was hissing and moving around the city with such a force you might think it was about to whisk everything away. I had been in the city for a couple of years after art school in Vermont, and the winter had sucked me dry. So far in New York, reality had been cold and bland. Too many roommates, mice-infested apartments, and living with people who were always turning off the heater to save money. A body-aching loneliness that seeped into my bones and never went away. The struggle had gone on for too long for me to appreciate the city. I was hating the place in silence, too afraid to tell anyone that after all these years, I didn't feel like I thought I was supposed to feel. I didn't feel at home; I felt tired. That night when Liam and I met, I was too aware of how much I had started gritting my teeth and taking deep breaths in order to not clench my mouth at all times. Before I met Liam, I'd started longing for home. I started toying with the possibility of going home for a while to "recharge," but that was usually shut down by Abuela. "It's normal to struggle, mija. It will all come together." I didn't press, because I wasn't ready to see Rafa.

"Are you okay?" Liam had asked, looking over my shoulder, studying the snack table. Chips and dips were spread out on a rough wood table that had seen better days. What I noticed first about him were his sea-colored eyes and his confident smile. He talked to me like he had known me my whole life.

"Yeah, why do you ask?"

"Well, you're taking deep breaths, and this is a party, I don't know." He swung his glass of wine to the side.

I chuckled. Most days I thought I was invisible, but it turned out people actually noticed me in this city. Or at least he did.

I opened my mouth and pointed at my bottom teeth. "See this?" I asked him, and he nodded, slouching a little to get a closer look. "I used to have perfectly aligned teeth, but now that I live here, my teeth are messed up. I'm gritting them too much at night."

"Are you sure?"

"Positive." I closed my mouth and took the last sip of wine.

"Mm-hmm. Well, I guess you could go to the dentist for a second opinion." Liam winked and rested his body on the snack table to mimic mine. I was aware of how close I was to this stranger at that moment. I could smell his pine forest cologne, which would be present in my life for years to come.

"Well." I paused and looked at my empty plastic cup. "Can't afford a dentist."

"Ah," he said dramatically, turning to grab a bottle of wine from the table. It was a screw cap, obviously. "An artist."

"By the way you're saying that, I assume you're not."

"Nope. Sold out a long time ago."

"That's good."

"Why do you say that?" I enjoyed the sound of him liberally pouring wine in our plastic cups.

"This wine is probably crap." He handed me my cup, and I took a sip, tasting the sweetness of cheap wine.

"I brought that."

Liam looked at me for a couple of seconds, his blue eyes wide. Then his expression shifted from an expressionless blank slate into a warm smile. He chuckled, and I laughed.

"You're good," he said.

"Oh, but I did bring it." I smiled back. "See, that's why I say that's good you sold out. I can't afford good wine either. Or to learn about wine so I can bring less shitty wine to parties."

"Oh, but . . ." Liam stayed quiet for a bit as if he was searching for something. "What's your name?"

"Violeta. But everyone calls me Vi. Yours?"

"Liam."

"I've never met anyone called Liam. It's like a name from a rom-com."

"Well, what I was going to say, Vi, is that no one cares what kind of wine you bring to these kinds of parties."

I looked around. People were drinking Tecates and taking vodka shots. Liam was right.

"That beer is probably warm," I said, looking at him and letting myself get lost in his blue eyes as he moved a piece of caramel hair out of his face. It had been six years since I had seen Rafa, six years since I had turned down his proposal and he had disappeared. And yet every time I met someone, I felt a stone in my heart—as if I were betraying him.

"It probably tastes like pee at this point," I said with a smile, trying to recover from my drifting thoughts to the past. I remember at that moment his arm was brushing mine. I was aware of how warm his skin was, and I wanted to move closer, to find a warm corner where I could take refuge from the freezing city.

"I know a wine bar around here. You know, they'll probably have better stuff."

"That's not hard," I said, taking another sip of the sweet wine and then putting it down. It tasted like waking up in the middle of the night hungover. "I need to say goodbye to Ollie," I said and quickly scanned the room to look for him. I saw him kissing a woman in the corner who was not his girlfriend. "Oh well." I paused, thinking about how I was going to hear about it the next morning. I rolled my eyes; hopefully they would have the fight at home instead of at Santuario. "Well, I can't say goodbye now. Let me grab my coat."

I walked to a stranger's bedroom where my coat was. I knew that this was a significant moment: I had met a person who would play an important role in my life. It was the way that he looked at me with such familiarity, and the way that we joked around like old friends. Liam from the first moment felt like home in a city that constantly felt like all other homes were occupied. I grabbed my burnt-orange wool coat, anxious to get back to him.

Liam was already at the door; I hadn't seen him say goodbye to anyone. Who had invited him? His gaze was confident and even happy when he looked at me from across the room as I made my way up to him. He gave me his arm, and it was solid and strong as we made our way down the stairs.

"I like your coat," he said, looking at my trench coat, never letting go of my arm. I held on a little too strongly, happy to leave the noise of the party behind.

~

Four years later, life with Liam was still as lovely as that first day. I called Abuela right after we ate. Ever since she got sick, a couple of years ago, I would call her every day. Sometimes we would talk for a few minutes, and sometimes for hours. The way her voice would light up on the phone every time she heard my voice had the power to turn around the worst days.

My fever was getting worse, and little drops of sweat were accumulating on my forehead. I had made some progress with the colors; every figure that had been blue was now orange and yellow. It didn't look right, but this was what Charlie wanted.

In a week I was going to visit Abuela. The cancer that had taken hold of her body was now spreading like a dark haunted vine. What had started as ovarian cancer had now spread to her lungs. The doctors said initially that she could live five more years; now it was only one.

I needed to go home, and I needed to be next to her. Now that the cancer had progressed, sometimes she didn't pick up the phone for our daily calls. She claimed that the disease had made her more deaf than before. But I knew that it was the pain. Sometimes talking took so much strength from her. My emotions oscillated in between feeling guilty and anticipating grief: a dread that I was able to feel from my head to my toes. Tears would come to me at random moments, in the middle of the night. I struggled to imagine what life would be without her, how I was supposed to go on in a life where she had always guided me.

I saw Abuela once or twice a year when I went home. She no longer stood up like a statue but now she drooped like clothes on a hanger. Her eyes had lost the spark of before.

Every time I called Abuelita, my heart beat fast—every call had the potential to be the last. *Please pick up. Abuelita, pick up.*

"Mija." Abuela's voice. I let out a sigh of relief. She sounded sleepy, and her voice was quieter than usual. But she was alive. *One more week,* I thought.

"What's new?" she asked.

I smiled as my teeth chattered, the cold seeping into my bones.

"Oh, nada. Liam cooked breakfast, Abuelita. Everything's fine." I paused. "Well, I'm still having trouble with that Charlie woman; she's so stubborn."

"Mija, but you can't let yourself be a doormat; you need to stand up for yourself. Those gringos are weird, and if you don't stand your ground, they're going to order you around."

I smiled, thinking that Abuela was quick to give orders, and she was okay with me doing what I was told, if it came from her. But with others I needed to be strong. Just as she had raised me. Without needing to close my eyes, I could see her shifting in her chair and putting her feet up, getting ready to give me one of her signature lectures.

My forehead was burning. I thought about telling her about my fever, but I imagined her so fragile. *No,* I thought, I mustn't disturb her. Abuela was many things: a gifted cook, a pillar of her community, and also a skilled healer. She knew exactly all the remedios that you had to take for relieving pain of the body, but not the spirit.

"Bueno, entonces—how is that gringo of yours?"

"Liam, Abuela," I said, laughing. "His name is Liam. He's good, working." I turned to look at him; he was organizing the art supplies I had left on the table. Ay, Liam, he never knew how to live with a little mess. "How are the treatments? Is Mami helping you?"

"Mija, por favor," she said and then released a string of coughs. "You know how she is. In out, in and out of our lives. She's here sometimes, sí, but not a lot."

"Abuelita, I have a ticket for next week. I'm not going to leave your side."

It had always been me and her growing up. When I looked back at my memories from when I was a child, it was her who I remembered getting me ready for school, talking to me when the kids were mean to me, helping with my homework at the restaurant counter in Caminito. Abuela took me everywhere with her, a parent at her older age. Mamá always had somewhere else to be; sometimes she'd even disappear for months and then appear right back, her spirit a little battered, ready to fall in love all over again.

The call was silent for a moment, and my thoughts started to get clouded. I was dizzy from the pain and the warmth of my skin.

"Si Dios quiere," she said. "Mija." She paused.

"Yes?" I said. Liam was telling me something in the background. But I knew I needed to listen. "Dime, Abuelita," I implored her.

"I think the nurse is here to put an IV in me. But promise you'll call me later. In an hour or so. I need to talk to you."

"What if you fall asleep? Call me back right after she leaves."

"I'll find a way to talk to you. I promise."

"Abuela?"

The line disconnected. My forehead was burning, and my mouth felt completely dry. There was a salty taste in my mouth; if I told Abuela about it, she'd say it was probably a premonition. Fever was always a way of announcing something, the body telling you that you needed to prepare.

"Liam!" I called him in what I thought was a scream, but maybe it was barely a whisper.

"Vi, you don't look good." Liam ran to my side and put a hand on my forehead.

"I don't?" I asked before my knees gave out and I collapsed.

CHAPTER THREE: RETURN

I woke up with the sheets covered in sweat and two missed calls from Mami. Now, when I look back, I understand more of what was going on that day—when I had fallen asleep, my dreams were tangled. I was there, floating, but no words from Liam could reach me. When I would see Abuela, she would tell me that she was somewhere that she didn't recognize but that she was okay.

A message. That word was engraved on my brain.

Mami never called. Had Abuela taken a turn for the worse?

"Mamá," I blurted out when I heard her voice. Liam woke up when he heard me speak. He turned to me, attentive to every word that left my mouth. He didn't speak Spanish, but he was able to understand a little, and he read my worried expression even in the dark.

"Mamá, qué pasó?" My heart was in my throat; I was scared I would swallow it. I was scared I was about to choke on it.

She released a long, deep sigh on the phone. "Lo siento, mijita." She said that she was so sorry without saying hello and continued in Spanish. "Mami died in her sleep," she said bluntly. I felt a pressure in my chest. Mamá's voice was distant on the phone, as if she was calling from somewhere with a bad signal. I wanted to throw the phone across the room, I wanted to scream, but no words came to me, just disbelief.

I was expecting harshness from Mami. I was expecting her to tell me that I was a mala hija. "See? That's what happens when you're never home." But Mami's voice was soft, childlike, barely a whisper.

"I thought we had more time. Hadn't the doctors said a year?" I heard in my voice the practicality of the question. In all those previous months I had thought about Abuela dying nonstop. What would I do if I got the call? Where would I be, if I didn't make it in time? Would I be in Charlie's office? Would I be asleep in the middle of the night? Would I be home, next to her, instead? But it all seemed like a lie now. The call didn't exist, really, because words weren't getting to me. I was listening, but I didn't understand. I had just talked to her. Abuela couldn't be gone. Not as easily as that.

Abuela, the wisest woman I knew, the woman who had the power to predict any storm, had not been able to predict her own death. She was also the most stubborn woman. If she had something to say, she would go through unthinkable lengths just to utter the words weighing on her.

"That was best-case scenario, nena. The doctor said these things are unexpected but they happen. No one can put an accurate timeline on death." Mami's words were mechanical, as if she'd memorized them. "You can take some comfort knowing that she died in her sleep. She was at peace."

She didn't sound like herself. Who was this woman uttering clichés on the other side of the line? I wanted her to scream at me, to tell me that this woman who had loved me so much had died without saying goodbye to me and it was all my fault. But nothing; after the clichés came silence.

Mami hadn't called me nena since I was a little girl. In fact, Mami rarely kept in touch. That was Abuela's thing; she was the one to call and tell me about the restaurant when she was still working, and then, when she got sick, she would tell me about running the restaurant from her bed, about the craft shows she watched and English royalty gossip that she sometimes occupied her endless days with. Abuela was obsessed with money and status, with people who were lighter skinned and richer than her.

"When is the burial?" I asked Mami in a tone that I also didn't recognize in myself. My voice felt alien. The words were coming out, but I couldn't really take ownership of them. I got out of bed and sat on the floor, wanting to feel grounded in knowing that at least the earth was still under my feet. Liam stood up as well and knelt in front of me.

"And what is it to you? It's not like you're here to help." Ah, there it was, the mother I recognized.

"I'll move my flight."

"Para qué, Vi?" *For what*, she said. "She's gone. You coming here won't bring her back."

We stayed on the phone in silence for what seemed like a minute that stretched until eternity. With Mami, things were often like that: we never had much to say to each other because Abuelita was the one who knew me, the one who had the authority to tell me that I was being stubborn, the one I looked to when I wanted advice and shelter. Mami? Mami was just there. Running around after men she couldn't keep up with anymore. Time was passing us both by. At least Mami had been by Abuela's side. At least she had that.

"Voy a ir. I want to be there." When I didn't get a response, I separated the phone from my ear to see if she was still there—my heart was beating fast, and my fever hadn't broken.

"Stay there—haven't you done that all those years? Para que vas a venir. She's dead, Vi. A week ago would have been good, a month ago, ahora, ya para qué?" *For what*, she asked.

"Mamá?" I called for her, but she had hung up.

In the dark, Liam kissed my forehead. He knew how important Abuela was for me. I sat there unable to speak, or to cry. My phone weighed in my hands like a grenade, but I didn't know whether to toss it or let it explode. I heard Abuela's words in my head: *"I have something to tell you."* I clung to those words, to the promise that if Abuela had to tell me something, she was so stubborn that she would go to immeasurable lengths to leave a note, a letter, a message, something. But she'd let me know. I was sure of it.

Liam took the phone out of my hand and wrapped his arms around me. He smelled like the winter, like cold air and pines.

"It's not your fault," he whispered, kissing my hair and forehead. "There's nothing you could have done." Liam hugged me even tighter. His body was warm despite the coldness of the room. I closed my eyes, feeling sheltered in his embrace.

He was lying to me. There were infinite things I could have done. I could have spent time with Abuela, in Barranquilla, playing cards with her or giving her pasteles de gloria con guayaba that the doctors thought were a bad idea for her diabetes (I could hear her voice saying, *"What's the problem? Me estoy muriendo"*). Asking her about her recipes in person and the plans for her restaurant. There were so many questions I had about the way she had lived, the life she had before Mami with Abuelo. How she had prioritized Caminito and us. Has she ever been happy? She smiled only when she was at the restaurant.

Over the years when I had visited during Christmas or the summer, she would never talk about the past. According to her, the past was good only to open poorly healed wounds. I had been determined to ask her about it on my next visit, thinking that maybe now that she was sick, she would be more eager to speak about her life. Abuela had always been reserved, telling me only what she wanted to reveal and keeping the rest hidden.

Now it was too late. Whatever had been left unanswered, I would carry.

Did I deserve to say goodbye? Why—para qué? Since I was a girl, Abuela would shoo me away from the kitchen because she didn't want me to have the same life she did. Did I deserve to say goodbye to the person who had loved me the most? But Abuela didn't love me for who

I was; she'd wanted to change things about me. Sometimes she was disappointed in how I hesitated about things. In the ways I lingered in situations where I wasn't appreciated. Abuela many times wanted to shake me and tell me to be better. Many times she did. She didn't love me for who I was, but she loved me fiercely, in the way that protective love goes with you wherever you go. In the way protective love follows you around, seeps into your head, and controls your thoughts. In the way that love wants to know everything you do and finds what you do is always interesting. The kind of love that feels like no matter what you do, you can never escape it.

But just like any other blessing, the love is limited. Finite. The kind of love that we can appreciate only when we lose it.

~

I spent the rest of the night sending emails to clients about Abuela's death and saying that regretfully I wouldn't be able to finish the work. Despite having several clients, I was always short on money. Some never paid on time, and none of them paid me what I was worth. I closed the laptop and waited for the morning.

After I received the call, my fever dissolved like a dream. Perhaps the temperature in my body had been a warning sign—my body trying to tell me that something was coming to an end. I paced around the apartment, trying to feel something other than guilt. I needed to cry, but tears would not come. I felt an urge to punish myself, to feel the abandon and the hurt that come from knowing that you are the only orchestrator of your problems. If I had been there earlier, if I had been there with Abuela in her last moments, if I had . . . those words played in an echo in my head.

I drafted an email to Charlie telling her that I had an urgent family matter. She could use the original illustrations or work with someone to adapt the work. I imagined her face, turning red and then purple, the color of violets. She would spit out her green tea, I thought. Oh well.

I took a deep breath and hit send. Hopefully she would still give me work when I came back home. After that, I searched for tickets. Abuela's burial would be in two days.

There was a flight for the next night. I put my credit card details on the website and gave a silent prayer that it would work. It was the most expensive flight I had purchased in my entire life.

It went through.

The next few days would be so intense. Abuela's burial, seeing Mami and Anton. Being home was always strange. I always felt like I didn't belong there anymore: I had left, and the city had moved on without me.

"Hey, you okay?" Liam asked in a sleepy voice and kissed my shoulder.

"All good," I lied. I was overwhelmed with the possibility of going, with the stress of having sent that email to Charlie. Liam turned to the other side and fell back asleep.

This was going to be a quick trip. I needed to be there to honor Abuela, and then I could be back and get in Charlie's good graces again. Keep working and keep trying to make space for myself in this city.

~

The next morning, as I made the coffee in the kitchen, Liam sat at the kitchen counter asking again why he couldn't come.

"I appreciate you wanting to be there, but there's no need. There will be other chances." I had never taken Liam back home—I dreaded going through the motions of introducing him to Mamá and Abuela and them asking him a million questions. It felt like too much. Liam always insisted on coming, and I always told him the next trip, or the one after that. Home was a complicated concept for me, still after all those years. He had always seemed understanding, but I wondered if he was starting to get tired of not being included.

"I just want to be there for you, Vi. That's all. Let me be there for you." I handed him a cup of coffee; he took the first sip and lowered the cup. "You don't want me there?"

"Liam," I pleaded and went to his side. I kissed him on the lips. "I do, but it's going to be so quick, and I'm going to be fine. It'll be over before you know it, and we'll talk all the time."

I hugged him, knowing I was being unfair. He wanted to support me, and I was pushing him away. But I didn't want to be responsible for helping him navigate a new place while also trying to deal with my grief.

I thought about Mami, how she would make everything about her own pain. And Anton, how devastated he was going to be. I thought about the impossible heat and the blazing sun. About the fact that Abuela wouldn't be there—how weird that was, it almost seemed impossible. It would be a rush of emotions, all at once, and then it would be over. Time to come back.

I released a deep sigh, suddenly feeling alone in the room, in the city. New York felt cold and immense.

But New York was home, I told myself. After all these years, and all that I had sacrificed, it had to be.

CHAPTER FOUR: LAS SANOGUERA

The heat hit my face like three quick slaps. Clap, clap, clap.

I arrived in Barranquilla at midnight, and I got off the plane as I had many times while visiting home from college, feeling disoriented and wondering if this was a real place. The heat certainly felt unreal as I navigated through arrivals as one navigates a past life. I thought about the last time I had visited Barranquilla a couple of months ago. Always a quick trip, no more than two weeks, always in a rush. Coming to Barranquilla always felt like too much, too many memories, the shadow of Rafa haunting the streets.

The old airport spread in front of me. The same ancient structure as always, the same clammy air-conditioned room that welcomed you as soon as you entered baggage claim, and the same smell of wet socks. My steps were slow and heavy; I was a tangle of grief and regret.

Anton was the only person who would be waiting for me. I hadn't told anyone else when I was coming, not even Mami. I didn't have the energy to start fighting just yet.

My face was burning with the recognition that I was returning under the circumstances of Abuela's death. Was it nerves or the city? Maybe it was both. I started walking in the familiar airport, passing the knickknacks and the stands with guayaba and coconut sweets.

Anton was outside the arrivals exit, in front of the long line of small yellow taxis people in the city called "zapaticos" because they resembled small shoes. He seemed skinnier and older since I had last seen him, but he was just the same boy with the long face and skinny frame he had always been. The boy who loved to cook and absorb Abuela's knowledge: he knew my family stories just as if he had been born in our house.

"Anton!" I waved at him, suddenly feeling how much I cared about him, how much Abuela had cared about him.

"Vi!" he shouted in front of the taxi booth outside arrivals. The airport felt so small in comparison to America's airports. Everything had reduced in size, from the people to the buildings and even the cars.

I walked toward him quickly, desperate to hug him.

"Niña," he said when he embraced me, "estás toda sudada. Don't they have AC on planes anymore?" He kissed me loudly on the cheek.

I pulled him close and hugged him again, not caring about the sweat. I laughed, feeling relieved; it was a balm to see him.

"Ni sé. I don't think I'm made para este calor anymore."

"Baby," he said, in a costeño accent, "what are you talking about? You belong to this heat. You were born here." He lifted a brow and grabbed my hand as we walked toward the line of taxis. "Cómo estás?" Anton asked how I was doing and then directed his attention to a man with a board and a pen. "Cuadro, un taxi a Prado," he said, using the deeper voice he reserved for these occasions.

The man wrote something down and walked us to the taxi and opened the door for me. "Señorita."

I thanked him and got inside, minding my head in the tiny car as Anton gave our address to the driver. "I'm okay," I said, sighing, and he squeezed my hand tight. "How are you?"

Anton put a hand on his chin and smiled softly. "Desastre. I'm a mess. I miss her too much. I've been crying nonstop. You sure you're okay?"

No tears yet, but a constant pressure on my chest. I still couldn't believe Abuela wasn't here anymore.

"I'm okay," I repeated, not being able to put words to my grief. "I'm okay," desperate to believe it.

I took the city in. The old familiar route from the airport to Barrio Prado was the same: first, the mercado at night. All the colorful little tents closed, waiting for the morning. Not a soul was walking en el centro except street dogs and stray cats. When you got a little deeper into the center, you could see the old art deco buildings in soft pastel colors, the church that people said was built with the doors inside out and the houses with big windows, all painted in different crackling colors. The dim lights illuminating the road. The city, even if everything had changed, felt the same.

Anton was talking and talking. Ha, he said, even the mercado in the city center is expensive. Even having a glass of water under a tree, they want to charge you for! And Mami! La doña was worse than ever! The house was falling apart. They had made some changes to the menu, but it was always the same customers.

I put my hand on top of his when the landscape changed to big colonial houses, with republican windows and wooden doors that were almost as tall as the palms on the street. I closed my eyes, preparing for the barrenness of a house without Abuela.

"Don't worry," Anton said, turning to look at me. "I have the keys, and I can stay if you want me to."

I hesitated. I doubted that Mami would be there; she would probably be spending the night in a new lover's apartment. She technically lived with Abuela, but she came and went as she pleased. Cold rushed through my veins at the thought of sleeping alone in the old house. We were getting even closer. I got lost in the familiar landscapes of Viejo Prado, the colonial yellow houses, the broad streets with palm trees and the majestic old houses. Barrio Prado was stuck in time, fueled by the ghosts of a more prosperous past.

"No, you don't have to stay," I said, reaching for my purse as confidently as if I had money to spare. I knew Anton wouldn't let me, because men in the Caribbean Coast were supposed to always pay.

"Keep the change," I heard Anton say to the driver: he had already given him a bill. Anton helped me out of the car and slammed the door of the zapatico.

We both turned to look at the house. I stared at it with him, in awe of how everything and nothing had changed. I felt the soil under my feet; I heard the echo of the voices of Abuela, Mamá, Bisabuela; I felt the midday sun on my cheeks even though from where I was standing, I could see the moon. I looked at him. Anton and I were under a spell—the shadow of the house was eclipsing us.

The old cream house with the big, now faded blue windows. The mataratón in front. The floor was covered in small pink flowers that smelled like tea candles and jasmine. I saw Caminito, too, at a glance. The restaurant and the house were connected by a small path, the yellow paint cracking and fading, the white windows standing tall, and although the lights were off, I could still picture it all lit up and full of people, their voices traveling throughout the cuadra. Abuela's pride and joy and our bread and butter. The restaurant looked old and decaying but still elegant.

So many times I had sneaked out of the house to see Rafa. He would always be waiting for me not far from the restaurant, always wearing the same smile. The blue of the night illuminating his face. No. I shook my head, trying to push away the memory. This was about Abuela.

Caminito was a well-loved ruin—the heart of Barrio Prado. Seeing it was like seeing Abuela's soul. This restaurant was more than its walls; it had been there my whole life. Memories of long afternoons doing homework at the bar before the customers rushed in, family and barrio parties, and Sundays of just losing myself in the customers' conversations—in the loud whispers of gossip, marriage proposals, and regular conversations that made a life. Caminito was the pounding heart of Barrio Prado.

What was the point of this house or of this restaurant if Abuela wasn't in it? After Abuela died, the house and Caminito should have dissipated into a cloud of dust.

"Segura, Vi?" Anton asked, as he helped with my bag and walked with me toward the house. The grass, usually manicured, was now overgrown and wet. It smelled fresh and vast like it did in Barranquilla after the rain. The crickets' midnight chorus guided us the rest of the way. "I can stay."

"No," I said, standing by the door. "I'll see you tomorrow, at the funeral."

Anton opened the door, carried my bag inside the house, and turned on all the lights, illuminating the little sala, the snail-shaped stairs, and the small kitchen hidden in the back. It seemed to me that Abuela was going to come out of one of the rooms all of a sudden to feed me a midnight snack of galletas and milo and tell me that I smelled like mapurito—that small mystery bug that all the sweaty kids in the Caribbean were told they smelled like so they would shower. But the house felt quiet and dusty.

A current of cold air entered the room. I brushed my shoulders trying to get warm. The house had always been big, but as I stood there, it seemed like the halls and the rooms would never end. The house looked emptier and bigger than ever.

"I can sleep alone," I said again, trying to believe it myself.

Anton stood by the door, waiting for instructions. He tilted his head, ready to insist again.

"Vi, mija, no need to be strong. Not with me."

"Baby, vete," *just go*, I told him, trying to reclaim the term that belonged to us. We used to call each other "baby" all the time, especially when we wanted to cheer each other up. We both came from families where sweet words or compliments didn't come easy for those who loved us. I blew him a kiss. "Don't worry."

He lingered for a couple of seconds, with his hand on the doorknob. "Chao, mi vida," he said, finally closing the door. "Call me."

Crik crik crik, the wooden sound of the stairwell as I went up the stairs at full speed. I couldn't stay downstairs for a moment longer. I ran through the hall, purposefully ignoring the family pictures on the wall. I needed to go to my room, get under the covers, and lie in bed until morning. It didn't matter if I didn't sleep. I just needed to wait; it would all be clearer in the morning.

I opened the door to my room, where the bed was made up and the flowery pink wallpaper had been taken down. The walls were cream colored like coffee cake icing. I got a whiff of fresh linens and lilies as I sat on the bed. My heart shrank with the thought that Abuela had prepared the room for me. The tears I had accumulated and carried with me pressed on my chest, making it tighter and tighter. But I couldn't cry yet.

I took my jeans and T-shirt off and got under the thin covers wearing only my underwear. I texted Liam quickly: I'm home, love. I'll talk to you in the morning. Guilt rushed through my veins, the feeling that I wasn't being a good girlfriend to him. A good girlfriend would call. But being home was too much, too overwhelming. Despite my being almost naked, my face felt warm, and I needed to breathe. I uncovered my head and released a loud breath. I let go the word on the tip of my tongue: "Abuela."

I wasn't sure if it was grief or the long flight or even my spirit conspiring to fool me, but I heard her voice as clear as if she were there.

"Mija," it said. It was coming from the hall, as if Abuela was just approaching the room. If I closed my eyes, I could hear her light steps in what had been her house. A chill climbed to the back of my neck.

No. This was grief. I resisted the urge to look around for her, to peek at the hall to see if she was there, waiting. Grief made you see your deceased loved ones closer, as if they were still alive.

I sat on the bed, biting my nails to stumps.

A current of cool air entered the window, and I closed my eyes, relieved by the brief break from the heat. I closed my eyes knowing that the comfort I wanted, I couldn't have.

Abuela's heavy hands that she used for cooking, spanking, gesticulating, and fixing things around the house felt warm on my feet. Abuela, as she had joked many times in life that she would do after her passing, was pulling them. She was a strong woman, with determined hands that curled on my toes and gripped them until she dragged me to the end of the bed where she was waiting.

"Abuela?" I asked, but the words didn't come out. What came out was a muted murmur from my mouth. "Mhhmm, mmm, mmm!" As much as I tried, I couldn't speak.

Abuela looked at me and tilted her head back with her expansive laugh. Abuela used to make fun of me when she was alive that I was playing victim or being too mopey. In Abuela's book, there was nothing worse than showing your emotions on your sleeve. Vulnerability was weakness.

I tried to speak again. Nothing. My mouth felt stitched together.

"Tranquila, tranquila," she said, touching my feet playfully. "If you're too scared, I can leave."

I didn't want to lose her twice in one day. As she stood up, the words that were stuck inside me came flowing out.

"Abuela, dónde estás?" I asked, and her face lit up. Her skin was golden and plump as if it was reflecting light in the otherwise dark room.

She sat back down on the bed and rested her hand on my feet. Her touch was warm, just as it had been in life.

"En la casa," she said. *I'm home.* And smiled with her white, small teeth.

I gasped for air, sat up on the bed, and released a sob. The dream had felt so real. I was grateful that I had seen her one more time. Was this the last time? I looked around my room; her spirit felt near, even if it couldn't be.

Ghost stories were part of everyday life in Barrio Prado. If you didn't sleep well, a reasonable explanation might be that an ancestor was velando your sleep that night, or if you heard a song at night, probably it was a ghost playing a song just for you. When you sat in the hairdresser's chair or you heard gossip on the street, you took in the stories—the reasonable explanation of a life lived twice. Once on earth, and once in the afterlife. Abuela believed in ghost stories. In the residue of the spirits that stayed on earth.

But could she have stayed?

Abuela, no estás aquí. "You are not here," I said, not wanting to believe it.

A tap, tap, tap on the door, as clear as if someone was knocking on my door.

I stood up with the resolve of a person who was about to meet their destiny.

"Abuela?" I asked, tentatively, as I forced my feet one in front of the other. "Abuela?" A chill ran through my spine as I opened the door. If she was on the other side, it would be terrifying, but also it would be so lovely to see her. To get to say goodbye.

"Abuela?" The hall was empty. No one was in the house but me.

~

In Colombia, we took care of our muertos quickly. I had barely had any time to settle, and it was already time to say goodbye to Abuela. Midday, smoldering sun and white flowers dangling out of funeral arrangements.

Abuela was to be buried in Barranquilla's best cemetery. One that defied nature's laws and managed to have a green lawn and lush vegetation despite the prolonged seasons of drought and the relentless heat.

The whole Barrio Prado was here, dressed in a sea of black. Abuela was a personality, the owner of Caminito, one of the neighborhood institutions, who had seen many weddings and funerals. Long ago, when I was little, Abuela still had energy to run around with pots and pans, tasting things and heavily seasoning whatever crossed her way. Heavy saffron in anything that appeared in her field of vision. Cilantro leaves floating in the air through her kitchen.

The restaurant, from what Anton had told me the night before, was more in trouble than Abuela had let on, but as I watched the regulars and people in Barrio Prado arriving en masse, it was clear that her place in the community was intact. So many regulars from the restaurant were there. Chanting their respects like a haunted chorus: "Doña Emilia, a saint."

"Mi amor, how's your mami taking it?" Doña Rocío asked, planting a wet kiss on my cheek. She was one of Abuela's neighbors and a family friend. I grew up with her beautiful daughters, who everyone called "las mellas," the twins, Sabina and Celina. Everyone called Celina by their last name, García, since she was the more serious of the both of them. While Sabina was dreamy and sweet, Celina was direct with no time for pleasantries. They were tall, with long black hair and yellowish-green catlike eyes. They always had a detached quality to them, like they couldn't relate to the world fully, only to each other.

I saw Doña Rocío at least once or twice a week when I lived in Barranquilla, when she brought platos of quibes and marmaón to our house. She was a warm presence in my life, a caring woman who was always overly preoccupied with Abuela and me. Always wanting to read our cards and have us over for sancocho, but Abuela, en vida, never had much time for her except what was strictly necessary, or when she couldn't escape Doña Rocío's firm and insistent grip.

"No sé, Doña Rocío." I confessed that I hadn't really seen my mother. I looked at Mami from across the room. I had been home for a quick Christmas trip a couple of months ago, when Mami and I fought about who forgot to buy Abuela's turkey (Abuela hated turkey and yet she insisted on having it on her table every navidad). Last year Abuela was going through chemo, and although she insisted on that cursed bird, she couldn't eat anything much. Everything made her nauseous. I would sit with her for long hours, playing cards and watching horror movies. Abuela always loved ghost stories and slasher movies.

I could still hear Mami: Por qué couldn't I stay for more than two weeks? Was I alérgica to Barranquilla?

Mami was a mystery to me. Even when I was little, I was always guessing her thoughts. Did she love me? Was I good enough? Her constant abandonment usually left me wondering if something in me was lacking, a missing segment that otherwise would allow her to stay.

The voices blended together in the funeral parlor. All I could see was her, with her long legs and needle heels. I hadn't seen her since I arrived because Mami was like that: elusive and mysterious. She had planned this funeral without my help, and when in between tears, I called to ask if she needed anything, she promptly barked at me. "De ti?" she said, *From you?* "I don't need anything."

Mami was dressed all in black, drying her tears with a thick black piece of fabric. Where did she get that handkerchief? I looked closer. The handkerchief was really a piece of fabric attached to a man's black sleeve. Típico, that was the Mami I recognized—looking for refuge in a man.

"Perdón, Doña Rocío. I'm going to check on her." Rocío nodded, and as I walked away, I could feel Doña Rocío's eyes following my steps. Barrio Prado and the neighbors knew that Mamá and I never got along.

I walked over to talk to Mami. I wanted to ask her so many things about Abuela's last words. For once in my life, I wanted to be told about what was going on. I was grown, I could handle it—growing up, Abuela and Mamá discussed my life as one discussed the fate of a rag doll. Studying in the States had never been my idea; it had been theirs—a way to give me another life, away from Barrio Prado, Caminito, and Rafa. Back then, I didn't have the strength to say no. I didn't know what I wanted.

I knew that I wanted to confront Mami. Why was this stranger more in her life than I was? How come I had not been included in funeral plans? My ballet flats seemed short and lacked authority against Mami's heels. Despite her artificial tallness, Mami was bending to bury her face in the chest of the small man dressed in a cheap, ill-fitting suit. She turned to look at me. I felt a shiver despite the sweat dampening the back of my dress.

Mami was the tropical queen of ice. I opened my mouth just to close it back. She looked at me with dead eyes. I couldn't stand that look, so instead I ended up meeting the man's gaze. He was short and had short-cropped hair. He stretched his arm to surround Mami, and she put her face on his shoulder.

"Mami," I said, trying to meet her eyes. In front of her, I felt small.

Mamá lifted her head slowly and locked gazes with the man. Her eyes were tender when she looked at him, full of love. Seconds after, she turned to look at me, her face devoid of all expression.

"Vamos." Mamá grabbed the man's hand and guided him toward the parlor. "The ceremony is about to start. We'll talk after."

I looked around the room, and the sobbing had just begun; people were just pulling out the rosarios. Horas, I thought. This could last hours. Bitter tears threatened to come down my face, but I took a deep breath, trying to keep it together. The stranger nodded and kissed the top of Mami's silky black hair.

I stood in front of her. Waiting to see if she would say anything more to me. My left leg started to shake, as I desperately wanted to keep it together. If Mami had something she wanted to say to me, it wasn't going to be now, in front of a new lover. She reserved a special sweetness for those.

What she had to say to me, she knew very well she had to say behind closed doors.

~

I couldn't hear the words the priest was mumbling. I was sweating, and although I grasped for reality, my head was still submerged in dreams. I kept seeing Abuela in my head the night before, standing in the doorway before dissolving into nothing. "Mija." Her voice was just the same, raspy and decisive. And yet reality was unforgiving: Abuela was not there. She couldn't be. Grief had the power of creating ghosts and making them walk the halls with us, forcing them to follow until we questioned the fabric of reality. Ghosts were just regret staring us in the face.

Mami had just stood up to speak, her stilettos getting buried in the grass, but she didn't care. She stood straight, persevering against the weather conditions that threatened to melt us all. Mami was wearing a pencil skirt above her knees that Abuela would have thought was too short. Abuela would have hated for us to speak at her funeral. We had to stay strong; we had to keep grief tight and close to the chest, like one clutches a rosary.

"Doña Emilia," Mami said gravely, "era una mujer generosa, of the people. She would wake up every morning trying to see who she could help. Her restaurant had an open-door policy and she was always eager to feed the hungry." Mami looked around; her mascara was running slightly, but her straight, freshly blown-dry hair floated around in the air, making her look like a beautiful grieving Medusa.

"Mami was kind to perros callejeros and the children in the neighborhood." Abuela hated dogs and children that weren't family, and just because she fed people, it didn't mean she loved them. I was standing next to Anton, and I tried to search for his eyes. But he was looking at her, immersed in the exaggerations Mamá had fabricated. Abuela would have thought this was too melodramatic, as if Mamá were the sole protagonist of her own telenovela.

Mami paused to cry. I turned to look at the man with the cheap suit. His lips were in a pout, and his eyes had a kind expression. He was nodding with every word Mami was saying, encouraging her to keep going. Was that what support looked like? Because Abuela would have told Mami that she was making a fool of herself. Abuela was bitter like a lemon, and sometimes her words cut like the sharpest of knives. Why didn't Mamá say that? Why not just tell the truth? Not telling the truth was also not seeing Abuela in full light. Abuela was bitter, yes, but she was also the first one to be there when you needed help. She wasn't sweet with words, but she was present. She was funny and sharp, with the survival skills of a lioness. Abuela was a leona for her family, and Mamá could have just said that.

Mamá was standing there, not saying anything but crying into the microphone. She buried her head in her hands, and the people from the barrio stared at her, whispering between them, gossip spreading like wildfire. No, no, no. I tried to make my way over there, but we were on opposite sides of the grave, and I had to walk following the square of land, bumping against people and trying to do it discreetly enough that she wouldn't yell at me. As I was saying a muttered "Permiso," I could hear Mami's sobs amplified by the microphone.

"Mami, Mami," I whispered as I stood behind her. I wanted both to hug her and take the microphone away.

I was about to touch her shoulders when Mami collapsed on her knees. She was bending forward, rocking herself back and forth in between sobs. I knelt, too, wanting to take away the microphone and get her up.

"Mamá, Mamá," I whispered, wrapping my arms around her as she continued to rock herself and risked falling on top of the casket. In the background, collective gasps.

"Señora Paula!" someone in the crowd yelled. My heart started beating fast, and the pressure in my chest returned.

"Ay, Mamá." I wrapped my arms tighter and tried to pull her up. She was frozen by emotion, as if she couldn't believe that the piece that had held her life together was no longer there. Tears welled up in my eyes too. I didn't want to be embarrassed or worried; I just wanted to be sad, and Mamá never gave me that privilege. She was used to eclipsing the room.

"Mamá, please get up."

The man with her knelt on her other side. His overpowering perfume was all I could smell. "Está bien, está bien," he said, rubbing her back. "Let's get up." Mami handed him the microphone, as if I weren't there, and the mystery man gave it to the silent priest. Mami, with the help of his hand, stood up slowly as if she were hurt.

I stood there, tears running down my face as I watched her get up for a man but not for me.

The sun was on my nose, and I felt my whole face burn. The people from Barrio Prado closed their mouths and took back their seats in the white plastic chairs. The scene was over.

This wasn't about Abuela anymore. This was about Mami and her all-consuming emotions. Mami was the kind of woman who always made you look.

I stood next to her as the priest said the last words: "En polvo eres y en polvo te convertirás." He sprinkled dirt on top of the grave, and Mami and I threw some roses on top of the casket; others from Barrio Prado followed.

Someone came to stand next to me and grabbed my hand.

It was Anton, half smiling at me, his face red and his eyelashes still damp from crying. As more dirt covered the casket, the priest said some words I couldn't distinguish. Guilt pressed on my chest for not being there for Abuela. I was home too late, and although I wanted to cry, I felt like I did not deserve it. I needed to sit down, and I needed water.

I took one last look at the grave as people started to walk away. Anton and I walked in silence. He was still holding my hand, his well-fitted, light-blue suit contrasting with the sea of black in the cemetery. Mami and I locked eyes again; hers were smudged and covered in mascara. She smiled at me, but her whole face twisted in an expression one could mistake for either sympathy or anger. I tried to sustain her gaze, but it lasted for only a couple of seconds before she locked hands with her man again.

I kept walking, desperate to leave the grave behind me. Abuela wasn't there.

"Beautiful, verdad?" Anton asked as we stood by the cemetery gates. That funeral was anything but beautiful or what my grandmother would have wanted, but I nodded, trying to keep the moment light. I looked back one last time, at the glowing grass, and I told myself again that Abuela wasn't there.

She was at home.

CHAPTER FIVE: CAMINITO

Caminito was for a long time one of the most elegant restaurants in the neighborhood of Barrio Prado in Barranquilla. It was the place where my mother got married twice and I had my first kiss. It was also the place that had been the center of our lives for all of us—Caminito was more of a home than the house was; it was the place where Abuela, Mamá, and I had eaten most of our meals and had had family fights and quarrels. It was the only place I wanted to take refuge in after a long day—it always smelled the same, like azafrán and tomatoes sizzling in olive oil.

There were now dust and spiderwebs in the corners of the restaurant. The wooden furniture was bitten by comejen. Termites, that bug that eats everything—the paper, the pictures, the furniture. The bug that eats memories. Our memories. My family's memories were destroyed by that white miniature bug. And yet.

Before her death I dreamed about Abuela almost every night. About her smell of bitter lemons, sugar, and salt. The smell of her kitchen. The sweet scent of the things she used to cook. I dreamed about the places she used to take me for pastelitos de guayaba. The places that were now closed. Of the hot smell of the sizzling oil that fried the hojaldre that she covered with a thin layer of granulated sugar while it was still warm. I dreamed about her lazy eye, which she got fixed later in life. I dreamed about her rudeness. Her awareness of how much, how often, and how far people will go in order to hurt you.

Caminito had an Argentine name even though it was Spanish food. The restaurant was named after an Argentine tango, but was dedicated to my Spanish bisabuela and the memory of her Spanish Colombian immigrant recipes.

That afternoon after the funeral, I walked around the restaurant. It was daunting to see the passage of time in a place that Abuela had fought so hard to maintain. I passed my hands over the old, dusty tablecloths. Abuela, who once was on top of every imperfection in the restaurant, hadn't noticed the browning edges of the fabric. There were signs of humidity damage on the walls; if Abuela had been healthy, she would have painted the walls herself. For her, everything always had to be spotless. I stood by the kitchen door, where she used to stand to observe the happy customers, the tables, and the infinite noise of a busy restaurant.

Soon my old memories of the restaurant would be replaced with the restaurant in its current form. A shadow of a place that had cost Abuela a life of sacrifice. Seeing the place like this felt like a second death of Abuela, one that would extend until the restaurant finally collapsed and became a ruin.

Caminito, our inheritance. I passed a hand over the tablecloth fabric, reminiscing about more opulent times. Friday nights in Caminito were an event in Barrio Prado. If I closed my eyes, I could see Abuela standing in the dining room, talking to customers and making sure that everyone enjoyed their food—she loved seeing empty plates, people asking for more food and complimenting her sazón. At home Abuela was strict, but in the restaurant she would laugh expansively, with a hand on her belly, showing her uneven teeth. Doña Emilia Sanoguera dressed up for her clients. She loved to wear black and pearls; she levitated around her restaurant proud in her steps—her way of bringing joy to the customers was through croquetas, good olive oil, fresh bread, and plenty of red wine. I could almost see her standing by the counter, tapping her red heels and telling me to go back home. There was no place in the restaurant for me; I needed to study. I needed to be better than the women in my family had ever been. Because, in her words, she was just a cook, but I could be anything I wanted.

"Are you going to help me bring the bags inside, or are you just going to stand there?" Anton appeared by the kitchen door. His hands were filled with at least four plastic bags of food. "Apúrate"—*rush*—"there's more in the car."

"Why do you have those? Don't we still have Jaime stocking the restaurant every morning?" I asked as I walked to the back door of the restaurant and brought more bags inside.

"Sometimes." He paused as he brought the last bag and put it on the kitchen counter. I started opening the bags and taking out the fresh vegetables first to rinse them in the industrial sink. "We owed him some money, so we had to stop getting so many pedidos and space them out."

Abuela never used to owe money. That woman had multiple notebooks full of information about orders, menus, and recipes. Everything was color coded, and in her neat handwriting she had several reminders for her and her staff. Even after cancer had spread in her blood, she was never able to forget anything.

"I bought this in the supermercado myself. I went after the funeral. I couldn't live with the idea that Doña Emilia wouldn't have a proper reception. If she were here, we would have started cooking three days ago."

I started rinsing the vegetables to keep my hands occupied. Why hadn't Mami told me that there were pending preparations? Why hadn't I asked Anton? Didn't I know Mami wasn't to be trusted? Abuela's passing meant that I had to take care of things, at least for now. The laundry list of what I would have to do appeared in my head: deciding what to do with Caminito and Abuela's things, making sure everything was in order. What were we going to do with the house? Did Mami think it was too big for her?

"Déjame pagarte." I told Anton I needed to pay him back for what he had spent. "This is not right. I'm sorry, Mami said—"

"No, I'm not going to accept un centavo. This is a gift for Doña Emilia. She did so much for me. It's the least I can do." He moved me to the side and put the rinsed vegetables on a chopping board, then washed his hands under the sink and put his chef jacket on. Without saying a word, Anton walked toward the kitchen pantry and threw me Abuela's stained pink apron. The one with the infinite pockets. I could still smell the sourness and the notes of salt in her sweat. I wanted to pause and take it all in, but instead, I just put it on and tied it loosely in the back. I didn't know grief could shift and materialize in the shape of a ratty apron.

"This is probably your first time cooking openly en esta cocina, no?"

I looked around. *If I teach you how to cook, you'll become a slave to a man. Is that what you want? To end up like me?* I had spent so much time here, watching Abuela be the boss of the kitchen and of a place she had invented and designed at her will, that it seemed crazy that now I didn't know where the knives were, or the chopping boards. I didn't even know where the spoons were.

"You know Abuela never taught me how to cook," I admitted, surprised by how ashamed I was of this fact.

Anton put a pan down and poured plenty of olive oil in it. He released a sigh. When I was little, and I'd stood in Caminito's kitchen eager to be given a job or any task, to be part of it, I'd resented Anton and the space he was given to grow in the kitchen.

While the olive oil was heating up, he unpacked the groceries and proceeded to chop a red pepper into big chunks; Abuela loved spice and bold flavors. Food had to taste of something. I thought about Abuela taking him under her wing when he was just twelve and an orphan. Anton used to live with his uncle and aunt, who made him work from a very young age. They also used to beat him. Abuela didn't do much about the beating, but she paid him a salary and taught him all the recipes that were unavailable to anyone else who was not family.

I couldn't be angry at him. I hadn't insisted. Even as an adult I didn't dare to try to cook a family recipe. In the States I'd anticipated my homesickness like a cold. I was an expert in the symptoms in my body: the impossible longing and the long sighs, the smells of home that suddenly would be everywhere. The smell of flan in a Mexican bakery, the smell of coffee in the morning or of salt in the air. It was dangerous then to take meals in Brooklyn that reminded me of Abuela and her kitchen. It was hopeless. Nothing would ever taste like she made it. She had perfected the art of comfort cooking so much that it belonged to her.

"You'll be in charge of making the tortilla Española."

A brief memory came to me: Abuela chopping and caramelizing onions in a sizzling pan, eggs beaten for not too long, poured in a cast-iron pan to create the perfect spongy circle.

Tortilla was a simple dish, and yet my palms started sweating. Being in Abuela's kitchen felt like being judged by her.

I had eaten tortilla many times with Abuela and Mami on Sundays with a piece of french baguette and a Coca-Cola. I had watched them make it in under half an hour almost every week. Tortilla in my family, just like everything else, had to be prepared a certain way, or else it was inedible: the potatoes had to be crispy and sweet, almost caramelized; the onions couldn't be soggy; and the eggs couldn't be greasy. The end result had to be thick and spongy. Like cutting into clouds.

I started with rinsing the potatoes, peeling them, and discarding the skin in one of the plastic shopping bags, like I had seen Abuela do many times before.

"Do you even know how to peel a potato?" Anton took the swivel from me and said, "Mira." His hands wielded the swivel expertly, moving downward quickly and in long strokes so the potato was naked in a matter of seconds rather than minutes, like it was taking me. "Ahora tú, go."

I took the potato and started peeling a little bit quicker, but it was still too slow. You never wanted to be the slow-moving piece in Abuela's kitchen.

"You can do it faster, apúrate."

I took a deep breath and held the potato with my hand bending backward, imitating Anton. I peeled another potato.

"Ajá, Vi, para cuando?" Anton was tapping his feet. Any minute he was going to take the potatoes away from me.

No. Anger flushed my cheeks. Those potatoes were mine; I belonged to this kitchen, and I had every right to be here—even if it was too late. I wiped the sweat on my forehead with the back of my hand. The heat of my city already consuming me. I kept peeling the potatoes.

"Just a little left," I told him.

"Vi, ve and see if people need some drinks. Some wine. I can handle the kitchen alone." Anton moved back to tend to the sizzling pans.

"No," I said. "I'm staying." I grabbed the bucket of onions. He said nothing but started chopping something in the background with force.

I realized that I would end up smelling like garlic and onions for the entire night, but I wiped off my hands on the apron and started to julienne the onions.

Anton was flying in the kitchen, tending to the many pots and pans just like Abuela did when she was alive and well. I continued chopping the onions as quickly as my inexperienced hands would allow.

We continued chopping and prepping without speaking. Our silence reminded me of our fights when we were children. Anton felt closer to Abuela than I ever did, and I resented him for that, so I would take it out on him—I wouldn't speak to him for days, but I would miss him fiercely. Anton was the only one who knew about how lonely it could get at home, how often Mamá would just leave. I wanted to tell him something about how the smell reminded me of Abuela's cooking:

butter, saffron, garlic, and olive oil. A smell that could guide anyone who was lost home.

But I bit my tongue.

~

People were starting to arrive, and we needed to make progress with the food. Anton gave a wiggle to the first tortilla, and after he had confirmed it was done, he took a plate and flipped it in a matter of seconds. Not confident in my ability, he flipped the second one. And the third.

"Déjame," I said. I flipped the fourth one and watched it collapse in the middle like a yellow, raw blob on the plate.

Anton let out a gigantic sigh that deflated his entire body. He put the tortilla back together with a fork and then proceeded to cut it into little square pieces.

"Toma," he said, pushing the plate into my ribs. "Put it on the tray."

The uneasiness of feeling like I didn't belong began to creep in again, but I didn't let myself break. "I want to try again." I pushed my shoulders back and tried to stand up straight.

Anton sighed and shook his head. "How many tortillas do we have to ruin?"

I rolled my eyes and grabbed the pan by the handle. I needed to move fast, or the tortilla would overcook and become too dry. I took the handle with an oven glove and held the plate beneath it. I remembered Abuela and how quickly she would do it, a flip that would consist of one single movement.

I counted uno, dos, tres in my head and flipped it—perhaps I hadn't done it fast enough; I didn't know if the weight on it felt right or not—but I removed the pan.

The tortilla was perfect: browned a little on top and in the shape of an even circle.

"Viste." My eyes searched for his approval; a smile appeared on my face.

Anton nodded quickly and approached with a paper towel to clean the rim of the plate. "I just want things to be perfect for Doña Emilia," he said as he delicately cleaned the edges. "I'm used to my ways, that's all. You did okay."

My lip started quivering. After I had cried the night before, I felt tears were always near. He was just trying to do right by Abuela.

I took my apron off and washed my hands for as long as I could. But the smell of what made a good dish stand out lingered. Mamá was standing in the doorway, saying hello to all the vecinos who came in. I walked out of the kitchen, and I didn't know if it was seeing all the people from the neighborhood who were there to pay Abuela their respects, or if it was just knowing that the day had a finality to it, or the silly fight with Anton, but my eyes started to well up with tears. The pressure in my chest came back. No crying, I told myself. I was not like Mami; I kept my grief on the inside—just like Abuela would have wanted.

I swallowed my tears, bitter and coarse, like a shot of salt.

Anton hugged me from the back and planted a kiss on my cheek. "Ve," he said. "There are so many clientes y amigos de Doña Emilia who have been waiting to talk to you." He went into the kitchen for a second and, like magic, came back with a tray of tortilla and tiny meatballs in a spicy tomato sauce. "Go and serve them this, with a smile and some dignity, like Doña Emilia would have wanted."

I could smell the saffron, tomatoes, and perejil in the meatball side dish. Abuela's receta. As I was getting ready to face the crowd, my phone vibrated in my pocket. A message from Liam:

> Baby, how are you doing? I'm so sorry I'm not there with you. I love you. Call me.

The acoustics in the restaurant had always been less than ideal. Familiar and unfamiliar voices blended in the dining room; the laughter traveled and the sorrow too—the tears and the low whispers. I would call him back later.

I approached the vecinas with the tray; many were laughing about something with the ease of old friends. All of them took a piece of the tortilla and stacked their little plates with meatballs and olives. They were eating in silence now; I had interrupted an animated conversation. Chisme. They were probably talking about me, the mala nieta, and the irresponsible Mami, la loca, about how I wouldn't be home enough, but the precious time with Abuela I had lost, I could never get back.

They were right. I stood there awkwardly as they took seconds. As I was walking away, I felt Doña Rocío's cold hands on my back. I turned back and saw her warm smile—she was probably ashamed that I had seen her with the neighborhood gossip crew. Whatever she was saying to fuel the fire, she had a right to. She had been here holding Abuela's hand, presenting her with dishes of sancocho my grandmother couldn't stomach, while I was in the States running around NYC to try and make ends meet.

As I stood there in silence with Doña Rocío, she opened her mouth to say something but was interrupted by Don Víctor, who had approached me to pay his respects. He was the oldest regular in the restaurant and one of my abuela's best friends; he shook my good hand and held it in between his.

"I can't tell you, mijita, how much Doña Emilia's illness affected me. Caminito wasn't the same after she got sick. Anton and the other cooks tried their best, but it wasn't the same without her running everything." Don Víctor looked from the corner of his eye to the table where he and Doña Ruth used to sit.

"Me, too, Don Víctor," I said, standing close to him and taking in the sadness of a man who had known loss. I could almost see him at the restaurant with Doña Ruth, eating paella and toasting with the bottle of rioja they bought every Friday.

Anton put a cold glass of wine in my hand and smiled, letting me know that all was all right. He got busy with a tray. He was serving crusty bread made in house with tomato paste and anchovies. He skipped me because he knew I couldn't stand the smell of anchovies. Don Víctor took two pieces of bread and ate them anxiously. He was a widower, and I wondered where he was eating now that the restaurant was temporarily closed. Barranquilla held to tradition as tightly as it held to its ghosts. Older men would rather not eat than to learn how to cook at an advanced age, or at any age. I smiled at Don Víctor, seeing his loneliness in the way his almond eyes pointed downward, in the way he spoke too fast and anxiously, as if he wasn't used to talking much anymore.

"Doña Emilia's sickness was so brutal—she was so skinny toward the end, barely able to eat."

I thought about Abuela's frame, robust and elegant. How her cheeks always retained a plump glow. If I could have named my shame right then and there, I would have.

More people came. Doña Amalia, a lady who was always trying to take Abuela to church. Melisa, the neighbor, and her cheating husband, who couldn't stop looking at Doña Rocío's daughters, las mellas.

Sabina and García, Doña Rocío's daughters, gave me their condolences together. Sabina put a hand on my shoulder.

"Doña Emilia is going to be missed so much. She made the best paella in the city."

García rolled her eyes. "A ver, Sabina, Vi's abuela just died and you're talking about food?"

"Ha," Sabina scoffed, taking her hand away and turning to her sister. They stared at each other in the way that only they could. They could read each other without needing to speak. "Vi gets it. You get it, right?" Sabina and García looked at me, and I was just happy to see a familiar face. Ever since we were kids, they had always been like this. They spent every second of the day together, and they argued the entire time.

"I get it, I guess."

García smiled. "See, Sabina, you just need to be more sensitive." I smiled at them and squeezed Sabina's hand. I walked to the other regulars, leaving their chattering behind. I saw Don Gilberto, the butcher who on one of my visits tried to set me up with his son who lived in New Jersey, not caring that I had a boyfriend.

Don Víctor never moved from my side as people were giving me the pésames. He just kept eating and nodding, agreeing with everyone's words about how wonderful and generous Abuela was. When he had finished with three pieces of boquerones and two glasses of wine, during a quiet moment, he said, "I miss Doña Emilia's food more than I miss mi esposa's cooking. Mi Doña Ruth. Que en paz descanse."

I put a hand on his shoulder. "Sí, I know," I said, wondering if Abuela could ever rest in peace as this incessant chattering about her was going on.

~

Mami arrived while Anton started sending the waiters to make the rounds with more food and more wine. I could hear him from the kitchen saying, "Rápido, rápido. Why is the sauce on this plate all spread out like this?" I recognized Abuela in his orders. If ghosts possessing living beings was possible, Abuela's ghost was taking up residency in his anxious body.

I tried to ignore Mami, to not pay attention to her loud voice that traveled through the restaurant and landed directly on my ears and the haunted clik clik clik of her heels, that sound that used to drive Abuela insane. She used to tell Mami that one of these days she was going to get a sprain or roll down the stairs. That day hadn't arrived yet; if anything Mami seemed more confident than ever, walking across the room to a rhythm that only she could hear, blowing air kisses like she was homecoming queen. I went over to Mami, cheeks burning, hands clenched into fists, to ask her why she hadn't told me that Anton was buying the food all by himself. We were supposed to be taking care of those things—no él, he had done enough.

"Vi!" Anton, who was standing by the kitchen door, called me. "I need your help." I looked at Mami wiping a tear with her index finger in front of a small crowd, her acrylic nails sticking out. I rolled my eyes. I would deal with her later.

"Voy!" I said, running to the kitchen. There were countless trays on the counter.

"I need you to help me put the coca bread pizzas in the oven." Anton was frying something, and I wondered how much food he needed to make. But he was like Abuela in the sense that when it came to food, he always preferred to serve more than enough. For most it was over the top, but for Anton and Abuela it was a generosity of spirit.

Coca bread was a family recipe of a thick dough with onions, red bell peppers, tomatoes, and plenty of spices. It was one of Abuela's favorite dishes. The balance between the paprika and the spice was perfect—the vegetables were always juicy and flavorful.

"You know, Mami is outside with the highest heels I've ever seen her wear. After arriving late—" I opened the oven, and a wave of heat hit my face. "That's so her." I grabbed a baking sheet and then another one.

"You know how she is, have you forgotten?" Anton said, turning to look at me, a devilish grin plastered on his face. "You know her better than anyone. Paula is all about her. That's how it's always been."

I really did. I did. When I was little, I used to think something was wrong with me because Mamá would never stay for long—she always had somewhere to be, sometimes for days and sometimes for months. If I asked Abuela, she had endless stories about where Mamá could be. Mamá was on vacation en Francia, she was on a work trip, or she was helping out a friend. Abuela fabricated stories so I wouldn't think of Mami's shortcomings.

I put the last baking sheet in the oven and took out the cake. "Ay, mi mano—my hand!"

Anton ran to me and closed the oven. "Ay, Vi, why didn't you use the glove?"

"I wasn't thinking," I blurted out, the pain only amplified and my vision turned cloudy. I breathed out of my mouth in quick rapid gulps, tears welling in my eyes.

Anton guided me to the faucet and ran cold water on my hand.

"Qué pasa?" Mami asked what was going on, standing at the kitchen door.

"Vi got burned with a hot baking pan."

"What were you doing in the kitchen, Vi?" Mamá said, here to remind me that I didn't belong. "Espera, I think I saw someone who can help." Mamá disappeared as quickly as she had appeared.

Anton kept brushing my shoulder and holding my hand under the faucet. "I think we have aloe vera here somewhere. Can you stay here with your hand under the water like this?"

I nodded, closing my eyes. I wondered if Abuela had ever felt pain like this—if this kitchen where she had created her most memorable recipes had also been a source of pain.

The sound of familiar footsteps. The blend in the air of a familiar smell that was always in my brain. My whole body shivered in recognition, and I didn't know if it was the pain or the anticipation of seeing that face.

His name burned on the tip of my tongue. A name I had swallowed again and again back home in New York. The name that tasted bitter like regret. Bittersweet like a secret.

Rafa.

This couldn't be—I hadn't seen him since that night. Hadn't heard from him, apart from the gossip that las mellas told me sometimes when I was home.

He ran to me and took my hand between his. What was Rafa doing here? My vision was blurring from the pain, and although I wanted to focus on reality, my head felt woozy, and I couldn't form any real thoughts.

"Ay, Vi," he said, examining my hand. "This looks bad; did you press your hand on the pan?"

I nodded, my cheeks wet even though I didn't know when I had started crying.

"Vi," he said.

The word cut me like a slap, after all these years. I had pictured this encounter many, many times in my head, but I couldn't have imagined that it would be like this.

"What . . . ?" I shook my head, trying to wake myself up. "What are you doing here?"

Rafa smiled; I could see the concern in his almond eyes. "I'm here to pay my respects. Anton, wait, do you know if Doña Emilia kept an emergency kit in the kitchen?"

Anton looked at him for a couple of moments, as if he couldn't fathom what Rafa possibly could be doing in his kitchen. "Um, yeah, let me look." He ran to the side of the wall where it should have been and opened the kit—nothing.

Rafa was holding my hand, and I realized that the last time he had held my hand was on that beach—the place where our story had come to a halt. Paying his respects? After all these years—why now?

Anton kept opening and closing cupboards and then opened a cupboard below the sink. "Ajá!" he yelled.

Rafa let go of my hand and opened the kit. "We have what we need."

The pain came in waves, and I closed my eyes, wondering if I was dreaming. Seeing Rafa brought back all those emotions from when we were eighteen and he wouldn't pick up the phone and Doña Magdalena sent me away because he wouldn't talk to me. The promise I had made him. I had come back, but he had never been there to see me return.

Rafa washed his hands under the sink and smiled softly at me. An involuntary shiver on my shoulders. His smile was the same, his big straight teeth and his easy laugh. If this was the past, I would have pulled him close and kissed him. Where have you been? I would have asked.

But this wasn't a dream—this was reality.

"I'm going to put a little bit of cream on you; it's going to feel nice and cold. And then I'm going to bandage your hand." Rafa tapped my hand with his index finger, putting the cream on the burn. I closed my eyes, trying to hide away from the pain.

"Ay, Vi, I know, I know," he said. His tone was soft and comforting. He tilted his head, and his deep-brown eyes were staring at me. I looked away.

Anton put his hand on my shoulder, rubbing it in a calming motion, and Rafa worked as fast as he could. In a minute he was bandaging my hand tight and giving me instructions. "You need to apply this cream twice daily—I suggest going to the store and getting a couple of tubes. It runs out really fast. You can shower as normal, making sure to clean the area with a gentle soap. Before you bandage it with clean gauze, make sure that the burn is dry. The skin might lift . . ."

Rafa, suddenly, seemed distant. As if I were another one of his patients rather than the woman he'd wanted to marry at one point.

"So you just came? Why?" I tried, but as soon as I asked that, Mamá entered the scene like she had saved the day.

"Rafa, is she going to be okay? Ay, Vi, pobrecita," Mamá said, caressing my cheek with her index finger, the first time she had touched me since I'd arrived in Barranquilla. She got close for a moment and then turned to Rafa with a big smile. As if they'd always been friends. "Vi is so clumsy."

I took a deep breath. My cheeks turned warm, and the throbbing of my skin was intensifying. It was as if the skin was palpitating. My emotions were a pendulum, and they were oscillating between confusion and anger.

"Yes, it's a second-degree burn, so she needs to be diligent with keeping the area clean and covered." Rafa secured the gauze, wrapping it gently around my skin. "Here," he said, locking eyes with me.

Anton and Mamá looked at each other, Mamá raised an eyebrow. She had been the one that had brought him to the kitchen—but was she wondering what he was doing here too? After all these years, what was the use of this?

"Bueno," Anton said. "I'd better go out and start serving the food."

Mamá put an arm on Rafa's shoulder. "Good to see you, hijo," she said, and her eyes traveled from his face to his chest. Years ago Rafa for her was just bad news, the simple son of a plumber. But now that he was a doctor, things were different—her behavior toward him had softened as quickly as caramel melts under heat.

Las mellas, the last time I had been in Barranquilla, had told me that Rafa had finished school and now worked as an emergency doctor in one of the biggest hospitals in the city. When they told me that, a rush of sadness and joy came over me. I was glad that he accomplished so much, but part of me was sad for him—I knew that wasn't entirely what he wanted.

Mamá gave him one last smile and waved goodbye. Rafa turned to pick up Abuela's emergency kit in the kitchen. I looked at him, feeling the love I had felt for him once. Nostalgia mixed with anger. He had never returned my calls, never came to the door, never said goodbye.

"What are you doing here, Rafa?"

"Do you want to get some fresh air?" Rafa's eyes were pleading, as if he wanted to tell me something but not here. I softened for a moment, imagining how it would feel to hold his hand then.

"Um." No, the answer needed to be no. We had both made mistakes. I should have been clearer about my reason for turning down the proposal, and he should have given me some closure. He'd owed me at least a goodbye. There was no use in messing with the ghosts of the past.

"Only for a minute, they need me here," I said. Always contradicting myself. I didn't feel good, my skin was tender, and I felt tired from the hurt.

Rafa nodded and followed me to the back door that connected the restaurant to the back patio. The night outside was balmy, and the sky was covered in stars. I could hear the beating of my own heart blended in with the sounds of the crickets.

"Vi," he said, and my heart stopped. When he said my name, my knees felt weak. No one else had ever said my name right, as if he were singing it, almost a whisper.

"I came here to see you." A sigh escaped his lips.

My heart stopped, all the hairs in my arms lifting up. I recapped how the day had gone so far: We buried Abuela today, I got burned, and now Rafa was here. To see me.

His black wavy hair was longer than he kept it years ago, and his dark eyes were still as bright and big as I remembered. His luminous brown skin looked golden under the backyard's dim light. "You know how this barrio is, todo se sabe." *Everyone knows everything.* "I knew how much your abuela meant to you. I wanted to say I was sorry for your loss in person."

"How did you know I was going to be here?"

Rafa looked to one side, as if he were searching for the answer in the air. "I just knew, Vi," he brought his gaze back to me and half smiled. I wondered if he was nervous, because he was moving from side to side, unable to stand still. "I knew you wouldn't have missed Doña Emilia's funeral."

My hand was still throbbing. The words on the tip of my tongue were coated with tenderness. I had missed him. Even if I didn't dare to think about it too much or admit it to myself, the truth was that I was angry too.

"All those years ago, you never said goodbye. I didn't imagine you'd be here."

I couldn't move closer. I wouldn't. All those years ago, after I returned home from that night at the beach, he wouldn't pick up the phone, wouldn't come to the door, it was as if he had vanished from Barrio Prado, and Barranquilla. I was going crazy with regret and heartache. The States was my only option to forget. And here he was, as if the earth had spit him back out. Why now? It wasn't until I'd met Liam that I was able to breathe easier.

Liam. I took a deep breath, remembering. The crickets intensified their noises, and although I was in Barranquilla and the earth was below my feet, I knew I needed to ground my heart in New York, to the life I had with him.

"Yo sé, I'm really sorry, I think I also came because—" Rafa stopped pacing and looked at me.

"Bueno, I sure appreciate you're here. But if you'll excuse me." I released a deep breath, turning to return to Caminito. I felt my mouth unclench. I wanted to sit down; my legs were weak, and the tiredness of the last few days hit me like a wave.

Seeing him was a reminder of everything one leaves when life folds in half and the two sides don't connect. This half, this man, belonged to the side I couldn't bring with me.

"Wait!" Rafa said. "Wait. I'm sorry, Vi. I was so immature all those years ago." He folded his arms. "I should have said goodbye. I should have picked up your calls and offered closure. I denied us both that." It was his turn to release a breath, and I caught a whiff of his scent: oranges and spices.

"Thank you for saying that. And for being here. Abuela wasn't always so kind to you."

Rafa nodded and turned his head to the side. "Yeah, she wasn't my biggest fan."

He laughed, and I remembered his sonorous laugh—more a cackle. It was contagious. It always made me smile.

"I'm sorry about Emilia—I really am."

I nodded, feeling softer. We were distant, standing on opposite ends of the patio. Rafa had been my first love, a significant love, and we both had been marked by the impossible weight of family expectations. Me, a life in the States. And him, a life as a doctor. We both complied. Was he happy? Was it enough for him? I shook my head; it didn't matter.

I marveled at his strong shoulders and the way he always stood straight, even when he was nervous. Rafa was of Lebanese descent. He had thick brows, eyes with long pitch-black eyelashes, and a strong build. From the moment I had met him at a party when I was fifteen, I had been drawn to him. He always made me smile, even when I wasn't expecting it.

"I used to look through the glass windows just to see what this place looked like on the inside. 'Over my dead body,' she used to say about me coming to her restaurant. I guess she was right."

"Abuela always kept her promises," I said, feeling multiple eyes on me. From the restaurant, you could see the patio. I looked over to see the people in the restaurant, many of whom had been witnesses to our love over the years, ever since we were teenagers and unable to escape something that felt stronger than us. The voices of the other conversations were traveling in the room, the constant clinking of glasses and the laughter reminding me of where I was, my so-called legacy. The family restaurant was heavy and burdensome, tangled and complicated with so many decades of pain, and yet here I was, my past looking at me, materializing in the form of a man I had loved once.

Rafa took a step toward me, risking being electrocuted by the invisible fence we had built. I wondered if his arm was going to burn or turn to dust, but he rested his hand on my shoulder with the ease of before.

"Vi," he said, his touch on my uncovered skin. "I'm happy to see you. You look great." Rafa's hand lingered; his smile was the same.

I took a deep breath, taking in the familiar weight of his touch. My body remembered, and every inch of me hurt with the desire of wanting it all back at once. But it wasn't possible; I didn't know this man in front of me. We hadn't seen each other in so long. We weren't the same.

"Sorry, I should—"

"Viiiiii." I heard Anton's desperate voice from the kitchen. "Viiiiii."

I took a deep breath and turned; Anton was in front of the kitchen, rolling pin in hand, waiting for me. I sighed, relieved to be needed.

"Perdóname, Rafa," I said, and I felt his hand moving away. I ran toward the kitchen without looking back at him.

"Cuidate. Take care of your hand." He was standing in the same place as I got farther away from him.

Bless Anton. I needed to be whisked away from Rafa and my past. I went inside and closed the kitchen door. I rested my back on a wall and shut my eyes, memorizing Rafa's touch and his eyes and the way that he said my name, like no one else could, and inside my chest a little fire burned: for what I couldn't have again, for what I felt I had lost and no return could bring back.

Mami was talking to Anton; they were whispering, and their shoulders were hunched forward like they were planning something. As soon as I entered the room, they got quiet. I was surprised by this; Anton and Mamá had never been close. Anton thought Mamá was lazy whenever she worked at the restaurant, and Mamá thought he took up too much space. I wondered what these two could be planning together.

"Ven acá, Vi. We haven't had a chance to talk," Mami said, standing tall and looking down at me, courtesy of her impossibly high heels. I wanted to sit down, but there were no stools. I put my hands on my knees to rest my back.

"Vi." Mamá looked to the side, searching for words.

"What? Dime, Mamá," I said, hearing the exhaustion in my voice.

"Mamá left Caminito to you."

The throbbing in my hand returned. Dreams upon dreams upon dreams. I stood up straight, the tightness in my chest getting worse. Caminito had never had a place for me—Abuela had made this clear. This had to be a joke. Abuela didn't want me near the kitchen. The first night I'd spent in Caminito's kitchen, I burned myself. Even after her death, Caminito found ways to push me out.

"Well, technically you have the biggest percent of ownership. You have sixty-six percent, and Anton and I have seventeen percent." She took a deep breath, her brown eyes staring at the door rather than at me. I looked back, a reflex, wondering if there was something behind me. "I mean, you don't live here. You never wanted anything to do with this place." She put a hand on her hip, her signature accusatory position. "I can't understand why Mamá would do that."

"That's not true," I said, still clinging to Mami's words. She had inherited Abuela's power: her words lacerated with the precision of blades.

"I love this place. This is Abuela's restaurant. What are you talking about, Mamá? This place means the world to me." I noticed I was raising my voice, and the words that came out of my mouth sounded high pitched, childlike. I looked over at Anton, who stood in front of the stove, hands crossed, looking at Mamá. Mamá was probably lying, I thought. This restaurant couldn't be more mine than theirs.

Abuela had never wanted me to be a part of Caminito.

"Mija, mija," she repeated. "It doesn't matter what you think of this place." Mami took a deep breath and pointed toward the dining space. "This place, mijita." Mami shook her head and poured herself a glass of wine. "Every second the lights are on, we're losing money."

Caminito was losing money, we had just lost Abuela, and I had lost a layer of skin on my hand. How much more could we lose in the span of a couple of days?

"Peráte," I asked Mami after a moment, my heart pounding. "You don't want to sell, do you?" I looked over to Anton, who shook his head and opened his mouth to speak.

Mami interrupted him.

"Bueno." She lifted a brow and smiled, although I could tell she wasn't happy. "Quién lo diría, you care after all. I can tell you what we both want and then you can decide, since technically this place belongs more to you than to us." She rolled her eyes, as if she couldn't believe what she was saying. "And I have been the one working here, not you. You are never here. Remember that."

I knew I hadn't been here. I had a knot in my throat I couldn't swallow. What was the point of telling me that? She looked at me and pushed a strand of her silky hair back.

"Pero . . . would it feel right?" She crossed her hands and looked at me, raising her chin up. "For you to make the decision after leaving for so long?"

"Mamá—"

"I think this place had its run. It was a beautiful number of years, and it gave us so much. But it's time to let it go . . . a property like this is worth a lot of money in a rapidly changing city like Barranquilla."

"Vi." Anton walked from the stove to where I was standing at the prep table in the middle of the room. He grabbed my good hand and held it. His eyes had a kinder expression than Mami's.

"Este restaurante means so much to me. And I want to run it. I want you to help me keep it open. I can't do it alone." He looked over to Mami, who was still crossing her arms. "I can't do it alone."

"No sé," I blurted out, overwhelmed. Anton leaned over on the metal surface of the counter. He looked tired and sad. Maybe we all did. "I live in the States. I have clients, illustrations I requested an extension on, rent, responsibilities. Liam."

"See, Anton? She doesn't have time. The best thing to do right now is to sell."

I tried to search Anton's eyes, but he looked away.

"Qué? Tell me," I said, hands in the pocket of my apron. Mami's eyes were open wide, her hand still over her mouth. What was so big that even Mami was lost for words?

"Dime, Mami," I said, desperate for someone to tell me whatever they were not saying.

Mami looked over to Anton, who met her eyes with worry.

"The restaurant owes a lot of money. Millones."

"What?"

Abuela didn't owe money. Not that kind of money.

"Impossible," I said, looking over to Anton, who simply nodded as if Mami was singing a tune he recognized.

"No me crees?" Mami opened her eyes. "Look." She grabbed from her pocket a folded piece of paper. "The restaurant is at risk of being repossessed."

I took the paper in my hands and opened it. The letter was soft and wrinkled, as if it had been read again and again and memorized.

Señora Emilia,

Aviso legal:

My eyes got cloudy. I had to stop reading. I knew what the rest said. We couldn't lose Caminito, not after losing Abuela. I looked around in the kitchen, trying to find my footing. Anton and Mami were staring at me.

"What do we do?" I said, searching for answers in Anton's eyes. I'm sure he had read the letter many times. I was sure he could recite it from memory. "How much do we owe?"

Anton sighed as if his body contained the weight of an impossible secret. "One hundred millones de pesos. We need to get them the money in forty-five days."

Twenty-five thousand dollars. I didn't have that kind of money. Anton didn't, and Mami sure as hell didn't have a centavo.

I tried to sit down and then remembered Abuela kept no stools in her kitchen. "I don't know anything about restaurants," I said, their eyes still on me. I looked at my bandaged hand, proof that I couldn't even function in Caminito. They looked at each other, as if they knew what I was going to say. "Tell me what to do," I said, hearing the tremble in my voice. For the second time that night I felt the tears already forming in my eyes—don't cry, don't cry, I told myself. Not in front of her.

"Quédate," Anton said. "Stay. Help us figure this out, at least for a month. Tu abuela arranged everything so you'd have the power to make a decision. She must have known you might be able to do something." His voice was quiet and his eyes were wide, pleading. I wondered if with his eyes, Anton was saying, *Don't leave me here alone with her, please.*

I knew how hard it was for him to ask for something like that. Anton was used to depending only on himself. Abuela had taught us that—to be strong, because people let you down. That was the life he knew, and yet he had gotten over his pride and asked me.

Mami said, hand on her hip, "Be reasonable. This place is a hole, just swallowing money. It has been like that for years. Do what's best for your family, for us. You owe me at least that."

There it was. The weight of family obligation. I started tapping my sneakers, my feet imitating Mami's restless heels. Abuela would have nagged us, telling us that we were about to make a hole in her floor.

"Un mes," I said, before I could think it through. "Let's try to do something for the restaurant for one month. And if it doesn't work, we can decide then . . . I just can't stand to lose one more thing. Not after losing her. I can't sell right now." I looked at Mami, who quickly shook her head.

"Ay, Vi. You don't know what you're doing."

I didn't. I had no idea what the hell I was doing. And yet I knew that the idea of selling made my stomach hurt.

"Un mes, Mamá. You can't give us one month?" I asked, standing up straighter.

"We're just going to get more in debt. What are you going to do? Or him?" Mamá turned to Anton. "We're losing money, mijita, despierta! What we need is to sell the restaurant and use the money to pay the debt and split what's left."

"How could you want to let it go so easily? Without a fight? That's how little you care?" I raised my voice. Mamá and I were face to face, anger sitting at the bottom of my stomach. I knew that if I dared to say something else, the damage between her and me could be irreparable.

"Okay, no more," Anton said and looked at us both. "Un mes, we can start with that." Anton walked toward me. He reached for my good hand and kissed it. I grabbed his hand, and the sweat on his skin made me feel a little better; it reminded me of Abuela and how hard she worked. Her hands were always clammy due to the heat of her kitchen, how much of herself she constantly was giving the world through her food. "Vi, you won't regret it." He planted a loud kiss on my cheek.

Ay, I thought, wondering if there was enough room for me and Mamá in this kitchen.

"I hope you don't regret this." Mamá and I stared at each other for a moment before she looked away, the distance lingering between us.

"We are going to save Caminito," Anton said, and in his voice I could hear a hint of the warmth that he'd radiated when we were kids. He always had a positive spin on everything, a kind word for everyone. His cheerfulness, from a young age, was a form of survival. Anton had always dreamed for all of us.

We were all there in Abuela's kitchen, the three people she cared about most in the world. I smiled, looking at her protégé, so wise and talented, his smile illuminating the room even as Mami remained skeptical and rightly so.

Where were we going to get that kind of money?

~

Before I called Liam, I stood outside on the patio, allowing my uncovered legs to get massacred by mosquitoes. I imagined him at home, perhaps asleep after an exhausting but exhilarating day of work. Liam loved working as an architect and the culture around it. The respect that he got from his peers and the praise. He was good at what he did. I, on the other hand, was always stretched thin and unhappy with the sheer number of hours I worked. I knew I was on the verge of reinvention; I needed to do something different, but I didn't know what yet.

It had been an endless night, and as time stretched in front of me, I yearned to talk to him. Liam had always been my shelter in an inhospitable city.

The phone rang, and I closed my eyes, preparing for what I should say. I didn't even know where to start.

"Vi," he said. His voice sounded sleepy, as if I had just woken him up. "I called you earlier tonight, but I didn't know if you were busy. I've been worried about you."

"I know, I'm sorry. It's been a very long two days. I'm still processing so much." I stayed in silence, and Liam did too. "I'm staying for a month," I blurted out.

The only noise on the patio was the crickets that seemed to intensify the longer I stood there. In the distance, I could hear the voices of the people still at the restaurant.

"Oh," he said. "Why?" Liam's voice sounded more alert. "Vi, your clients and work. You have so many projects going on. Did something happen?"

The pain in my hand was still constant. Thoughts about Abuela, Rafa, Mamá, and the restaurant were all swirling in my head. Liam and I had never been apart for so long. I wondered how the distance was going to affect us. And Rafa. He was a scene that replayed in my head over and over. I had surprised myself by how anxious he still was able to make me.

"Vi?" he asked, nervously. "I'm sorry, I just . . . didn't expect this. What made you decide that? Do you want me to come?" Liam had gone into superhero mode. This was one of our fights: I didn't always need sheltering, protecting, or him rescuing me.

"No, I don't want you to come. The month is going to go by so quickly." I walked around the patio, waking up the mosquitoes that danced around my ankles. "I mean, I do, of course I do," I said, worried that I sounded too harsh. "But the truth is there's so much happening. I don't know if it would be good for you to be here." I paused, examining the reasons I didn't want Liam here. It would be too much to have him here while trying to navigate saving the restaurant. It didn't have anything to do with Rafa. I wouldn't see him again; I would keep my distance.

"Abuela left the majority of the restaurant to me."

"What? I thought you said she never wanted you there and that she always kicked you out."

"Well, that's what she did. Yes, but Abuela didn't do things without a reason. She was extremely calculating. If she did, there must have been a reason why."

Liam sighed into the phone. It was a long sigh, full of tiredness and unsaid words.

"What are you going to do, Vi?"

"I haven't even thought that far ahead. Liam, the restaurant is struggling so much. We have so much debt. I don't know what to do but to stay and help. Besides, Mamá wants to sell—" I looked around at the overgrown grass, the flowers torched by the sun. "I can't let her do that, at least not yet." Abuela loved her plants and her garden, and now it was all in ruins, overgrown, brittle and unkempt. I reached down to touch the dirt with my fingers. It was dry; no one had watered it in months.

"What could you possibly do? You know nothing about working in restaurants, Vi. What do you know about running one? Let alone saving one?"

"I don't. I don't know, but I have to try. This restaurant was Abuela's life. She fed and clothed us with this place. There's also Anton. He has worked for Abuela his entire life, with so much care and devotion. I can't disappoint him like this."

I checked the time. It was late. I imagined Liam sitting up in the bed and pulling off the covers to get out and walk around like he did when he was having trouble wrapping his head around something.

"For who?"

"I've told you about him. He was the boy who used to help Abuela with the restaurant. Anyway, I don't want to talk about this right now. I want to hear you're here for me and that you respect my decision even if you don't understand it. You at least could have some faith in me, no?" I touched my forehead. Little droplets of sweat were accumulating. I closed my eyes, feeling the balm of the Caribbean air at night.

I couldn't believe Liam had forgotten about Anton. Many of my childhood stories took place in Caminito. Stories of me sneaking out to the kitchen and Anton and me creating recipes in the kitchen, pretending to cook when he was working. I was trying to carve myself space in a kitchen that didn't want me, while Anton was carving himself space in the kitchen in order to survive.

"I know you can do something for the restaurant, Vi. I'm just concerned, a month is a lot." I heard his steps, pacing around the room. "I'm just going to miss you. That's all. I'm going to miss you," he repeated, as if he needed to make sure I would hear him. His voice was softer now. Liam couldn't stay mad very long. I imagined going to bed with him that night, escaping the New York winter and fitting in the perfect nook he always had for me when I arrived late from work. New York was never easy, and yet, it would be so much easier to be there right now. In the home we had built together.

"I miss you, too, my love," I said, my voice softer as well. Now that things were quieter, I let myself miss him. "I got a little burn on my hand," I said, looking at the wrapped hand; the skin still felt vulnerable.

"It's nothing, though, a friend of the family who is a doctor took care of it." The lie slipped off my tongue so easily. It was easier this way. Liam didn't know many particulars about Rafa and me; he just knew Rafa was my first love. But Liam had always been adamant about not dwelling on exes, and that story had always felt too big to put into words. Liam also didn't know Rafa was a doctor, and he certainly didn't know that he was there in the restaurant—I looked back, feeling the weight of my past with him. I was grown now, I reminded myself: Rafa was an old story, and that was that.

The burn was an open heart beating under my skin.

"What? Are you okay, Vi?" The concern in his voice returned. "Can you even work in a kitchen with the wound on your hand?"

Missing him was replaced by anger. My cheeks started getting warm again. "Liam, I'm not some wounded bird. I made a mistake."

"I'm just saying . . ." Liam paused. "I'm worried."

"I'm fine. Please don't be mad. But can we talk in the morning? I know I haven't been in touch as much, but I need to go back. They are doing this reception for Abuela in the restaurant. I need to be there for Anton. I'll call you tomorrow, yes? I promise," I said, still annoyed that he didn't think I was capable.

"Okay." I heard the rustling sound of the sheets. "I love you." His tone got quieter, like a candle dimming. "Don't forget. Call me." Liam wanted to keep talking—I knew him—but he also wanted to sleep. He liked being early at work, being fresh and well rested in the morning.

"I love you too," I said and hung up, my body suddenly sucked dry. I closed my eyes and let the salt in the air wash over me. An image of Liam at the wine bar, that night we met, appeared in my head. He was looking at me with those sea-blue eyes and telling me that he could tell I was going to stay in his life for a long time. He was sorry to be so blunt, he didn't want to scare me, but he could feel in his bones that this was true.

"Yeah, right," I remembered saying, taking a sip of the expensive wine he had bought us. Liam half smiled, and I melted. He had a sharp jaw, and he confidently touched my hand, as if he was used to touching me all the time.

"You probably date a lot," I said, moving my hand away.

"I did." Liam looked down before meeting my eyes. "That was then."

I opened my eyes and felt a hand on my back. I jumped, fully aware that if such things as ghosts existed, my family house and Barrio Prado were overflowing with them.

"Doña Rocío?" I asked, expecting to see her behind me. I was standing in the middle of the backyard with my back to the restaurant, moments after hanging up with Liam. A cold current of air brushed around my legs, and I braced myself for the possibility of seeing Abuela in the flesh, ready to tell me that my elbows were ashy or that my hair was too long. Something insignificant compared to the magnitude of what was shifting in our home and in Caminito.

But it wasn't Abuela. It was the familiar voice again.

"Hola," I said to Rafa, who stood in front of me in the dark. I was shivering despite how hot it was. I tried to push my hair behind my ears, but I could feel several curly strands escaping my ponytail. I gave up and instead used my hands to wave away the mosquitoes that were continuing to target my uncovered legs. I didn't dare move closer. Seeing Rafa after all these years was confusing, sure, but that was all. I couldn't let myself be sucked in again. I was only going to be in Barrio Prado for a month.

"Sólo . . . I only wanted to say goodbye. I have to wake up early tomorrow for a shift." Rafa looked at me with his brown eyes squinting; all the lights in the dark patio were dimmed, and I could barely see his face.

Rafa's scent lingered in the air—when Rafa was near, I always knew he was in the room. The air in Barranquilla had a way of announcing him; the sound carried his steps.

"You're a doctor now," I said, smiling with joy for the first time since I had arrived in Barranquilla. Las mellas had told me once when I came home for Christmas. They'd said it so casually. And I'd pretended that I didn't care, but just the mention of his name made me shiver. Rafa had become what his parents always dreamed for him to be. And he did that despite losing his dad and having to take his place around the house. "Doña Magdalena must be so thrilled."

Rafa put his hands in his pockets and looked at me. I wondered if in the open air, my garlic scent could be masked in the smells of the overgrown grass and the dirt. He was studying me, as if he could tell I was lying to him and making small talk to make him stay. Did I want to make him stay? No. He had turned the page as soon as I said no, showing me that if we weren't on his terms, then it wasn't meant to be.

It wasn't meant to be, but then, why was my left leg shaking?

"If she could, she would wear a pin that announced it. She's thrilled." He rolled his eyes. "It's her favorite sentence in the Spanish language now." He laughed, and I was unable to resist. I laughed too.

"She must be so proud."

"Ajá, too proud." Rafa shifted from side to side, and when he moved his arms, he brushed my elbow. It was as if someone had lit a match and thrown it on my body.

"How long are you staying?" Rafa asked. "We should go out for coffee before you leave. I haven't seen you in ten years." He reached into his pocket and pulled out his car keys, playing with them on his index finger.

No, what did this man want coffee for? He had shut down. He hadn't said goodbye. What could there be left to say? Although it had been many moons ago, I could still feel the wetness of my cheeks from crying myself to sleep.

I bent to slap a mosquito. "For a month or so." I stood straight again and brushed a flyaway strand off my forehead; like magic three more reappeared. I wasn't naive. I knew that Rafa had a pull on me, and I couldn't entertain this any longer.

Rafa leaned forward and softly brushed one curl away and put it behind my ear. I inhaled, holding my breath.

"Your hair . . . it has a mind of its own,"' he said, suddenly closer to my face. My hair obeyed in that instant. At that moment, I swore that I could hear my heart beating. I took a deep breath in, trying to pull myself together.

"I'm going to be very busy, I'm not sure if I can fit it in," I said, lowering my gaze.

Rafa nodded, as if he understood what I was really saying. It was best to not disturb the past. "I'm here, if you need anything. Please take care of your hand, sí?" His voice was soft, almost a whisper. "Vamos adentro. They're going to eat you alive," he said as I followed him back into the restaurant, again. A memory of a starry night in Barranquilla came to my head. I was in the audience of an outdoor patio, when we were both seventeen. I was so proud of him: it was his first time playing his original songs in front of people that weren't his mother or me. As he played a song on his guitar, everyone was mesmerized by his voice. At that moment I had thought that there was no one else that I would ever feel that way for. Yes, I was young. And yet, I knew.

With every step, I told myself: I was wrong, I was wrong, I was wrong.

Our love story was a written chapter from a forgotten book. It was done.

"Hey, Vi," he said softly, turning to me, before opening the door.

"Yes?"

"It's good to see you."

I nodded, scared of saying another word. He walked away, and I went to the sink to wash my hands as if I could banish his smell imprinted in my skin. We had barely touched, and yet, I remembered it. It lingered in the air. Should I have said yes? For what?

It was better this way. It was better to end the cycle before it began.

~

"Violeta! Vi!" Abuela's voice.

I woke up looking around at both sides of the room. It was dark, and I couldn't see much, but my heart was beating with anticipation. I was dying to see her, and at the same time, nothing would scare me more.

"Mija," she said, in a voice that was very matter of fact, as if I had just seen her the day before and she was waiting for me at home with cafecito y galletas. In my dream, she was sitting by the end of my bed.

"You sleep so heavy these days! I called and called."

My entire body shivered. Her touch was warm and damp, as it had been when she was alive. Was she real? I shook my head, wanting her spirit to leave. Wanting it to stay.

"Abuela?" My voice quavered, and tears were close. I could feel them.

"Quién más? You don't remember me anymore?" she said, crossing her legs. Abuela was sitting by the bed. Her face was younger and her hair fell nicely on the sides of her face, black and thick. No white hair anymore. She was beautiful, younger than I ever remember seeing her. She lifted her chin, and her posture was flawless; she was orgullosa, proud as the most majestic tree.

I was going crazy. Or I was dreaming. I was dreaming, I was dreaming, I was dreaming . . .

"No estás loca. I told you these things happened," she said, as if she knew what I was thinking. Abuela always talked about ghosts. When I was growing up, she would tell me stories that would leave me sleepless for days. We came from a bloodline of folks whose spirits stuck to them like gum. Abuela was barely a couple of inches away from me, so close that I could touch her if I wanted to, and yet I didn't dare move. My teeth were chattering as if I were naked in the snow.

"Abuela." I swallowed and leaned back on the bed, hoping that I would wake up. "Qué puedo hacer por ti?" I asked her, desperately wanting to know what I could do for her. I had always heard that ghosts stayed among the living up until someone helped with a task they needed to complete. Something they had left unfinished. "I'll do anything, just say the word."

Abuela's laugh was expansive. She tilted her head back and unleashed her bruja cackle. She shook her head.

I had so many questions. What was death like? How was she a ghost? Why had she left the restaurant to me if she never wanted me there in the first place? But words didn't come easy when you had a ghost in front of you. All the blood left my face.

"Mijita, I just realize that I misled you in so many ways."

"Are you really here?" I said, lifting the sheets from my body. I didn't know what to do. If I stood up, would she leave? If I touched her, would she dissolve?

They said that when people died, you took them with you everywhere. Perhaps I was talking to my grief, and my grief was talking back. Abuela was still sitting there, smiling at my question.

"Estás bien?" I asked if she was okay. That was the most important thing.

She tilted her head and stared at me. Her dark eyes were the same, small but expressive. I couldn't see too well, but her eyelashes were long and curled, not sparse like they were when she was older. Her expression was clearer, wiser than ever. When she looked at me, I felt exposed in a way that made me want to run all the way back to the States. It was as if she knew something about me that I didn't.

"Bueno." She hesitated; her voice was quieter, and she wasn't smiling anymore. Her hand was still on my ankle, but she wasn't gripping it any longer. "Sí, hay algo. There's something you can do."

"Qué?" I asked. I could hear the beating of my heart as loud as a drum. I put my hand over it so it would be quiet, but it persisted.

"Duermete. Go back to sleep. There's so much that we need to talk about, and we have time," she said softly. Before I could say anything, her body was already leaving the room.

"Abuela?" I asked again from my bed, unable to move. "Don't go," I said, my voice breaking. I had already lost her once. I wasn't ready for her to leave again. "Abuela!" I called out, wanting to hold on to her just a second longer. "Where are you going?"

I wondered if ghosts hid between the cracks of the house, if they slept in the beds that had belonged to them, or if they didn't need sleep at all.

This house had so many secrets, and some of them, I realized, were best kept in the dark.

CHAPTER SIX: BARRANQUILLA IN THE RAIN

The next morning, Mami had brought in a couple of chairs for the kitchen. Mamá, Anton, and I were sitting in silence, staring at our warm tea. I looked over to her, soaking her bag of tea over and over again. She finally looked up.

"It will take a miracle to save Caminito," Mami said, slouching forward. She always was so proud of standing up straight, and now her shoulders pointed to the floor. She was sitting like I did. She took a sip of her green tea and stared at me intensely, as if she wanted me to think this whole thing was my fault and it was on me to solve it.

She shook her head and looked down at her cup. "Mami took that loan to send you to the States, and for a while, the restaurant was just paying that off. She didn't have any money for updating the decor or to keep this place up to date."

Abuela had put herself in debt to send me to the States. The failure of Caminito was my fault. "Did you know this?" I asked Mamá, who was just going over a laundry list of everything that was wrong with Caminito: the decor screamed nineties. No one wanted to come to an old restaurant anymore. We needed new appliances.

"What? That you made your abuela go in debt with the bank?"

My cheeks turned hot, and I felt my jaw clench. Mamá always put things in a way that made me look like the villain.

Mami put her elbows on the metal surface and smoothed the lines on her forehead with her fingers. "I'm exhausted, Vi. You want this to work, no? Is this the time to go over family drama?"

Mami was wearing golden bracelets that went up and down as she moved her arms. Under the dimmed lights, she looked young and upset. When I was little, I would observe her getting ready: two pumps of perfume, always Chanel No. 5, on her wrists and on her neck, a cherry-red lip, and her hair (already mostly straight) blown upside down for volume. In this kitchen, in front of Anton and me, she looked flawless. Not as if she was ready to put on an apron and work in a sweaty kitchen but about to rush out the door to meet the love of her life. I, on the other hand, was freshly out of the shower. My hair was wet, and I had no makeup on, which meant I looked like a child.

Mami stood up in one quick movement and started pacing around the room, shaking her head simultaneously. I looked over to Anton, who just shrugged.

I bit my tongue; my teeth were pressuring the tip of the flesh. I thought about the night before, how my guilt manifested in the form of Abuela. Ever since I came to Barranquilla, I had felt her presence everywhere.

"Vi!" Mami insisted. "Where are you?" she said, hands on her hips.

"Qué?" I asked her. "I'm thinking," I said, just as sharply as she'd spoken to me. I heard a sigh coming from Anton, who was still sitting next to me—he always hated being caught up between the two of us.

"Entonces, what are you thinking, Paula?" Anton asked, trying to diffuse the thick air in the kitchen we were all breathing. His tone was clipped and exasperated. Anton was scratching his hands and pulling on the sleeves of his chef jacket. He was itching to get to work.

I stood up and grabbed a bottle of wine I had hidden under the sink. I opened it and poured myself a large glass.

From the kitchen window, I saw that our third customer of the night had entered the restaurant, followed by another regular. I nodded at the customer, saying hello from afar, wondering if he even recognized me. I poured Mamá a glass and served a little one for Anton.

"No, Vi, you know I don't drink at work," Anton said, staring at the glass I was putting in front of him.

"Bueno, you drink now," I said, putting the bottle of wine to the side but close to me, in case we needed it. The only waiter, Berto, entered the kitchen and left with a plate of meatballs with saffron and dill that Abuela served with crunchy crusty bread and basil from her garden.

"It's Friday night, and there's like three people here." I took a sip of the red wine; if nothing else made sense right now, the oak flavor of the wine and the notes of vanilla were comforting.

Comforting. That's a word that I didn't use too much in New York. Work, friends to see, Liam, my illustrating hustle. I was constantly worn thin and exhausted, dragging my barely there body around Brooklyn and Manhattan to make ends meet. My life in Barranquilla had been all about comfort. Friday nights with Abuela when she wasn't at the restaurant, watching movies on the couch. My memory traveled to Doña Rocío bringing us food that she had made for the weekend. Her Lebanese plates: the fragrant quibes made of meat, mint, and parsley that she would serve as soon they came out of the fryer: warm, soft, and perfectly spiced. Her creamy labneh drizzled with olive oil and fresh herbs. How soft and pillowy her almond-and-chicken rice was. The sweetness of her syrupy rose pastries. My stomach growled thinking about her mastery of garbanzos and lentils that never came out of a can. How she could transform the cheapest of ingredients into something rich and luxurious.

"What if we change it up?" I said, suddenly arrested by the memory. "Let's serve Abuela's family food and introduce other things. Like who says that we can't serve Rocío's mint quibes as an appetizer? We can play around with Caribbean-infused Mediterranean tapas. I've worked in restaurants for a couple of years now. People love little things to share while they drink. We can attract a younger crowd like that. You've been craving cooking differently, too, no? How long has it been since you've wanted to try to cook your own food?" I said to Anton, who grabbed the glass of wine and started taking baby sips.

Anton stared at one corner of the room, thinking.

"Ay, Vi. You think it's that easy?" Mami said, drinking half the glass of wine in one gulp. "Caminito needs a real solution. The accountant said that for the restaurant to stay afloat, it would have to earn double what it's making currently for a year plus what it owes. How do we pay that? With a tapas night?" Mami took a deep breath. "Pff, Vi, por favor. Please."

"Mamá," I said, raising my voice. "We can't keep serving the same food if we want our finances to change. What's so hard to understand?"

Anton stayed quiet. I stood up and peeked through the kitchen window, and Anton followed to tend to some pots he had on the stove. The kitchen smelled like spicy bell peppers and paprika. We had a few tables and one waiter. Soon, we would have to stop fighting and do something if we didn't want to lose the few customers we had.

"Ajá, Anton. What do you think?" I asked. Purposely not looking at Mami.

"I think that we can also do grilled bell peppers stuffed with crispy chickpeas and mint. Garbanzo croquettes filled with chèvre, kale, and red pepper flakes for a kick of spice. Maybe something sweet that plays with plums and dough . . . ," Anton said, quickly jotting down everything in a little notebook he produced out of his pocket. It was a similar notebook to the one Abuela used to have.

"Jesús. Anton, you too? A tapas night is not going to save this. We have no customers!" Mamá said, pointing to the front of the restaurant. "No one new is coming. I know all the clients by name. How does one make a successful business work like that?"

"We don't know if it's going to work if we don't try it. We at least have to try new things, get some new people into the restaurant," I said, raising my chin up to fake confidence.

"And what about the deudas, the overdue bills, 'jita? Are you going to pay for those with your tapas?"

"Quibes are not experimental, Ma. At least I'm proposing something new. What are you doing besides complaining?"

I took a step, getting closer to her. Mamá stood up straight, towering over me.

"Well, you need to keep your feet on the ground. Be grounded in reality. I don't know which universe your head is in right now. But in this plane"—Mami moved her hands in a big circle, like she was tracing the earth with her small hands—"this restaurant is drowning in debt. Do you understand?"

"I think we can do it." I stared at her. I wasn't afraid. I was not a child anymore. I turned to Anton. "Dime, what should we cook, Anton? Let's try new things." I walked to the sink to wash my hands, walking away from her.

Anton faced the stove. He plated one of Abuela's classics out of a big caldero. The customers had ordered two plates of the sticky arroz de cerdo with peas and carrots. The smell of the brown sugar and the soy carried the whole dish and left a trail in the kitchen. That was the dish Abuela used to make when Abuelo's salary was stretched too thin (which was often) and there wasn't enough money to cover good cuts of meat at the supermarket. Abuelo had been in and out of our lives, for as long as I could remember. As Abuela got sicker and sicker, he disappeared for good. So when there was more food in the house, they ate pork, and when there was less, they ate arroz con huevo, fried brains, and other cheap cuts like kidneys and liver that Abuela would serve with crispy papa amarilla. "Poor people food," she used to say, but the truth was that those were the dishes that stood out in my memory the most. The dishes that tasted like creativity mixed in with dignity—just because my ancestors were barely surviving didn't mean they couldn't eat well.

"Perhaps we can also play with some of Abuela's more humble dishes. The restaurant can go from being classy Spanish Colombian food to a mixture of affordable Mediterranean and Spanish food that's a wink to the immigrants who came to Barranquilla with very little." I looked over to Anton and Mami, who stared at me wide eyed. No one had ordered any food for a while, and Anton was standing still. Like he didn't know what to do with himself.

"Qué tal . . . what about . . ." I got closer to Anton. "Arroz con huevo. Abuela's classic weekday dish with curry, herbs, and soy sauce. Could be a hit como una entrada or a tapa. We could serve the rice like Abuela used to serve it: from the bottom of the pot. So crispy it was almost a little burnt—cúcayo—we could add crispy papa amarilla on top . . . some cilantro." My mouth watered just thinking about how that dish could warm you up instantly. Abuela always had a magical touch for knowing which herbs could make a dish comforting and at the same time keep you on your toes. Every bite would be different. Spicy, sweet, more herbal. My stomach rumbled with hunger—I put a hand on it, trying to quiet it down. Although I was ravenous, this was no time to eat. This was the time to show Mami I deserved my place in Caminito. To show myself.

"So we make this into a simple restaurant where people could have lunch every day?" Mami crossed her arms. "That's not what Mamá wanted."

"What do you know about what she wanted?" I said, standing in front of her. Mami remained seated like a queen, arms folded above her flat belly. She looked victorious although she hadn't even fought yet.

Mamá lifted her chin, dignified. I wanted to stand tall, but I felt small. Insecure from the fact that I hadn't been here for Abuela. That everyone in this room knew more about the restaurant than I did.

"Mija, por favor," she uttered, laughing and looking at the side of the kitchen as if she couldn't bother with me. With every word she made me feel smaller.

"No más." Anton stood in the middle of us. "So tired of you two. No más. Either you behave in my kitchen"—he spread his arms between us, as if he thought we were going to hit each other—"or you leave. Entendido?"

Mami sat there, her mouth a frown. She didn't move.

"Vi. Understood?"

I nodded, although I didn't know why I had to be the one to understand if she was the one misbehaving.

Mami poured herself another glass of wine, and before Anton could protest, she put a hand in the air. "Déjame," she said, *let me do it.*

"Doña Emilia wanted the restaurant to survive. You can't save something that doesn't exist," Anton said, turning his back on us and lighting up the stove to make more food that nobody was asking for. His restless hands needed to do something—that's what Abuela had always taught him. In the kitchen, you needed to be kept on your toes.

"Bueno," she said, dropping a hand and hitting her hip. "I trust you." She looked at Anton. "But if this fails at the end of the month, we're selling."

Naturally, Mami didn't trust me.

"Boy, stop!" Abuela would have said, moving him from the stove and turning it off. "Vete a tu casa," *go home.* Rest up and save your forces for when the restaurant had customers again. But she wasn't here, and I knew that the only thing that could keep Anton's head at ease was feeding people, even if there was no one to feed.

"Anton, what are you going to make?" I said to him, standing by his side, watching him get his pots and pans as an artist gathers his tools. He poured olive oil on a pan liberally and started the stove. Mami took a sip of the wine, sighed, and stood up.

"Bueno," she said, "tell me what to do, Anton."

I watched him as he started dancing around the kitchen: cutting vegetables, seasoning them, and starting bases for sauces. I watched him as the whole world dissolved around him.

"We can't keep wasting food. We don't have a lot of customers, but it's raining—" I looked at the window; it was raining hard, which meant that no one could go anywhere. Not in Barranquilla, where the streets turned into streams with the ruthlessness of rivers. They washed away entire cars, buses, and even people who attempted to walk in the merciless rain.

Anton looked at me. "Why don't you tell the customers that we need some testers, and maybe you can also look at the books?"

Of course, I didn't expect to have my place in the restaurant instantly. But I did, didn't I? I expected to be cooking and moving around the restaurant like I'd always belonged here, like I had never left. "Bueno," I said, leaving the room. Mami and Anton moved around the kitchen like they owned it.

Caminito was what they called a "Restaurant Tradición" in the city. Which meant that the architecture was so old and characteristic of the city that it had to be preserved by law. You didn't have to spend too long in the restaurant to understand this. The restaurant had high ceilings and beautiful big windows with elaborate white arches on top of them. Black-and-white-checkered floors that weren't for sale anymore, and if you stepped in the middle of the room, there was a huge candelabro that hung from the ceiling: delicate teardrop crystals hanging from its center. Stepping in the restaurant, you could feel transported to another era in Barranquilla. One where people were still amazed by the first steamboats arriving to the Caribbean Coast. Tradición, as we had learned already, didn't pay bills.

"Don Víctor." I sat at the table with him and his friend. He was with a man I knew from the barrio as well. I didn't remember his name, but he was often playing dominoes in the park, in the late afternoon when the sun didn't burn your skin anymore. "We're going to be bringing some dishes that are going to be courtesy of Caminito. We would love the feedback. You know how Abuela was—she didn't love when people lied to her. Can you be honest with us? Excuse me, what's your name?" I asked the man whose name I didn't remember.

"Edilberto." A slender man wearing a vintage watch extended his hand. Barranquilla was hot, and yet he was wearing an old-looking jacket.

"Can I trust you, then?"

"Mija, pero claro! Of course," Don Víctor replied for the two of them. I looked at the table—they had only had two cups of coffee, which Berto hadn't picked up, and a glass of wine. Of course Caminito was sinking: people weren't even eating at the restaurant.

I sighed, getting up and going to the other two tables to repeat the process. More regulars and one or two new faces. People were delighted by the possibility of new food. Roberto was the waiter, our only waiter, who did a lot of sitting because there wasn't much to do. I grabbed Berto, who was in the kitchen taking a break—from what, who knows—and we put some tables together to seat everyone there so it would be easier to gather the feedback.

Anton had that manic energy he only had when he was in the kitchen. Tasting things, chopping things, seasoning things, he was doing it all. Mami was helping, but Anton was like Abuela—they both had trouble delegating, because they did it better.

"Everyone is ready," I said, entering the kitchen with Berto, ready to serve.

Anton took a deep breath. "Listo." He plated his creations: pimientos rojos with crispy chickpeas and col rizado—Anton had a way of sautéing kale that made it taste salty and buttery all at once—chickpea garbanzos with chèvre that melted in your mouth, a thick-dough pizza with brie and apples, and a simple kale salad with green apples, apricots, almonds, sourdough croutons, and a honey-lavender vinaigrette.

Barrio Prado customers clapped when they saw the food—how lucky they were to be here, at this exact time, when we were giving away free food. I squeezed Anton's shoulder, who was radiant. He loved a job well done. Mamá took her phone and took a picture of the table. It looked simple but elegant with candles and fresh flowers.

Anton went through all the dishes. "Buen provecho," he said. Berto, Mamá, Anton, and I stood to the side of the table, watching customers try everything. Most people, at first, ignored the salad—going straight for the croquetas or the pizza.

Remedios, a woman who owned a house with a colonial fountain in front of her doorway, said between bites, "These are the best pimentones I've had in my life."

"This salad," Edilberto said. "I don't even like salad."

A woman in her twenties I'd never seen before said, "This pizza is good." She chewed, and Anton opened his mouth, waiting to see what she would say next. "But the cheese is weird. Too mushy?"

Anton's face turned red. We hadn't exactly talked about how to deal with criticism, and brie wasn't exactly everyone's cup of tea. I started taking notes on my phone about the feedback.

"Are the chickpeas too salty?" Mamá asked, and Anton turned to look at her, as if he was saying, *How dare she insinuate that about my chickpeas!*

"Mmm," the same woman said. "A little." I took the note, while fumes came out of Anton's ears.

People kept eating. When the desserts came out—flan and pineapple upside-down rum cake—everyone commented on the sweetness and the spice of the pineapple, the depth of taste the rum gave the cake. The flan tasted of vanilla and caramel; according to everyone, it was perfect.

I placed my hand on Anton's shoulder. I could tell he was conflicted by the feedback, but people loved the food—it was a step in the right direction to serve food that was more casual and that people could share. We could attract new customers that way.

When the last person took a bite of the flan, letting the spoon linger in their mouth, everyone started clapping for Anton. I pointed at Mamá, too; it was only fair. She had helped. I joined in the applause and watched them as they smiled. I knew we were all feeling it. It wasn't too late. The possibility, perhaps, we could still do something to save Caminito.

~

I stood in the kitchen, my arms deep in the sink, scrubbing a pot. "I'm going to look at the books tonight. See where we can cut some expenses," I said. "Why don't you go home, Anton?"

Anton opened his eyes wide, as if I was speaking to him in a language he couldn't comprehend.

"Vi, I can't . . . I could plan the menus for tomorrow. I could clean the fridge, redesign the menu."

I wiped my forehead, my hands covered in soap. "Mañana."

"Bueno, Vi, you're taking care of the books and redecoration," Anton said, as if he couldn't help but remind me of my tasks.

I sighed. I wanted to do more. I wanted to be in the kitchen with them, but perhaps this would do for now, at least until we were out of the woods.

"I'm going to take care of social media," Mamá said.

I raised an eyebrow, soaking the pot in warm water until my gauze was wet too. I needed to go home and change it soon. "You?"

Was Mamá into social media now? She'd owned a flip phone until not too long ago. Anton shook his head and opened his recipe notebook; he didn't want to comment.

"I am very good at it. And we're going to need it if we want new people here."

"Okay? Anton, you're in charge of the food, I guess."

"Claro. Y quién más?"

Who else? he said, and I kept scrubbing, ignoring the pain in my hand. The memory of me sneaking in the kitchen when I was around thirteen and heating caramel for a flan. The caramel bubbling up and spilling over the pan. I had been scared: Had I burned the pan? Had I stained the stove forever? Anton had come behind me and swiftly turned off the stove.

"I messed up, I'm no good," I'd said, panicked.

He'd handed me a rag and smiled. "You can't make caramel without a little heat."

Anton had always been wise for his years.

~

I practically had to push Anton to the door, but Mamá was easier. She just took her purse and went out, leaving me with the mess of the kitchen. I left the kitchen as clean as I could, up to Abuela's standards, and sat down to look at the books.

They were a mess. As I studied them, two things became clearer. One, the entries were in solely Abuela's handwriting in all the first years of Caminito from the 1980s to around 2010. The last five years, the records of Caminito's expenses became less and less clear. Abuela wasn't tracking every penny that entered the restaurant and every penny that left. I recognized Mamá's handwriting, and even Anton's, but they weren't as meticulous with their tracking. And two, Caminito had too many unnecessary expenses and too many customers consuming barely anything.

Abuela was a firm believer in the best quality for everything, and all her expenses had remained the same over the years. Even if she didn't have the same number of customers anymore as she had when the restaurant was in its prime, she kept spending the same money on first-quality meat, and tons of it, and on organic vegetables and on wines from Argentina and Chile, which accumulated in the basement.

We needed to use what we had. I noticed from the books the people whom Abuela had let go until she was left only with Anton and Berto. My heart wrinkled at the thought of Abuela having to make that decision. She had always loved a full kitchen—she was more alive when she was giving orders in her kitchen, dancing from pan to pan and trying everything. I turned the page and arrived at the end.

Abuela had always had the most elegant handwriting, cursive but readable. The first years of Caminito, it was neat and organized; it could have been displayed in a museum. The last page of the book was written in a faded pencil. The handwriting was barely legible, but it belonged to Abuela, that was for sure.

It stated clearly the number of the debt. And the balance remaining: one hundred millones. Around $25,000.

I closed the book, as if I had seen an apparition. I was going to need to dig into my already tight pockets to keep Caminito running for a month.

My eyes were closing, but with a pen I turned a new page and started making notes about all the ways we were going to scale back. We were getting meat only every two weeks. Anton would go to the market to get the seafood every day, and only in small quantities. *ONLY WHAT WE NEED,* I wrote in bold caps. *No more purchasing wine; we only will offer what we have.* I felt as if I were opposing Abuela's spirit of generosity. Caminito was a symbol for ever-flowing wine and abundance.

This was a moment of scarcity, I told myself, as a long exhale escaped my lips. As I scribbled furiously, I reminded myself that if Abuela had taught me anything, it was that scarcity, like almost anything else in this life, wasn't permanent.

~

I closed the door behind me and double locked it, as Abuela would have wanted, and went upstairs without looking around. Being in my childhood home scared me. The house seemed bigger and darker than it ever was—it was missing Abuela's warmth and touch. The stairs appeared longer and steeper, and the only room that I could enter was my own. Abuela's room was in front of mine, and although the door was closed, I was sure it was still occupied. I imagined her there, flipping through the pages of an old gossip magazine or newspaper, sitting in the dark and reading with the help of the moonlight. I turned on the light bulbs in the hall and my room, but the house was never bright enough. It remained dark and bigger than ever—a ghastly silence coated the walls.

I took my clothes off and got in between the covers. Too scared about what or who I might see if I wandered the halls to go to the bathroom to take off my makeup or brush my teeth.

"Abuela: we're trying," I told her as I covered myself quickly with the sheets. "We're trying to save Caminito," I said, my eyes closing themselves from sheer exhaustion. These past few days had been a tornado. The truth was the house had always been scary. The halls were long, and the amount of wood made it look dark. This was a house of spirits. I imagined the spirits tangled like vines along the stairs, listening behind doors, dormant but waiting to be woken up. I drifted into heavy sleep lulled by the sound of the steady rain and the wind rattling the glass.

In my dream, Abuela was not in the dark anymore. We were in the only mall in Barranquilla, sitting together at a coffee shop like we used to do when we were bored and wanted to do something in a city where otherwise there was nothing. Always just the two of us. In the dream, I knew she wasn't well. She didn't have long.

"I have something for you," she said. Her hand disappeared in her huge Louis Vuitton bag, the one she always kept full of receipts, her huge wallet, and her unused lipsticks, which she kept in a makeup bag just to have them.

A little white jewelry box emerged. "Para ti," she said.

I opened it. I felt my hand reaching for something. I couldn't find an apparent bottom to the box. I finally felt something. It was hard and light. I pulled it out of the box, a little pastel-blue diary.

"It's mine," she said. "For you."

I woke up. I felt something tap, tap, tap me on the shoulder, a crisp breeze on my cheek despite my whole body feeling warm and sweaty.

But when I opened my eyes, my heart quickening its beat, I realized I was alone.

CHAPTER SEVEN: LA BRISA

Thwack! Anton was cutting through wagyu beef with a big kitchen knife for a steak tapa with truffle mayonnaise and shiitake mushrooms that he had invented. I checked on the caramel for the flan I was making. Despite my distracted thoughts, the caramel was still in its liquid form and hadn't crystallized on the pan. As I stirred, I let myself take in the notes of brown sugar, vanilla, and the smoky scent of the hot caramel; it calmed me, if only for a moment. I was fidgety after having told Mamá that Caminito was spending way too much money. Anton protested. He was scared of running a restaurant with less food than he was used to. Mamá just shrugged. "We should just close. All this trouble para qué."

"Vi! Ajá," Anton said, tapping his feet. "I need the flan. I trusted you with this—"

"Sí, capitán," I said, turning off the heat and putting the saucepan away from the fire so it could cool down. I wiped my forehead with the back of my hand. The kitchen had no AC, and although all the windows were open, I was sure that this was what hell felt like.

"Dos minutos."

Mami paced around the room. She had created a new Instagram account for Caminito and was frantically posting stories of the restaurant. I rolled my eyes.

She was delusional—I wondered what she knew of social media. And even if she did know how to use it, how would she get people to care? How were the Barranquilleros going to learn about all the things that Caminito was and represented? "We could use some help in the kitchen, sabes," I said to her. "We are short."

Mamá barely lifted the eyes from her phone. "And I'm busy."

I sighed; would Mamá and I ever have a normal conversation? I took the mold of flan from the fridge and drenched the dessert in the warm, velvety caramel. The air smelled like burnt brown sugar. I sprinkled a dash of cinnamon on top and thought about how Abuela would do this mechanically but with precision. She had prepared thousands of flans in front of me when I was little.

"Toma," I said, handing Anton my perfect flan.

"Ya era hora," he said, unimpressed. "It took you an hour to make this flan."

"Ay—" I was going to protest, but he took the flan so fast I didn't have a moment to get a word in.

He shook his head. "An hour. Move faster."

At the restaurant, it was another night of a few tables. But no rain. Outside, the weather was humid and warm, and the sun hadn't set yet.

"Vi," Anton said. "Apúrate. Ve and check on Berto, see if he needs help." I opened the kitchen door slightly and saw him smiling at one of our three tables. He told them the specials: wagyu steak, paella de camarones, and seafood bisque.

Berto came inside, with a kitchen towel hanging on his shoulder. I pulled it and threw it into a corner of the room.

"Berto, por favor," I said. "You can't be walking around with that dirty rag on you. You're the only waiter. People eat here."

He shrugged. "Sí, señorita. They want one paella and one steak."

"Nada más?" Anton raised his voice. "What about the other table?"

"They just wanted the croquetas and the salad. They asked for the check."

Anton faced the stove and took a deep breath. I walked to stand behind him, but I didn't dare touch him.

"Let me check on the paella, Berto," I said, but he was already leaning on the prep table; his phone was out. Anton turned back, and I knew this couldn't be good.

"Berto! Go and make the rounds, see if someone needs anything."

"Pero—"

"Ve." *Go.* "Vi, check on the paella, don't let it get dry—"

I nodded. "Yo sé." I lifted the lid; the paella was swimming in a bubbly broth. It smelled like a good day at the beach and olive oil and tomatoes.

"Not ready, capitán."

Anton wasn't listening. He was hitting a steak so hard you'd think he was trying to send it to another dimension. From where I was standing, I could see drops of sweat accumulating on his forehead.

"Anton, you're going to kill that steak."

He stopped and started to rub the meat with salt.

"Dios mío." He looked up. "What are we going to do?" His voice was breaking, and he was about to cry.

Mamá came back to the kitchen. I didn't know where she had gone. Her cheeks were red, as if she was embarrassed—but that woman didn't know shame.

"Vi," she said, looking at her phone instead of me. "Te buscan."

I didn't have any friends left in Barranquilla. "Quién?" *Who,* I asked, wiping my hands on Abuela's apron. I smelled like garlic and butter, probably even paella since I was just stirring it.

"Ve. Go look," she said.

"Plate the paella," I told her, taking my apron off and giving it to her before walking out of the kitchen. "If we let it get too dry, Anton might cry."

Mamá put her phone in her pocket and took the apron reluctantly without saying a word. I exited the kitchen, wondering who it could be.

Rafa was there, studying the menu and sitting by himself. The thrumming of my heart was beating faster and faster. Carajo. Rafa was looking around as if he was meeting someone here. I waited for a woman to come in behind him. A morena with a cascade of jet-black hair, perhaps, or a blonde woman wearing a thin silk dress. Thousands of scenarios crossed my head before I took another look at him.

I waved, unsure if he could see me from my place by the kitchen door. I was wearing an old yellow summer dress that I wondered if he recognized, and my hair was up in a lazy bun that was threatening to unravel at any minute. He pointed at the kitchen with his hand, and I assumed it meant he wanted to come see me. I waited for him, unable to take a step forward or a step back. Why was he looking for me? There was nothing to talk about.

Rafa got up. I felt my jaw unclench, the sea storm that was my heart coming to an abrupt end.

"Buenas noches, Vi," he said, standing in front of me. His lovely dark hair was messy, and I wanted to run my hands through it. No, I told myself as if I were slapping my hand away from something overly sweet I wanted to devour. I was with Liam. And these desires were just a reflex from the past, a learned behavior that had reared its head but that, like everything else, I had to learn to forget.

"I was hoping to get a bite to eat. Can we talk?"

No, no, no, the answer is no. There was a voice inside of me screaming, demanding. But when I opened my mouth, the word "Sí" slipped from my tongue.

"Whatever you want, on the house." Everything that was coming out of my mouth made no sense. This wasn't the time to give food away for free. And yet I wanted to. Rafa smiled at me, and I was a tongue-tied fifteen-year-old again. No one wanted to be that age—before meeting Rafa, I'd never thought I would want to. But many times, the memory of him opening the door to his parents' house, his warm smile, his wavy hair would appear in my head. Any moment of the day, it didn't matter.

The words that he always would say to me: Vi, pensaba que no venías. *I thought you'd never come.*

Our bodies were one big knot of anxiety and devotion then.

He looked down and chuckled. "Vi, no, I can pay. I just . . ." He released a deep breath. "Needed to see you."

I took a deep breath, too, trying to swallow everything, trying to feel nothing.

"Are you working?"

I wanted to nod, but I didn't move.

"It seems like you are. I can wait—I'll be sitting there, if you want to come. For a bit." He tilted his head, waiting for my answer.

"Yes. Claro."

Rafa moved his arm forward, and his skin brushed my arm. The hairs on my arms stood up. "I'll come when things are calmer."

The steps back to the kitchen felt longer, as if the checkers on the black-and-white floor were stretching in front of my eyes. My head wanted to turn, but I maintained my gaze forward. I couldn't do this to Liam. I wouldn't like it if he was talking to an ex he had loved once. Yes, that was it, I told myself. I had loved Rafa once—not anymore. This was infatuation, a memory. I exhaled when I entered the kitchen, the smells of spicy tomato sauces flooding my nose. I wondered what Mamá and Anton were thinking, seeing me talk with Rafa when Abuela had put an ocean between us, risking the restaurant and her livelihood in the process.

Anton pointed at a board that had a handful of cilantro resting on top of it and at another one that had mushrooms.

"Vi, por favor, chop the cilantro. It's already rinsed. And the mushrooms, in thin long slices. And when you're done, you can go and check on Rafa. I imagine that he didn't come here to hear about the specials." Anton quickly looked up at me and winked. "Te conozco," he said as if he were singing one of the boleros he liked to play in the kitchen when he was cooking alone. *I know you.*

"What is this for?" I said, waving the kitchen knife in the air. "There's no one here," I barked at him, putting my hands on the wooden table. Barranquilla wasn't one to lay ghosts to rest; it was one to present them to you on silver platters. I wanted to open my mouth wide and swallow my past.

Anton shrugged and kept dicing some onions. "Ay, Vi, you never know. Maybe tomorrow it will be better. We need to prepare regardless. Chop the cilantro and then go go go." Anton kept slicing. "What is it with you anyway?"

I tried to focus while chopping the cilantro, but I was failing miserably. Anton could tell something was on my mind. He could tell my head was flooded with thoughts of Rafa and seeing him again.

"Vi," he insisted.

Anton's preparations for the next few days looked at me: colorful vegetables and thick dough. Was he listening to me? I'd told him we needed to budget. A deep, long sigh escaped my lips. Had I forgotten how to speak Spanish? No one ever listened to me.

"It's a lot to see him again." I shivered.

"Vi, lower the knife."

"Oh." I realized I was waving it like a sword. I put it down, and Anton nodded, relieved. He didn't trust me with knives. "Vi, you don't have to figure everything out right now."

"I can't leave you, anyway," I said, turning to chop or butcher more cilantro. "You're alone in the kitchen."

"Baby." Anton looked up from his preparations and pointed with his lips formed like a kiss to the front of the restaurant. This was something Barranquilleros did when they didn't want to use their hands. "There's like three people here. I can manage. If you want to close this chapter for good, it might be a good thing to go talk to him—see what he wants."

When we were teenagers, I told Anton everything about Rafa. How I used to sneak out to see him, how Rafa spent his nights composing songs, how Rafa played football on Sundays, and how we always fell asleep on the phone. We never ran out of things to say; we didn't want to miss a minute of being with each other. It was as if we knew that someday this would be taken away from us.

After we ended things, I realized that love was more than just passion. Right after I left Barranquilla, and when I was in college, I had been cautious about romance. While my classmates and roommates were excited about dating, I was guarded. Never letting a moment of vulnerability shine through. Never letting anything go past a couple of dates. The key word was *never*. Back then, I used to think love was something that wasn't for me. It hadn't ended well for the women in my family. Why would it be different this time?

It was only when I met Liam that I dared to think things would be different. I knew Liam wouldn't disappear.

It had been more than ten years, and yet I could still feel the wetness of the pillow where I rested my head night after night, after Rafa left. I started chopping mushrooms. I concentrated on making them look even, but I knew it didn't really matter. Anton was going to use them in a sauce. Abuela's voice appeared in my head: *You're playing with fire.* The caramel bubbling and spilling all over.

My head kept thinking about Rafa, that last time I had seen him on the night of the proposal. Shame shame shame. Chop, chop, chop, my hands moving as fast as they could, with every chop a flash in my memory of his confused expression. We were getting ready to say goodbye, and it had felt wrong—irreversible. So many things I had wanted to say to him ever since that night—things that I thought I would say into the night, on a warm beach, because no one would ever hear them, and now he was here.

Why? For what?

Even if I didn't want to admit it to myself, the truth was that I had missed him, like one misses an old part of themselves. Losing Rafa felt like losing the part of myself that believed in a love that could move mountains and alter reality. But when Rafa disappeared, that willingness to let go vanished with him.

Anton was right. I needed to talk to him. If only to close the chapter. If only to say goodbye to that part of myself.

"I'll be back in ten minutes." I put the knife down and washed my hands.

"Mm-hmm," Anton said, while stirring something in a pot.

"Saving resources, sí? Don't get carried away, te conozco."

As I exited the kitchen and walked toward the dining room, my heart started to beat faster, to the beat of that accelerated drum that played whenever Rafa was around.

I sat down at his table and smiled. Rafa looked at me, and I felt the weight of the years we had been apart hit me suddenly.

"I ordered a paella de mariscos and a glass of rioja."

"Do those things go together?" I smiled.

"No sé." Rafa shrugged, relaxing on his chair. "I just order what I like."

Rafa and I hadn't been from as different worlds as Abuela used to think. Rafa's family were immigrants. Some had set off to build fabric and jewelry empires while others had ended up having to struggle to make ends meet. Abuela's great-grandma had arrived on a boat, running away from the civil war in Spain. Our Spanish ancestors were potato farmers who'd had even less than we did here. In Colombia they fared better than they had in Spain. We both descended from poverty and hunger. Abuela wanted more; she had made a vow to never have to go to bed without dinner, to not have to ask for loans to pay for her daughter's school. Rafa, for her, represented everything that her family had been running away from for generations. The promise that she would do everything it took in order for me not to struggle.

Rafa and I were alike that way: we didn't know much about wine or fancy food. Liam was the one who knew about wine pairings and food, the one who saved me from ordering a sweet wine that would trigger my migraines. Oh, Liam.

"Entonces," I said as I looked at him and picked at the complimentary bread Anton served warm and with creamy butter de pimentones rojos, spiced with cayenne and red pepper flakes.

"Entonces," he said, taking a big piece of bread with butter to his mouth. "I'm sorry I came here when you were working. I wasn't sure when you would leave." Rafa paused, leaving the bread on the plate and looking at the table.

Berto came and served him a glass of wine. Then he turned to me, raising an eyebrow.

"Vi, vino?" Right, he was asking if I wanted wine because I was working. I shouldn't. Red wine had the power of making me tongue tied and emotional. Naturally, the answer should be no.

I nodded. Berto poured me a little glass.

"Más," I said, and Rafa half smiled, meeting my eyes. By the time Berto was finished pouring, I had a full glass of wine. Thank god.

I grabbed the glass and took a big, breathless gulp.

"Wow," he said, laughing, awakening something in me. His laugh sounded the same as it had all those years ago, maybe just deeper.

"Sitting here makes me feel old."

Rafa laughed. "And me. I mean, sitting here and drinking wine and about to eat paella?" Rafa took a sip of the wine. "Do you remember when we used to go to eat empanadas in the corner? We would have to sit in the dark so no one would see us and go with the gossip to Doña Emilia."

Now, we didn't have to hide, and yet everything was so different.

We had two options: We could linger here and make small talk. About the impossible heat, the restaurant, or his day at work, or mine. Or I could ask him what he was doing here. Rafa was holding his glass of wine between his index and middle fingers, examining the amber tones of the wine.

“Hey, Rafa,” I said, careful not to come across as accusatory. “Why did you never say goodbye? I mean, I get the anger. But I looked for you, I called, I was worried.”

What I left out was that I was devastated. I could hear Abuela’s intense knocking on the door, threatening to break it down. My eyes shut and a pillow over my head—wanting to sleep my love for him off, wanting to wake up somewhere else. Because it couldn’t be, no podía ser, that we weren’t together anymore.

Rafa inhaled and then deflated. He held his glass of wine and swirled it around.

“I’m my father’s son, Vi.” Rafa put the glass of wine on the table and lifted his eyes to look at me. “My pride is one of the lessons that my dad taught me.” He furrowed his brow, and in his expression I could see his dad’s handsome face. The same chiseled jaw and dark eyebrows. The same intense gaze Rafa had inherited. “Pride has taken me very far in life. I was able to graduate, pride fueling me through the nights where I was worried about being short to pay for tuition, or paying for electricity in the house. Pride was what allowed me to ignore Doña Emilia when she’d say I wasn’t good enough for you. When I knew—”

When you knew what? I wanted to ask, my heart beating fast. “Right,” I said, trying to change the subject.

Rafa did not peel his eyes away from me.

“Pride has been good for me. But it has also been terrible.” He shook his head. “Vi. I was hurt and stupid. I was so immature to disappear. I never wanted you to think—”

“It’s okay, it doesn’t matter now,” I said, but my eyes betrayed me. I could feel the tears threatening. It was grief. My feelings were all mixed up. I felt vulnerable. I allowed myself to put together a list of excuses in my head.

“Vi,” Rafa pleaded, his voice softer. It took me back to the words he’d say to me when he would whisper in my ear, the song that he wrote for me once. It was one of those December nights when the wind was colder than usual. He took his guitar out on the beach and sang it for me. I was in a rush—it was almost midnight, and Abuela was going to kill me when I got home. My curfew, at sixteen, was 11:30 p.m. But when he started to sing, all my worries melted away. This song would haunt me for years to come. It played in my head when I got on the plane to New York ten years ago. It was in my head at random moments when I was just living life and I thought I had forgotten about Rafa—about his buttery voice, the way he closed his eyes when he played his guitar.

"Your name is a song the wind carries."

Without knowing, Rafa had predicted our future when we were sixteen. Our names would be songs the wind would carry wherever we went, but nothing else.

"It does matter. Once we mattered to each other very much." Rafa grabbed my good hand between his—his touch was as warm as I remembered it.

No crying, no crying, I told myself. But alas, I could already feel the tears wetting my cheeks.

"I'm sorry, Vi."

I kept his hand in mine for a little longer than I should have. Feeling all the things I did for him once came back to me all in a rush. I wanted to climb up on this table and kiss him. Tell him that it didn't matter, we could start over. As if my life in the States was a piece of paper I could just crumple, throw away, and start over.

"Rafa." I inhaled, taking my hand away and using it to wipe a tear away. "I have someone."

Rafa straightened himself and moved away. "Me too." Under the lights, I noticed Rafa's eyes were moist too. Was he crying? "Her name is Marta. She's a doctor. A pediatrician. We've been together for a while."

"Married?"

"Not married." Rafa took the wine to his lips. It took him a second to ask me. "You?"

I shook my head, thinking about how months back Liam and I had started talking about if we were ready to get engaged, and what our life together would look like. I had been more calm during the talk than I'd expected. A future with Liam felt nice, safe, and comfortable. We agreed to keep talking about it, but the topic had been tabled after Abuela died and I had to come to Barranquilla. Now that I was sitting across from Rafa, it felt more complicated than that. Getting engaged to Liam meant that I needed to leave Rafa behind forever.

I had already left him behind, I reminded myself. This was just an echo of the past.

"Look at us," Rafa said.

"Look at us," I said, feeling that we weren't supposed to be here. There was a stuffiness in the air, sitting here, that we never had together. We were supposed to be at the beach, or eating empanadas, having a beer maybe, but wine? Us?

"Are you still making music?"

Rafa nodded and learned forward, as if he had a secret to tell me. "I do, but just for me these days. I play in this bar sometimes, but I don't tell anyone that I do. It's more of a hobby nowadays. You and your art?"

"I illustrate for a living now," I said.

"Vi." Rafa's eyes lit up. "That's so amazing. You've always been such a great artist. I knew you would be big someday."

"Ha, well, I am not there yet."

Berto appeared with the paella, because of course he would bring it at the worst/best possible moment. I studied Rafa at the other side of the round table. Things didn't feel normal again because of course they wouldn't. I thought about calling him over and over again without an answer. Doña Magdalena's face when she told me he wouldn't speak to me, about how I thought he hated me. I wanted to tell him, too, about how I thought I'd never love again. At eighteen.

But it didn't matter now; it really didn't. Rafa served me some paella, and then he served himself.

"So do you like the US?"

"Ha, you know. I like it fine. It's so much work to live in NYC. People say that you have to love it to live there, but I don't even think I have time to think about that. Do you like medicine?"

Rafa's eyes were on his plate. He took a spoonful of paella and then opened his mouth. "This is so hot. How are you eating?"

I was already swallowing.

"You've always had a boca de hierro." An iron mouth, able to eat anything no matter the temperature.

"That's me." I winked at him, and he laughed, probably thinking about all the meals we had shared when we were together, how we sat across from each other with pizza boxes, empanadas, his mami's arroz, Chinese noodles, quibes and arepas.

"That's you," he said, eating more rice. He sighed. "Do I like it? I like helping people—is that clichéd to say?" He smiled, eating quickly. He always ate as if someone was about to take the plate away.

"Ajá, súper clichéd."

"I've always been cheesy. I don't know, I guess it's a symptom of growing up that I don't think about being a musician anymore. I am good at what I do, I care about people, I've always liked studying. My parents always thought I'd be good for it, and they were right. I am very practical—"

"Hm . . ." I looked at him from across the table, putting the fork down. "You are, and you aren't."

Rafa had asked me to marry him at eighteen. That's not practical—that's madness.

"What do you mean?"

"I mean—" I opened my mouth to speak, closed it.

"Vi."

"You did ask me to marry you when we were eighteen. That's something a dreamer would do, in my opinion." The words slipped through my tongue so easily. I told myself it didn't matter. We wouldn't see each other again; I was with Liam. Rafa was with Marta.

"Vi, I don't know. Does it happen to you?"

I shook my head, not knowing what he was talking about.

"Every year, I lose a little bit more of who I used to be. I know that it's here." He put his hands over his belly, moving them as if he was looking for something. "But I don't know. I don't think that person that was there is here anymore. Do you know what I mean?"

I nodded. "I do," I said, although I ached for things to be different.

After we finished eating, Rafa and I walked outside and stood in front of his car. I hugged him first, tight, his smell staying with me. I closed my eyes, wanting to retain the memory of his embrace, how when he held me, he always did so with so much urgency.

"Vi," he said, and I touched his hair, holding him for a moment longer. "I'm sorry about how I behaved with you, I've been having this apology in my throat for so long. I've been wanting to tell you—"

I held him for what felt like seconds, and also hours. Forever and nothing. I took a deep breath and took a step back, separating myself from the embrace. Knowing it was time to let go.

"It's fine, Rafa, it was so long ago."

"It isn't." He swallowed. All that could have been. I touched his hand, by reflex; it was cold like the rain.

"It isn't. But I appreciate your apology now. I am sorry too."

Rafa nodded and took out his keys. "Thank you for tonight." He walked away, and I stepped back as I watched him get in his car. I should have been used to it by now, I thought.

I should have been used to losing by now.

~

"Liam," I said as soon as he picked up. "I am sorry about not calling a lot. I've been working." I hadn't worked the hardest tonight, that was for sure, but I was still thinking about seeing Rafa earlier. The power of his embrace.

"We've barely talked. How're you doing?"

I looked down, studying my sandals, the old white-and-black tiles that were so emblematic of Barrio Prado. I let out a sigh. If I had told the eighteen-year-old that I was once that this was how things were going to end up, what would she have said? Would she have told me that I was wrong? Would she have urged me to fight harder? I couldn't have fought harder; the only thing that had been left to do was to beg him to see me.

"Vi?" Liam asked. "Are you even there?"

"Sorry," I said, realizing it took me longer than I'd thought to reply. "I know, I know. There is just so much to figure out. I've had a lot on my mind."

That wasn't a lie.

"How are you?"

"You know how it is, working a lot. Hey, Vi."

"Yes?"

"You would tell me if something was wrong, right? Ever since you've been there, you've been a little distant."

"Abuela just died. I'm processing."

"I get that, it's just . . ."

"I would," I said, biting my lip. There was already so much I wasn't telling him. "Hey, Liam, I should check on Anton. I need to make sure he doesn't need anything, we're short staffed."

"Call me."

"I love you, I will," I said quickly.

"I love you too," he said, hanging up first.

Liam didn't deserve a half truth. The truth was so complicated I suspected it would take me a while to understand it myself. I was done with Rafa, and yet that night I had felt something I'd thought long forgotten. When he hugged me, it was like no time had passed at all. I entered the restaurant, passed a few tables, and went into the kitchen. The heat always took me by surprise.

"Do you need me?" I asked Anton, who was putting containers in the fridge marked with best-by dates.

"No," Anton said simply. He was washing pans and pots, moving and reorganizing the kitchen. I could tell he was having a moment. Anton had this mad-scientist energy around him sometimes that was best left undisturbed.

"Mamá?"

"She left, claimed she had somewhere to be."

I closed the door to the kitchen, knowing he needed to be alone. To grieve, probably, to stress out about all the money we owed.

The clients had all paid and left promptly. I sat down at a table in the restaurant. The only sound in my ears was the clinking of metal in the kitchen. I opened the books. Okay, besides cutting expenses, what else could we do?

I looked around. I needed to deep clean and remodel this place. I could ask around to see who had new furniture in the barrio I could repurpose; in exchange, I could leave some of Caminito's old pieces on the street for the taking.

What else?

I could call some investors? I didn't know anyone that could invest, but I could ask Mamá or even Doña Rocío, las mellas . . .

What else?

I could buy a ticket, get on a plane, and get back to NYC. Forget about this place.

Ha, I thought. As if I ever could.

I stood up, feeling that mad-scientist energy myself. I was desperate to do something. I took out the cleaning supplies from the cuartico where we kept them, and I began to dust the corners that brooms hadn't graced perhaps in years. An old magazine rag in the corner—threw it out. The art, old gold frames of pictures of Barranquilla in the twenties—took them down. I looked at the wall, painted colonial red. We need to do something about that.

I cleaned until my arms ached and I couldn't even hear Anton anymore in the kitchen. My eyes were closing. I turned off the lights of the restaurant and closed the back door. Exhausted but glad that I had put my energy to good use.

The house was dark and empty. I leaned back on the door. I should have felt accomplished, and yet I felt anything but.

Barrio Prado was a museum of all my mistakes. All my shortcomings were large and shiny on display, staring back at me. A timeline, with labels and dates and everything, of all the ways I had ruined everything: I had run away from Rafa, I hadn't been there for Abuela, and the loan Abuela had taken out to send me to the States had bankrupted Caminito.

As I reached the staircase, I saw a blue notebook on the table in the living room.

I glanced again, thinking that perhaps I was finally losing grip on reality. Grief was making me delirious. I walked toward the table. My vision felt blurry, and I decided that maybe I was dreaming. The house was the constant backdrop of my dreams; maybe I was dreaming and I was back in Brooklyn and none of this had happened. Abuela was still alive, and we weren't about to lose the restaurant.

I picked up the notebook and studied the pages, tracing the words in black ink and taking in the musty smell. It felt more solid than in a dream. The handwriting was neat and elegant. It was unmistakably Abuela's. My hand started to shake. This was her notebook, the one from the dream.

How could this be possible? Had the notebook always been here, and I just hadn't seen it?

I passed the pages, looking for answers. The paper smelled like cake and scotch.

Perhaps Abuela had left it here for me before her death. Maybe this book had some insights about saving Caminito. Maybe the names of investors to call. The entries were different lengths, and in some the handwriting was rushed, as if she was running out of time.

"Abuela—" I said out loud, wanting to cast a spell to make her appear. This was futile. The house was silent like a morgue.

I craved for her to help me navigate this, to tell me the stories she had never been able to articulate because no one had let her. No one had ever listened.

Barranquilla 1961

> *Mamá of course didn't approve of the marriage.*
>
> *She took me aside the morning of the wedding while the parientes of the novio were arriving at our house to greet the novia, and said to me that if I wanted to, we could kick everyone out. Go back to Santa Marta and start a new life, just the two of us with our cake business and my magical hands to make fondant flowers. We didn't need anyone else, solo nosotras—only us—she said as she tugged the lace sleeve of the wedding dress she had made for me. Mami's expression was clouded, her eyebrows were low, and her ojos verdes were as wide as if she was seeing the future. Mi futuro. I felt a tingle on the beds of my feet. A whisper that uttered: "Corre." Run. But it was the nerves, of course it was just that. Mamá told me I was a terca. And I hugged her, inhaling the sweet scent of her skin and I told her that it was okay—I knew she was just scared of losing me. Her unica hija. Her light, as she used to call me when I hadn't met Amadeo yet. Mi marido. The man who changed our world of two.*

I stood there, notebook in my hands and my legs still shaking. Abuela was a practical woman. She had never encouraged me to trust hunches: "Listen to reason," she would say. "The heart is capricious."

The heart liked to throw tantrums. This was true. My heart had thrown multiple tantrums since I had arrived at Barranquilla days ago. Abuela had been in love with Abuelo once. This revelation made my blood run cold. Their marriage, from what I had seen, had been distant. He was barely ever home, and she moved in life like she wasn't married to him, like she had no one to depend on but herself.

Abuelo had always been a stranger to me. The few times I saw him over the years, our conversations didn't transcend past hellos and goodbyes. It was as if we weren't related at all. I slid my hands over the paper, took the notebook to my chest, and closed my eyes.

"Abuela," I said.

"Mija," her voice replied. I felt her presence behind me, as if she were standing there.

"Volviste," I said. "I knew you would return."

CHAPTER EIGHT: BARRIO PRADO

Barranquilla 1962

To make fondant flowers you have to have a lot of skill and a lot of patience. Mami says that I make the most beautiful fondant flowers in the barrio, in the whole city even. My cakes—our wedding cakes—are sought out by everyone in the neighborhood.

But for Amadeo I can't do anything right. I'm no good at anything at all. I'm stupid, a buena para nada.

Our cakes, even if it hurts him, are the only thing sustaining our home and putting food on our plates. That beautiful arroz con huevo that Mami makes when Amadeo brings home nothing but rum breath and curses. The arroz pegao tastes like salt and aceite, like a perfectly runny egg that blends with the arroz and fills me up with joy when everything in life with Amadeo is as dark as the clouds announcing rain in abril.

Mami hasn't told me "I told you so," pero I see it in her face, I hear it in every sigh as she sets the table. In the way she puts the bills that we make from the cakes in her only good bra. She's saving for something.

I hope it's for our escape.

I closed the blue notebook and stared at the street.

I always knew Amadeo, Abuelo, was a bad man. Although she didn't speak about it, I knew he had given her a life full of unkindness. The few times he was at home, he would yell at her and make her feel worthless. Abuela was Doña Emilia Sanoguera, a woman who took no nonsense from anyone, and yet, around Abuelo, she always kept her head low. She always preferred not to engage in his name-calling, in his huffing and puffing around the house, about how everything always was unsatisfactory. Abuela couldn't cook anything right, even if she was one of the best cooks in the city. I thought Abuela was rising above him, but I knew now that the woman I thought was fearless was scared of him. Bisabuela had told Abuela not to marry Abuelo, and she had done it anyway. Were all the fears she had for me justified?

The men selling tinto and the grandmothers walking their grandkids home after school. I hadn't been in Barranquilla for all that long, and that day, everything reminded me of Abuela. Grief wasn't linear and all-consuming. I was working on the books nonstop and selling some pieces of furniture and old china that were antiques. I was only able to get a couple hundred dollars, and when Mamá saw the restaurant, she screamed at me. "Now it looks empty, Violeta!" And it did (especially now that it was white—I had gotten rid of the red on the walls), but there was something nice about having more space to fill it in with something new one day. Anton was adapting to cooking without so many ingredients. So many sighs and complaints under his breath, but he was doing it, and Mamá, reluctant as ever, was on her phone all day—claiming that she was gaining followers and for us to trust her, because she knew what she was doing.

I sat outside the restaurant drinking Coca-Cola out of a long glass bottle. It had been my first break in days. Abuela's favorite dinner was Coca-Cola with a piece of baguette, no butter, no anything. Abuela wasn't there, but I could see her beautiful black hair that she would keep in a neat bob and that she washed with bar soap until the end of her days. I would think about her all the time, even when I wasn't thinking about her necessarily. I wanted to grieve, but I didn't want anyone to know about it because it would mean sharing her with others. If I kept my grief to myself, I could carry it in her ratty apron with infinite pockets everywhere I went.

There were men selling coconuts and aguacates, collecting AC and junk pieces, and selling raspao. I heard the horn of the man selling peto, the constant clinking of a knife against a ponchera de metal of the man selling butifarra. There were ladies dressed in bright colors running to catch the bus and people with big umbrellas trying to shield themselves from the midmorning sun. The skin of my nose burned—there was no escaping the sun. It was scorching us all. I sat outside, trying to ground myself in the landscape that had been familiar to me growing up.

I took another sip of the Cola-Cola and tasted the sweetness. Our streets were wide and colorful, a reminder of another time when they had been beautiful and new. A signaling of the future. I closed my eyes and let myself be washed by the sounds and the rhythms of a city I still loved.

Before getting up to go back to the restaurant, where Anton was frantically running around like he did every day, I remembered Abuela and me holding hands to catch a taxi in these very streets. I was a kid, and her clammy hand never let go of mine. Taxis came and went in a rush like cars always did in these streets, without stopping for us.

"¡Mandan huevo!" Abuela said, pointing at the taxis that would get stuck in the holes in the street and that then would fly through the narrow streets, flying in between buses and motos as if they were invisible.

"¡Abuela!" I said, shocked by the swearing. The nuns in my school said that it was for truck drivers and sinners. "No swearing."

"Mija," she said, brushing my cheek with her index finger. "That's half the fun in life. That and drinking." She half smiled, revealing her yellow teeth, courtesy of the blue Belmonts she chain-smoked in the patio that, when I was little, I used to hide or destroy by tossing them from the second floor. I could still remember the spanks that came after.

Abuela never denied herself any pleasure in life, even if she was constantly ashamed of taking up space: of her lazy eye, her yellow teeth, and her limp. I took a deep breath, staring at those streets, wishing I could take away some of that shame that we felt just for existing and make it disappear.

~

"There's a big table of eight outside."

I peeked outside the kitchen window, and a large group of eight business-looking men sat at Caminito's largest table. They were sharing bottles of whiskey and wearing crisp white shirts.

"They ordered paella, steak, and fish a la mediterránea. Vi, everything has to be perfect. We can't afford anything but perfection. Take those croquetas and take them to their table, tell them you're the owner."

"What about Berto?"

"Vi, it's good for business for customers to know who the owners are."

I took the tray without saying anything more; he was right. I needed to start taking ownership around here seriously. That's what Abuela would have wanted. Large groups in restaurants always intimidated me. When I was a waitress, I always had trouble keeping track of the demands of the group—there were more expectations for the night to be perfect.

Abuela's croquetas marineras were one of Caminito's best appetizers. They were breaded corn dough with seafood inside. They were always fluffy and warm when you cut into them.

"Señores," *gentlemen*, I said, announcing my voice and putting two plates of croquetas on the two opposite sides of the table. "Croquetas de langostino. On the house." I smiled at the men, who made a brief pause in their conversation. I looked back at Anton, who was smiling at me, mouthing, "Diles." *Tell them.* I took a deep breath and collected myself. I had big shoes to fill. Abuela's shadow loomed in Caminito, her big welcoming smile. I could never replace her, claro que no, but if I wanted to save Caminito, I had to own it.

"I'm Vi," I said. All their eyes were on me. They waited for me to continue speaking. "I'm the owner. This is our family business. We've been operational for more than thirty years."

"Ah," the man who was sitting at the head of the table said. "I used to come here all the time with my wife. I suggested it because the seafood here is among the best in the city." Then he looked around. There was only one other occupied table that night—Mamá had started advertising on her Instagram, and I had quickly done some graphics for her. We advertised promotions of two-for-one cocktails and set prices for a couple's dinners. But no one wanted to come. Probably the poor man was thinking that this place was past its prime. It had been a mistake to bring these people here.

"It still is, señor," I said, clearing my throat. "I'm glad you gave us a chance. Berto is going to be your waiter, but I'll be making sure everything is excellent this evening."

The men nodded, and I started to walk back. As I entered, I saw Berto leaving the kitchen with a tray, almost running. I made a mental note to train him, once and for all. Or at least to tell him to not run in the restaurant.

"They seem happy," I told Anton, who was searing some steaks. "How can I help you?" I carefully put on Abuela's apron. Anton was running around, grabbing the olive oil and dressing a perfectly plated octopus with it.

"I don't know, can you make salad?"

I rolled my eyes. "Who do you think I am. Of course I can make a salad," I said, going to the fridge to take out vegetables. "Don't you remember?" I started chopping kale and slicing dried peaches for his salad. "When we were teenagers, I used to help you in the kitchen. O no, se te olvido? The older you get, the more possessive you become."

"Claro, of course I remember." Anton stayed in silence as he pan-seared cod on a pan with olive oil, butter, and spices. The smell was fragrant, and I let myself be carried away by the aroma. "You were so insistent." Anton turned to me. "Oof, niña, a pest. But you're good, Vi. All you need, or all you needed back then, was some confidence." It's funny that he said that because I had gotten that a lot with my illustrations too. All I needed was confidence.

I mixed in the ingredients for the honey, white wine, and lavender vinaigrette.

"Delicioso," Anton said when he tried the salad. "It will complement the steak and the calamares al ajillo perfectly." Squid in a butter and garlic sauce.

Anton stood up by the fridge, thinking about what in the world he could tell me to do next.

"Okay." Anton let out a deep breath. "You can do the asparagus and take out the potatoes. Can you do that? Without burning your other hand off!"

I tried to hide my smile. I had graduated from the salad to pan-searing the asparagus. He was letting me use a pan. As I took out the asparagus from the fridge, Anton gave me instructions. I had to wash the asparagus and then put it on a baking sheet with olive oil, salt, and pepper. When it was done, I could braise them for a couple of minutes with white wine and butter. The potatoes were almost done; in five minutes I needed to put well-minced garlic on them and let them roast for ten more minutes.

"Fácil," I told him. But he wasn't listening; he was busy with the steaks and the grilled fish. Anton wasn't a talker when he cooked, and my head drifted to Rafa. Ever since that night, I had told myself no. No thinking about him. Not thinking about the past. For what? Abuela's diary was proof. Proof that when you insisted on what wasn't yours, what wasn't meant to be, you ended up with regrets.

I needed to focus on my future with Liam.

"Are the asparagus in the oven yet?"

"Sí, capitán," I said, smiling at him. Caminito was crumbling, but it felt right to finally be in the kitchen. Even if Abuela wasn't here to see it.

~

There were so many dishes for the table of eight that Anton and I had to come out to help Berto serve the banquette. There was a big paella in the middle; a salad; a golden grilled fish with herbs, olive oil, and lemon; and some steaks to share. The potatoes that I'd almost burned, but Anton had rescued, smelled like butter and garlic, and the asparagus was perfectly cooked. As we set the table, the laughter and chattering shifted to the admiration of the dishes.

"Todo se ve buenísimo," a client said, and I looked at Anton, who was mesmerized by the experience. Getting to serve his food to people who were going to appreciate it.

I knew then that I needed to save Caminito, in order for him to have this opportunity again and again. Without a kitchen, Anton was a performer without an audience.

We observed them through the kitchen window, silent for a moment as they enjoyed the feast Anton had prepared. Anton watched as one watches a TV show: he delighted in the anxious bites, in the second servings, and in the compliments to his food.

"You did good, baby." I looked at him. Anton's face lit up from the inside.

Berto came in to tell us the table had ordered flan, pineapple upside-down cake, and pie de manzana to end their meal on a sweet note. Anton walked to the oven to turn it on to heat up the pie a little so it would be warm when he added the homemade ice cream and the caramel, nutmeg, and cinnamon sauce.

"Vi, what was the last thing you did in this oven?"

"Turning it off," I said, as I scrubbed a sheet pan in the kitchen sink. "Why?"

"Are you sure? Did you touch something?"

"No." I walked over to see. The oven was completely unresponsive. "Berto!" I yelled, and he came running. "What happened to the oven?"

Berto started tinkering with the buttons and then opened the massive thing. Nothing. No sign of life.

"Did you do something? You were the last person . . ."

I shook my head. "Anton, I swear. I did nothing but turn it off. I mean, this oven is so old. Abuela perhaps hadn't replaced it since Caminito opened."

Anton started pacing back and forth. "Okay, first things first. I'm going to heat up the pie on a pan for a minute."

"We don't have to heat it—" I said, but Anton shot me a look that stopped me in my tracks. "Okay, you do that."

"Vi, call Paula and tell her to find someone to repair it first thing tomorrow." Anton turned off the heat and looked at Berto. "See if the other table needs anything, and when you're done, take them a piece of the pie." Berto started quickening his pace. "No running." Anton rolled his eyes. Berto started walking so slowly that Anton had to raise his voice. "Not that slow. Normal." Of course, the minute things started going right, the oven had to die. "Ay, Vi." Anton shook his head.

"Perhaps it won't be that bad," I said, lip quivering, lying through my teeth. Ovens were expensive.

Anton put an arm on my shoulder and let out a big sigh. "Let's hope you're right."

My phone started to ring—Liam. I wanted to talk to him. To tell him about how Caminito was crumbling. Was it my fault? Had Abuela been right?

"One second, I'll be back," I said, getting out of the kitchen and picking up the phone on the patio.

"Honey," I said. "I'm so glad you called—I've been so stressed about Caminito, and now the oven just broke. It's going to be so much money." I was running out of breath, and I was crying yet again. It was exhaustion mixed with fear.

"Oh honey, I'm so sorry," Liam said. "I have some good news, though."

"What's that?" I said, stopping the crying for a moment. Growing up, I was never comfortable crying freely. Abuela had trained me in keeping my feelings on the inside. *"You have to be fuerte,"* she used to say. *"People take advantage of the weak."* But I was who I was; in adulthood, her words had run straight through me like water. I was always quick to cry when I was overwhelmed.

"I'm coming to Barranquilla. I asked for a leave from work, and I am coming. I know that you said I didn't need to—"

My eyes dried up. I didn't need Liam here—we had so much to do. A plan to figure out. I couldn't be playing tourist with Liam.

"Liam, I'm just working here. Things with Mami are tense—what are you going to do with your days?"

"Whatever you need me to," he jumped to say. "I just don't think it's right. You're my partner in life. I need to support you—you're going through this massive thing all alone."

Did I deserve this man?

"Liam," I said. "I don't know, what if the city is too hot for you? You get bored of working at the restaurant? You won't get to rest much."

"Hey, Vi," he said, laughing. "I'm going to be there for you. I don't care. I'll do whatever."

"My mom is a lot."

"Doesn't matter."

"It's like three hundred degrees here."

"Great."
"I think our chef is losing his mind."
"I am a good listener."
"I think I am losing my mind too."
"Then I am coming just in time."

CHAPTER NINE: FLAN

I didn't sleep, thinking about the oven. What are we going to do? I lay on my bed, thinking whether Liam coming here was going to work out—there was so much to do with the restaurant.

Rafa. I was still not over seeing Rafa that day. I told myself that it was natural to feel this way—we had meant so much to each other—and yet, and yet, and yet it didn't make it okay. The only person in my heart should be Liam.

I felt Abuela's presence in the house, but I didn't hear her. What would she have done? I closed my eyes and tried to think like her. Abuela was practical, not prone to emotion like Mamá and I were. I tossed and turned, trying to come up with the answer. By dawn, I was covered in sweat but without any solutions.

~

Mamá had gotten to the restaurant earlier than anyone.

"Why do you punish me, Dios?" I heard Mamá saying as I opened the back door to the kitchen. It wasn't even 8:00 a.m. yet, and Mamá was turning up the drama already. This was going to be a long day.

No, Mamá, I wanted to tell her. This wasn't something that Dios had done to you personally—we were all affected.

The oven-repair man was already here. I looked around for Anton; he didn't seem to be in the restaurant yet. Good. We didn't need one more person to add more fuel to the fire.

"Buenas." I said hello and put my purse on the table. The man was checking the oven with a flashlight.

"Do we know yet how much the repair will cost?"

The man closed the oven and turned to us. He started putting his tools in his bag, as if there was nothing else to say.

"Perdón," *excuse me*. "Entonces, so, how much?" I took a step forward. Mamá didn't say a word, and that seemed even worse. Mamá never ran out of things to say.

"Lo siento," he said. His gold chain was dangling on his chest. "But I don't think I can fix this. It's so old. It's going to be more expensive to fix it than to buy a new one."

I put a hand on Mamá's back out of instinct; it was so warm it was burning. Mamá covered her face with her hands. She was worried for the future of Caminito, after all. The first night I had been here, she was convinced she wanted to sell. My chest felt tight, and tears were threatening to roll down my face. Pero, no, I needed to be strong.

"No te preocupes." *Don't worry*, I told Mami. "We'll figure something out. How much is a new oven?" I asked as the man took his tools and headed to the door. "How much?" I turned to Mamá. Her hands were still covering her face.

"Como twenty-five millones," Mamá said. Around $6,000. On top of the restaurant debt.

I had to close my eyes. I suddenly felt drowsy. This could not be happening. It was as if everything were conspiring for us not to be able to save Caminito. I wasn't one to believe in signs, but everything since I had arrived was pushing us to let go.

"No te preocupes, Mamá." I brought her closer to me, hugging her as tight as I could. I wondered if Abuela had ever held her like this. If Mamá had never hugged me like this because she had never learned to.

We weren't ones to hug each other, or touch much, but we both needed the comfort. I closed my eyes, letting myself feel enveloped in her familiar smell, the warmth of her hug. A rush of tenderness washed over me.

Mamá hugged me back for a moment and then took a deep breath, liberating herself from the embrace.

"Bueno." She sighed and took a step back, as if she realized what was happening.

"Should we wait for Anton and see what we come up with?"

"Ajá, sure," Mamá said, biting her nails and looking to the side. Mamá never bit her nails. They were always red, long, and perfect.

I closed my eyes, taking a deep breath. Uncertainty filling my thoughts.

~

Anton took the news as badly as I expected.

"Ay, Vi. Perhaps Paula was right. Do you think we need to sell?" He took his nails to his mouth and started pacing around the room.

I shook my head no. Anton could not doubt. If Anton started doubting, then the whole operation would break down.

"Anton, mijo!" I clapped my hands to bring him to reality. "I told Mamá already; we're going to figure it out. I have no idea how, but something will come up. Resolver, remember?"

Resolver. That had been one of Abuela's favorite words. If there was no food in the house and we were hungry, we needed to resolver, to whip something up as if it was magic. If I had a problem at school, she'd promptly say "Resuelve." Don't dwell on it, just do something already.

"Violeta," Mamá said, as if she had just remembered something. "Didn't you tell me ese novio tuyo was coming?"

Yes, I had told Mamá Liam was coming that morning. Mamá had just nodded and said something vague about how it would be good to meet him. I thought about Liam red cheeked and sweating buckets, unable to take the heat. Was I happy that he was coming? I was stressed. But one could be happy and stressed at the same time, right? I took my nails to my mouth and started biting them.

"Vi! Stop biting your nails. Disgusting."

I knitted my brows. When I did it, it was unacceptable.

Mamá stood up from a stool and shook her hands in the air. "Bueno, we need to start making pasteles. If he's going to be family, he needs to try one of the most special family dishes."

This was typical of Mami, to deflect and self-sabotage. Who cared about pasteles right now? Our debt just went from $25,000 to $31,000. In dollars perhaps it wasn't much; in pesos it was a lot. And it became worse for the fact that we didn't know investors or anyone that would have that kind of money. None of us had good credit.

"Mamá," I pleaded with her. "He doesn't care about pasteles. He knows we're struggling." When I'd arrived, Mamá wasn't even at the airport waiting for me. Why did she want to cook for him?

In Barranquilla, it didn't matter if you were swimming in debt. What mattered was what you projected—Mamá had always loved to appear to have the most riveting love stories, that Caminito was always doing well, that we were opulent. But this was too much—we needed to save our energy for Caminito.

Anton rolled his eyes and let out a sigh. "Qué pasteles? The oven!" he said, dropping a washcloth on the sink. At least he was on my side.

"Nada." Mamá was already opening the recipe notebook to search for the page. "Pasteles. He's a guest. Vi, that's what your abuela would have wanted. Imagine, your abuela would be mortified to know that your novio visited and we received him with nothing."

I wiped the sweat from my forehead. I couldn't tell what Abuela wanted anymore. Was Mamá insisting that she wanted pasteles because she thought we were done anyway? She knew we would end up selling?

"Okay," I said, knowing that there was nothing else I could say to stop her. "Fine. But we do the pasteles, and then it's all about Caminito again."

"Get me the shopping list."

As Mamá wrote down the ingredients, I thought about Abuela. How I would have loved for her to meet Liam.

"Apúrate, so we can get started."

"Okay, while I'm gone, Anton, can you research if there's any event we can cater? Anything, we should be able to do anything. Did you research investors, Mamá?" I had asked Mamá to ask around to see if anyone knew anybody.

Mamá shook her head. "Rocío told me she might have a lead. But I don't know. Maybe give her a call."

Anton took his phone out, which he never did in the kitchen, and disappeared to make a few calls.

"Mamá?" It felt wrong to order Mami around. I was so used to the opposite. "See about the Instagram page, more promotions, whatever you can do to get more people to come." I didn't know if it was actually doing anything, but it felt right to give Mamá a task.

"Bueno," she said, to my surprise agreeing with me. I left the restaurant with the note. The sooner we got the pasteles out of the way, the sooner we could start worrying about this oven.

On my way to the store, I passed multiple pastel-colored houses, rosebushes that somehow survived the heat. I wanted to memorize everything. I knew my pass through Barranquilla was temporary. NYC was calling. It was a matter of time until Charlie would start emailing and texting, and my clients got antsy. This was just a moment in time, and it would go quicker than I knew it.

"Doña Rocío," I said when she picked up. "Mami told you I've been looking for investors. She said you had a lead." The supermarket was the same, the same bright lights and the customers with the same slow rhythm. People in Barranquilla went to the supermarket for fun, lingering in the aisles and snacking on bread with sugar and Coca-Cola. It was an outing to go to the supermercado.

"Si mija, mira. I do know someone—someone who invested in the restaurant many years ago. But I don't know—"

"What? What don't you know?"

"Where he is, or what he is doing anymore. I need to locate him first."

I grabbed a basket and started with the vegetables. It was a long list; pasteles had so many ingredients. I was going to be here for a while. We didn't have the money to spend on these kinds of things. But it was impossible to tell Mami no.

"Can I help?"

"No, no. You can't help. If I know anything, you'll know."

Doña Rocío had a mysterious air around her. She always did. It was always better not to ask.

"Okay, but we really do need—"

"Sí, sí, sí," she said and hung up.

~

Watching Liam pass through customs and through the gates made me feel as if my heart was about to burst. He smiled at me as if nothing had passed between us. As if I hadn't been super uncommunicative these past days. He looked at me, and my heart jumped, a single word escaping my lips: "Liam," I said, and I waved frantically as he rushed to me with his arms open. We both smiled as we ran to each other.

"Vi," he said and dropped his bag on the floor. He hugged me with such intensity that it reminded me instantly of all the safety he emanated. Liam felt like a refuge in the Barrio Prado, which was always shifting and throwing things my way.

I grabbed his face in between my hands. Tears welled up in my eyes, but I was so happy to see him.

"Oh, Vi. No, don't cry. What's wrong?" Liam said, placing his now-warm hands on my cheeks. Liam had been in Barranquilla for less than a half hour, and he was already sweating.

"I don't know," I said, my voice breaking. I was confused. What was going on? I had seen Rafa days before and had been so overcome with emotion I'd had to fight hard to contain myself. And now seeing Liam, all the feelings I had toward him rushed back.

He held me tight and kissed my forehead, then the tip of my nose, and then my lips. I closed my eyes, delirious with happiness to have him here. Our kiss was urgent and sweet, a current of electricity through my veins.

His kiss was like coming home after a long day.

"It's like you described it," he said, holding my hands between his. "Like putting your head in a hot oven."

"I told you it was three hundred degrees out." I laughed with him and buried my face in his chest. "Take this off." I gestured to his jacket. "That's not helping."

Liam took off his jacket and long-sleeve shirt until he was only in a T-shirt. In his clothes, I could smell our Brooklyn apartment. Our life together.

He grabbed his bag, and I took his hand, as I always did. We started walking to the exit, where not too long ago I had taken a taxi that had dropped me off at Caminito.

"You okay?" Liam asked, squeezing my hand in front of the row of taxis. His voice was soft and comforting.

"Yes," I said, looking at him. I kissed him again. "I can't believe you're here."

Liam smiled, looking at me. "If you need help, there's nowhere I wouldn't go."

I took a deep breath, absorbing the magnitude of those words.

"Ready?" he said, making eye contact with a taxi driver. As soon as they saw his blue eyes, I knew they were going to try and charge us double.

"Ready," I said, not wanting to let go of his hand.

We got in the taxi, leaving behind the airport where I had left for another life more than ten years ago, the airport where now two of my different lives were colliding.

~

Pasteles were a big seller at the restaurant and for encargos around navidad and año nuevo. It was one of the things I missed the most when I was in the States. It was also one of the things I dreaded when I was younger. Abuela would fight with the kitchen staff and Anton to get them right. The hours of preparation, sudor y lagrimas—sweat and tears. Pasteles, in my family, was a recipe made of two meats: chicken and pork. The color of the dish was from the peppers, green peas, cabbage, and garbanzos. The rice always had a boiled egg that had been marinated for an entire day with the rest of the ingredients. The boiled eggs were always my favorite part, and Abuela always made sure mine was the one that had two. The regular customers at the restaurant said my abuela's pasteles were her gift to the world.

But Abuela's gift came with a lot of guilt. Whoever wasn't doing enough was always called out. Mamá, according to Abuela, would never learn enough in order to be able to make them on her own. Anton always complained too much and left the pasteles for too long on the stove. "All that food, all that effort, and they're overcooked. Who's going to eat that?" Anton would take the pasteles home, defeated, knowing that this defeat was temporary because he would have to go back the next day and help make a new batch. His pasteles were never good enough for Abuela or Caminito. And I wasn't allowed to sit in the kitchen without Abuela practically throwing a book at me.

All that inheritance in one dish sat in front of Liam, who stared at it with respect. Almost frightened by the size of the dish.

Despite Mamá's intentions to entertain and be liked by the guest, the air in the room felt dense. We were alone with Mamá, because Anton and Berto had to take care of the restaurant by themselves—it was a lot, but due to the few customers, it was probably manageable. Mamá knew basic English from school, and her words rolled heavy on her tongue. Most of the time she stopped herself from forming full sentences out of self-consciousness.

Mami was at the head of the long table, and there was an empty seat next to her. I wondered if Abuela's presence was sitting there, if she was already judging how slowly he ate.

Liam and I were on the other side. The only sound at the table was the clink-clink of the cutlery.

"Mami, él te oye. He can hear you. He understands a little even if he doesn't speak it." I had been trying to convince Mami to speak English, but she would start a sentence and stop herself. She would pretend to be too busy eating. Everyone was supervigilant around Liam, who was going to wake up with swollen cheeks from smiling so much. He was nervous, I could tell. He was usually very talkative and warm, but now he sat with his arms to the side without moving them.

Below the table, I put my hand on his knee and squeezed it. I turned to look at him, but he was focused on Mami.

"I see that he's not eating all of the tamal?"

I rolled my eyes. Mamá was judging Liam already. If Abuela were here, she would be interrogating him about not eating. "Está comiendo despacio. Muy pesado? A los gringos no les gusta la comida picante." *Gringos don't like spicy food.* Mamá intercepted the question, as if she had been to the States or was an expert in the matter. Mami kept observing him without shame, as if he were something to watch on the TV and not a person in front of her.

"Mami, no es verdad. He loves it," I assured her. I glanced over at Liam's plate. He still had more than half of the pastel left. I feared he wouldn't finish it. Mami and Anton had cooked for so long, and I didn't know if Mamá had it in her to forgive Liam for not eating the whole thing.

On the coast, the rules were simple: men ate a lot, while women pretended to have small appetites. I, on the other hand, was about to finish my plate. Since I had arrived in Barranquilla, I had been surrounded by delicious plates of food, and seldom did I have a chance to eat them.

I told him what she was saying. Liam, still with a smile on his face, tried to speak the broken Spanish that he had learned in the Mexican spot we liked close to our apartment. He loved talking to the beautiful Mexican woman with black shiny hair who owned the restaurant and telling her that everything was "delicioso, siempre." He understood a little but couldn't speak back.

"Delicioso," he said, looking. "Muy rico." Liam gestured an "okay" sign with his hands.

I knew Mamá was hoping for a more detailed answer from Liam. She wanted to know if he had eaten anything like that dish ever before. She probably wanted to know what his favorite part of the pasteles was. Was it the notes of spiciness? Or how the chicken pulled off the bone perfectly? The vinegar-boiled egg? But her English couldn't reach that far.

Had I been expecting Abuela? Knowing her, she wouldn't miss something like this, but my eyes widened when I saw her. Ghosts were a possibility in Barrio Prado, or the heat was making me delirious. I gripped Liam's knee so much that he turned to look at me.

"Vi? Everything okay?"

I nodded absently. Abuela was moving from the corner of the room to sit in the free, open chair. That was it: the lack of sleep, the stress of losing Caminito, how surreal it was to see Rafa again. I was losing it. A current of cold air entered the room, breaking the heat, and I rubbed my naked shoulders. I swallowed hard, wondering if someone would notice that all color had left my face, that my leg was shaking under the table.

Abuela smiled breezily at me as she sat.

I looked to Mamá and Liam, both smiling at each other, without a care in the world.

"Mija," Abuela said, although I was the only one who could see her and hear her. She was wearing the same red dress. She looked the same, just as young.

I closed my eyes, hoping I wouldn't see her when I opened them back up. She was still there.

Liam put his hand on my shaking leg.

"Vi," he said, with a concerned tone. "What's going on?"

"All good," I said and tried to look at Mami, who seemed to have found her voice.

Mami started talking about how I never had friends as a child and Abuela and Anton were my only friends. Abuela pointed with her mouth to the guest, arms folded on the table, since she wasn't eating. I started to play with my food just to look busy, but I couldn't look away. What was she going to do?

"Este es?" she said, asking if this was Liam. As if she didn't know. As if, even in the afterlife, she didn't have the power to know everything.

I looked at Liam saying yes to everything Mami said. I nodded, hoping they would think I was nodding at Mami saying I was a lonely kid and who knows what else. Mami went on to say that she was always being called to school because I never paid attention, always daydreaming and doodling stuff in the corners of my notebook. What she failed to mention was that it wasn't her who went to the school meetings; it was Abuela. Liam smiled politely and looked at me with so much tenderness in his eyes.

"No," Abuela said quickly. "No me gusta." *I don't like him.*

I tried to be expressionless. To not react.

"He is not the one for you, escucha, I know these things."

"Abu—" I stopped myself. Mamá raised an eyebrow.

"Eh . . . I just, ah, wished Abuela was here, that's all. She would love to meet you." I looked at Liam. "She would love you."

"No," Abuela repeated. "I wouldn't."

I moved my head, trying to shake off Abuela's presence. Mami gave me a quick glance and then kept talking to Liam, who was just nodding.

"No," Abuela said again, bending over the table as if she were going to melt on it. I looked at Liam. He was so kind with Mami, so patient. Listening to her every word.

"Ajá, and who do you like?" I said bitterly. Thinking that he was what she had always wanted for me. She hated Rafa because his family was too poor. Liam's family was respectable; he had a good job. What was the problem? Who was the right one for me, then?

Mamá and Liam stopped talking, all eyes pointed in my direction. The silence was so stark that I wondered if they could hear Abuela's murmur. Every time she was in the room, her presence, even if she wasn't speaking, sounded like she was emanating a certain frequency. The low hum of an old machine.

How could they not feel the current of cold air? How could they not see her smile? I touched my cheeks, trying to see if I was burning. No fever, just me losing my mind.

"Nada, Mami. I was just saying that I was a weird kid. Nothing wrong with that."

Liam squeezed my knee under the table, agreeing with me.

"I was a weird kid too," he told Mami. "I got beat up almost every week." He smiled at me, and our eyes met. I was grateful to be there with him—to feel protected by his words.

Mami leaned in and smiled, crossing her legs. "Un muchacho tan buen mozo como tú." So handsome, she said, she couldn't believe that.

"Ay." Abuela let out a sigh. "Ahí está pintada. Típico. Vi," she said, "your mom can't release a breath without flirting."

The words sat heavy in my stomach, heavier than the full dish of rice and chicken I had eaten. I felt sick. I wanted to yell at her that she didn't know who was right for me. She didn't decide for me anymore, and then I looked around—Mamá's wrinkle on her forehead pronounced like thunder on a dark night, Liam looking at me. Waiting.

"Vi," Liam said, squeezing my knee.

"Yes?" I said, distracted. Mamá was still talking, but I couldn't concentrate. Abuela was here, in this house, and she still didn't trust me to make my own decisions.

"I've missed you," he said.

I kissed him softly on the lips, desperate for the fear to go away. My hand was shaking. I closed my eyes, giving in.

When I opened my eyes again, her presence had vanished.

~

Mamá had decorated the house with flowers in every room and with our family pictures. On a big wooden piece of furniture in the kitchen, Liam laid his eyes on a picture of Mamá in her lace wedding dress. She was holding her wedding bouquet of white flowers with ramitas of cilantro sprinkled throughout. I hadn't seen the bouquet in so long, and I had forgotten how vibrantly green it was. How fragrant it had been when you stood next to Mamá and her flowers.

"It was a cilantro wedding bouquet," Mamá said to Liam, when she caught him looking at the picture. She delicately wiped the sides of her lips after finishing the last bite of her tamal. "It was my wedding. Fifteen years ago."

I was born out of wedlock, and that was Mamá's second marriage. I didn't know who my father was, though there was a time when that had mattered to me very much. When I'd searched for him. But growing up, I had realized that by him not being in my life, not doing anything to be, he had shown me all I needed to know.

It had always felt like enough to grow up in this house, surrounded by Abuela and Bisabuela, Mamá sometimes.

"Mi mamá, Violeta's abuela, put some ramas of cilantro in the bouquet because she didn't like the arrangement the flower woman made. She said it looked so . . . Vi, cómo se dice? Sin vida?"

"Lifeless."

"Lifeless. Gracias. So Mamá went to the restaurant and grabbed some cilantro sticks and put it in the arrangement so it would look more vibrant. It smelled like heaven."

"Abuela said she always wanted to get married with a cilantro bouquet, but Abuelo said it was ridiculous and that the church would smell like a kitchen," I said, remembering how glorious the combination of the smell of the flowers with the cilantro had been. Abuelo had been in and out of my life; sometimes he would spend periods in the house, but he always had a foot out of the door. I never knew where he went. Abuela would simply say he was with his amantes. The other women. She said that in a tone so removed that I wondered if she had trained herself not to care. Or at least to pretend like she didn't.

Abuelo was consistent with his words. All that ever came out of his mouth was unkindness.

All the guests had been so enamored with the bouquet and how beautiful Mamá looked with her lace dress, the contrast of the bouquet's shades of bright green, and her bright-red lips.

I didn't remember what Mamá's second husband, Roberto, had thought about the bouquet. If he, like Abuelo, had said something about the smell. Probably not. He was a kind man, until he wasn't.

That marriage didn't last long; I was already thirteen years old when they got married. As if she had the power to predict the future, Abuela told Mamá to get settled, find a home, and then to have me move in with them. They never found a home big enough, and as her husband started to reveal the truth about himself, Abuela clutched to me. She protected me from what we both knew was going on. The bruises, the lies, the sudden bursts of emotion.

"So much history in this restaurant," Mamá said, looking longingly at the picture of her from the day of her second wedding and running her fingers over the silver frame. She released a deep, dramatic sigh that hid so much. How a picture could hold joy and sorrow all at once. "So much history, and she doesn't want it."

What? Mamá didn't want Caminito. She wanted to sell.

I shot Mamá a look for doing this right now. That was typical of her: to shower with attention the man who belonged to my other life in the States while also pretending she wanted me to stay and keep the restaurant alive. It made no sense. She knew I couldn't have both.

"Mami, not now." Did Mami ever get embarrassed? I thought. Did she ever stop to think about when to say things?

"Qué?" Mami asked with a smirk. "Te da pena? Did you tell Liam?" She directed her eyes at Liam, who was taking small bites of his pastel. He was slowly but surely eating his whole portion. I released an exhale of relief: one less problem. If he didn't eat it, Mamá would ask why. Liam took the ají and drenched the uneaten half in the hot sauce. "Liam, didn't Vi tell you? She wants to sell the restaurant. Get rid of Caminito. All that her abuela worked so hard for!" Mami put a hand on her face as if she were witnessing the most shocking tragedy.

"Mamá." I paused, my cheeks burning and my hands in fists. "Are you crazy?" I raised my hands in the air, as if I was on the top of a roller coaster. "You were the one that wanted to sell!" I rose up from the table. "No, no. I said that we needed to try. And you know it."

He was a stranger to all these kinds of dramas. His family didn't do these types of scenes in front of each other. They always had kind words for each other, room for understanding. Well, this was a good introduction to how things were around here, then.

"Vi." Mamá looked around the room as if there were more people in it. "Please lower your voice—there's no need." Mamá looked at Liam and shook her head slightly. "Calm down, Violeta. Is she like this with you?"

I took a deep breath and threw my napkin on the table. "You don't get to do this." I turned to leave the room, but then I heard Liam speak.

"I don't know, Paula." Liam lowered his face. "I am sure Vi wants the best for the restaurant. Why else would she be putting her life on hold for it? She has a lot of clients in NYC. I'm sure her business is going to take off any day now."

Mamá leaned on the chair and opened her mouth wide in surprise. "Ha," she said. "As she should. We have sacrificed so much for her."

I put a hand on Liam's shoulder, trying to stop him from getting into it with Mamá. "Liam," I said softly. "It's not worth it."

"I'm just saying . . . Vi has an illustration business that she's been working on for years, and she's putting that on pause for the restaurant." Liam looked at me and shook his head. "You could give her some credit."

Mamá rolled her eyes and smiled at him. She had that look on her face that made her seem as if she knew more than everyone else. "I gave her life, I don't need to give her credit."

"It's okay," I told Liam, locking eyes with him. "Leave it." The heat in that room was suffocating. "I don't need you to defend me, you know." As soon as the words came out of my mouth, I desperately wanted to take them back. "I'm sorry." I shook my head. "I'm just upset."

"I know, it's just . . ."

"Mamá, look, I need you to stop talking about me being here as if I've been trying to sabotage Caminito when all I've done is work to save it."

Mamá lifted her hands in the air as if saying "fair play."

"And you," I said to Liam. "I feel like you don't understand what Caminito means to me. It's almost like you don't understand what I'm doing here."

Liam released a chuckle. "Vi, all I've done is be understanding. I had to get on a plane here so you would talk to me. How do you think that makes me feel?"

"Excuse me," I said, finally walking out of the room. It was a big house, with long halls and snail stairs, but inside of it I felt small, incapable. The night was warm but with some breeze. I closed my eyes, letting the breeze caress my face. Nothing that I could do at that moment felt like it would ever be enough. Not for Mamá, not for Liam, not for Rafa, not for myself.

"Vi," Liam said, following me and almost whispering. "I'm sorry, I realize I've been not giving you space to figure this out. I told you I'd wait, and I will."

I turned slowly. "Tell me how you really feel about this whole thing. About me trying to save Caminito."

The only sounds in the night were the crickets and the horns from the buses. I walked closer to him. "Tell me," I insisted.

"I don't know, I think that if this is something that means something to you, and you think it's worth doing—"

"Liam." I put a hand on his shoulder. "Don't lie."

"Vi, I don't know. I mean, it doesn't seem like the restaurant is going to survive anyway. Your mom is so rude with you, I just don't get why you want to stay or what you're after." He looked down to his shoes. "I think you're wasting your time."

I took my hand back. And there they were, the strings of tears sliding down my face. The bitterness in my throat. I felt so naive.

"That's the faith you have in me."

"It's not you, it's just how things are," Liam said, putting his hands on my arms. "Vi, I love you, but I wonder if you're running from our life. You knew it would be hard for your business in New York to take off. It's NYC, for god's sake, of course there will be competition. We were even talking about getting engaged . . ."

Months ago, when he had first mentioned it, I'd started laughing, first out of nervousness and then out of happiness. After four years of being and living together, it was a natural progression for us. We were used to each other's quirks and rhythms. I loved our life together—I held his hand and confessed that I, too, was picturing a future with him. I felt ready to jump, to commit, to marry him right then and there. My feelings, I understood now, hadn't been a lie. Back then, things felt clearer to me and more straight cut. I looked away, the beds of my feet tingling.

"Liam, not everything is about us. I want to do this for Abuela." I cleared my throat. Suddenly the memory of sitting on our couch, holding hands, came to me. Everything had felt possible for us at that moment, even forgetting my past with Rafa had ever existed. Was I running away? Was this about me or about Abuela? "Abuela's memory."

"She's not here, Vi. You gotta do what's best for you. For us."

"You don't understand, Liam. It's my family. It's important for me to be here for them."

Mamá opened the door of the patio and peeked her head out like an ostrich.

"Dessert?" she asked, and although I couldn't see her face clearly, I swore she was smiling. I wondered if she was enjoying seeing Liam fight with me.

"Sí," Liam said, turning to her.

"I'm not done with this," I said between my teeth. "I can't believe you don't think I can do this."

"Vi, let's talk about this later? Let's just get this over with, yes?" Liam put his index finger on my chin, and I took a deep breath. "Please?"

I walked a couple of steps farther, without saying anything, not ready for his touch.

The bitter taste on my tongue wouldn't go away.

Mamá had set the table beautifully. There was a golden-brown flan in the center decorated with cherries. She got up and started cutting pieces of flan for everyone, without saying a word, just a smile. Mamá couldn't be quiet for long, and I started to wonder what she could say next.

Liam put a hand on my knee, and I knew he wanted to make things right, but I couldn't let this one go. I moved my knee to the side so his hand would drop. Even if I was guilty, too, guilty of letting myself spend time with Rafa. Guilty of not letting him know what was going on with Abuela. But how could I tell Liam? I saw him smiling at Mamá when she gave him a generous portion of flan. How could I tell him that when I had arrived in Barranquilla, the ghosts of my past life were waiting for me, ready to have a word?

"So," Mamá said, sitting down. She hadn't given me a piece. She put a hand on her forehead. "Ay, Vi, serve yourself, I forgot." I was about to get up, but Liam beat me to it. "Allow me."

Mamá smiled. "Qué caballero." *What a gentleman.* "So what are you planning to do in the next few days?"

She seemed to get more fluent the more she drank. Liam put a slice of flan in front of me, and I started eating it anxiously, without saying thank you, trying to concentrate on the food instead of what everyone was saying. This was the first time that I had eaten something at home that tasted exactly the same as it did when Abuela made it. The caramel wasn't too dense, and it was liquid, so it didn't overwhelm the flavors of the vanilla and the flan. Under it all, there was a hint of rum. I closed my eyes and I could see Abuela, garnishing her famous flan, the light of the kitchen window illuminating her brown, freckled face.

"I don't know, Vi." Liam looked at me. "What are we doing?"

I took a deep breath, feeling Mami's expectant eyes on me.

"Working," I said, taking a break from the flavors of caramel and vanilla. "Tonight was nice." I took a huge spoonful. "But we have an oven to buy."

CHAPTER TEN: AGUA

Mamá opposed me and Liam sleeping in the same bed. We explained to her that we lived together in an apartment in Brooklyn. We shared the bed every night. And yet Mamá wouldn't allow it. She stayed in the house with us instead of with her boyfriend. Mami installed herself in her old room, and that was that. "Liam can sleep in Mami's room," she said, inserting a fake sense of morality.

I kissed Liam before bed like I did in Brooklyn every night. I was still angry at him, but I didn't want him to go to bed without a kiss—I didn't want the distance to land in Barranquilla, too, and seep into our relationship until we couldn't get rid of it. He caressed my hair and brushed a frizzy strand out of my face.

"I'm sorry, Vi. I let myself get carried away."

I nodded as he put his hands on my cheeks. His hands were warm and cupped most of my face.

"I'm excited to see you tomorrow." Liam half smiled. He was amused by Mami's self-righteousness. Liam still couldn't believe Mamá needed us to sleep separately. "I've missed you so much." He really didn't get how things worked around here. He pulled me close to him and squeezed my shoulders. He hurt me when he pulled me so close. His touch was abrupt and urgent, his nails digging against my exposed skin. He took my bandaged hand and examined it in between his.

"How is this going, love?"

"Healing," I said, ready to get up. My head was heavy with thoughts of him not understanding what Caminito meant to me. The fact that he didn't think I had what it took in order to save it. Liam took my hand and pulled me on top of him. He started kissing my shoulders and neck until he got to my lips. I suppressed a moan when his warm lips touched my neck. I had missed this; I had missed him.

"I can't stay," I said, pushing him away, the anger returning. I started buttoning my blouse. "Mami is right next door. I know you don't understand," I said, already by the door. "But this is how they do things here—it matters to her." I usually told myself that I didn't care what Mami thought. But I wanted to avoid a fight with her. Perhaps also a part of me, despite how much I denied it, still wanted to please her.

Liam looked at me from the bed. His legs were spread wide, and he was sweating.

"I get it. I love you, Vi," he said, looking at me from afar.

"I love you too," I said, closing the door behind me. None of this felt real.

Ever since I arrived in Caminito, I realized I had descended into a space where Abuela's ghost was roaming the halls of the house, where Rafa was walking in the neighborhood—his presence looming behind me. I was Vi, and I was Violeta. I was eighteen and twenty-eight. I was dreaming, and I was awake.

The next step I took could lead me to losing it all. I opened the notebook, as always looking for answers, knowing that life wasn't as easy and clear cut as that. The next entry was short.

Barranquilla 1963

> *Mamá hadn't had the words to warn me about what she knew would happen, but even if she had articulated it perfectly, would I have listened? Every morning I wake up, and I yearn to wake up somewhere else. Every time I*

feel the sun on my cheeks, I feel rage. I can't believe every day is the same, and yet, every day it gets worse.

My heart hurt for Abuela as I read those words. She had survived poverty, an abusive husband, and loneliness, and I knew that she was just trying to protect me from her same fate. She wasn't able to save Mamá entirely, and although I wasn't sure she was here, I wanted to tell her that I had learned. That I wasn't going to make the same mistakes. My life, in part due to everything my ancestors had sacrificed, wouldn't turn out the same as theirs.

~

I was heavily asleep when I heard it. First, the steps up and down, and the steps that sounded against the wooden staircase with their crik crik crik and crak crak crak, and then the bang on my door. I thought it was Mami wanting to see if I was sleeping alone or with Liam. I woke up annoyed at this thought. "Voy," I said, slowly waking up. My toes curled at the first touch of the freezing floor. I opened the door to Liam, who was pacing around the room from side to side. He was in a T-shirt and boxers. It was odd that he hadn't put pants on to see me. What if Mamá saw him walking through the halls in his boxers?

"What's happening, Liam? Sit," I offered, sitting on the bed myself. His hair was messy. I wanted to run my hands through it to smooth it, but he seemed frazzled.

He sat next to me. His legs were shaking next to mine. I put a hand on his leg to calm him down.

"What's wrong?" I said in a barely there voice so as to not startle him.

Liam lifted his head and looked at me. His face was as pale as if he had seen a ghost.

"No." I felt the hairs on the back of my neck stand up. "No," I muttered again under my breath, trying to understand what was happening. I squeezed his knee hard, wanting to ground him in reality.

"There was a woman in that room," Liam said, gaze lost in a corner of the room. "I was asleep, and when I woke up, I saw a woman sitting on the couch that faces the bed."

I'd been convinced Abuela's presence was a product of the grief that had taken residence in my body. How could he feel her too?

"What did she look like?" I tried, pushing his hair behind his ear, caressing it in calming motions. But the tightness in my chest returned.

Liam shook his head and stood up, pacing around the room. I watched him from the bed, knowing that even if I had the words to explain what was going on, he wouldn't understand. I didn't either.

"Maybe it was a nightmare?" I offered, my voice low and not confident enough in the lie.

"Maybe." Liam stood still, biting his nails. "No." He shook his head. "I was awake, Vi." He opened his eyes wide. "I saw her."

Her. That younger version of Abuela. Her spirit, I knew then, would always get the last laugh. She was defiant and rogue. Larger than life itself—Abuela had warned me about this. About how the spirits in our family lingered.

Liam looked around the room. On my nightstand there was a picture of me and Abuela when I was a little girl. My hair all frizzed out and my belly poking out of a pink shirt. I hated how I looked in that picture, but I loved that Abuela had her hands on my shoulders and was smiling. It was a rare picture of Abuela wearing bright-red lipstick—she looked happy, without a care in the world.

Liam lingered on the picture, his eyes getting lost in the image.

"Liam," I said nervously. "What is it?"

He took the picture in his hands; they were shaking. I wanted to take the portrait from him. I didn't want it to break.

"Liam?"

"It was weird because since my eyes were half-closed, I couldn't see her clearly, but she was there. Wearing what looked like a red-and-brown flower-patterned dress with midlength black hair. She was looking at me. I couldn't see her clearly, but I felt her eyes on me. I was sure that it happened. That I saw her. I was sure I was awake—"

"Maybe you just saw a picture of Abuela and then . . . a nightmare," I tried, taking the picture from his shaking hands and putting it on my nightstand, where it would be safe. He wouldn't understand. Liam didn't believe in ghosts; he believed that death was the end of it all, and I was too exhausted to make him see.

"Liam, it's been a long day . . . maybe—"

I had to send him to his bed before Mami heard us and before Abuela did anything else. I planted a kiss on his cheek and pulled him closer, standing on my tippy-toes, wrapping him in my arms, kissing his ear, his neck, and his hair. Wanting to protect him from her, from this house.

"You can't sleep here. Mami would hear us. You can sleep with the door open," I offered, kissing his ear again, not letting him go. "Hey," I said softly. "It was all a bad dream."

"Maybe I'm just jet lagged," he said, as I planted the soles of my feet on the floor, pulling my arms away from him.

"Maybe," I offered. "Do you want me to walk you to your room?"

Liam shook his head.

"No, I . . ." His eyes looked lost. "I don't believe in ghosts."

Liam had always been methodical, a man of science, and that hadn't left room in his life for knowing that things weren't always as expected. No room for the in-betweens. Liam was being presented with the evidence, and yet he couldn't believe it.

"I love you," I offered as he turned to walk away, his head hanging low. I tasted salt on my lips—the bitterness of knowing that he couldn't, wouldn't believe me even if I told him the truth of what I thought. Although he was close, there was a distance between us.

"I love you too," he said as he walked into the hallway without closing the door behind him.

I closed my door. The house was humid and stuffy, the air heavy with something. One step, two steps, as I went closer and closer to the darkness.

A current of cold air blew in the middle of the room. I brushed my arms and closed the window. The air carried the whisper of her voice.

I felt her eyes on the back of my neck. The humming of the machine that her spirit produced, her smell of rain even if the clouds outside were dry. I was scared, scared of feeling her with me, and I was angry that there weren't words in the dictionary to explain to Liam what was happening. The realization that there would always be words missing between us. And could I live with that?

"Abuela," I said as I turned but didn't see her. I got up and opened the door again, starting to go down the stairs to the living room.

She was sitting in her favorite chair, legs crossed and hands folded on her knees as if I was a visitor in her house and she wanted to keep her posture. She lifted a hand, her arm long and elegant, and gestured for me to sit.

I shook my head, no way. "Abuela, no más juegos, dime." I stood my ground, far from her. "Tell me what you want me to do for you . . . Abuela?" I asked when she didn't say anything. "Dime."

When she finally spoke, her voice was raspy and low, as if she had been crying. "Tu sabes porque estoy aquí . . ."

"No." I shook my head, standing in place. "I *don't* know why you're here. You have to tell me so I can help."

"Mija." Abuela stood up, again, her body unfolding rather than moving naturally. She didn't turn to me, no, she moved to the staircase and started going up. I wondered about following her, but I was scared, petrified of what she was about to show me.

"Abuela, why are you here?"

She put her hand on the staircase railing and turned to me.

"So you don't make the same mistakes I did." Her face wasn't the same childlike spirit that had appeared before. Her eyes looked tired, and her expression was blank, as if she was disappointed.

"There's nothing I want you to do for me. Don't you see?" She gripped her hand on the railing as if she could fall. "It's more what I can do for you." She pointed at me with her free hand.

"Qué?" I said, my voice breaking.

"Even after death I'm still looking after you."

"I didn't ask you to."

"Ay, mija." The sigh of a ghost sounded like the murmur of the wind. "It doesn't matter. When you see someone you love making a mistake, you intervene. I led you astray, mija. I see that now."

"Abuela," I called. We, las Sanoguera, were terrible at letting go. Even in the afterlife she held on. "What are you talking about? What do you mean?"

"Just because I felt fear, it didn't mean that you had to feel it too." She continued going up, and when her body reached the second floor, it disappeared, leaving me to wonder if she had been here in the first place.

I sat in Abuela's chair, still warm as if it had just been occupied by a body. I wondered if Abuela was here to prevent me from giving in to fear. Fear had been too much part of my life at this point; I didn't even know how to make a decision. I held on to things: to the past, to my jobs, to Caminito . . . to Liam?

No, this wasn't about Liam. The chair smelled old and musty like the rest of the house—not like her. After a while I stopped hearing the static noise her spirit produced. I shifted in the chair, trying to get comfortable enough to fall asleep. This wasn't about Liam because being with him had felt right from the first moment; when we were together, I felt safe.

I rested my head and closed my eyes. I wanted to sleep downstairs, away from her ghost. Away from the weight of my own guilt about not spending her last days on earth with her. If I closed my eyes, just for a second, I didn't have to figure it all out right away.

~

I woke up in Abuela's chair, my neck bent in a weird position and my whole body hurting from sleeping on the chair. It was early, and Liam was still sleeping upstairs. I would be back before he woke up. I dressed in a rush and left the house to look for the only person who could give me answers to what Abuela's spirit was looking for.

Doña Rocío.

Her house smelled like a blend of tobacco, marine breeze, and something earthy like the grass after a long day of rain. She opened the door with a smile, as if she knew I was coming. Doña Rocío, Abuela used to say, had the gift of premonition. She predicted and felt things before they happened. She greeted me with a cup of coffee that had so much sugar it tasted like a syrup rather than something I could drink.

She took me to her office and spread her tarot cards on the table just to gather them back.

"No," she said. "No cartas. It has to be the caracoles." She stood up and brought two handfuls of small shells. "Two rolls."

"Doña Rocío, tell me something," I said, sweating under my summer dress. Terrified of what she was about to say.

"Drop the Doña," she said without looking at me. She threw the caracoles on the table and studied them as if the position of the shells spoke to her. She counted them. Rocío closed her eyes and became quiet. The sugar from the coffee was going straight to my head. I hadn't had breakfast, and my stomach was rumbling in protest. Drops of my sweat dripped from my forehead.

"Rocío?" I asked, and she opened her eyes. Her face was as relaxed as if she had awoken from a nap.

"Si sigues así . . . you're going to hurt many people."

I cleared my throat. My indecision and cloudy thoughts were hurting the people I loved the most. It wasn't enough to try with Caminito—I had to do something that mattered. Fear. Abuela had talked about that the night before. My emotions these past few days had oscillated between scared and confused.

"Cómo así?" *How come?* She lifted my right hand, covered by the bandage.

"Are you taking care of this?"

I was telling everyone that I was. And yet my hand felt weaker every day. Every night I put the cream on without looking, rushing to wrap my hand, too scared to see what was underneath.

I nodded, lying.

"You can't really heal and close cycles if you don't look. What good has ignoring done to your familia? Mira, Vi, you can lie to other people. But are you lying to yourself? You are confused now, but if you're honest with yourself, Vi, you already know the answer. You've known all along. You're wise. Listen to yourself."

What good had come from listening to myself? I was in New York, and then I wasn't. I had listened to Abuela, and I had run away, built a new life. But I had run away from myself so much, I no longer recognized my own voice.

"That's not why I am here," I said, feeling feverish. Taking my hand back. "She said she doesn't want me to make the same mistakes." I bit my nails. "She's here."

Touching the shells softly, Rocío looked as if she was in a trance. Not really alarmed by any word I pronounced. She lifted her chin and looked at me. "Of course she's here, mija. She is always going to be here."

What did that mean? Of course Abuela's presence would always stay with me. But there was more, her spirit around the house; how could I hear with such clarity?

"She left a diary," I said, thinking about Abuela's life when she was young, her private thoughts that provided a more complicated version of her story that she never let us see.

"Do you think you have permission to read it?"

"Sí." I nodded. I bit my lip. "I don't really know."

"Ay, Vi." She shook her head softly. She gathered her shells and held them in her hand. She threw them on the table and studied them for a couple of seconds. Doña Rocío lifted a brow and then looked at me.

"Mijita, you know I love you."

I nodded, fixed my posture, and sighed, not feeling comfortable in the chair. I was desperate for answers, for Doña Rocío to tell me what to do.

"I love you, but you can sometimes be a little self-centered." She swallowed. "If she left the restaurant to you, she has a reason for that. Are you trying your best?"

Yes? No? I wasn't really sure what to do with Caminito. It felt like I never knew how to take space in the restaurant, and it was showing in my clumsy attempts.

"No."

"You know what to do, mamita. That's why she's here." She left the shells on one side and wrapped her hands around mine. Her hands were soft like silk. "Perhaps she can't rest until she knows that you don't need her anymore."

I thought about Abuela. Ever since she was young, all she did was take care of people. As a result, she had lived a vida prestada. A life where she was never the protagonist, her desires always at the end of the list.

"What can I do?" I asked Rocío, who was gathering her shells with her index fingers.

"Take care of her. Listen to her. No one took the time to really listen to her when she was alive. She needs that before she's able to rest."

I watched her hold the shells in her palms as if they were treasure. How did one take care of a ghost?

She was right. Abuela had been strong for all of us. But none of us had ever returned the favor. My chest felt tight thinking when the last time was that I had asked her how she really was.

Rocío shook her head and grabbed my hand. "Portals are delicate and temperamental. One day they are here, and the next day they go poof! And the way to communicate with our muertos is no longer there. This is a delicate time, aprovéchala. See her, mi vida, see her and talk to her because you never know when will be the last time you'll be able to."'

I got up, the knowledge hitting me like a bullet. Abuela wouldn't be here with me forever. I needed to hold on to every second. "Hey, Doña Rocío, did you ever hear from the investor?"

"Rocío. Simply call me Rocío." She got up, too, her chair screeching. "No, not yet. I'm working on it."

CHAPTER ELEVEN: PAELLA

"What difference is a rice festival going to make, Mami? Isn't that more money? We need ingredients, a logo, a banner for the table." I stood up in front of the dead oven as if I were guarding it. Anton was prepping for tonight's service, which basically consisted of dishes we didn't need an oven for.

Mamá was lately always on her phone. She lifted her eyes briefly to look at me.

"Well, we have the best paella in the city. People love seafood in this town. If we sell enough, maybe we can get some money to at least cover the first payment of the oven," Anton said behind me. Mamá broke into a smile, pleased that he was siding with her. She loved to be right.

"Anton, but isn't that more work?" I raised my voice. I was worried we were going to take on something else that wasn't going to be successful. At that moment, I wondered if Abuela had given me Caminito for me to learn to let go.

He shrugged. Mamá put her phone on the counter, and Anton shot her a look. Phones were unsanitary.

"Do you have any better ideas?" Mamá asked. Touché.

I shook my head. I really didn't. Liam had offered me money to pay for the oven, as a loan. But something was telling me not to take it. Maybe the fact that then we would be tied by money, and that would put unnecessary strain on our relationship. Abuela didn't want me to depend on a man, let alone be tethered to him by money.

Abuela wouldn't have wanted me to let go, not yet. She would want me to fight.

"Let's try."

"I'm going to make a call, see if they can fit us in." The festival was in a few days. In my head, a to-do list appeared.

Mamá left the room, phone in hand, and I caught a whiff of her floral perfume, the sound of her high heels.

Anton and I locked eyes. He cleared his throat.

"It will work," he said, his confidence dwindling.

"Sí," I uttered, looking down. "It will work." We were both trying to hold on to hope.

~

While people in Barranquilla were quick to underestimate me in the kitchen, they didn't doubt my drawing skills. I sat in the living room, at home, throwing piece of paper after piece of paper in the garbage as Liam refilled my glass of wine.

"I think you're putting too much pressure on yourself," he said, sitting on the couch and taking a sip of cold white wine. The heat was relentless, despite it being late at night. The restaurant service went up till ten, a few tables here and there. At least customers drank a lot tonight. "Vi, you do this for a living. Just take a deep breath—"

I made another ball of paper, the paper crinkling on my hand. I breathed in, breathed out, and closed my eyes, picturing the waves, the relentless midday sun. Caminito—what did Caminito represent? Food, tradition, family, history. Those concepts were larger than life, and logos needed to be simple.

I placed my hand on the paper and drew a simple teal-blue pan. Trash.

Then, I decided to try red, Abuela's favorite color. Perhaps it was a cayenne flower, like the emblematic flower of the city. I ripped the paper apart.

Liam placed a hand on my shoulder. "You okay? I might go watch a movie on my computer or something." He leaned in and kissed me.

"Go," I said, already placing a fresh piece of paper on the table.

A wave. Trash.

Time passed slowly as I stared at my old friend, the white page. I was drifting to sleep when I finally felt it. The wind. The beach. What was it with the beach? Abuela's words about the infinite caracol: time was a circle, not a line.

"We're always returning."

A chill ran down my spine. I woke up, as alert as one wakes up from a nightmare.

My hands gripped the pencil softly, and as if I were learning how to draw again, I let myself slowly trace a shape, discovering what it was. It was the shape of a snail. A caracol.

It seemed right to me to represent something that was family history. I picked the paper up.

What color would Abuela choose? I asked the wind, deciding on a cerulean blue, the color of the sea.

Those days, I felt Abuela's presence in the house whenever I was there. Whenever I needed grounding, I would touch Liam's hand and tell myself that this was the life I had built for myself, with him. The rest—this house, the restaurant—would have to accommodate itself around it. Hell, if nothing else, I needed to start standing up for myself. I thought about all those years ago, Abuela telling me to go to the States. Abuela fighting so I wouldn't see Rafa. Her cutting words. But no, not this time: Abuela would have to get used to the idea that this was what I wanted.

Liam didn't feel or notice these things. Ever since he had seen her, he would tell us he didn't remember that first night. It was probably all the food, the heavy dreams, being jet lagged. Not a ghost, because in his world ghosts didn't exist. I didn't say much. I would hold his hand like it had the power to tether me to the earth, to what was real, in front of me.

But most nights, I worried I was lying to myself. Mamá came in and out of the restaurant, as if it were a revolving door. Most nights, she didn't stay at home, and on those nights we slept in the room together, I searched for his body despite the heat.

In the dark, my hands recognized his chiseled chin, his broad shoulders, and even the sound of his breathing. Over the years, I had memorized it all. The way when I kissed him, he would immediately put his hands on my cheeks, urgently needing me.

~

Three days later, and multiple fights with the printing company to get the color and the lettering right, it was time. The rice festival in town was one that hosted individual chefs and restaurants where Barranquilleros were presented with the opportunity of selling dishes such as shrimp rice, coconut rice, arroz chaufa, cod rice, and other rice dishes that were unique creations.

For the festival, I spent the few dollars I had in my savings account getting the banner printed and the ingredients for the rice. Anton had worked day and night on the paella, and Mamá had been relentless on social media, dedicating herself to it.

As Anton and Mamá fought over how to turn on the little stove to heat up the paella at the table—which Doña Rocío had gotten someone to loan her for free—I smiled, looking at Mamá making an effort. Perhaps she cared after all. This was her way of showing it.

"Do we like the banner? The table?" I said, a hand over my eyes to cover the sun. The table looked simple but elegant. The only decoration was the banner that had the new logo, and the crisp white tablecloth. On one side of the table, we had wine bottles to accompany the paella.

I had made my calculations. We still needed all the $25,000 that we owed. Then, the oven was going to set us back another $6,000, but we could pay it in installments. If at least we got a little over $1,000 today, we could start paying for the oven. We could also get the word out about the restaurant. The calculations and the heat were making me feel weak. I hadn't eaten anything all day. I remembered Liam telling me about lending me the money for the oven. Possibly some for the restaurant. No, that would be a last resort. I needed it to feel right.

"Vi! Where do you want this?" Liam arrived with a box full of bottles of wine. His skin was red from the heat. He had been helping Anton with the paella and had waited tables with Berto to help out.

"You're the best," I said, pointing below the table. My stomach was rumbling, and I didn't know if it was from fear or hunger. Fear that we would fail. That this would land us even more in debt.

"Vete." Mamá told Anton to leave. "I got it."

The plan was for Anton to be at the restaurant and for Berto to drive the car back and forth as we needed more paella throughout the day. Anton froze in front of the stove. "What if it doesn't work?"

Mamá started stirring the rice. The saffron rice was pillowy and well balanced, and since it was Abuela's recipe, the shellfish were always fresh with a hint of picante that made them stand out. The end result was lush without being too moist.

"What did Mamá always say?"

"En boca cerrada no entran moscas."

No flies will enter closed mouths.

"No." Mamá laughed. "She used to say that where one sticks the head in, one has to take it out. We have already decided to do this. We have to see it through."

Anton stood behind her, as if he wanted to take her place. He didn't trust others to do anything.

"Okay?" Mamá turned back. "Now go."

Anton ran to the car, as if he were a doctor and he were running to perform a lifesaving operation. Liam took my hand.

"It's going to be okay," he said, locking eyes with me. "I promise."

I squeezed his hand, letting myself believe him.

~

People in Barranquilla and in Colombia liked to have lunch at exactly 12:00 p.m. The long line started forming. I was managing the money, and Liam was handling the customers, handing them the plates of paella Mamá gave him.

Mamá knew that the secret was not to overcook the paella, or it would become too dry. She was slowly plating the portions, making sure they were neat and well presented.

"Mamá, you need to be quicker," I said as the line progressed. "We can't afford to slow down."

Mamá ignored me, using her glacial pace to plate another paella. I rolled my eyes.

"If you rush me—" she started.

Liam turned to look at me. His blue eyes under the sun had hints of green. "We're doing good, Vi," Liam said. "Don't worry, I think we'll get some money for the oven."

I nodded, going back to my task of handling the change. We urgently need the money, the new customers. I overheard clients commenting on Liam's eyes and what on earth was a tall white man doing in Barranquilla serving paella.

"Está soltero?" A lady in her early forties wearing big gold hoops and with big curly hair asked if he was single. I smiled and shook my head, shooting him a loving look that Liam returned. He made me feel so certain, so supported, when everything felt on unstable ground.

His "everything would be okay" sounded right at that moment. I held on to every word.

"No. I'm sorry." A smile on my lips, proud that he was mine.

"Lástima," she said, taking her paella. "That's too bad. He would be perfect for my daughter."

I laughed. People on the coast said everything they were thinking, no matter how outlandish it was. It was nice to be working side by side with them. Mamá was still slow but kind to customers, smiling and bantering with them. Perhaps she, too, had trouble letting go.

The money box was almost filled. Of course, there were a lot of small bills, so who knew if we were close. But this was something in the right direction.

I looked up to take a break and wipe the sweat off my forehead when I saw a familiar woman.

Tall, golden-brown skin, and short curly hair. She was wearing long brick-red pants and a white linen shirt. She was holding her son's arm as he paraded her proudly around the festival.

A client talked to me to order some paella, but I could not hear. What were the chances that they'd be here? Barrio Prado was a small neighborhood, and Barranquilla didn't have many things to do. So when there was a festival of some sort, most people attended.

Liam touched my back. "Vi, are you okay?"

"Yeah, yeah," I told him, shaking my head, trying to snap out of it. "I'm okay. What do you need?" I asked the client in Spanish.

As Liam plated the paellas, and I counted the money from the customer, I saw Rafa coming my way. Rafa stood behind the line, not coming closer to our stand. I understood the distance, and yet it hurt me that he wouldn't even say hi. He wouldn't even meet my eyes.

"Violeta!" his mother said, approaching the table.

I gave a look to Mamá, who nodded and called Berto, who was taking a smoke break from the car runs between Caminito and the festival. "The till!" she yelled.

I walked around the table, my hands smelling like money and my apron smelling like the bottom of the sea. I was happy to see Rafa's mother, and yet I felt sheepish being in his presence. We stood on such unclear ground. I had told myself the last time I saw him, that was it. I knew why he hadn't said goodbye; I knew we could never be together. We both had other people, and too much had happened. And yet, whenever he was around, more unanswered questions reappeared.

Doña Magdalena had always been such a warm presence in my life, when everyone in my family opposed Rafa and me. She had been our refuge and our confidante. She wrapped me tight in her arms and cupped my face in between her hands.

"Mija, you look so beautiful! Doesn't she, Rafa?" She looked behind her, expecting him closer. But Rafa stood far away. I looked at him and nodded. Trying to communicate that I understood why he kept away. The night of the proposal would linger over us forever. Had he seen Liam? Liam was too busy serving and taking money with plastic gloves and then taking them off to see what was going on. I worried Liam would figure out Rafa was the ex, the man who I could have ended up married to. But I looked over to him, and his hands were moving at the speed of lightning, trying to be enough.

"Gracias, Doña Magdalena," I said, taking in her beautiful face untouched by time. She was a widow, and yet she didn't look a day older than when I last saw her. All those years ago. I looked over to Rafa, trying to make him see me while also desperately yearning to be invisible.

"Mijo!" She turned to Rafa and extended her hand to tell him to come. "You have to say hello to Vi. Don't be rude."

His mom didn't know that we had seen each other a couple of times. That was expected.

Rafa walked slowly toward us. He put a hand over his eyes to cover his face from the inclement sun. The fact that these two men would meet felt wrong. They were never supposed to be in the same corner of the world—oh god, oh god, oh god, the rumbling in my stomach returning. I had forgotten English and Spanish, all the languages I bounced between.

"Buenas," he said coldly. He looked over to Liam, who lifted his hand and gave the pair a warm smile.

"Friends of yours?" he asked, and I wasn't sure what to say, so I nodded and offered him a weak smile in return, my face burning.

"Yeah, friends," I lied. Rafa was standing there, awkward. Not saying a word.

Liam offered him his hand, with a big smile on his face. Clueless about who he was.

I watched them shake hands; my forehead and my face were covered in sweat. They locked eyes, and Liam still didn't erase that smile. Magdalena watched the scene, turning to look at me. She knew who Liam was.

"Enchanted," she said, in broken English, grabbing Liam's hands. "Vi is a great one. You're lucky."

Liam looked at me. "She is."

Rafa, who was standing there as if he had seen a ghost, with his hands in his pockets, turned to leave.

"We should go, we don't want to distract them. Vámonos. I need to eat before my shift."

Magdalena gave me one last hug, so tight I felt my lungs being squeezed. She put a hand on my cheek. "Cuídate, tesoro." Rafa waved simply, and Liam had already turned his attention to customers.

I saw them walk away, arm in arm like they always walked when they were together. Rafa said something to his mom, and she nodded, putting a hand on her chest and clutching to a rosary. As Rafa walked away, I let myself grieve everything we would never be. My eyes watched them until they disappeared. It was better this way.

I directed my eyes back to the line, and Liam was so busy he didn't have a chance to ask who they were.

I would never see Rafa again, I decided. And if I did, it was best to be quick like this. Rip the Band-Aid. My love for him would always linger, but that didn't mean I needed to seek him out.

"Buenas." As I took money from a customer, distracted, I saw Magdalena and Rafa appear again in my field of vision. They stopped at a stand. He turned to look at me, and I couldn't look away.

For a moment, I wanted to go over there. Tell him that we weren't done—there were words stuck in my throat. But hadn't we said it all? Our love was over. We'd been teenagers. We hadn't known any better.

Berto was saying something to me, but I wasn't listening. Rafa and I locked eyes, across the festival. Always far from each other, leaving words unsaid.

"Liam, take a break, honey." I turned back to the man who had been there for me, for us, all day long. "I got it from now on," I said, taking his place.

~

Although Mamá was reluctant to take on more debt, we had no other choice. We talked to her friend who fixed and sold ovens and told him we could give him our earnings from the festival. Five millones, around $1,000 for the initial payment, and then we could make the rest of the payments in installments, which meant we still had $5,000 left to pay.

That was on top of the $25,000 the restaurant owed. But he installed the oven the same day and took away the old one. We could open Caminito, and Anton could finally get his oven. I could finally take a break from his incessant commentary about not having one. Every time we did something right, and we got closer, it felt like we got further away immediately after. I didn't know what to do. Was this how Abuela had felt after Caminito began decaying? Was this what got her sick?

It was painful to think about how she had to figure it out all alone. She always felt she needed to be strong, and we, I had started realizing, had left her by herself to figure it out. We never insisted; we trusted her when she said she had it covered.

But perhaps Abuela hadn't been strong enough to admit she needed help, and we hadn't been strong enough to ask.

~

After we got the new oven, we started working the same day. With the rice festival, new customers were starting to come to the restaurant. It had only been a few days, so it was too early to say, but things seemed to be looking up.

Three days after the rice festival, there was a blackout. That night, while my pineapple cake was baking, the lights went off. Apagones en Barrio Prado, and in Barranquilla, were frequent. You could hear the collective sigh of the neighborhood, the people going to the street to ask neighbors if they knew something about it or if they had called Electricaribe yet. But of course, in the kitchen, the only thing I could hear was Anton.

"No, no, no, no," he said, hands on his forehead.

Liam looked at me. His hand was still holding the wooden spoon he was using to stir the cake batter. "What happened?"

"Apagón," I said, looking at Anton, who stood in front of the oven as if he would make it turn on with his voice. That night, the restaurant was fuller than ever since I had returned home. Between the festival and Mami's Instagram campaign, there were at least twelve tables in the restaurant—a bunch of orders for small, colorful plates that needed electricity.

"Maldito Electricaribe," Mamá said, writing something on her phone. "I'm telling customers we need to close early."

We couldn't close early—we had food we needed to sell. We needed the money. Anton cursed under his breath and stormed out of the kitchen, with his kitchen rag still in his baggy pants, apron still on. Mami, Liam, and I just watched him leave. I had seen Abuela do many times what he was about to do: look to see if there were any trucks doing the rounds or try to get as many neighbors as he could to call Electricaribe to see if a miracle would happen and someone could come in a timely fashion.

"Mamá, don't tell them that yet. Let's see if we can come up with a solution."

"Will Anton come back?" Liam asked, setting the batter aside. I shrugged, knowing how usually things with Electricaribe went: slow and unreliable.

Berto, the waiter, entered the kitchen. His face was as pale as if he'd caused the entire thing.

He asked what we should do, without closing the kitchen door.

I stood up taller, trying to invoke Abuela's persistence and clarity of mind in me.

"Get everyone some olives and some bread. Me and Liam are going to take care of the meat. Tell people the light will be back in fifteen minutes. If they try to leave, offer them a glass of wine on the house."

"Is that true? Fifteen minutos?" Berto said, gathering the bread baskets.

I shook my head and clicked my tongue. "Ay, Bertico. You live here, you know the truth. Mami, go with him." Mamá raised an eyebrow; she was usually the one who ordered us around.

"No." She shook her head, looking at her phone. "I'll stay here."

I tried to breathe in some patience. "Mami, there's enough to do here—go."

We locked eyes. For a moment, I thought she was going to leave, but she put her phone down and followed Berto.

"I have to do everything around here," she complained. I shook my head and smiled at Liam.

"Wait!" I stopped them. "Candles. We need candles." Berto had the secrets to this kitchen; he knew where everything was. In a matter of seconds, he produced multiple white candles from a package and colorful farolitos to put them in.

We came out to distribute a candle in a farolito to every table. People were fascinated with Liam. That was such a sight to see, a gringo in a Colombian kitchen, wearing an apron and everything. He smiled at everyone without saying a word as he put candles and bread on every table.

"Isn't my son-in-law so handsome?" Mamá asked some old ladies in the neighborhood, not caring that we weren't even married.

"Qué ojazos," a woman, Abuela's age, said, referring to Liam's sea-blue eyes to her granddaughter.

Liam smiled at them, as if he understood.

We went back to the kitchen and placed a couple of gas lanterns where we could. The lights were dim, and Liam was so attractive to me at that moment, working without being asked.

I grabbed his shoulders and turned him toward me. We were standing in front of each other, and I could see from up close the eyes others were admiring. They were all mine.

"Vi?" he said, half smiling at me. "What is it?"

"Nothing," I said. I was hoping Mamá didn't sleep at home that night so I could spend another night with him. I missed the warmth of his body, the way his kisses were always soft and slow. "We have to do something about the meat. Or Anton will kill us," I added. Liam followed me to the freezer. We put two big bags of ice in a cooler and packed as much meat as we could inside. The meat had been so expensive—such a stretch for the little survival money we had. For this order, I had put the last of my very dire savings to pay for it. I had no more.

"Keep going," I said to Liam, who kept going as if this was his restaurant.

I lifted the lids on the pots and pans on the stove. We had patatas bravas, a freshly made tortilla, some pulpo a la gallega, and Abuela's fideuá negra. Fideuá was a similar dish to the paella, but instead of having rice, it was made with thin noodles, and Abuela used black ink to make the dish creamy and flavorful. I took a spoon to the fideuá and tasted it, knowing that Anton would kill me if I served something cold. But the food was still warm and delicious.

"Vi, people are leaving," Berto said, entering the kitchen, his white shirt sticking to his body. His hair was wet, covered in sweat.

"Platos," I told him. He passed me a few plates, and I plated as many small dishes as I could.

"Tell customers we have a limited menu but that tonight we're serving a designed small-dishes menu. Actually," I said, looking at Liam, who still was bent, working his way through the freezer. "Liam, join Berto and Mami. I think they won't say no to you."

"Why don't you go?"

"Trust me," I said, "you go."

~

I watched from the kitchen window as they distributed the small dishes. They poured generous wineglasses, and at some point, Liam sat with the grandmother and granddaughter, as if he were the chef. People were so happy eating by candlelight, having a gringo serving them food. Such an odd sight. For once, the Caribbean Coast saw the roles reversed.

Mamá and I watched from the kitchen. It was such a sight for us to see too.

"You know, Vi," Mamá said, in a moment of softness. "This man really loves you."

I looked at him, floating around the tables, being so kind. He did. He really did love me. Maybe I was being unfair to him, for him not getting exactly what this place meant to me. He didn't get it entirely, but he was here, working alongside us.

Liam came back to the kitchen, his cheeks beaming with pride.

"People are so nice here," he said, emptying the dirty dishes into the sink.

I kissed his warm cheeks, not telling him that people in the Caribbean were especially nice to people like him. That there was a currency to white skin and blue eyes.

"You're so wonderful," I said, cupping his face. He kissed me on the lips. "Which is why you'll also bring them the check."

An hour and a half later, Barrio Prado miraculously had electricity again. We were replenishing the freezer and cleaning the kitchen when Anton came back.

"Did everyone leave?" he said, standing by the counter. His voice was low and raspy, as if he had been screaming to someone for a while.

"No." I shook my head, not being able to hide my smile. "We sold everything. Not even a crumb left. Everyone loved it."

Anton looked at Berto for confirmation, who just nodded.

"We sold it all," I told him, walking toward him. He was covered in sweat, despite it being night. I hugged him, resting my head on his damp shoulder.

~

It was Liam's last night in Barranquilla. After closing time, right before I finished washing my last pot, he asked, "Why don't you come to the front for a little bit? I'll finish washing later." I dried my hands on my apron and walked with Liam to the main restaurant room. The lights were dimmed, and there were candles all over. We sat down, and on the table there was a little bouquet of white alstroemeria with cilantro leaves coming out of them, just like Mamá's flowers. I stretched my hand over the table, and Liam took my hand.

"Thank you," I whispered, the memories of the bouquet swirling in my head. Liam had also baked Abuela's vanilla, cinnamon, and almond cake; the sweetness of it permeated the air. At the beginning of his trip, at dinner with Mamá, I'd thought Liam didn't understand what this place meant to me. But looking at the cake and the flowers, I realized that his time here had taught him what Caminito meant to us. Pieces of my past life were looking right back at me, and yet looking at him, appreciating everything he had done for us, I only wanted to look forward.

"I know that there's a lot going on. I'm so sorry it took me a while to see it. I know that maybe me coming here wasn't what you wanted. You needed space, and I didn't give it to you—and me pressuring you to go back if you're not ready wasn't right." Liam took a sip of water and looked at me. His hair had started growing back, and it fell nicely on his ears.

I took a deep breath—it was good that he was able to recognize that at that moment I'd needed space. But I was so glad he'd come. I took his hands and squeezed them. In Barranquilla, time went quickly. Some things vanished—just like that. But this, I was holding on to.

"I know, I understand," I said, leaning forward to smell the cake. Butter and vanilla. It was fresh out of the oven, and it smelled right, like Abuela's cake did. My cakes never smelled or tasted like hers. Maybe this was a sign, from her or from the universe, to not get caught in the past. Liam was the future. "I'm sorry I haven't been that great about keeping in touch. I've been so overwhelmed."

Liam shook his head and squeezed my hand harder. "Don't worry about that."

"What changed?" I crossed my hands on top of the white cloth, my left hand covering my bandaged right hand.

"It was being here, surrounded by your family. And this place. I know now why you wouldn't want to leave it behind." Liam looked around. I took in the historic arches over the windows, the candelabro in the middle of the room, and the vintage air that Caminito had. The restaurant had magic in it: it held inside it the story of a city that didn't exist any longer. Liam was starting to get why this place was so important to us, even to Mami—who wasn't quick to admit it. I couldn't help but smile. It was one of those moments in life where everything aligned and things seemed just right.

Liam put one of the pieces of cake in front of me.

It was spongy and syrupy, decadent.

"You like it." Liam smiled, watching me eat.

I nodded and kept eating bite after bite, not being able to get enough. All of a sudden, a tingling appeared on the back of my neck, my body trying to alert me that something was about to happen.

If I closed my eyes, I could see our life in the States, our routines. The way the sun always hit our Brooklyn apartment, always right. Our mornings together, waking up and being able to curl up next to his always-warm body. The way he always had the right word of comfort. When I was with Liam, I could be the new version of myself that wasn't tied to family obligation. I was just free to reinvent myself and to change. To lead with what my heart wanted, instead of what the women in my family said I needed to do.

I thought about Liam in the kitchen, moving around as if he owned it. His work during the blackout and working side by side with Anton. Liam was a man who, when he cared, he cared so deeply. If Liam wanted to talk about our life together, I decided I was ready for it.

"So are you coming home soon?" Liam took a piece of cake to his lips. His eyes lingered on me, as if he was waiting for a particular answer I wouldn't deliver.

I couldn't leave yet; we hadn't come up with the money yet. I pushed the plate of cake in front of me.

"I need more time. I know I said a month, but you've seen how Caminito is doing, we need—" The restaurant's dimmed lights made me feel as if we were in another time. I reached for his hand and squeezed it tight. "I'm here, Liam. I am with you, but I need you to give me more time. Go home if you need to, but I need to stay here for now."

Liam shook his head and took a sip of coffee. "But when are you coming back?" In his question I could hear him getting anxious.

"A month, perhaps?"

He pursed his lips. "Vi, what about home? Your responsibilities?"

An image of Charlie appeared on my head, smoke coming out of her ears. "Where is Vi?" she would bark at Alma, her secretary. Promises of never hiring me again would follow. It had taken me sweat and tears to build relationships by designing menus and sometimes wedding invitations or even kids' birthday party invitations for rich parents. But now, that part of my life seemed far away. I looked at my arms, covered in paint. Caminito was anchoring me home for now.

I took a deep breath, ready to tell him again what was keeping me away from them. I couldn't believe we were here again. After the week he had spent here, didn't he understand?

"Caminito . . . ," I started, the words not feeling quite right.

Liam opened his mouth, hesitated. "Vi . . . but it was never a priority for you. I understand helping now, but you have to let Anton and Paula handle it after. You have a life to go back to." Liam leaned forward, closer to me. I stood back, trying to keep my sanity and my ground. He ran his hand through his hair.

"You don't even know the first thing about running one. For god's sake. Look at your hand! And there's people who are willing to do it. For you. And better than you, probably."

I shook my head. Anger sat in the base of my stomach. "You don't get it."

"So explain it to me. Because it seems to me that you're just avoiding your life with me in the States because things aren't going so well with work right now. But every career starts like this, Vi, you just have to keep working. You're good, Vi. Don't run away from it." Liam looked away, assessing the words. "From us, Vi. It feels like you're running away from me."

How could I explain to him that I wasn't? That if anything I was running deeper into myself, figuring out what I really wanted. After years of not listening to myself, my voice was low and distant. I needed to learn how to listen to it, and it wasn't easy to figure out what it was that I wanted. When I was eighteen, I wanted to have a place in the restaurant, a life with Rafa. I didn't really get to process losing all that, getting another life entirely. My love for this place was in my roots, in my body.

Liam leaned on the chair and stayed silent for a while. I knew this had been as surprising for him as it had been for me. I wasn't necessarily one to talk too much about the past, or my life here. I realized now why. It hurt.

"Vi." He took my hands between his again. "This is not yours. Don't you want to build something that is yours?"

"Don't you see, Liam?" I told him, my voice getting louder than I intended. "I have to fight for my place in this restaurant—for once. Didn't you just say you wanted to support me? I don't want to come back in four years and discover that it's gone. And I did nothing. I want to keep building my life with you. I'm certain. But you need to give me time. I want to know that I did everything I could. No regrets. What am I supposed to do? What do you want me to do? Turn my back on Abuela?" I said, moving my hand back in the air like I was showing him what was behind me. And there was something I carried with me everywhere. The burden of what little I had done for my family since I'd moved to the US.

This last thought haunted me. In the States, I thought about only my life: the clients, paying rent, Liam . . . but I had forgotten about Barranquilla, Barrio Prado, the roots that pressed on my ankles, currently gripping them, wanting to plant me here.

But I also belonged in the US. With Liam.

"Vi." Liam took a deep breath. "I know you."

"What does that mean?" I lifted my eyes. "Tell me."

Liam leaned on the chair, his legs dangling in front of him. "You'll lose steam, you don't even have a clear plan. And when you do, I'll be home, waiting."

I stood up. My blood was boiling, and my cheeks were as warm as two furnaces. I lifted my hands in the air like I was calling for rain.

"You don't have to wait for me. Don't think for a second that you have to do anything, because I don't need you to. Leave if you want. Don't come back if you don't want to. No one is asking you to do shit. But you don't have to come and tell me what I'm going to do or not because you aren't me. You don't know what I am capable of."

"Maybe I don't," Liam said, getting up, too, and looking at me from across the table. "You know what. I get it. You have a lot going on—you don't know what you want right now. But you'll have to decide eventually," Liam said. "And that moment will come sooner than you think. Not deciding is also making a choice."

"I know that," I said. We were squared off, standing across from each other, separated by the table.

"That's it? That's all you have to say?"

I crossed my arms and looked at him. I didn't have anything to say to him. I was angry that after the week he had been here, he hadn't learned anything about how much Caminito meant to me.

Liam took a deep breath. "I think we should just leave it. I'm going to have a drink somewhere. Let's talk later," he said, walking away.

I stood in the same place watching him walk away from me on his last night in Barranquilla. I was scared of losing him. This moment felt definitive. If I didn't run after him, we might never come back from this. There would always be that distance, lingering like a stench. But if I didn't stand my ground, he would never understand that he had hurt me deeply. This was part of who I was too. And he had dismissed it as if it were nothing but a fantasy of mine.

I didn't know how he was going to communicate to the taxi driver or if he even knew where to go, but I let him go. That was his problem. The anger returned, and my steps were fueled with fire. I walked toward the kitchen, turning lights off as I made my way to the back door to close Caminito.

As I walked home, I thought about all that tethered me to my two very different lives. In order to be free, I needed to listen to myself. If I thought I needed to be here, then I did. He needed more time, and if not . . . it was too scary to think about the alternative.

I remembered Doña Rocío's words about already knowing the answer, about being wise.

But I didn't feel wise—I felt lost.

~

The next day Liam grabbed my hands in his, his touch warm and soft. I had always loved his soft hands and his carefree smile that lit up his whole face. Liam kissed my cheek as we stood in front of international departures, and at that moment, I wanted to make him stay, but he had said so much. I was left wondering if he knew me at all.

The night before, he had arrived home smelling like whiskey and cigarettes. It was strange; Liam didn't really smoke, but perhaps people were smoking around him. I wasn't really sleeping very heavily, and when he came back, I let out a sigh of relief that he'd arrived safely. Even if I was still angry. But that morning, the fact that he was leaving made me soften toward him. I rolled over in bed and touched his warm cheeks. Pushed his hair away from his forehead. I kissed him, knowing that he would be gone. We made love, and it was soft and sweet. The same.

Back in the airport, Liam stood in front of me, wearing dark glasses due to his hangover. "I love you. I'm sorry I said all those things yesterday. I didn't mean them."

I nodded, knowing that he'd meant every word that had left his lips. The anger returned. I swallowed hard, worried that he would never understand that other part of me. The part that belonged to Barrio Prado.

I wrapped my arms around him, and I hugged him as tight as I could. The tears were coming. I breathed in his clean sharp smell and kissed his neck, the nook that was always warm even in the winter.

I whispered in his ear that I loved him so, so much.

I knew he'd meant what he'd said, about me running out of steam and that I was only here because of Abuela's passing or else I wouldn't have returned. And still, I felt myself unable to let him go from the embrace. Anger and love mixed inside me.

"We'll see each other soon. I know it."

I nodded. My cheeks were wet, but I didn't care.

"Vi," he said, standing outside the door of the departures terminal.

"Yes?" I held on to him tighter.

Liam let go of my embrace for a moment and took my hands between his. He was observing them, as if he couldn't look at me.

"I . . ."

"Yes? Liam?"

"We need to talk about what's going to happen moving forward. Getting engaged—"

The tightness in my freaking chest. Anyone would be thrilled about these types of conversations. A year ago, I would have been overjoyed. But now, all I felt was worry.

Liam looked at me. "Vi?"

"I would love that," I said, my tongue getting unstuck. "Let's talk more about it."

Liam kissed me for one last time before he left. His embrace was long and passionate. "Don't forget," he whispered into my ear. "I love you."

"I won't."

Liam waved and started walking to departures. He waved once more and then went in, his backpack blocking his face. As he walked toward the gates, I lost sight of him.

I stayed behind, rooted to the earth despite the urge to run after him and get on the plane, forget about this city that brought nothing but confusion. I stayed in the same place for what seemed like a long time, unable to make a decision about where to go next. The city for me was the house or the restaurant; there wasn't anywhere else. I made my way slowly out of the airport, my steps dragging with the heaviness of all that I was carrying.

CHAPTER TWELVE: DIARY

Barranquilla 1964

I won't make it till old age. If he keeps hitting me and spending his sueldo on drinking and other women, I don't know how we're going to survive.

I'm convinced that Paula senses our fighting, my fear whenever he raises his hand in my direction. So much hatred in his eyes, so much fear in mine. Mamá says that she can hear him shouting at me. That she knows. A woman knows. A mother knows.

But there's so much shame. Pena. Pena. Pena. I should have listened. I should have taken my baby and disappeared so Mami wouldn't have to take care of me. I should have killed him in his sleep, when he was snoring in his boxers close to the window, sucking all of the air out of the room. Pero no me atrevo.

I have someone else to think about now besides myself.

The day I left home to go to college in America, I was terrified. I was eighteen and had never left the country. I was pacing anxiously in the living room trying to remember if I had forgotten something—as if it mattered what I brought. I was going to university in Vermont, and I later learned that all my warm-weather clothes were useless in the cold months. Layering would be a hard lesson that I would never quite learn.

Abuela was sending me away, and I was going. Oh, was I going. Rafa was so hurt that he wasn't calling me back. Going away felt like the only possible answer—I was getting as far away as I could from Mami, and from the city, and the heat. Rafa for me was the real deal, the love that was destined for me, and I did nothing but mess it up. Rafa was going to be a doctor; I could see it. He was ambitious, a good student, and a good man. Dios. I doubted my decision of saying no so much those days. Those days, I desperately wanted to go back to that night, to just take the leap.

"Vamos," Abuela said. "Esa mamá tuya." She grabbed her black leather purse and shook her head. "I guess you'll see her when you come home for Christmas. Me importa una mierda. She wants to see her daughter? She should be here on time!" She moved to leave and signaled me to follow her with her hand. Mami not coming to the airport was not a surprise, and yet I was on the verge of tears. She was supposed to be there; I was terrified and heartbroken about leaving. I wanted Mamá to be there. I was convinced she would advocate on my behalf. Mamá had bet on love again and again. Maybe she would know just the right thing to say to Abuela. I was so young, and it was one of those moments where I needed Mami; instead, I had Abuela, who was desperate to get me out of the country.

Abuela thought that if she unrooted me from Caminito, then I wouldn't be pining after Rafa anymore.

We left the house and passed the restaurant, which was right next to our family home. The big roble morado that covered the houses was in full bloom, and the whole street smelled like cotton candy and warm spring. Abuela turned to me and gripped my arm: "See that?" she said, pointing to the restaurant. I nodded. "Headache. My life with your abuelo?" I nodded, wanting to liberate my arm, but instead she gripped even harder. "Another headache! This effort that I'm making, sending you away, is so you don't have to live like me. Como nosotras. Like your bisabuela or your mom. You're not tied to anything." She let go of me. "You are not tied to anything. Mija, you don't have to be."

What Abuela didn't know then was that I was desperate to have what she was taking from me. Caminito, Rafa, home.

She kept walking to the main street, and I dragged my heavy useless bag with me. The street was busy, and she looked around, as if she was looking for someone.

"Let's go before tu mamá comes back with excuses and I have to murder her and you miss your plane." I nodded and we both lifted our hands, calling for a taxi on the street. I felt Mami's absence in the tightness in my chest. I gripped the handle of my suitcase, trying to get used to the weight of my decision.

She turned back to me, and with her free hand, she brushed my cheek.

"Mija," she said softly. "Te voy a extrañar."

My heart ached at the memory. I, too, would never stop missing her. Home. Rafa. The life I wanted and I would never get to live.

~

After he left, things between Liam and me were better. We were talking on the phone regularly. We were feeling his absence at the restaurant. Anton had left that night early. Early! For the first time in the history of Caminito. He always was the one insisting to be the last person there to prep for the next day and organize the fridge. "Ay, Vi, if we don't know what we have in the fridge, then we won't know what to cook! We can't throw food away, Vi, no cuando la cosa está tan dura."

As I was organizing the fridge and cleaning the kitchen before closing, the hardship of the situation weighed on my shoulders. We had less than fifteen days to pay the debt. Caminito was getting by, but we didn't have enough.

The thought of disappointing Abuela kept me up at night. The risk of losing it all.

I double-checked that everything was as clean as Anton expected and took the keys to lock up. As I put the key in, a grave voice sounded behind me.

"Buenas noches."

I jumped and whirled around.

Rafa was standing in the badly lit street with grocery bags in his hands. It was confusing to see him here, so soon after Liam had left. Although Rafa had been my first love, Liam felt like an anchor: safe and strong, there for me. Rafa felt sudden, like a wave that threatened to wash me away. The decision, most days, was obvious, but whenever I saw Rafa, my knees trembled, and I felt light headed, suddenly craving his touch.

"Buenas," I said quietly, nervous about seeing him.

"You're still here."

"For now," I said, looking down at my apron and tucking my hair behind my ears. "And you?" I laughed at myself. "I mean, I know you live here. I meant to ask you how you were?"

Rafa kept smiling. He knew the effect he had on me.

"I'm good," he said, hands in his pockets.

We stayed in silence, and I tried to guess what he was doing here. I didn't know; what I knew was that my heart was beating in my chest, my face immediately getting warm. My swirling thoughts of wanting to say the right thing. Whatever that was. But I was with Liam; my whole heart was with him.

Rafa and I really didn't know each other as adults—we didn't know anything about each other. We had been part of each other's lives at one point, and that was it.

"I just made a new dish the other day, and I remembered how you loved spicy food. Have you eaten? I thought about making it for you if you were free," he said, standing on the sidewalk.

I hadn't eaten, and my stomach was rumbling. I wasn't sure if it was the lack of food or out of nervousness.

"How do you know Liam is not here?" I asked. Hadn't Rafa seen him the other day?

"I heard," Rafa said, pushing his glasses up.

"From who?"

"Ay, Vi, are you surprised? In Barrio Prado gossip travels faster than lightning."

I hesitated. Rafa had waited until Liam left to show up. What did he want? This was a bad idea. Liam, Liam, Liam, the name resounded in my head like an echo—and yet, and yet. Perhaps this was the last chance I would ever get to see Rafa. Yes, we had said goodbye. And yet all the unsaid words were weighing on me. I felt as if I would never be finished talking to him about the past. Closure didn't exist—I wasn't naive.

But I wanted to be with him, even if it was just for an hour. I wouldn't do anything. I knew that. Liam and I were solid. But just this once, I told myself.

Just this once.

"Entonces?" Rafa lifted the bags, his eyes bright under the lights. The night was warm and balmy, and there was a full moon.

"Um, I already locked up."

Rafa lifted a brow. "I could cook for you in your house."

I was surprised he even asked. It was such a risk. Mamá wasn't there, but we hadn't been alone in so long. The intimacy would be disconcerting. Where would I put my hands? What would I say? Would there be anything to say?

Did I trust myself? I had to. I wanted this. I wanted to spend some time with him. Maybe it was curiosity, nostalgia, the past. Perhaps it was just him. For a while it had been him all along. Now that it wasn't, the memory still tugged at my heartstrings.

I told myself I was doing it for her—for that past version of myself that dropped everything to be with him. Rafa and I couldn't be friends. That was for sure, too much history. Too much hurt.

"We eat and then we go, bueno? I have an early morning."

I turned and opened the door to the restaurant, turning on the lights. Rafa placed the bags on the kitchen counter. I was glad that Anton wasn't here. I imagined all the questions it would raise if he saw us together. He liked Liam; he liked how helpful he was. Mamá told me that Liam loved me very much. I wondered if Mamá had ever thought that about a man she was dating, if she had felt loved like that.

Rafa started chopping the red peppers, and when I asked what to do, he told me to open a bottle of wine. So I drank, and I watched him sauté onions and tomatoes into a sofrito. It was weird to be so close like that. To be in this kitchen, of all places, the place that I loved so much with a man that I'd once, a long time ago, considered marrying.

For a moment I wondered if this was a parallel universe. One where we'd never left each other.

"What are you making?" I asked as the aromas of fried onions lifted from the pan, filling up the room. I stood in a corner of the kitchen, far from him, hugging a glass of wine.

"A surprise," Rafa said, dropping cubes of chicken into the sofrito. When he smiled, I could see him in his kitchen when we were sixteen, moving as if he were performing a dance. At sixteen, he could cook, clean, and play music. Magdalena had raised no inútil. "Can you get me a glass of wine?"

"Ha," I said, getting down from the counter and pouring him a heavy glass as he hummed to a bossa nova that was playing on my phone. This moment felt like us, years ago. When his mom wasn't home, he would cook for me. Liam was a recipe chef, while Rafa was more inspired. He would make concoctions from whatever was in the kitchen: soups, stews, arroces, anything. Dancing around in his kitchen until I eventually would dance with him.

"Vi," Rafa asked, jolting me from a reverie.

"Dime," I said, pouring myself more wine. Self-restraint, self-discipline, not getting close. Not breathing next to him. No. No. No.

"Oye, where does Anton keep the spices around here? I need red crushed pepper and parsley."

I went to the spice drawer and took out the spices and the salt. I put them on the table so I wouldn't have to hand them to him and accidentally touch him.

Rafa spiced the dishes liberally, just like Abuela did. Ay, if she knew that they had that in common. Using the flavor with abandon, not measuring anything.

"So how is Marta? You didn't talk much about her the other night." I put my hands on my chin, as if I were preparing to hear a story. I thought that if she became more real in my head, if I made her a presence between us, nothing could happen.

"She's okay. I mean . . ." Rafa lifted his head while something was bubbling in the pot. He raised an eyebrow. "I didn't think you wanted to talk about her."

I didn't. But I had questions. Did he love her? How long had they been together? Did Magdalena like her as much as she liked me? But I didn't dare ask. I knew the answers, even after all this time, would hurt too deeply.

Rafa cleared his throat. "How is your guy?"

My guy. So weird hearing him say that.

"He's an architect." I took a sip of wine. "He loves museums, bike rides, and cooking, just like you. It's funny, I'm around all these people who cook well, but I had never found my confidence in the kitchen."

"I think I know why."

Rafa slid some red peppers in the sauce.

"You just listen to everyone but yourself."

I looked at Rafa from across the room, my whole body leaning on the counter. I stood up straight, realizing that my body language was pulling toward him. My face was warm—that he could say something so personal.

That he was right. Liam would always be there for me, but Rafa told me the truth.

"Do you want to try the broth?"

I got closer, step by step, cautious as if I were walking on moving sand. He put the spoon to my lips. The sauce was full of vibrant flavors of tomato, herbs, and spice.

"It has a kick to it," I said, licking my lips.

Rafa took a different spoon and tried the sauce himself. "Hmm, pepper." A cloud of pepper descended on the sauce.

"And what about you? Are you good at listening to yourself?"

Rafa lowered the spoon and smiled. I ached when I saw his dimples I'd always loved so much.

"Touché, I'm terrible. Look at the music thing, where that ended up. I go to a bar on Friday nights, it's pathetic. No one knows me there. Look at what happened with you—"

I shook my head, not ready to get into it.

"Maybe because I see it in myself, I recognize it in you too. I suck." Rafa laughed. "Pointing out something in you that I should see in me."

"You see the mote in your brother's eye . . ."

"Quoting your Bible."

"Something good came out of Catholic school."

I almost always wore my uniform when I would see him after school. If I went home and changed, I risked having Abuela ask me where I was going, who I was seeing. It was easier to call her and tell her I was studying at someone's house.

I chose a table by the window and lit a candle. Rafa was behind me with two perfectly plated dishes. He set them on the table, and I handed him his glass of wine.

We sat down, studying each other's faces brushed by time, how different we were now, and how much the same.

"Entonces, qué es?" I said, looking at the dish.

"It's a creamy red roasted chicken with poblano peppers and a green rice I brought from home, already made. Mami's recipe." The dish smelled like butter and spinach.

I took a bite to my lips, tasting the notes of azafrán and red pepper, the buttery chicken. "Mm-hmm."

"Bueno?" *Good?* Rafa asked, taking a bite.

I didn't answer but instead took another bite. "Rafa, this is incredible. If you weren't a doctor, I would hire you to be a cook here."

Well, I would also need the money for that, I thought. Money I didn't have. I thought about how much Anton and Rafa would clash. They were both incredibly creative and incredibly stubborn.

"Okay, so tell me what's going on around here?"

Ever since Rafa had arrived with groceries, I wondered what he could possibly be doing here. Now I realized he wanted to talk. Life had given us the small window of opportunity to see each other again—we wouldn't do anything, of course, and we would never be friends, but we could talk, even if it was just for tonight.

Nostalgia invaded me. I could feel the aching in my bones from head to toe.

"We need to get money. I am terrible with money." I took another spoonful, the spice lingering on my tongue. "The oven broke the other day—then the lights went off, no investors, no nothing. We are all three at a loss about what to do."

"You know, you're always so stubborn."

I raised an eyebrow. "Thank you?"

"No, no. That didn't come out right. You're so stubborn. When you get your mind on something, you do it."

"We have that in common."

Rafa nodded, taking a sip of wine before continuing. "If you decide that you're going to save this place, then you'll do it. There's no doubt in my mind."

"Didn't you feel that way about music?"

It was hard to see Rafa so disillusioned about it, when once in his life he was always working on a song, always humming a tune.

"I did, but I felt that I had to honor the memory of my father." Rafa knitted his brows, the pain in his face indicating that this was an open wound for him. "It didn't feel right not to fulfill the promise I had made to him. And as I said, I'm good at it. I like being good at things."

I thought about those words. Was I good at illustrating? I wasn't the best businessperson, but my colors and my art resonated with people. Then did I do it because I loved it? Or because others thought I was good at it?

"I get that." I toyed with the glass of wine. "What if we just did whatever we liked?" I smiled, catching his gaze from across the table. This moment felt like we had been here before. Again, again and again, stealing glances but not doing anything else because we couldn't. We shouldn't.

"Hey, I should go. I just thought that maybe I could see you once more. I'm sorry, I know it's not the best idea. I have no right."

"Are you done?" I laughed. "I'm glad you came. It's nice to see you."

I've missed this, I wanted to say. Rafa and I had been lovers, but we also had been friends in a time when we thought that everything was possible.

He stretched his hand across the table, and in a stolen moment I grabbed it, squeezing it, holding on to his touch. Our eyes lingered on each other.

"You should go," I said.

Rafa stayed for a moment.

"Go," I repeated, letting go of his hand.

When he left, I remembered a night when we were listening to My Bloody Valentine. We were lying on our backs, looking at the glow-in-the-dark stars he hadn't bothered to get down since he was a kid.

"I think you're the only person that has ever played this song in Barranquilla," I said, turning to him, probably raccoon eyed. Later that day, when I looked at myself in the mirror, I would learn that copious eyeliner and the heat didn't mix well.

Rafa pulled me close, kissing me under the corny green lights.

"Don't you wish we could be grown-ups already? Living together, you doing your art, and me playing my music."

At that moment, Magdalena knocked on the door. "Everything okay in there? Turn on the light, Rafael."

Rafa got up and shook his head. "Sí, Mami." He turned on the lights, and his mom went away.

"Don't you wish we had that freedom?"

I looked at him, and I nodded, not sure of what to say.

Standing in the restaurant, about to turn off the lights, I wished I had known. We would never know so much freedom as we did back then.

~

After cleaning the kitchen, I went home and sat in the living room in the darkness to listen to the quiet movements of the house. Outside, there was a gentle light, and I wondered what time it was. I was looking at a corner of the room, frozen in time still.

Liam. It had been him since the moment we met. But why did it have to hurt so much? I wiped tears from my cheeks with the back of my hand. My only company was the crik crik crik of the stairs. Although I was alone, it sounded like someone was going up and down them.

I sulked in Abuela's chair, and I thought to myself that it was time to stop blaming a ghost for my past mistakes. Not wanting to come home had been all me. Not fighting to be a part of Caminito, yes, all me.

Our first kiss had been in the house. When Mamá and Abuela were asleep, he was waiting for me at the door. I opened the door as quietly as I could, and we went inside in silence. We didn't even bother turning on the lights. Rafa pushed me against the wall and kissed me for the first time. There was no doubt, no rush, no fear. The kiss was soft and sweet. Back then I was sure of everything.

"I've been waiting for this," he said to me, cupping my face in his and planting a kiss on my forehead. "Our first kiss."

I was fifteen and Rafa was eighteen. I had hated school and everyone in it. It was a private school, and Abuela was doing her utmost to afford it, but being able to pay for that school meant very little money for anything else. Abuela, Mamá, and I never went anywhere. We never vacationed as a family because work always came first. We never had any new clothes, and while my classmates were planning quinceañeras and trips to Europe, I sat alone in school dreaming about living in New York, the city that I had only seen in movies. I dreamed about the food, the different cuisines, the vibrancy of the art. The city combined my two passions.

I forgot about NYC when I met Rafa. He was at a party that las mellas invited me to. I never went to parties. Dresses and skirts were always tight on my hips. My hair didn't cope well with humidity, and my forehead resembled, as Mamá liked to remind me, a piece of corn.

Rafa, as he had reminded me many times over the years, approached me as soon as he saw me. My friends and I were in a corner talking to each other to avoid talking to the boys that they came here to see. My sole purpose at the party was to tell them when the boys were approaching us so they could be ready and act caught off guard. So when I saw Rafa walk in our direction, I thought that he was also in competition for my friends' attention. Rafa's hair was dark and wavy. The first thing I noticed about him were his almond-shaped dark eyes and long beautiful lashes. Although he was young, he had a sharp jaw and a confident expression. When he walked toward us, my knees shook. He was looking at me. I told myself it couldn't be happening. Boys didn't notice me. Not him, not anyone. They always noticed the twins, with their long black hair that reached the smalls of their backs. The twins were getting ready: I saw them push their long curls back and prepare a cold hard stare in his direction. But Rafa didn't look back at them. He stood in front of me, as if I were the only person at the party, and said, "I've never seen you here before."

Years later, Rafa told me that when he saw me, he felt like he needed to talk to me. "It was your thick glasses, esas gafas gruesas," he said. "I'd never seen anyone at that age wear them with such ease. I thought you looked beautiful with your big curls and glasses—you looked like yourself at a party where everyone looked the same."

That night at the party, we sat there looking at each other without saying much. Slight smiles from across the couch and my nervous laugh. Rafa was not drinking like the rest of the boys; he wasn't trying to touch me or impress me either. He was a boy who held a lot of weight on his shoulders.

One of the first things he said to me was, "My parents want me to be a doctor." Followed by: "Have you ever read Raúl Gómez Jattin?"

Days after Rafa and I first met, we talked every day on the phone. If the phone rang three times and then I picked up just to hang up, it meant Abuela and Mamá were here and it was best not to speak because they could easily lift the other phone and hear what we were saying. Whenever I was alone and able to talk, I would pick up immediately, ready to spit my heart out of my mouth.

We always had things to talk about. Movies we had seen, music, art, the weather. Back then, we were hungry for consuming as much art and music as we could. We were catching up on the decades we weren't alive, on everything that had come before us.

We would watch movies at the same time on the phone. *Los amantes del círculo polar*, Almodóvar movies, silent movies, anything. Rafa would talk about the music, and I the colors—the freedom that these characters had to mess up. Abuela and Mami wanted to shield me from all that.

"Would you like to live in Madrid?" Rafa said, his voice getting sleepy on the other side of the phone.

"Me? Madrid?" I said, hearing the excitement in my voice. I lowered my voice, reminding myself to be careful not to be too loud in the house. "Only if you come."

I couldn't see him, but I knew he was smiling. "I would follow you anywhere, Violeta."

CHAPTER THIRTEEN: PUERTO

Mamá was busy posting day and night, posting promotions, anything that would engage potential clients. One night we would have eight tables; other nights we would have ten or twelve. The restaurant was blooming. People were spreading the word, and just like animals returning to their environments, people in Barrio Prado were returning to one of the first restaurants in Barrio Prado. I had doubted Mami, but she was good at connecting with people. She adapted.

That Friday, we were struggling to keep up. Anton even hired a few extra cooks, and although the money wasn't enough, we were starting to get our heads above water a little bit. We still owed around $27,000. The little profit we had made had been used to pay part of the debt we had from the oven. Now that things were a little better, we needed to keep pushing. I was in the prep station, and my hands were getting used to the rhythms and the demands of Anton. He was divided in between the sauté station and reading the orders.

"Vi, two cheese boards, three pan con tomates and—" Anton paused to look at Berto, who entered the kitchen with his hands full with dirty plates. "Mijo, haven't I told you? You're going to break something!"

Berto rested one of the plates on the counter and shrugged. "You need to hire more people. Yo así." He stood up straight, and I could see that he had a tomato sauce stain on his white shirt. I said nothing. "No puedo. I can't. It's too much."

Caminito was vibrant with noise. People were enjoying conversation, and every time the kitchen door opened, we could hear the boleros and we could feel the breeze coming from the AC. It was a wonderful night—when I was younger, I dreamed about this. About being a part of the kitchen, seeing clients happy with their meals. I had begged to be a part of this, and now that I was, it felt as good as I had dreamed. It was as if I were inside Abuela's beating heart.

"Berto, table four is waiting. Let me finish this and I'll go help," I said, putting the last touches on a cheese board I was assembling. I thought about New York and the charcuterie boards I loved to make whenever Liam and I had people over. It was like forming a piece of art. I liked playing with the sizes, arranging the cheeses from tartness to sweetness. Arranging the almonds so they would be in the center of the board or scattered around the cheeses. Every cheese board could be different, and when I was making them, I could zone out of the rhythms of the kitchen. Anton's orders went to the background of my head. His voice was static, and the only real thing was the sweat on my forehead and the roses I could make with cheese.

"Para hoy, Vi." *For today*, Anton said, standing behind me. We needed them quickly. I released them, fixing some last touches. I heard Mamá's steps without having to turn back, the clik clik clik of her heels. Mami was the only person on earth who wore heels in the kitchen, and yet I couldn't imagine it any other way.

"We're short," I told her, cutting some thick slices of bread.

Mamá put a hand on my shoulder without saying a word. I turned back, scared by how quiet she was being.

"Alguien se murió?" I asked if someone had died.

She shook her head. "They are going to start repossessing stuff. I just got a call from the bank."

I looked over to Anton, who was sautéing gambas in butter and olive oil. He didn't stop shaking the pan, which made me more nervous for his reaction. This was it. I put my hands on my knees, trying to breathe. The debt so far had seemed an abstract thing. I was thinking about it all the time, but also it didn't really seem real. Perhaps we could convince the bank—we could throw a small sum at them and beg them for more time.

After a moment, he turned off the oven and put a hand on his mouth.

"I thought we had more time." Anton's voice broke. This was exactly what I'd said to Mami when I'd learned that Abuela died.

"How do you know? We were going to—" I thought about our options. I could call Liam and ask for the money. It had never felt right. Something inside me told me no—maybe it was Abuela's voice. Maybe it was my own intuition telling me not to depend on him, not this time.

Mamá took a hand to her ear, her bangles moving up and down, making a clin clin sound when they came together.

"When?"

"At the end of next week."

"Can you ask for an extension?" Anton said as he put the gambas he was cooking on a caldereta. He covered his face with his hands; he didn't want us to see him cry. The pressure in my chest returned. I hadn't done enough. I had failed Abuela. She had trusted me with this, and now it was slipping through my fingers like sand blowing away on the breeze.

"I can try, but we need to get the money," she said, her voice cracking. Money. We had been slowly paying off dimes from the loan, but it wasn't enough. Of course it wasn't.

Berto came back to the kitchen. Food was taking too long. The asados, the pan con tomate, the tortillas, people wanted them right now. Mamá turned her back to slowly put on an apron, delicately drawing it over her head.

"If we have to let it go . . ." She paused, her eyes welling with tears. "We do it." She shook her head. "We do it."

Mamá no longer cared about disguising her love for Caminito. She really wanted to save it as much as we did. I was so tired. Exhausted from all the emotion these past few weeks, I wanted to give up. I did. But I couldn't let this go; it felt like giving up for all of us.

Anton was next to the stove, as if he couldn't move. Couldn't say anything. Couldn't let go. I believed him capable of chaining himself to that stove, to that kitchen. I believed him capable because this was all he knew.

Images from my childhood. Abuela smiling from ear to ear at a Friday service, Abuela rearranging the flowers and candles for a Monday wedding for a customer, Abuela fixing napkins so every table would look perfect. Letting go of Caminito was letting go of Abuela's soul.

"No." I let out a long breath. "We won't let this go. I'll go to New York, every penny that I make, I'll send back. Money in dollars will be a lot in pesos. We could make a dent in the debt."

I wasn't ready to leave Barrio Prado yet. But I needed to be home eventually. I could ask Liam to not lend me the money but instead cover the costs of our life for a bit. My clients trusted me; I could tell them that I needed the money sooner than usual. Every penny I made, I would send back.

"Vi." Anton put a hand on my shoulder. I hadn't seen him like this since Abuela's funeral. He was scared, and I was scared too. "We need you here."

"No, you both stay, keep the restaurant open, and we make it work. I'll be more helpful if I'm making money."

Mamá stared at me for a long time; then she lowered her head and studied her shoes.

"Vi," she said finally, her voice low like a little girl's. She swallowed before speaking again. "I wish you didn't have to go. I just don't know what else—"

I walked to her, the anger and the disappointment and the hurt all dissolving for a moment. I extended my arms and pulled her close, hugging her tight. "I wish I didn't have to leave either."

I meant it.

This was my way of not letting go.

~

Once again, I found myself in the same position: not being ready to leave. Angry tears ran down my face as I packed my bag, throwing clothes in the suitcase, wanting to think of a way of being able to stay. Leaving again felt like losing home all over again.

If I was leaving for good, then this was the last time I could see Rafa. I called him the next day, right before going back to New York. I didn't really have anything to say to him or any plan.

When I told Liam I was coming back, he told me that perhaps it was for the best. Caminito had had an incredible run. We should be proud! I was on the other side of the line, putting a hand on my mouth to muffle my tears. Liam's practicality was wonderful. I believed that it was one of the best qualities as a couple: my dreaminess and sensitivity kept things fun and creative, and his practicality sustained us. But it was in moments like this that I wished he would open up. Hear me a little bit more.

Rafa would understand. Rafa and I had always been good about being honest with each other, listening to each other. We had understood our family dynamics more than anyone else could.

I arrived at the beach in a manic state; my hands were slightly shaking, and I couldn't get the idea of losing the restaurant out of my head. It seemed like in Barranquilla I was always in a state of losing: losing Abuela, losing Liam, losing Rafa, losing Caminito, losing myself.

I chose the beach because it meant so much to us. It was the place where everything ended, but it was also the place we had come to again and again. It seemed to me that I was always dismissing places just because there were bad memories in it. But wasn't that just life? The good mixed with the bad. History tarnished even the most beautiful places.

I sat down in a plastic beach chair and began furiously sketching the beach and the foam that hit the sand. I hoped that the familiar colors would calm me, that doing something with my hands would prevent my head from exploding.

The shades of blue, yellow, and brown, the colors of most of the beaches in my hometown. A beauty obscured by darkness. The heat, and the tracing of the colors, helped me gather myself.

"Rafa," I said, looking up at him from my beach chair. He had come. I wanted to extend my arms and hug him. Rafa's curls sprouted over his ears. His sun-kissed, freckled shoulders that I wasn't able to see under his shirt but that I remembered.

"Vi," Rafa replied, sitting next to me in the chair I had saved for him. His expression was distant, as if he could only stay for a couple of minutes. Despite his initial coldness, seeing him always felt like letting out a long-awaited exhale after holding my breath.

"I think we're going to lose it."

I didn't dare to turn to him. He stared at the beach, too, wrinkling his eyes due to the sun. Rafa scratched his forehead and passed a hand over his hair. We were both already sweating.

"Just because it feels you're about to lose it, doesn't mean you will." Rafa turned to me, the sun in his eyes. "Vi, I know you."

I stared at his hands, so far away from me. I craved to grab them.

"You won't lose it. Something will come up."

"What if I have to let go? What if this is Abuela's lesson? Just learning to let it go. I—"

With Rafa, I was never scared of crying. When Mamá and Abuela were pestering me, I would come to him and cry and cry. Letting him see me in a complete mess. With Liam, I always measured myself. It wasn't because he told me to but because I felt like I needed to.

I let myself cry, the wind drying my tears.

"You will figure it out. Something will come up."

Rafa smiled at me. Whenever he did, I would always stop crying, wiping my tears with the back of my hand, eager to laugh with him.

"So you're going to New York for good?"

I nodded. "It's the easiest way to get money. I don't know what else to do. Me being here wasn't particularly helpful."

I didn't regret my time here. I got to feel Abuela and talk to her. I worried about her being alone in the house, not being able to rest. Mami all alone. I worried about Anton, dealing with the restaurant, that massive weight on his shoulders.

I didn't worry about Rafa. But seeing him had made me realize I was always in a state of making myself not think about him, not miss him. If I wanted to turn the page, I would need to confront all the ways that he had stayed with me.

"I'm glad I saw you," I said, even if it was confusing.

We were so close I could grab his hand and touch him. I was looking for a distraction, yes. But there was always something pulling me closer to him.

"Let's walk."

Rafa and I walked on the beach we both knew so well. Street vendors started appearing out of thin air. First a woman offered a foot massage and then braids for me. Then a man offered coconut water, and finally a man selling sunglasses and stone jewelry. We shook our heads, said "No, gracias" what felt like a million times. I rehearsed many things to say to Rafa. About our past, our future, even wanting to be friends. Friends? I could never lie to him like that. As soon as I returned to the US, I knew this was something I needed to forget.

He took a deep breath. "Okay, I'm going to tell you something, but you can never say anything to anyone."

"Who would I tell?"

"Fair." Rafa laughed, looking at his feet. "I have been writing more songs lately. I think I'm ready to do a bigger show, and actually tell people about it."

Rafa. I tapped his shoulder, feeling so much joy for him. Rafa wasn't Rafa without his music.

"When?"

"Next month—you won't be here."

"Right." Even if I were here, I wouldn't be able to go. Marta would be there. "Rafa! That's amazing. I'm so proud of you."

"You know, that night . . ."

I looked away; Rafa couldn't speak of the proposal by name, and I was in no shape to hear it either. It was better to talk around it.

Rafa continued. "I realized I needed to change. I needed to be different, not this person that disappeared on those who they loved because they said no to them. I needed to be solid for my parents. I wanted to be so different that I changed so much, I became this person I no longer know. I want to start recognizing myself."

Loved, past tense. I swallowed. I, too, wanted to recognize myself. But who was this person? If I were to reconstruct those pieces of me, where would I even start?

"You inspired that," Rafa continued, looking at me with those wide brown eyes. "Thank you, Vi. For reminding me."

My hand was shaking when I slowly placed it on his face. His skin was warm, and I knew that I shouldn't, but I needed to touch him. Rafa closed his eyes and leaned his face into my fingers with the ease of before.

"You'd tell me, right?"

"Tell you what?" I smiled, taking back my hand and putting it in my pocket.

"If I sucked."

I laughed. "Of course I would tell you." We kept walking, the winds and the waves intensifying. "You probably are so rusty."

~

We talked for what felt like hours. Time was passing quickly and slowly at the same time. I told him about Charlie, and Ollie, my friend who was always forgetting stuff but made the most incredible margaritas. I told him about how Liam and I met.

Rafa heard the story about the party without saying a word. When I was done, he looked at me with a soft smile.

Rafa told me about Magdalena's cancer (I didn't know), how she was possibly out of the woods; he told me about how Marta loved classical music. When he was telling me about her, I looked away, not ready to hear more about her. If I had stayed, if I had said yes, would we still be together? Would I have met Liam or he Marta?

He told me about how when he couldn't sleep, he would drive around. His dad lost his car at one point, and Rafa learned how to drive later in life. He loved driving; it reminded him of everything he had accomplished. Everything he promised his dad he would be.

It was the afternoon, when the sun started to get a little orange, that we knew it was time to come back. It was always time to leave.

"Would you tell me if *I* suck?" I said.

"What? The restaurant, your art?"

"Both, anything."

"I would tell you." Rafa exaggerated a nod.

"I'm about to suck right now," I said, starting to walk back to the car. Had Rafa or I ended things years ago? I had said no, but he had disappeared shortly after, motivated by hurt and confusion. That imprint would mold every relationship I would have and not have shortly after.

The fear that would take hold inside my body—fear of loving again, giving in.

"I think we need to let go. It's not fair to see each other like this. I know I called—" I stopped walking and planted myself on the beach. I looked at him; his eyes were on me.

Rafa nodded. "I agree." He released a sigh.

"I just remember this person I used to be when I was with you. Full of love for home, and freedom, and this urge to rebel against Abuela and everything she planned for me—" I waved my hands in the air, feeling the energy of those days. Anything was possible. I had so much fight in me.

Rafa sighed. "I feel the same." His voice was quiet, almost a whisper. I could hear the sadness in his voice.

"But we can't do this. We have a life. You have one—"

I didn't know if it was the finality of everything, but my voice was breaking. I was about to cry.

Rafa looked at the beach and then at me. He bit his lip. "I do. But Vi . . ."

"What?"

Was I really that different from the girl he proposed to, all those years ago? Maybe I was just more jaded, more tired.

"Nothing." He released another breath. "Get in the car, I'll take you home."

"That's it?" I raised my voice, suddenly full of anger. Residues of old and new.

"Vi." Rafa smiled softly and grabbed my hand. It was warm and soft. "What do you want me to say? You have a life in the States. You're leaving, you're not coming back. I have a life here. I need to take care of my mom. I can't leave."

"I want you to do something, to say something. All those years ago . . ." Are done, are the past. No use in reviving that, I told myself. But why did I have trouble believing it? All this time, I had pushed those years away from my mind, and now I was throwing my hurt all around this beach.

"Tell me what you would have told me all those years ago. Tell me that you would have fought for me."

"Vi." Rafa took a couple of steps closer to me, putting his hand over my hair and caressing it. We were so close that if I wanted to, I could get on my tippy-toes and kiss him. I could blow my whole life up. His.

"There hasn't been a day that I don't regret who I was then. I often think of who we would have been. Do you know?" Rafa smiled, and I noticed his eyes were welling up with tears. "I never drive past your restaurant, or your house, because it hurts too much. I have to take a huge detour to get to my house. It drives Marta and Mamá crazy. They don't know why, claro—"

I sighed, tears threatening for me too.

"But I know I have to live with this."

What if we didn't?

No, we did. We didn't know each other anymore; too much time had passed. And I loved Liam.

"Tell me to stay," I said, tears running freely. Wanting to feel eighteen again and like everything was possible.

Rafa shook his head. "I can't do that. I tried to propose to you before you were ready, and look how that ended up."

"Then I'll go," I said, walking to the car, already hearing the immaturity in my words. I wasn't going because he was telling me to go; I was going because I needed to go.

I opened the door, and we stayed silent for a moment before he turned on the car again.

"I'm sorry," I said. "I'm just emotional. I'm going because of the restaurant. It's not your responsibility—"

Rafa put his hand on my good hand. "I know. I wish I could say anything to make you stay." He swallowed. "But I know that I no longer have that power. I never did. You left because you felt you needed to."

I nodded, sitting with those words as he pulled out of the beach parking lot and started to drive home. I left because I wanted new experiences, because I was scared of who I would be if I stayed home. I didn't want to repeat the story of Bisabuela, Mamá, and Abuela. What if passionate love burned me like it had burned them?

What if I never found my place in the restaurant? I left because I was full of fear. Fear that I wouldn't have what it took to fight for my place in the life I wanted.

We drove in silence, and I knew we both wanted to say everything but instead said nothing. Words were too heavy; they were nothing in the big scheme of things.

Rafa pulled over in front of Abuela's house. I wasn't ready to get out of the car.

"You're home." Rafa turned to look at me, smiling weakly.

"Rafa," I started.

He shook his head. "Go. I know, this is hard for me."

"I'm sorry, Rafa, I really am," I said, pulling him close and hugging him, as tight as I could. "For everything."

"We were so young. I'm sorry too."

His skin, his smell. The way that Rafa made me feel like anything was possible.

"Rafa," I said, wiggling the door handle as if I had suddenly forgotten how to open a door.

I started opening the car door, when he touched my arm.

"I'll always love you, you know that?"

My body burned, and I started feeling feverish again. "I'll always love you too."

Our eyes connected for a moment, and I knew then that this was it. We couldn't turn back time, there were no right words, it was just time running its course. This was it.

"Bye, Rafa."

The finality of our words was the push I needed to open the door and practically throw myself out of the car. I walked as fast as I could the short distance from the car to the house. Tears threatened to fall, like the thunder had threatened rain a couple of hours ago.

I closed the door behind me, wanting to hide in the house. I imagined Rafa driving away, getting away from this house, from the memories, from me.

I felt a throbbing in my hand and went up to the bathroom to check on it. I turned on the lights and uncovered the bandage. Despite the cream I was applying twice a day, the skin still stuck to the bandage, especially on really sweaty nights. The rain had probably made matters worse. The skin was still purple, and one of the skin bubbles had burst. I moaned in pain.

A wound without attention refuses to close.

I remembered Rocío's words: "Solo tienes que mirar." As always, I had refused to look. Now it was too late. I hadn't been checking under the bandage, so I didn't know how to assess the problem. I hadn't asked for help.

Someone stood by the door, behind me, saying my name softly: "Vi."

I felt the hand caressing my curls. Mamá took my hand in hers. I saw the worry in her eyes.

"Ay, Vi. Muchacha," Mamá said, opening the medicine cabinet. She took the alcohol and cotton and washed her hands thoroughly.

She wet the cotton ball. "This is going to hurt, but it will be one second." She pressed on my skin, and I bit my lip, trying to not scream. Carefully, she passed it around the charred skin.

"Mija," she said softly, a whisper of Abuela's voice contained in that word. "It's all okay. I'm here now."

I cried. For Caminito, for Abuela, for Rafa, for Mami, for us.

She tapped tapped tapped softly on the skin. "We're okay," she said, lifting her eyes to look at me. "You're okay."

I let myself cry in front of her, feeling the tears like a release. Mamá had never been maternal, she had never been tender in her words, but at that moment we were both for the first time really trying to meet halfway. She was trying to be what I had needed when I was younger.

"Gracias, Mami," I said. It had been hard to say it, but it felt good to acknowledge it.

CHAPTER FOURTEEN: NEW YORK

Was it possible to say goodbye to a house?

I stood outside, my skin still throbbing under the bandage, but I was unable to pay attention to that pain. Anton and Mamá stood by the door; my bags were still packed. I had been at home for less than a month. I had failed. Okay, not failed yet. I could still work really hard, send money . . .

"Vi." Anton hugged me first. He squeezed me like a lemon. "Please come back soon. Don't let it go so long."

"I promise." I closed my eyes, the familiar sun on my skin. "Mami." She got closer. She wasn't one to hug, so I figured she'd tap me on the shoulder. Instead, she put her arms around me and placed her head on my shoulder. "I'll miss you," she whispered in my ear.

My eyes welled with tears. I didn't want to cry, but this was as good an occasion as any.

"I'll send money. We'll figure out something," I said, breaking out of the embrace and walking to the taxi. They couldn't take me to the airport; they needed to work at the restaurant.

"Mamá," I said, looking at her from afar.

"Vete," she said. *Go.* "You're going to make me cry harder." Mamá was crying. All those years ago, we didn't get to say goodbye. Life came full circle.

I looked at the house. Abuela's presence in it. I waved at it, too distraught at leaving her a second time.

"Vete, Vi, you'll miss the plane."

I turned and waved one more time, knowing that if I didn't go right then, I would stay.

~

It had been three weeks since I first arrived in Barranquilla and since I'd been away from the apartment in New York. Opening the door felt strange, like the space was mine and at the same time it was someone else's. While Liam told me about how he had kept the plants alive and how he had bought some new ones for the terrace, I looked at him. The distance lingered, weighing on our bodies. Although not a lot of time had passed, I felt far away from him. Maybe I just needed time to adjust.

My heart was heavy from the day before with Rafa. A last goodbye that played on repeat in my head and that burned on the tips of my fingers. My hands felt warm and heavy, as if they were still carrying the heat of home.

"I have a surprise for you," Liam said, dropping my bag on the floor. I hadn't taken much to Barranquilla, expecting to spend only a week or two. I sat down at the kitchen table, exhausted from the trip and the last couple of days.

When we met in the airport (Liam and I had made a promise to always pick each other up from airports), he kissed me as if he hadn't seen me in months. I kissed him back, unsure at first, my head still heavy with thoughts of Rafa. But after a moment, my lips opened up, recognizing his kiss, his love, our love. This city that I had devoted so much love to.

"What is it, baby?" I said, trying to disguise a yawn, feeling the exhaustion of my time in Barranquilla. "Sorry, I'm so tired."

Liam shook his head and entered our room, not even fazed by my yawn. "Close your eyes!"

I did as told and focused on our Sunday mornings. I would always start the day by drawing, and he would play jazz and cook, or do some work. Sometimes, after I was done with work, we would sit on the couch watching movies or go for a walk. Saturdays and Sundays were sacred for us. Days of big breakfasts that he would make from scratch, bike rides, and long afternoons drinking beers and playing cards. Liam for many years had been the only home I had in New York. The only home I wanted.

"Liam—" I started to speak, a breath tangled in my throat. Thoughts about Rafa, Caminito, and home spiraled in my brain. But for the moment, I kept my eyes closed.

"Now. Open."

I opened my eyes slowly, one first and then the other.

In front of my eyes, there was a little painting easel he had built for me with painted sky-blue wood. He had already put a big white canvas for me to paint on it.

"Because you said you wanted to try to do more oil paintings."

I felt my chest making room for the breath I was holding. I had said that in passing one time we went to the Whitney and my eyes had lingered on a painting. The vibrant colors had reminded me of home, of the flowers and the mural I had painted once. I took a step closer, overwhelmed by emotions. My hands knew the way to the back of his neck. I pulled him closer and kissed him, welcoming back the part of myself I was in the States. The winter breeze still entered through the closed windows, and the cold woke me up to my New York self. Life in full English, with Liam and our apartment. Our plants, which had gotten through the winter and my absence after all. The plants were stronger than I was.

"I've missed you," I said, grabbing his hands between mine. Liam was so thoughtful; he held on to every word I told him, in a way I wasn't sure anyone else in my life did. I bit my lips, guilt sitting on the bottom of my stomach.

"I've missed you, too, baby," he said, kissing my cheeks and my face. He pushed me gently on the couch and started kissing my neck and my hair. His kisses moved down and covered my whole body. I closed my eyes, trying to focus. I was here, in NYC, with the love of my life. There was no use holding on to the past.

The lights flickered, and the winter rain started hitting the windows. No menace of it flooding the city here. In New York, the rain would travel through the gutters like it was supposed to.

"Funny," I said, stopping his kisses to watch the rain for a second, "how nature follows you to places. It's been raining in Barranquilla too."

He turned to look at the rain, without saying anything. The weight of his body was familiar and comfortable. I pulled him back up again, toward me. Missing him already.

"One second, one second." He planted me to rush kisses on my lips, before running to turn off the lights. He came back and pulled my curls back, kissing my uncovered shoulder.

"I've always loved your shoulders." He placed his lips on my bare skin.

The darkness of the apartment made it easier for me to touch his face with the same hands I had touched Rafa's with days before. Our lips touched.

In New York, at least I was free, I told myself. I was free to do and undo my life, however I wanted. I was Violeta instead of Vi. I was an artist, free of obligation to a family restaurant. I could do what I wanted, and no one cared. There were no neighborhood gossips here or the ghost of Abuela looking over me. I was free.

I climbed up on top of Liam and took off his shirt, button by button. Making him wait. I kissed his warm neck, his thick eyebrows. I felt his breath on my skin.

"Liam." I said his name like there was no tomorrow, fearing that there wasn't. "Liam."

~

A thunder that seemed to have the force to split the sky in two woke me up.

I woke up sweaty, my naked body stuck to the sheets. Liam was sleeping, hugging the corner of the blanket as he always did.

The diary gleamed under the light. I hadn't been able to leave it at home. If I was going to leave Abuela behind, I needed to take something of her with me. I'd put it on my bedside table to remind myself that I had debts at home: the need to save the restaurant and to find out what it was that Abuela needed in order to rest in peace.

I lay back on the pillows, the silk ones I had insisted we buy two years ago when I saw everybody was switching to silk and I thought the material would be kinder to my messy curls. It didn't do much.

Barranquilla, 1966

> *Today I went to eat Frozomalt with Gabriel in the town center. It was a rare treat, one that I couldn't afford regularly but that he offered to pay for. La Heladería Americana belongs to some Greek brothers who introduced the city to chocolate shakes with a mystery sauce. I'm convinced it is a ripe papaya jam. Gabriel says que no, that it couldn't be. It has to be cherry. Cherries? Around here? I ask him. And he laughs. With that laugh of his that travels to every corner of every room, that stays with me, that follows.*
>
> *Gabriel. He likes the sun, the beach, and to fish. He likes to visit his mother and take her places. He has never been married because he says he was waiting to meet me.*

Gabriel? Abuela was with another man that wasn't Abuelo? I put down the diary. Many nights, when I couldn't sleep, I wondered if Abuela had ever known love. If she'd ever felt loved.

But Gabriel and I met too late. I tell him I have a little girl, a house, un marido. A bad one but I don't tell him that because what difference do the details make? I belong to someone else. Especially now that Amadeo is too busy to insult me or beat me, I really can't complain much. I'm left to hustle with Mamá, who loves my little girl and helps me with her endlessly.

Gabriel, while eating ice cream and dipping sweet cookies in the sauce, told me that he would wait for me.

Let's get you a divorce, he said. As easy as if he were saying: "Let's get you a new dress."

But what does Gabriel know about me? About my past? Does he remember I haven't even finished high school? I can't remember if I told him or not. He doesn't know enough about me to start a life together. He knows the good but not the bad.

What he does know about me is the little parts of my day where I laugh with him. When I tell him that my girl is doing well in school. That she is good at mátematicas because I teach her. That Mami gets so many pedidos for wedding cakes that I can barely keep track.

Let's open a bakery, he says, with resolution in his voice. With that smile of his that makes his eyes twinkle when he gets an idea that he wants to execute. Right now! There's nothing more exciting for him than to build things quickly, while they're still fresh.

A bakery? What do my mom and I know about bread? What does a young lawyer know about bread?

I laugh and push him a little. Then I look around, scared that someone might have seen me touching him. You don't know anything about bakeries, I tell him with a smile. He smiles back, more deflated but pensive. Ready to offer another alternative.

Emilia, he says, I want to give you a place that is yours.

Gabriel? Abuela never told me about this person. I couldn't blame her—until the end of her days she spoke only about her bitter marriage with Amadeo, my abuelo. Whenever he disappeared, I could breathe easier. When Abuela got really sick, Amadeo disappeared from our lives completely. Abuela said that it was the only thing that had been good about her disease.

He was mean to Abuela, bitter. The marriage that limited her happiness and her opportunities in life—she'd opened the restaurant to survive and as a refuge from the man who gave her nothing but unhappiness and hard times. But of course, there were always two sides to the story. Abuela had another love.

I thought about her warning me about infatuation, telling me that I was going to get burned. She knew boys like Rafa.

Gabriel: I said his name out loud, and it sounded light and airy, like a tale that you would tell again and again but that would never become real.

The lights in our room flickered. A lightning strike made Liam turn; I waited to make sure he wouldn't wake up. I put a hand on his shoulder to see if he would, but he stayed still, snores escaping his half-open mouth.

A spot on the paper. I brought the diary to my nose and smelled coffee and butter. I pictured Abuela smoking and making a cake perhaps to sell, maybe for Mamá's birthday. Her famous Sara Lee that she used to call "Sarali." When I was a little girl, Abuela said "Sarali, Sarali, Sarali" so confidently I thought it was her own recipe she and Bisabuela had invented.

It wasn't until I grew up and American products started occupying the shelves of Colombian supermarkets that I realized Sara Lee was a famous cake that everyone in the world made—there were multiple versions of it. She hadn't invented Sarali, but her own version was even better than the store bought. It was spongy, the sweet notes mixed in with vanilla and the butter, the cream dissolving in your mouth like the softest of clouds.

~

That night I dreamed of roots.

"Despierta." Her voice echoed in a dark, empty room. "I'm going to help you." I lay on a bed, alone and uncertain. I was able to move my torso but not much else; my feet and the bottom of my body lay heavy on the bed.

"Abuela? Eres tu?" *Is that you?* I asked, searching from one side to the other.

I tried to wrestle. To move my arms and my legs, but every part of me was too dense for me to move it. I let out a scream, but no one came; my voice came out like an exaggerated whisper.

Although I wasn't moving, I felt my body splitting in two. Stretching like gum and expanding to the dark corners of the room. Someone or something was playing with my insides like dough, and Abuela was doing nothing to stop it.

I let out a quiet screech of horror, my voice finally coming out in full force. I gasped, trying to gather as much air as I could.

"Abuela!" I yelled. "Abuela."

"Touch your feet." Her voice came out from the darkness, an order.

I shook my arms to see if my body had gone back to normal, and then I touched my feet as Abuela had instructed me to. They were as cold as ice.

"If they're cold, that means you don't trust your decision. Listen to yourself, mija. I beg of you."

Roots in shades of purple, deep green, and blue started popping out of my feet and growing in all directions. I stared at my side of the bed, at nothing, just darkness without an end. Once the roots were tangled around my legs, they pulled me over toward the door. They swept me like I was weightless, with a force that pulled me forward and threatened to split my body into nothing. I was succumbing to the roots, becoming part of them.

I gasped.

"Vi, Vi." Liam shook me awake. His expression was worried; he looked at me as if I had been screaming. He put a hand on my cheek. "You're warm, baby. You were kicking with your arms and legs. I've never seen you do anything like that."

"I'm sorry. I must have—I don't know," I said, reaching for the glass of water on my bedside table. Too fast—my head felt cloudy, and I had to close my eyes to get grounded. "Bad dream," I said, acting like I had forgotten already. *Trust your decision. Why. Don't. You. Trust. Your. Decision.* Abuela's words echoed inside my head.

"I'm going to bring you a cup of tea to help you relax," Liam said, jumping off the bed. "Do you want something to eat?"

I shook my head no.

"Just the tea." I stretched my legs on the bed, reveling in the sensation of being able to move them. I melted on the pillow like butter, thinking that even if I didn't realize it, just like in the dream, my feet were tied to the other side of the world.

CHAPTER FIFTEEN: WINTER

The next morning, as soon as my toes touched the cold floor, I reminded myself of my main goal for the next weeks: money to save Caminito. Almost as soon as I landed, I swallowed my pride and called Charlie.

Of course Charlie did not pick up. Alma, her assistant, did. Her voice was as low as ever, full of doubt. I could never tell if she was sorry for me or for herself.

"Oh hi," I tried, sounding breezier than I wanted. "I just wanted to talk to Charlie about possible work for the next few weeks."

"Uhm, yeah," Alma said. "I . . ."

"Alma, I'll pick up." Charlie came onto the phone, and I held a breath. "Hi, Violeta. Took you a moment to call back. Longer than you said—"

"Yeah, I'm sorry. I just—" I thought about explaining, but I didn't owe her anything. "Look, I need anything you have. I'll do anything. Any colors you want, no protesting."

I could hear Charlie smiling through the phone. "Anything?"

"Anything and everything. Multiple projects if you have them."

One of the things that was nice about Charlie was that they paid immediately upon delivery. It wasn't like my other clients who took months.

"Anything," I repeated.

"There's this super-extensive project. The illustrator messed up the illustrations, and we need someone to do them again."

I thought about what it meant when Charlie said "messed up." They probably just didn't do exactly what Charlie wanted but didn't dare to speak up.

"What's the project about?" Did I even care, did it matter?

"It's about a little girl who can't find dancing shoes for her recital night. It's about trying different things until you find the one that is not perfect but fits you just right."

It sounded terrible. I had illustrated so many ballet books for children already. "Sounds great!"

"Wonderful. I'll send you a color palette and a style guide."

"Amazing." I said, hanging up. Already exhausted by the prospect.

~

I had brought the blue notebook home with me. I opened it, searching for Abuela's presence right now. Maybe answers about what she would have done.

Barranquilla, 1967

> *A married woman has to keep secretos in order to stay alive.*
>
> *Gabriel is an elegant man. When he comes to the restaurant to supervise the place and the workers, their wives outside selling tamales and bollos turn their heads to look at him.*
>
> *Gabriel and I never meet in the restaurant. We meet in the center far away from Barrio Prado, and we sometimes have big fish lunches with fried plantain and arroz de coco that leave us sleepy. Then we walk the streets*

tumbling around, looking for a cafecito with panela to cure our midday slumber. One of my favorite things about Gabriel now is how he's always buying things from people in the street. He can't resist a rose, incense, bollo, empanadas even if we have eaten, whatever crosses him that he can offer to me.

Gabriel bought me a little house in Barrio Prado so we could build a restaurant. Mamá and me.

Abuela hated the idea of me depending on a man. And yet she'd had no issue taking this place from Gabriel. Caminito had been a place that had started with charity from a man. Abuela hated depending on others and hated taking help from people. But she had no problem with taking property from Gabriel? I closed the notebook and started pacing around. It was okay for her to be vulnerable, but not for me.

I reread the entry. Yes, Caminito had started because of an affair. I released a breath, not knowing what to do with myself, who to talk to about this. We probably didn't know this, because Abuela had been ashamed. It went against everything she had ever taught us.

I took a moment before diving back again in her words. This side of her story left me wondering if I'd ever known her at all. If the side she had shown me was the side that all the hurt in her life had shaped. Abuela was hardened, a strong presence who never faltered. And I had been molded in her likeness.

I knew the carefully packaged version she fed me. The stern, intense matriarch. But her softness was all here, immortalized in the notebook.

We told Amadeo that Gabriel was a distant cousin, and he wanted to help and invest in a restaurant that we would open together. Amadeo, back then, was so consumed with his own interests of drinking and disappearing for days that he said nothing but urged me to bring him a beer. After a while, he told me that he was sure it would fail, like everything else in my life did.

Gabriel has told me that this restaurant doesn't come for free. He will love me until I say yes to divorce Amadeo and marry him. I tell him he's in love with the idea of me. How can one love someone that they only know through heavy lunches and occasional beach afternoons? How can one love someone that they only know in the stolen moments of the day?

But I want a life with him, a restaurant. Something that I can't make mine, and his. A place where we feed the neighborhood, and there's parties, weddings, vibrant nights full of food and love. I want to give my family a place to love and take care of. A place that represents the Sanoguera women.

Because I can't talk to anyone about this, I ask myself questions in front of the mirror and try to guess my true answer. What I really want to do. If I bat my eyes, I want him. If I stare at myself and my face turns pale, I want to stay with Amadeo and live a quiet life, una vida respetable. One where Paula doesn't get kicked out of private school like I did because Mamá was separada. Away from her esposo. Improper. I don't care for people thinking I'm a loca, desquiciada, but I care about my daughter thinking that. One more sacrifice, for her. Thinking that maybe at the end of my days I'll look back at my life and that's all that I'll see: a life amounted to sacrifice for Paula. An old woman on a cross.

I already knew the ending of the story. Abuela ended up with Amadeo. A life full of bitterness and unsaid words. But I wanted something different for her, something better. I wiped a tear, glad to be alone in the apartment.

I always thought we were so different. I was weak, in love, irrational. But once, I wanted to tell her: once, Abuela, we were the same.

> *If everything goes to plan, Gabriel and I will open the restaurant next week. Amadeo spends so little time with us nowadays that it is easy to cook him a good dinner and close my eyes when we turn off the lights at night. The only good thing about Amadeo is that he always has one foot out the door.*
>
> *I wonder if Mamá knows about Gabriel? Who she sees sometimes when she goes to check on the construction and to bring the men lemonade and sometimes almuerzo that we can't really afford. But Mamá is always like that—even when she can't, she stretches the little she doesn't have. She sees Gabriel and smiles at him with her kind eyes, with a certain tenderness I haven't seen her use on anyone else, as if he were her son or a beloved grandson. He tells her that he wishes he had her olive-green eyes.*

Abuela had her Rafa. I wondered what mine—he wasn't mine, I corrected myself. Had been mine?—was doing now. I imagined him revising charts at work or having lunch with his mom somewhere nice.

Maybe he was with Marta. I had been careful to avoid that subject with him. If I didn't know about her, it wouldn't hurt me. It was almost like that side of his life didn't exist. I was afraid that if I knew more, it would cut me deeper than I wanted to admit.

I thought about calling him, but for what? What was there left to say?

"Rafa," I uttered under my breath, his name lingering in the air like a secret.

I opened the email attachment from Alma and Charlie. The writing was subpar, and this wasn't going to be the next *Goodnight Moon*, but at least it wasn't too long. I scrolled down: $10,000 upon delivery. This wasn't much for illustrating a whole picture book. But beggars can't be choosers. I heard Mamá's voice: *"They're going to start repossessing stuff."*

I thought about them taking away the new oven we hadn't even paid for in full. The thought motivated me to email Charlie back: I'll get started right away.

I'd told Ollie I needed work, and now he was calling me back. "Ollie," I said. "I'll do anything."

~

I sat at my writing desk with a couple of sheets of paper, my colors, and my iPad, and I had no idea where to start. All that came to me was Abuela's kitchen, Caminito with its white tablecloths and red velvet chairs. Barrio Prado. Home.

Those thoughts were juxtaposed with money—the big debt we had.

I opened the white page on the iPad and started sketching without thinking too much. The soft, long lines of Abuela's kitchen counter. The vibrant green from the cilantro that was always scattered around the kitchen, the plethora of olive oil.

No. This was not what I was supposed to be doing. I saved the page, exited it, and opened another blank page. One deep breath. My feet and my whole body were freezing. How does one get used to the cold after reveling in the heat?

I had no time for this. My chest felt tight, and I closed my eyes, remembering Abuela's words in her diary—how many sleepless nights she'd had, with all the worries of maintaining a family. Surviving. I had to deliver the illustrations. Caminito's future was dependent on it.

Flowers came to me. White alstroemeria with cilantro stems coming out of it, white petals floating in the air, adorning the big wedding bouquet. The colorful sign that said "Caminito."

I decided to start with Ollie's work because it was easier. I looked again at his instructions. The first ad was for a DJ session night with a Korean chef taking over the restaurant for the entire weekend. I looked at pictures of this chef and of his food: a color palette that was in different shades of velvet red and deep, dark blue. I put my iPad away and took the paper out, blue and red colored pencils in front of me.

"Ok, Vi," I told myself. "Concentrate." *Focus.*

I took a sip of coffee, followed by another, and I stared at the window and the strong winter breeze.

After a couple of minutes, I ended up sketching Abuela's restaurant table. The one we used for chopping vegetables and making the dough for the coca bread pizzas and our homemade bread. I took out my watercolors and started wetting the paints. I mixed deep brown with the different shades of blue. I painted her favorite vegetables, like rábano and cauliflower. I painted the old-fashioned black-and-white tiles, Abuela's favorite part of the restaurant. I closed my eyes, and I thought back to when I was around ten years old and she would help me with school projects when Mami was too busy going on dates: her hands covered in paint strokes of white and blue, her holding a thin brush so delicately, trying to paint flowers for my Virgin Mary school assignment poster, squinting her eyes, trying to make sure they were perfect.

Hours went by, and Abuela's kitchen stared at me in the face. I had nothing.

~

When Liam arrived home at 6:30 p.m., I had switched back to a digital page—it was also blank, and I was almost in tears. Liam kissed me on the cheek, and when I lifted my eyes from my board, he kissed me on the lips.

"Baby, I love this." He lifted my drawing of Abuela's kitchen. "I love the colors."

I nodded, looking at the vibrancy of home. "Well, no one is paying me for that one."

"I'll get started on dinner," he said, pointing to the kitchen. "I'll make my working girl something good."

"We can order out," I said, not lifting my eyes from the iPad, scared that if I stopped staring at it, the right idea wouldn't get to me.

"No takeout for you, tonight. Only the best that this kitchen has to offer." Liam took out a couple of bottles of wine and put them in the fridge.

I sighed loudly, trying to concentrate on work. I had promised him I wouldn't work at night, and yet I was behind on everything.

"What's wrong, baby?" Liam said from the kitchen, as he was washing some vegetables.

"Oh, nothing. Just tired." I watched him from afar, all the words on the tip of my tongue. I was scared that if I told him what I was really thinking about, I would lose him. I was thinking about Caminito nonstop. What if I hadn't left?

In the in-between moments, I would think about Rafa. His scent, his words. *I will always love you.*

"Nothing, I'm just distracted."

"Oh," he said, putting the rinsed vegetables on a cutting board. "I'll be as quiet as a church mouse." Liam smiled at me, and I just gritted my teeth, wondering if I deserved him.

I started drawing a couple of lines just to get out of my head. Liam kept working on dinner without saying a word. Lime, notes of sake, and chili started floating in our tiny apartment. Tonight's dinner was salmon on a bed of white rice and vegetables with a teriyaki soy sauce.

Liam was in the kitchen, carefully following a recipe to make the sauce, the last step.

"Take a break," he told me while putting some herbs on top of two perfectly plated dishes. "Time to eat." I looked at my white page, with scattered lines on it. I felt defeated but hungry.

"Proud of you for trying to make this work," he said as he put the food on the table. I smiled at him, and without letting go of his hand, I ate the first forkful of salmon and rice. The flavors were comforting. The rice was pillowy and spiced with herbs and a hint of what was maybe red pepper. The salmon was buttery and salty, and the roasted vegetables were crunchy and perfectly seasoned. I was grateful to be in our place, with him, eating the food that he had crafted with so much love. I squeezed his hand once more, taking it all in and feeling grateful and guilty. I wondered if he could see it in my eyes.

"What's the plan with the restaurant?" Liam asked as he took a bite of salmon.

I shrugged. "Who knows?" I wanted to tell him that we were short. They had started repossessing things. But I didn't want to talk about it anymore. If I kept it to myself, it didn't have to be real.

But if I started keeping secrets, could we come back from that?

I forced myself to speak. "I have to make enough money this week to send it home so we can start giving the bank something substantial. If not—"

Liam grabbed my hand across the table and squeezed it. Not really saying much. He had doubts about us, or rather me, being able to save the restaurant. I stood up, picked up my plate, and left it in the sink, letting the water wash over the porcelain.

We had one week and a couple of days. If not, we were done. I was going to try to make as much money as I could. I contemplated borrowing the money from Liam, something that would tie me to him. Abuela had done it. Caminito was the result of that.

If she could, I could do it too.

"Mamá has all these plans for it. Theme dinners, promotions, maybe a party, god knows what else, but we're short, nothing feels like enough. Earning money in dollars, I know, will be a big help. But I'm scared."

I shook my head, washing the first dish.

"We could lose it, and the bank would take it all."

"Ay, Vi." Liam stood up and came behind me, putting his hands on my shoulders and sliding my curls to one side so he could kiss my skin. "Leave them, keep working, I know you're stressed."

"But . . . ," I said, looking at the pile of dishes. Liam had cooked. It was only fair.

"Nothing, go," he said, gesturing at the living room table, where I always worked. "I'll bring you a glass of wine in a second."

I looked at him, rag on his shoulder, water running on the pile of dishes. He started working as I moved away.

"Liam," I said from my place at the table.

"Yes?" he said, lifting his eyes.

"Thank you," I said quietly, and he nodded. My chest felt tight. I looked at him, working on the dishes as if he had no other care in the world.

"I love you," I said while opening a new page on my iPad. He didn't say anything. I wondered if he could hear me with the water running. "I love you," I said again, this time louder, getting choked up.

"I love you too," Liam said with a confident smile, not even noticing the change in my voice. "But you know that already."

~

If I had to see another ballerina, I would lose it. The color palettes were soft pinks and light blues, the color of clichés. It was past midnight, and since Liam slept with the door open, I could hear him snore. He slept so peacefully, while I was contemplating throwing the iPad out the window.

The first line of the book started, *"Mom told me I needed new shoes."*

And I needed a new life.

I started the first page. I hated every line I traced, every strand of hair, every color I chose.

Ballerinas. If I had to see another one, ever again. I yawned, wondering how many projects like these were left in my future.

~

Despite my promise to Liam, there was no way I could not work nights. I had worked full nights and full days, barely sleeping a couple of hours every day, divided between Ollie's and Charlie's projects. The days felt longer and at the same time faster since I was working every waking hour, conscious that I couldn't procrastinate because it would cost me. My little free time was with Liam and sleeping.

It was already Wednesday, four days after I'd arrived. Ollie told me to come to the restaurant in Bushwick to have a drink tonight. I was tired; bouncing between the two projects had been a lot. Anton texted me that Mami was looking into loans, and that Caminito was fine. I didn't need to worry, but was he saying that just to protect me?

The iPad was glaring in front of me, as if it was motivating me to pick it up again. I took a deep breath, the cold seeping through my bones.

One drink, I texted Ollie quickly before I regretted it. I have to go straight home and work some more.

~

Ollie's white-and-black hair sat on top of his head in little waves, thick for a man his age. He had a salt-and-pepper beard to match and a ratty red velvet sweater that was a couple of sizes too big, and when he waved at me from the bar, I noticed it had a huge hole in his sleeve.

"Vi, cariño!" he said, blowing me a kiss from across the restaurant.

I walked toward him and waved. I left my bag on a bar seat and hugged him. His smell of unwashed sweaters stuck to my nose.

"You look more tanned, how is that possible?"

"Home. I was home," I said, realizing my mistake, a wave of sadness coming over me. "Sorry, I was at Abuela's house. Really sunny down there."

"Oh," he said, taking a sip of his margarita. "Want one?"

"Claro." I smiled. The restaurant looked the same: open under the glass ceiling and the big windows. I loved how close to the sky it felt, even in the winter when all everyone wanted was to be inside. The restaurant / cultural center still had this playful atmosphere of possibility. When you went through those tall wooden doors (an impossibility in the middle of industrial Bushwick), it felt like you were being transported to somewhere else: colorful chairs and murals, and hundreds of plants that were green and lush even in frigid weather.

Ollie put a margarita in front of me and raised a "salud" for old friends. He looked great, and I wondered if he was doing better. Last year, he was going through a breakup and was drinking a lot and constantly looked tired and overextended. But now, apart from the sparingly washed clothes that gave him his signature smell, he looked well rested. He didn't even smell of cigarettes.

"Doing okay, Ollie?" I asked. "You look great."

He took a sip of his drink. "Better than ever. I'm thinking about selling this place at the end of the year and moving to Latin America, not sure where."

"What?" I asked, putting my drink down. This restaurant was Ollie's life. New York was his life. This man prided himself on going through Hurricane Sandy and 9/11 and staying in the city. It was part of who he was, what had made him the man he was whom everyone loved so dearly.

But also—I got that impulse. The desire to move where it was always warm, where the sea was minutes away and the night breeze was cool and gentle. Life flowing like a river instead of running like a well-oiled machine.

"It's time. The restaurant's ups and downs are finally getting to me. I feel like I have barely had a second to discover myself and what I want. Writing has become an afterthought, something that I do here on a slow night or the rare morning that I wake up early. I feel the exhaustion in my bones. I need a change if I don't want to die an alcoholic." Ollie was writing a memoir about being a restaurateur in New York City, and starting as a dishwasher in his twenties.

Ollie lifted his margarita glass and smiled. I could see the tiredness in his expression, the sleepless nights worrying about being able to pay staff. This business aged you, and although Ollie carried his age well, I wondered if I would have as much resilience as the people who had succeeded in this business had.

I took a long gulp of my margarita, feeling the tequila burn my throat. "So, I should update you. I came back to make money, and I left my mom and the chef working on the restaurant. We have a week to come up with everything we owe."

Ollie put his drink down. He was familiar with these conversations; after he had turned around the future of Santuario, people sought him out all the time.

"So how are you going to come up with the money?"

"Um, well, working for you and for Charlie."

Ollie rolled his eyes. He hadn't met Charlie, but he had heard enough to not like her. "Okay, and is that going to be enough?"

Ollie asking the hard questions. I grabbed the drink again. "Mami is looking for loans, but she has terrible credit—I was thinking maybe it would soften the bank if we gave them something."

"When are you going over there next?"

"I am not sure. I'm trying to make money in dollars to send home. I wasn't being much help there anyway—"

"Vi." Ollie put a hand on my shoulder. "I hope this is okay for me to say. But you have this thing." He took his hand away and exhaled, looking for the right way to say it. "How to put this? Violeta, you just get in your own way. You always think people think a certain way about you, and it's not the truth. You're talented. You're good, you make an effort. You care."

"But that's not enough," I said, taking the last sip of my margarita, the sugar and the tequila descending down my throat.

"Are you thinking about staying with it?" Ollie asked. "For good?"

"No," I said. Thinking about what it would entail to keep Abuela's memory alive. Even if we saved it. Would that mean going to Colombia every few months? Despegarse. I thought about how hard it would be to leave every time, Abuela's whisper in every corner in the house. "I want to. Caminito always felt like home—even when everything and everyone were pushing me away from it, I knew it was a place that was important to me," I said, choking up. "I do, Ollie. But I'm scared. I don't know how to."

"Vi, you just have to go home. Make as much money as you can this week, and take it to the bank yourself. If the ship goes down, you're there for it. If it keeps sailing, you're there. But if you really want this, you have to be at Caminito."

I tasted the salt from my tears. "I can't leave," I said simply, thinking that if I left, I just didn't have it in me to come back. Saying goodbye to New York . . . another thing to separate myself from Liam. I feared that we couldn't get past it.

"Just tell me what you did to save Santuario."

"I just woke up every day wanting to do something for it. I called investors—who said no. My community rallied for me, and I just stayed with the space as long as I could until I could come up with the real solution, which was crowdsourcing like crazy. It was the community that really helped me make it through."

I remembered the rallies, the support of the community that embraced Santuario as this place where everyone could come together.

"Ask for help. But to ask for help—"

"I have to go home." I completed the sentence, in between sniffles.

Home.

~

Ollie and I drank three margaritas that night. The exhaustion from working endlessly and staying up with Liam and trying to finish stuff made me get drunk faster. It was around midnight, and people had started to get up from the booths and tables and dance to a Stevie Wonder song. I texted Liam to see if he wanted to come, but he was too exhausted. I hadn't planned to stay here for so long, but I need to just not think for a night. Just one night out of my head.

"Let's go." Ollie pulled me to the middle of the restaurant where some people were dancing.

I started moving my shoulders and my hips slowly.

"C'mon, Colombiana!" he said. "You can do better than that."

I moved my hips with more direction and range, my feet moving from side to side with my eyes closed to feel the vibrations of the music.

Ollie started singing the song and moving his long legs side to side awkwardly and his arms back and forth like he was doing the mambo.

"See? I don't know how to dance, and I still do it."

I imitated his mambo arms and laughed a deep belly laugh; it felt good to laugh again.

"It's liberating to do shit that you have no idea how to do," Ollie said, grabbing my hand and giving me a little twirl.

"Ollie!" someone called him as they approached him. Ollie introduced me to a couple, but I didn't catch their names or what they were saying; they were drunk and their words were slurred, but we all danced together without talking.

I danced with Ollie and the strangers, and I thought about how in Barranquilla, I'd be more self-conscious about taking up space. Was my hair okay? Was my dress too tight? People there were always noticing and commenting on how you looked. It was a form of capital: sometimes you had value, and when you didn't look as good, your value diminished or even disappeared.

But here, in New York, it didn't matter as much. For that night I was allowed to just exist.

"Stay for another drink," Ollie said, half smiling. He was just getting started.

I shook my head, thinking about the pile of work I had at home. "These freaking ballerinas." I said goodbye to Ollie quickly, with two kisses on the cheeks.

"Suit yourself, aburrida!" he said, waving from the dance floor and taking another shot with his new friends.

I stood in front of the restaurant, watching the snowfall in March. The temperature didn't feel as cold as it had before, the snow warming up the night. I put my hands in my pockets, too drunk to look for my gloves at the bottom of my purse. I walked to the train station and opened my palms to gather the thin flakes falling from the sky.

My clothes got wet from the snow as I walked home from the station.

I took everything off but my underwear and went under the covers quickly.

"Hey," Liam said as soon as he felt me in the bed. Without opening his eyes, he stretched his warm arm and cuddled me tight. "Your body is cold."

"It's snowing," I said, turning my head to kiss him. "You didn't come."

Liam said nothing, I could hear his breathing rising and deflating. He had fallen back asleep instantly. I closed my eyes, feeling that tiredness that arrives after you walked a long time and you thought you would never get home. My body relaxed, savoring this moment with him.

If I had learned anything this past month, it was that nothing was eternal.

CHAPTER SIXTEEN: THE HIGH LINE

I slept two hours that night, and woke up at 4:00 a.m. to do something about those posters. I was going to finish both projects even if it killed me.

How are you holding on? I WhatsApped Anton.
Fine, he replied, already up.

Mami had told me about the failed loans last night. I wasn't holding my breath on those. Community. I woke up groggy, thinking about that word and what it meant. Would Barrio Prado rally around us? It couldn't, if we didn't ask.

For now, money was the most important thing. I looked at the white pages, thinking about the women from home. What would they do if they were in my situation? Rocío would light some candles, Mami would spray herself with some luxurious cologne for confidence, and Abuela would glue her behind to the chair, not letting herself get up from it until she was done with the work. The house was dark and quiet. I made myself a big pot of coffee, sprayed some cologne on my neck and wrists, and lit all the living room candles. I closed my eyes, channeling my grandmother. Abuela's hands always knew what to do; they didn't need to wait for inspiration because they were always ready for work: chopping, seasoning, arranging, kneading. Abuela created art with every breath.

The room felt colder for a second, and the flickering light trembled as if an invisible force were threatening to blow it out but didn't. I took my white paper and colors and started thinking about the posters Ollie needed me to do. I started with lines like I always did and called her again.

"Abuelita." A chill ran through my uncovered shoulders, and as I started to get more and more into the drawing, I felt someone sit next to me at the dining room table. I couldn't see her, and I wasn't sure if this time I was imagining her, but I could feel her presence in the room. She was on the seat next to me, watching me draw as she'd done sometimes when I was in high school. When I was still drawing because I wanted to, not to make money out of it. Abuela was never a passive observer; she would tell me to add more of this color or that one or question me about my placing of things or proportions. This time, she stayed quiet.

Although I couldn't see her, I could feel her smiling: watching me return to something I'd thought lost.

~

By 8:00 a.m., I had a couple of illustrations ready, or at least the idea for them. If I had Ollie's illustrations, plus a partial of Charlie's work, I could make around $5,000—which was not enough to cover everything we needed at the restaurant, but in pesos it was something to give to the bank. I didn't know if they'd be okay with us starting to pay, rather than having the whole amount, but we had to try.

I got on the subway to Charlie's office. I took a couple of breaths—seeing her always gave me anxiety. I never knew I could feel this bad to see someone; her presence always put me on edge. Fearful of saying the wrong thing, of not standing up for myself, or rather of letting her walk all over me.

The doors opened wide, giving me the illusion I was welcome. Alma let me see Charlie right away, which was unusual, since she was always seeing people and approving things (mostly disapproving). I took a deep breath, as if I were gaining courage to see the dentist.

"Oh hi, Charlie," I said casually. She was wearing a black turtleneck and small baguette diamond earrings; her usual bob was in a tight short ponytail.

"iPad," she said without acknowledging me.

I handed her the iPad and sat down. As was my usual, I started babbling about my process. "So I did the color palette you asked for, and I tried different things for the storefronts. I wanted it to feel very Brooklyn but also—"

"What are these colors? This storefront looks unfinished."

I stood up to take a peek at what she was seeing. I had worked so hard on this that I'd barely slept all week. Before I could utter the words "Let me see," Charlie turned the iPad to show me what she was seeing.

"See?"

The colors were what we'd agreed on, soft colors. The storefront was inspired by my favorite coffee shop: a blue storefront with wide windows and dogs standing outside, with a big tree giving it shade. The lines were soft and watercolor-like because it went nicely with the themes of the ballerinas.

"It's a style." I cleared my throat. "I thought it would be—"

"Vi, you need to go home and send me a better draft. What is it with you? You usually are impeccable with your work."

This was the first time she'd given me anything that resembled a compliment, but it was really an insult. "Nothing is wrong. I worked really hard on this." My voice was getting louder.

"Well." She scoffed. "If you don't give me a quality product, I can't pay you."

I stood up; the chair screeched. "Sure, some of it's unfinished, but we agreed on a partial, not the whole thing yet. I've been trying so hard to complete this project per your specifications. I just thought—"

"I'm used to a certain standard. Go home and do your job—"

I didn't realize I had agreed to sell my soul to the devil. Charlie was dismissing me like she was the principal, and I was the misbehaving student.

"You know what? I'm done." The words came so quickly that I didn't have a chance to take them back. "Pay me a kill fee, it's on the contract," I said, taking the iPad from her hands. I turned before she could see me cry.

"I'll never hire you again." Charlie stood up.

"Great!" I said, storming out of the office, tears running down my face. Alma saw me before I got in the elevator.

"You did the right thing," she said softly and then turned back to see if Charlie was looking before she walked away.

I got in the elevator, finally able to cry freely. I had messed this up. Now I didn't even have enough money to give to the bank. Ollie's part would be only $2,000. The kill fee couldn't be much. I let myself cry until I arrived on the ground floor. The doors opened wide.

This had been another mistake, and yet I had stood up for myself. I hadn't let her bury my style—yet again—with her specifications.

It was nice to step out of the building, to feel the crisp air of March on my face, to know that the next drawing I did wasn't tied to a project, or for pay. It would be only for me.

The feeling didn't last long. The uncertainty returned as soon as I opened my eyes. I didn't have enough to help Caminito. I had so little to show for my years in the States.

We were running out of time.

~

That night, Liam decided to take me out to cheer me up. For Liam and me, going to the High Line was our adventure. It was an elevated park built on a decommissioned rail line. We loved feeling the vibrancy of the city from above, walking with linked arms as the seasons changed. We would have to take the train from Brooklyn and then get off at Union Square and walk twenty minutes to get there. We sometimes would stop in Chelsea to get fish tacos and Mexican beers at a taco stand close to the market; other days, we would just fill our tote bags with snacks and make a picnic day in the park with olives and fresh-made hummus. But that night, we did nothing like that. Liam said we were doing something different to change things up.

The first clue was the blue shirt that he was wearing that night. Silk and custom made, one of the only shirts like that he owned, a gift from his grandma. It was the shirt he wore at weddings, funerals, and important events at work. I was wearing jeans and a sweater, thinking that we were going to stop for fried fish tacos, so when I saw him arranging the sleeves of his shirt, I knew I had to change. I put on a dress in a panic and the only heels I had that didn't blister my feet after half an hour, sure that we would take the subway. And that's when I heard him, standing by the door.

"Vi," he said, the door already halfway opened. "Our cab is here."

The third clue was how when we entered the restaurant, the hostess called us by name as if she were expecting us. The waiter said, "We have prepared a special table for you." I walked to the table slowly, just behind Liam, who grabbed my hand confidently. I was floating in the restaurant, having the sensation that someone else was living this, not me. My spirit was still in a certain hot kitchen in Barranquilla, caught between the sauces, the tamales, and the tapas station. Anton's nervous energy making the rounds.

My heart was beating fast, and I was scared of what I was about to say, what I could do. My body was split in two—between the possibility of staying here and making a life with him, a life that I was sure would be good, happy . . . and then a slow simmering feeling in my stomach. What if I had to return home? I hadn't been there for Abuela, and that was something I would regret for the rest of my life.

If I wasn't there to see the future of Caminito through, could I live with myself?

"Vi." Liam's voice was serene. He moved the chair for me so I could sit.

We sat in front of each other, and he reached for my hands from across the table.

"I'm so happy you're here, where you belong."

I attempted a half smile. He still didn't get how complicated it all was. NYC was where I wanted to be. But that didn't mean I belonged.

"I wanted to do something special for us." He caressed my hands as he spoke, his face dimmed by the candlelight of the restaurant. "I know I haven't been the best. I know I pressured you."

Flashes of seeing Rafa a couple of days ago warmed my cheeks.

"I—" I said, knowing that I had to tell him I was thinking of going back home to figure out the future of Caminito. It was the best I could do.

I looked at Liam across the table. He was smiling, looking around without a care in the world. I was so happy with him, with the peace that traveled with him wherever he went. Liam had a curiosity about the world that I loved.

And yet, I couldn't stop thinking about Caminito.

"You've been great," I said, holding tight to his soft hands. "So supportive. I'm sorry I haven't been there for you this past month."

A waiter in a black suit came to interrupt us. He went through the ritual of handing the menus to us and asking if we wanted a bottle of wine. I thought about home, Berto running around the restaurant, trying to do everything. His casual tone with the customers, the banter. This waiter stood there as if nothing could touch him.

"Wine," I said simply. "You pick it."

Liam had a conversation with the waiter that I didn't hear; he showed him the menu, and the waiter smiled, pointing at other places on the menu. My head was underwater. I was here and yet I felt submerged, not able to think straight.

When the waiter left, Liam spoke, his smile radiant.

"I read this is one of the best restaurants in Chelsea. They're famous for their fish," Liam said, studying the menu. I thought about Abuela and Gabriel eating fish close to the market, the idle mood from eating heavy lunches in the midday Caribbean sun. Abuela knew that this was the man for her—the man she was destined to be with. I wondered if I would ever be lucky enough to have that certainty.

I put the large menu in front of me. I was sweating. Cálmate, I told myself, get a grip. Rafa is in Barranquilla; he's with someone else. He is not for you. But was I hearing Abuela's voice or mine? I closed my eyes and tried to listen.

But you love Rafa, a voice in my head said. You love him.

I loved him? Maybe I still loved him. Breathe in, breathe out. I took an exhalation that sounded like the waves hitting the sand.

"Vi?"

I lowered the menu. Liam had a worried expression on his face; he knew something was on my mind. "Crab cakes?" I said casually, but I knew my voice was breaking.

He nodded and smiled at me from across the table and squeezed my right hand, still covered by the bandage but healing properly at last after Mami had taken care of it.

"You look so beautiful," he said, bringing my hand to his lips to kiss it. I was wearing a burnt-orange dress I had found in the back of the closet. It was silk, and it usually stretched around my hips. That night, it fell on my hips and legs like it had never before. The constant worry was making me lose weight.

I leaned back in the chair, and I felt myself relaxing, something in my body giving in.

I opened my mouth to speak, closed it. Out of ideas. Words were una maraña, *a mess*, on the tip of my tongue. I could say a million things, or I could say nothing.

"I've had a lot on my mind lately."

Liam nodded from across the table. He exhaled in recognition. "I know that. I was there, remember?"

The waiter interrupted us once more; he showed us the bottle of wine. Poured me just enough.

"Delicious, thank you." I didn't even know how it tasted. It was red wine, and that was good for me.

Rafa crossed my head. Pictures in my head of Abuela and Gabriel, in a restaurant that Abuelo could have never, would have never taken her to—not even if he could afford it.

"Liam," I asked, taking a sip of red wine for courage. "I think I need to be in Barranquilla for now."

Liam half smiled and looked at the other side of the room and laughed. He passed a hand through his longish straight chestnut hair and looked at me, his blue eyes piercing me.

"Is this a test?"

I shook my head.

"I would support you."

"No." I hesitated. "I think I need to go alone."

I cleared my throat. My heart was beating fast, and my chest was as tight as ever, but I knew that I was saying the words I needed to say. For once, I felt that I could trust my voice, my decision. This was right. I knew Rafa wouldn't be waiting—that was a chapter that we had both closed. I was coming home because I knew that that's where I wanted to be.

Liam leaned forward in his chair.

"Vi, where is this coming from? Are you breaking up with me?"

"No, no." I shook my head. "I just need to be there for now, until we figure things out with Caminito. I just know you're tired of me leaving."

"I knew we had our issues, but a month ago I thought we were happy," Liam's voice got louder. He looked from side to side, careful not to make a scene. "It's not so much about you leaving, Vi. It's me fearing you won't come back."

I swallowed hard. I wanted to tell him that I had that fear too.

"We were." I paused, closing my eyes. "But after I went back, I realized that I wanted to be home. I need to be home. It has nothing to do with you. I love you." I searched for his hand. "I don't want to let go." I put a hand on my mouth as if that could stop the tears, the mess that my face probably was.

Liam leaned in from across the round table and pulled my hand away from my mouth. He took it to his lips and kissed it.

"I don't want to let go either." Liam's voice was breaking. "We don't have to let go. Vi, you were just there! What did that accomplish?"

"I know, I know. Not enough. Which is why I need to—"

"There we go again." Liam looked up as if he were searching for mercy. "Why do you care about that? It's the past. We have to live here now. Is it money? I'll lend you some money. Send it, and then we can see how it goes."

I didn't want to let go of anything; I was clutching to everything so hard. And yet something had to give.

"Vi, I love you so much. I'm just worried that you're putting our life on hold for a place that won't survive. You know this."

"I don't," I said, louder than I wanted. "Yes, sure, everything points in the direction of failure. But I just have this feeling—maybe it won't fail. Something will come up."

Liam shook his head. "Don't be naive."

We stared at each other, neither of us giving in.

"Vi, trust me. We can continue building a life. I know this means a lot to you—"

"You don't know, that's the problem."

He was closer, and I could see his eyes were watery, threatening tears. Liam never cried. "If I am honest with you, I could tell something was going on. Your distance—" Liam didn't even need to finish the sentence. Yes, the distance I had put between us.

"Are you sure this is not a rushed decision? Vi, we made a life here. I love you. When I picture my future, our future, you're always there."

Liam and I took a good look at each other. I studied his blue almond-shaped eyes, his long nose and pointy chin. The mole that sat just above his thick lips that I loved kissing. I wasn't touching his face, but I knew his soft skin by my memory, how if I reached and touched it, my hand would run across it like butter.

"I need to go home and think, but I don't want you to put your life on hold for me." At that moment, I wondered if the distance had come from anticipating that going back to Barranquilla would change me. That I feared I wouldn't come back the same.

I put up my hand to caress his cheek, wet from the tears.

"Are you breaking up with me?"

"Yes," I finally said, scared by the finality of what I was saying. "I am. It's not fair to make you wait," I said, fat tears running down my cheeks. Liam didn't say anything but rested his face on my hand.

"I don't understand it." He stared at me, wide eyed.

"Me neither," I said. Wishing I could make it work, that we could be together, but there was something that didn't fit.

"I love you," I said, across the table.

"I love you, too, don't forget."

"Never," I said, wanting to stop time.

~

That night after dinner we walked hand in hand in Chelsea. We had broken up, but we wanted to spend time together before we left; no need to spend our final moments fighting or saying sour words to each other. We were interested in making our hours together last.

We walked the New York streets. People coming and going in taxis and by foot. With grocery bags and Prada bags, with bottles of wine and colorful flowers that contrasted with the eeriness of a March winter night. We walked by people wanting to rush home to their children and by people who were just walking slowly, trying to escape routine. Everyone we walked past was ignorant of our situation, of how much our life was changing in that very moment. Our life was stopping and staying still, and the people of New York kept walking.

Our city, that night, stayed still so we could have the memory of a love that still remained—that never stopped—just for a little longer.

~

"Hey," Liam said to me later that night, when we were in bed. I closed my eyes, wanting to memorize this sacred ritual between us. The things that I loved from my day-to-day life that I wouldn't get to keep. "What was it that you were reading the other night?" He sat next to me, opening himself a little nook in between the messy sheets.

I sat up, wondering what I should say. I opted for the truth.

"It's my abuela's diary. She wrote it when she was young and newly married to Abuelo."

A pause, followed by another kiss. Every time we touched, I wanted to take my words back and our decision. I wanted to stay, even if I knew I needed to go.

"You know," he said, "I never imagined that I wouldn't meet her. That four years would pass and that we wouldn't get around to visiting together."

I nodded, thinking that in a way he had gotten to meet Abuela. Abuela's spirit was as restless as it was in life, as determined and as critical.

I put my head on his chest so I could close my eyes.

"What are you going to do tomorrow?"

I'd come home last night and bought a ticket for tomorrow night. I needed to get home as soon as possible. "I need to call Ollie and send him some stuff. Probably go for a walk too."

"Say goodbye to the city?" he asked.

At dinner he had held my hand like there was no tomorrow. These were our last moments together; after this trip, I didn't know if I would see him again. We both knew that in front of our eyes, our lives were bifurcating.

Liam dropped his book and kissed me. His familiar smell of mint and the warmth from the sheets his body still emanated. At that moment, I wanted to believe in reincarnation or in parallel universes. It didn't seem fair that we were running out of time, that I could love him and still need to let him go.

As we were kissing, I thought about our sea of things. Liam told me he was going to move; he needed a clean break. This apartment that was ours was now going to go to someone else who was going to inhabit it and make it theirs. Liam, whose skin was always so soft and whose blue eyes always calmed me. He knew me, and he had never doubted my ability to be a successful illustrator. I couldn't say that about my family or even about Rafa, who didn't know about my career. With Liam, I felt free in ways that I never would with anybody else. I wanted to cry. To never leave this apartment, but inside my chest, I knew that something stronger than me was pulling me home.

I wondered if a version of us would live in this space, trapped inside the places that had made our love what it was.

Perhaps the next tenants, whoever they were, would be able to hear that version of us.

~

After I ordered a glass of wine on the plane, I sat with a blanket over my legs and took a couple of sips. My eyelashes were still wet from crying over Liam and leaving New York. I didn't have a chance to say goodbye to Ollie or other friends; I just left. My presence in it left the city unchanged.

Liam took me to the airport, and whoever saw us kissing would probably imagine that we would be coming home to each other, that we always would. I caressed his soft brown hair; I memorized the scent of his neck; I kissed every corner of his neck. Knowing that this was the last time.

When it was time to go, we looked at each other, and I put a strand of hair behind his ear. His hands were comfortably sitting on my waist.

"You were home to me," I told him, meaning every word. Liam didn't say anything but kissed me on the lips again, one last time. I walked to departures knowing that homes didn't need to be forever for them to become a safe memory in your head.

I couldn't stop crying on the plane. It was as if I were mourning the death of a loved one. Liam had given me an easy love; he'd never made me doubt his feelings for me. He never withdrew, never played games. He gave me the love I needed after Rafa, a love that was safe and life affirming.

Cramped in the airplane seat, I opened the notebook and wondered what was next for Abuela after she had said goodbye to the love of her life. I thought about how, generations later, I was living a similar life to hers. My body was split in two, between the love that I had left behind and the place that I owed everything to. I thought about what we both owed, our burden, how despite everything we were still chained to what others expected of us. I opened the notebook and wished that if nothing else, I could help Abuela finally be free.

Another entry, this time without a year, just words.

> *Mamá fell in love with abandon and ended up raising a daughter on her own. Bisabuela: who knows if she ever loved anyone, but she ended up on another coast, struggling to understand life in another language. Stranded, sola, in a country she didn't want and as an early matriarch to an offspring who would never be able to understand her native tongue, Mallorquí. Who was I to love then and be loved equally? Who was Gabriel to lift the curse? Gabriel. Mi único amor. The only one I will recognize when I go to the grave, so maybe it's better if it ends like this, like nothing, brief and almost without consequences to the outside world. Something that can be removed from the world as easily as dust.*

I set the diary on my knees and peeked out the little airplane window. It was a dark night, and I could barely see any clouds.

Being in New York had opened me like a faucet. I tried crying quietly this time. I didn't want anyone to ask me if I was okay; I wasn't. I hadn't been ready to say goodbye to Liam. I wondered if Rafa hadn't been in my life, if I would still be with Liam. If maybe in another parallel universe, we were still together, curled up in bed, my face taking shelter in the always-warm corner of his neck.

Gabriel. Abuela's Rafa. I struggled to find a face for him, but a man surfaced in my memories, tall and gray haired, one of Abuela's friends who used to come to the restaurant when I was little and told me I was so smart, like Abuela.

Was that him?

Barranquilla 1967

> *A life with Amadeo is not life.*

I thought I could hold on for Paula, but I couldn't take it anymore. After a year apart, Gabriel and I are going to flee. First, just the two of us, and then we'll send for Paula, who every day understands more of my sadness. I fear for her and for what she sees, and in the same way, in a way that others won't understand, I'm doing this for her too. Gabriel and I have to go far first, and then we can move closer, perhaps even move back to the city and reopen the restaurant, but all of that is in the future, and right now, I'm concerned with packing my bags. Mamá will take care of the restaurant and break the news to Amadeo, who I don't think will be too bothered to look for me. He hates me.

Amadeo hasn't been home for a week, so tomorrow Gabriel will pick me up at night, and we'll drive to Bogotá, where he already has a job waiting for him and contacts who can help us find an apartment. I've never been to Bogotá, and when I think of the cold, I feel the hairs on my arms stand up. It feels exciting to start over in a city that doesn't feel familiar. Will it be too much for me to start over in a city where I don't know anyone? Will it be too much for Paula? I fear leaving Mami behind, I don't know life without her, but she wouldn't leave. Her feet are well planted in Barrio Prado; she wants to live and die here.

Despite the fear, I know there's so much more love in me than fear. I want Paula to have the opportunities that I never had.

Because I love her, I want her to grow up knowing she can be free.

I took another sip of wine and finished the plastic cup. Abuela always had so much love for us. I try to memorize those words, love over fear. I closed my eyes to try to sleep, but I kept reopening them. I couldn't stop thinking about Caminito. The debt. Without the money from the ballerinas, we were in even worse shape. What the hell were we going to do?

I closed my eyes again and took a deep breath, melting into the airplane chair. That night on the plane, I dreamed about Abuela again, but not like I usually did. This time she was young, in another life with Gabriel and Mamá as a little girl, reaching for her hand. She was in Bogotá, and no one knew who she was, but she was happy, her very straight black hair curled at the ends. And when Gabriel looked at her, he did so lovingly. They walked on a street very close together until they disappeared out of the picture of my dream, and all that was left was the darkness of a life that never was.

CHAPTER SEVENTEEN: CASA

The day I returned to Barranquilla, I focused on the heat. The way that my cheeks felt the burn first and then the rest of my body; how if I closed my eyes, I could feel the brisa marina; the way the city was carrying his name: "Rafa." Returning felt tight in my chest. A string of words I could say to no one because Rafa had closed the door on us and rightly so. Right now, I needed to focus on Caminito.

I told Mamá and Anton I was coming back, but to not worry about picking me up from the airport. I needed them focused at the restaurant. I opened the door to the house, left my suitcases on the floor, and greeted Abuela.

"Abuelita," I said, talking out loud in the living room as if the house could hear me. I took off my shoes, and my soles touched the ancient wood. This was home, and a warmth took over my entire body. I had given up so much in order to complete my circle, and I'd arrived here, but for now, I decided, I would let myself feel the joy.

"I am here," I told her.

The windows were open, and although the enormous house was quiet, I could hear her. In the susurros of the wind, the brisa, I could hear the whisper of her voice.

"Bienvenida," her voice said, the word resounding around the house.

Every step of the old wooden staircase sounded with the familiar crik crik crik. Every step recording the decision I had made, the life I had left behind.

This is home, I told myself. The entire house felt enormous, and at the same time, it belonged to me. I took in the immensity of the halls, the checkered floors that had been there my whole life, the windows that led to Barrio Prado, a place stuck in time. This was mine to inherit, the good, the bad, and the stories.

I walked up the stairs, taking in once more what was always meant to be mine.

~

When I was little, Abuela always told me that when she died, she was going to pull my feet. If I didn't shower promptly when she told me to, she would pinch the fat on my arm and tell me that when she died, one night she would put cold hands on my toes, just to remind me she was there.

I felt the pull in the middle of the night, the grip on my big toes.

"Abuela." I woke up, that name on the tip of my tongue. My body was burning, and my bata was soaking wet.

Abuela was sitting on the end of the bed, her face as brown and freckled as ever. Her smile intact.

"Mija," she said, her voice sonorous and calm, as if she were singing a song we both knew. I held on to her voice. "Volviste." *You came back.*

I sat up, careful to not move too suddenly. I didn't want her to disappear.

"You read the diary."

"Gabriel—" I let out a sigh. Gabriel and Abuela had loved each other; every word in that diary was an unfulfilled promise, a caracol that had never returned to the center. "Is that why you're here? You want me to look for him?" My heart beat fast with the thought that she would say yes—where would I even begin looking for a man who perhaps didn't want to be found?

I heard Abuela's laugh, as sonorous and deep as if she were alive.

"No, mija, that story is closed. What had to happen already did. I have you and your mom, and that's enough."

"Pero Abuela—"

They always say that ghosts long for love that they've lost, but Abuela's voice seemed serene.

"I gave you that notebook because I wanted you to learn from my mistakes. I know that I tried to separate you from Rafa. I see now that was wrong. It was you who had to make the choice. Not me. That's what I wanted to tell you."

It made so much sense. Abuela had told me that she needed to tell me something and to not forget. The diary was all there. Her fear and overcoming it: the desire to choose love over fear.

"I'm still scared, Abuela," I whispered. I was scared that I wouldn't figure out how to save the restaurant; I was scared, now that I was here for a while, of seeing Rafa with his girlfriend, walking the streets we had walked together many years ago.

"Tu qué quieres, Vi?"

What do you want? That question was privilege, one that was rare in our family. How rarely had I asked myself that question.

"I was afraid—all those years, I'd been terrified of repeating the same story." I was so anxious, scared of saying the wrong thing. "What do *you* want, Abuela? I want to listen to you."

I looked out the window. The mataratón was shaking from side to side. The whisper of the wind made it sound like ghosts were circling around the house.

Abuela's spirit sighed. "I want you to stop being fearful. That's what I want."

I stayed silent for a moment. Contemplating how fear had been at the center of her life. Had she fought for Gabriel?

"Vi, just because I felt fear doesn't mean you should too. If you want Rafa, go find him. If you don't, then stay put. If you want to stay with Caminito, do it." The room suddenly felt colder, and I felt something getting close, as if Abuela was placing a hand over my heart. "Cierra los ojos." *Close your eyes.* "Listen."

I closed my eyes, and I listened to the impossible quietness of the house, the old wood and my old friend the wind. I listened to the sound of Abuela's spirit, like rain. I knew she wouldn't always be with me. I took a deep breath. Feeling something I hadn't felt in a long time, ever since I was a teenager and I would sneak out to the kitchen to cook, in Caminito, even when I wasn't wanted, I always felt a deep-rooted belonging.

Abuela and I hadn't held hands much when she was alive. The Sanoguera women were short with their words and also with their touch—I always thought Abuela wanted me to grow up strong, not sensitive, so I could be prepared for life, and yet—I was who I was. Tears were always around the corner for me.

"Is this what you want, Vi. A life here?"

I nodded, my body shaking with recognition. I didn't want to stay here just for a moment, not letting go of my life in New York fully. I was done with things halfway; I wanted this. "Si. That's what I want." I pushed my shoulders back and stood up straight. "I think this is what I wanted all along and didn't let myself have."

My heart ached for the things Abuela had wanted as well and never let herself live fully.

"Even if Caminito fails?"

I thought about it, the nightmare of Caminito becoming a ruin. "Yes, even then."

"Mija." Something pressed against my chest. Was it her touch? "Where I am, I no longer feel fear for you. Just trust."

I opened my eyes, and Abuela's spirit had left the room. The tears that were running down my face would not stop—as if someone had opened a faucet, the tears were abundant and ever flowing. I had a past life to mourn; the list of ghosts that followed me was long. An image of Liam and me wrapped between the sheets in our apartment in New York flashed in my brain. But these ghosts were also a part of my history.

Returning meant choosing a life I had run away from many years ago and realizing that it was the life I was destined to live.

I looked at my nightstand and picked up my cell phone. It burned on the tips of my fingers. I wanted to call Rafa, but I needed to be respectful. All those years ago, I had made a decision. Now, he had made his. We had decided to let it rest. I needed to find my place in Barranquilla, in Caminito, without him. If I looked for him, I risked losing the real meaning of why I had come home.

I went to Abuela's room and searched in her closet for the cofrecito—the little chest of wood—in which she kept the pictures of us and the pictures of the restaurant. I opened it to the odor that everything had in this house: salt and moistness. The comejenes, termites, were getting to the pictures too. I shook them to get the dust away, a sadness in my chest seeing how some of them had little holes around the edges.

"Malditos comejenes," I said. It made me feel like time was running out, that if I didn't do things fast enough, the house was going to disappear and be eaten with everything inside of it, including me.

I picked up a picture that had Bisabuela, Abuela, Mamá, and I standing in front of the restaurant. I was around eight in the picture, and I was wearing a dress with blue polka dots. Mamá had her arms on my shoulders and was looking ahead as if the future stood in front of her.

I felt a warm hand on my shoulder. I jumped.

"Nena," Mamá said, standing behind me. "It's just me."

I laughed, not sure if relieved or amused. In this house, anything was possible. I stood up and wrapped my arms around her, holding her as tight as I could. Mamá smelled like jazmín flowers or like a spring afternoon. Mamá and I didn't ever talk about things too much; I wasn't sure we ever would. And yet, something was shifting for us. We were closer than we ever were.

"Ay." She was surprised by the hug. Slowly she placed her arms on my back. "You were only gone a week," she said as I unwrapped my arms from hers. Mami had a full face of makeup on, and her lips were a shade of bright carmine red. There was something hopeful in the way she was always so put together, always ready for whatever life threw her way.

"Still." I turned to the pictures on the floor. "I missed you."

Mamá looked at me for a moment, unsure of what to say. Las Sanoguera had been raised with stern words. Sweet words were reserved only for deathbeds and, on occasion, every time someone achieved something or did something right. Mamá turned her eyes to the pictures and knelt on the floor; the heels on her shoes stood out like daggers.

"Qué buscas?" she asked, shaking the pictures to liberate them of the dust, but too much had settled; by now it had become another layer of the picture.

"Gabriel."

"Who?"

I sat Mamá down, and I told her the story about how I had felt Abuela's presence ever since I came back home. I didn't spare details about the dreams, her words about not wanting to live afraid. I told her about the pulling of my feet—Mamá laughed and wiped her tears at the same time. I showed her the notebook.

I waited on the floor as Mamá read the pages. I sat in front of her with my legs crossed, waiting. From time to time, I lifted my eyes to gauge her expression, but I couldn't guess much. Her eyes were focused on reading what had been an unknown part of her childhood.

When Mamá was finished, she handed the diary back. Her thin eyebrows met in the middle, and Mami, who was not often speechless, paused for a couple of seconds, staring at the window.

"Maybe I met him, and I didn't even know."

"Parece. Bisabuela did too. But you were probably very little, do you remember?"

"No. Why would Mamá want you to read that diary?" she asked, still looking at the pages. She traced Abuela's handwriting gently, as if she were staring at a picture of her rather than her words. "Why not me?"

"I don't know." Many things were still a mystery to me. The fact that Abuela gave me a greater percentage of ownership of Caminito, or that she had manifested herself to me instead of Mami. Perhaps, just like I had done, Abuela wanted me to tell Mami. She didn't want us to live lives dictated by society or family expectations. She wanted us to choose what we wanted.

Even if we made a mistake.

Mamá held the notebook open, her eyes still lingering on Abuela's words.

"We missed you at the restaurant. Not that Anton would tell you that." Mamá half smiled.

"I wouldn't think you would tell me either," I said, still sitting across from her on the floor, wanting to get closer to her but not daring to move.

Mamá put a hand on my knee. Her eyes got lost in the corner of the room, as if she was in deep thought.

"We need to save this place. For her."

"I brought home some money—not as much as I wanted, but at least we can give some to the bank. What are we going to do, Mamá?" I asked, hands on my knees.

She stood up, shaking the dust from the back of her flowy white dress.

"Ay, Vi," she said, putting the notebook on the table and smiling wide, as if she had a plan. She put her hands together and said, "Vi, in this family we always find a way."

I took a deep breath, hoping that she was right.

~

Anton, Mami, and I went to the bank bright and early the next morning. We had money in an envelope and knots in our stomachs so tight we were struggling to breathe. The woman from the bank was stark and quick.

"I think you don't understand, Señorita Violeta," she said, lowering her glasses and looking me straight in the eye. "This doesn't even cover fifteen percent of the debt."

"Give us ten more days." Mamá lifted her head, dignified. "I know Mamá was late in her payments, but for many years she was a good client of this bank. She always brought her business here. When we recover—"

The woman closed the file and stared at the table. She sighed. "There are procedures in place. I can't simply—"

"But you can, no? You certainly can."

"Ten days. Not a day more."

Anton squeezed my good hand as tight as he could. We both stood up straight, trying to hide our smiles. "Ten days," Mamá said and shook the woman's hand. She turned to us, smiling quickly, before the manager could see her.

The bank told us that in order to qualify for a payment plan, we had to come up with $6,000 more to make a dent in Abuela's debt, our debt. I lay awake at night, sweating and thinking about what it would be like to really lose it all. I had dreams about driving in front of Caminito knowing that it didn't belong to us anymore. In some nightmares, Caminito was a car wash; in others it sat empty and decaying, a playground for ghosts.

In my restless nights, an idea came to me. But it was an idea that wouldn't be easy. It came packaged and wrapped in shame. Abuela would not accept it; Mami wouldn't either. But it was the only way.

We had given so much to the community, and now it was time to rely on them.

~

Mamá came up with an idea to reinaugurate the restaurant, to make an event that showed people that we were still here. I had put all the food for the evening on my credit card, and although I was terrified by taking personal debt, I wanted to trust it would work out. Everyone was invited, new and old clients. People from outside the barrio and from within. Even if we were not able to save it, at least we could give it one last hurrah. A send-off before they would sell the house to become a real estate company or something of the sort. No, I admonished. I couldn't tell myself this. We would make it work—but how?

Mami was at the kitchen counter absorbed in her notes. Papers were scattered around her, and she was biting her nails. She was looking at the books I had organized when I first came here. She was not very good with numbers, but she could probably identify all the ceros and minuses.

"Vi." She looked up.

"Qué pasa?" She opened her eyes wide. "Pasó algo?"

"The bank, Mami, you're seeing the evidence. We need more money, or they are going to take it all." I sat down at the counter. I felt weak; I rubbed my eyes to wake myself up from the nightmare of losing Caminito.

"Something will happen, Vi. I know it."

Anton came from behind with a basket full of vegetables. "What are we talking about?"

"The restaurant," I said. It was the only thing we had been talking about lately. I wished for Mamá's unwavering faith. That was typical of Barranquilleros: they took positivity and turned it into delusion.

I shook my head. "The reinauguración needs to be a fundraiser. We are going to have to shift direction, ask for money," I said, wondering if that had been Mami's intention when she came up with the idea.

Mamá left her papers on the table and laughed as if I had told the funniest joke she had heard in her entire life. Anton, as was usual, was caught in the middle of us. He put the basket on the floor, and I wondered if he was going to back me up.

I knew what she was going to say: Abuela would die of shame. She would never allow it. Abuela would rather be dead than to—

"Ni pensarlo." She stood up and served herself a cup of coffee. It was midnight. "No. Imagínate. Tu abuela would die again, we don't beg for money. We are days shy from the event. How would we do it?" she shook her head and sat down on the kitchen stool, chuckling again. "Estás loca."

"Mami." I reached for her arm and locked eyes with her. "We don't have any other choice. You were there at the bank, you negotiated. We just don't. It's either getting the money or letting the bank take Caminito. Do you have someone that could lend us the money?"

Mamá looked down and sighed, her body rising up and down. She sat up straight, gathering her dignity.

"No."

"Vi is right." Anton spoke up. "I don't think right now is the time to clutch our pearls."

Anton and Mamá looked at each other. He nodded, as if he were telling her that even if there was doubt and resistance, we needed to do this. It was our only choice.

I brushed her arm softly. "Get on Instagram. See if you can get the word out." Mamá approached social media with the charm she had in real life. It came naturally to her to come up with banter and mini essays about food and history below every picture. Mamá was a beautiful writer. I pondered if she had perhaps inherited her gift with words from Abuela. Caminito had become a sort of warm, constant presence on social media, always talking to people and with constant commentary—like ladies gossiping in rocking chairs. Mamá was always replying to comments and posting.

She put a pencil above her ear just like Abuela used to do.

"Do you have a plan?" she asked, gathering her pages to take notes.

I nodded, telling Mami and Anton the plan I had crafted in my restless sleep.

~

The next morning, Mamá's hair was braided in two shiny buns. She looked beautiful in the morning light, and her brown skin had a reddish tone that it hadn't had when I'd seen her more than a month ago. She was flipping some arepas for us for breakfast, and the kitchen smelled like freshly ground coffee.

"The reinauguración is in six days. Mamá is doing great on the Instagram campaign. Now, Anton, how's the menu coming along?"

"Perfect, capitán. I made these fried chicken colombinas that are deliciosas." Anton kissed the tips of his fingers. I half smiled, thinking that Abuela would die again if she realized we were going to serve fried chicken in Caminito. I served everyone a refill of coffee in Abuela's minuscule coffee cups.

Caminito was entering a new phase. One that Abuela hadn't conceived. She had liked that the restaurant was upscale but still was a place beloved and cherished in the neighborhood. She loved it when couples who thought they couldn't afford to celebrate their wedding in the restaurant asked anyway, and she lowered the price so they could. But it was precisely those free and lowered prices that had gotten us where we were. That, and the unforgiving passage of time. Now, under Anton's direction of his food, the restaurant had a more casual vibe where people could enjoy a glass of wine and some apps. But also a good meal if the occasion required it. We were shifting to be what the neighborhood needed.

"I think we still should keep the neighborhood feeling. Whatever comes next," I said as Mamá put an arepa in front of me. I went to the fridge and took the butter out, which would slide smoothly on the arepas.

"There's queso blanco," she said, pointing at a block of fresh cheese someone had probably gifted her. In the neighborhood Mamá was quite the personality. People were always giving her little gifts.

"What do you think, Mamá?" I asked, brushing my hot arepa with a layer of butter and sprinkling it with cheese, and for a moment, I felt thankful. For being home, for eating the food of my childhood. For the impossible. Mami and I were not good at getting along, at understanding each other. And yet here we were. Making an effort to stay in each other's lives.

"I think she wanted us to try, and we're trying." Mamá ate her arepa plain. She took her first bite and looked out the window, the day sunny and warm already.

"Why do you think she didn't teach me, then? Why did she never want me in her kitchen?"

"Ay, Vi," she said, lowering the arepa. I could hear annoyance in her tone. "What do you think she did when she left the restaurant to you?" Mamá shook her head as she ate another bite. "Isn't that worth anything?" She smacked her lips, smiling and looking at her plate.

I nodded and took a deep breath. The knowledge made me feel warm inside. Abuela's love was so big that even if she didn't have the words to say it, she proved it with her actions. She trusted me with the place that had meant the world to her.

~

Anton had left to prepare for the service that night. We were working on the Instagram announcement when I heard a knock on our door. I opened the door and saw Rocío, but she came in so quickly she didn't even turn to look at me. Mamá said hello to her while pouring herself another cup of coffee.

"So did you finish reading the diary?" she said, entering the living room in an ample white dress that made her look like she was floating.

Mami and I looked at each other. Rocío poured herself a coffee as if she was in her own house. "She never left," Rocío said as she sat with her purse resting on top of her legs.

"What?" Mamá asked. "What are you talking about?" Mamá poured herself more coffee too.

Rocío made a sound with her teeth indicating that she didn't want to explain.

"Ay, niña." Rocío sighed. "Escucha. She was getting ready to leave with Gabriel to Bogotá, packing her bags and arranging everything with her mother, and then the day that she was supposed to leave, she didn't come out of her bedroom. She hid there for days. I remember because I was a child back then, and from our house we heard the alaridos, the screams, of your bisabuela yelling at Emilia to get out of the room."

We stared at her.

Rocío took our silence as a cue to keep speaking.

"Entonces Gabriel waited and waited outside, and Emilia's mother, que en paz descanse, God rest her soul, had to explain to him that she wouldn't come out of her room. She didn't know what was wrong. He went up to ask her, knocked on her door until his knuckles hurt, but Emilia wouldn't open. Emilia's mother told him to come the day after to see if she would come out the next day, but after several days of coming to the house, he gave up. He knew Emilia would never come to the door." She looked around the room. Mami's face was as white as paper.

"She didn't shed a single tear, Vi. Not in front of me, at least." She locked eyes with me. "After a while, Emilia opened the restaurant like nothing had happened, and the rest is history."

My eyes welled up with tears. For all the things she wanted and she didn't get. Fear had gotten the best of her. I could see her room, in this house, staring at the window, wanting to go but not being able to move.

I recognized a lot of myself in Abuela—in that desire of wanting to jump but being scared.

"Y ya? That's all? She didn't look for him or nothing?" Mamá said, her chin resting on her hand and her long red acrylic nails curling on her cheek.

Rocío let out a big sigh and rested her hands on her knees, as if she were gathering strength and paciencia.

"Niña," she said to Mami, her brown eyes wide and bright. "She lost a part of her that day, no ves? What good would it have done to look for him?"

"He wasn't going to wait forever, Mamá could have gone after him, she could have looked for him . . ." Mamá stood up and started walking around with her cafecito.

"Mami, she didn't feel ready," I said, standing up, trying to meet her eyes. "Who are we to judge?"

Rafa had also cut ties after I'd declined his proposal. He hadn't even picked up the phone again.

Would Rafa and I be destined to the same fate? We weren't because there wasn't "Rafa and I." And yet it was in my head how the stories were linked. Gabriel and Emilia had loved each other very much and had never taken that step.

"Niñas." Rocío clapped to dissipate the air. Mamá and I were standing in front of each other. We turned to look at Rocío. "She stayed because she thought it was the best for you, Paula. And then, sí, quizás she wasn't brave enough. But she always said that if it wasn't for that, for that horrible marriage with Amadeo, she wouldn't have you, and if she hadn't stayed, maybe Vi would have never been born. Life as it is exists because she stayed."

Mami and I sat back down on the couch as if we were kids and our teacher had told us that it was enough. I turned to look at Mami; she had a hand on her mouth, as if she was deep in thought. Abuela had chosen her—she had chosen us. I wished someone had told Abuela that she didn't need to always be strong, that it was okay to sometimes choose herself.

"Gabriel left for Bogotá without her shortly after. I know that she played around with the idea of tracking him down to ask him how he was doing, but I don't think she ever did. She always wondered what would happen—if he would even want to see her. She said she was too ugly and too old for those kinds of things."

"So that's it?" Mamá said, waving her delicate hands in the air. "She instills this fear of men in me my whole life. She stayed with Amadeo, who was good for nothing, and then I grew up with him in and out, in and out, for what? All that complaining and all that bitterness, and you tell me there was an out all this time? And she didn't take it. Mami was a coward."

It was all too much. Mamá, instead of hearing that Abuela loved her, and sacrificed her happiness for her, was hearing that Abuela became bitter because of it.

"Mami." I turned to look at her. Her face was as young as always. I shook my head, thinking that perhaps she still looked like a teen because she had never assumed any responsibility. She had always let Abuela take all the bullets for her. I was done blaming Abuela for our mistakes; we had done plenty by ourselves. "Don't say that, you don't know."

"I would have rather grown up with someone who was a bad mother and happy than a bad mother who was angry," Mamá said, perhaps to herself.

I could have told her that she didn't know what she was talking about. Mamá had always chased around after men, perhaps looking for happiness. And as a kid, I knew what it was to have feelings that you couldn't name yet. To miss someone whom you didn't know but whom you saw every day. The memories I had of Mamá during childhood were of her doing her makeup in her room, always giddy at the possibility of new love. But she never seemed worried for me.

I had a string of bitter words I wanted to say to her on the tip of my tongue, but I resisted them all. She also had known having a mother whose body was there but whose spirit was elsewhere.

"I think she was trying to let you know what she was too scared to tell you when she was alive," Rocío said, turning to me, her voice calm and unaffected by Mamá's outburst. "Vi, she wanted you to know that she had been wrong to send you away. She was scared that you would repeat the old story. Yo nunca te dije, I never told you . . . I thought it was not my story to tell, but enough time has passed. I just wanted to make sure you knew."

I closed my eyes, knowing the ways that Rafa resembled Gabriel. The way that both our loves seeped under our skin until they followed us everywhere. Abuela had been scared for me to have a love like that. After all, it hadn't turned out for her—she didn't want me to suffer.

"We can't say we have been too skilled at love either," I said, assuming the *we* instead of the *you*. Looking at her and her rage against the woman who had carried so many of the burdens of her life, I decided I was done with that cycle. Now, it was time to understand my mother.

Mamá moved her slender neck and stretched her head from side to side. She sat up straight and took a deep breath, lifting her coffee up for a toast. "Mami," she spoke. "Te perdono."

I forgive you. Her bottom lip was trembling, as if she was about to cry. I resisted an eye roll and smiled, biting my tongue. Her eyes were looking ahead, focused, as if she was seeing her in the kitchen with us. She raised her coffee cup to an invisible figure.

Mami, te perdono, I said in my head, too, as I looked at her. Her beautiful face was untouched by age. The skin around her eyes was full of little wrinkles but not hardened.

"To Mamá." She raised her coffee cup, and we all followed, my anger toward Mami dissipating.

CHAPTER EIGHTEEN: COMUNIDAD

Abuela was not on board with the reinauguración.

Shame had followed Abuela to the afterlife; her spirit tangled in the qué dirán, and the vecinas would never stop talking about us asking for money to keep Caminito afloat. Ni pensarlo. No way, we had to think of our dignity!

"Pero Abuela," I said, spreading butter on toast late at night. I leaned on the kitchen counter and ate it slowly. "We don't have a choice." I was deliberate with my words. Pronouncing every syllable. After I'd told her I was staying, Abuela had been overjoyed—she was hoping that I realized my place was here.

"Volviste," she said, the word resonating in the house. But the happiness didn't last long; when I told her about the plans for the crowdsourcing, she was angry again.

"Vi, we have a reputation." Abuela had always told us that the only thing we had was our dignity. Nothing else—todo lo demás el tiempo se lo lleva. *The rest, time takes away.*

It did: time took everything away. Love, places, possibilities . . .

"Abuela, it's not like we won't give people things for their money. I'll do illustrations for people of the barrio, some friends of Anton's will play music. It will be a whole event. Caminito is a Barrio Prado landmark, the community will want to help—"

"No." Whenever she spoke, the windows trembled, and I could hear the sound of her spirit, the ruminating of an old machine. "I won't let you do it."

I clenched my jaw.

"Las Sanoguera never take money from anybody."

"Pues yo si," *but I do*, I told her, taking the last piece of bread to my lips. "Abuela—" I tried, knowing that Abuela held grudges. This wouldn't be something that she would get over in a couple of hours. Abuela would be mad at me for a while, and yet I remained there, standing in the dark eating another piece of toast. The pressure in my chest was not there. I felt content, clear minded, calm.

This was what we needed to do.

I took a breath, and fully, for the first time ever in my twenty-eight years of life, I trusted myself.

~

The day of the reinauguración came quicker than we all expected. Abuela was still not talking to me, and although I didn't hear her, I would feel her around the house. Late at night, when I was up planning things for the party or early in the morning, before I fully woke up. Abuela was on the breeze that entered the window, in the creaking of the wood, and in my dreams. I could tell that Abuela was there even if she didn't make herself visible.

All I wanted was her bendición, and yet, like the stubborn spirit she was, she wouldn't give it to me.

For the reinauguración I wore a dress that had belonged to Abuela. It was made of a red satin fabric, and it had a V-shaped neckline and a cinched waist. The dress was long, past my ankles, and it had a wave of drama to it. When I looked at myself in the mirror, my shoulders covered in bright-red satin, I wondered if Abuela ever got to wear this dress with Gabriel. If this dress carried the secrets of their impossible love. Images of them dancing in old salones came to my head, of them kissing when they thought no one was looking.

I wore her pearl earrings, which she didn't wear so often but that I had seen her wearing in pictures. I pinned my curls up and put some of her palo santo cologne on my neck for good luck. I uttered a prayer under my breath and said the name that now lived under my tongue: Rafa.

I prayed that tonight would go well—that a miracle would save us.

"Lista?" Mamá said, opening the door of the room without knocking. She was wearing a green silk dress and diamond earrings. I wondered if they had been a gift from her new lover.

"Lista," I said, looking at my phone once more.

I was hoping to hear from Rafa. Maybe he had heard about the inauguration. I knew I had to respect his choice, but I couldn't help wanting him to be there that night, even if we didn't speak. I could see him, wearing a black shirt tight on his shoulders, standing across the room. My whole body would unravel wanting to speak to him. I offered Mamá my arm, and we walked down the stairs and outside the house without saying much but arm in arm. In my head, all the things that I hadn't told her in all these years. All the time that was lost was now circling back and giving us a second chance.

We stood outside the restaurant, and we saw it all illuminated under the fairy lights: with a salsa band playing and full of guests, old and new. I exhaled a sigh of relief. For Mamá, for Abuela, for Anton, for me. The night was perfect, clear skies and heat. I closed my eyes and took it all in. This was the start of our miracle, or this was the end of the road for Caminito. There were no in-betweens.

Mamá grinned as she saw the place she had grown up in, the place that had signified so much heartbreak and loss. She squeezed my arm.

"This is going to work, mijita." Her voice was full of hope. I bit my lip, incapable of saying anything.

"Go to your booth. I'll be in the kitchen checking on Anton." I imagined Anton running around the kitchen like a chicken without a head, agitating every cook, every waiter. "Ve," I urged her.

I sat in the illustration booth on the patio. I was making portraits for people from the community. People had many ways to donate that night: neighbors could donate by paying for their seat at the table or giving more money if they could afford to. The illustrations were also by donation, and the band that was playing "Tres Gardenias" in the background was a gift from Mamá's boyfriend. Everyone from Barrio Prado and beyond was here. Mamá called the event "Salvemos a Caminito," *Let's save Caminito.* Abuela would not have approved.

On the patio, under a string of fairy lights, was a big sign that said "SOS Caminito," and although no one had asked her, Doña Rocío walked around with a midsize collection bag that would send Abuela to the grave for a second time.

"Donation for Caminito," she would say, approaching tables of people who dropped loose bills in her bag. Neighbors and customers were already here, enjoying the salsa music and drinking Old Parr and wine like someone was getting married. Long flowy dresses and long silky blowouts that still smelled like heat: this was how the people in Barranquilla attended events, like they were Hollywood stars and not like this was the Caribbean where the heat melted makeup. I scanned the room for Rafa. Men were wearing roomy and well-ironed guayaberas, nursing drinks that we were charging more for than every other night.

I took a deep breath and leaned back in the chair. No Rafa but my first customer glanced at me, her eyelashes impossibly long.

It was one of las mellas, Doña Rocío's twins. Sabina, like a model, posed for a portrait. I traced the long lines of her neck, the way her slender nose pointed upward, and the slight wave of her hair that, past her shoulders, dissolved into straight locks.

Sabina had always been the most romantic one and the softest. Sabina was sweet, and Celina García was practical.

"Your earrings," she said, touching hers. "Where did you get them?" Abuela's earrings were little Spanish abanicos made out of gold.

"They are my abuela's," I said, passing my fingers over the smooth finish of the gold and pearl. I wondered if they had been a gift from Gabriel, perhaps a parting gift. The last thing he gave her before he vanished.

Sabina smiled and pointed at the midsize diamond that rested between her collarbones. "It was a gift."

I nodded, wondering if she would have a happy ending, unlike Abuela. I shaped her eyes the way I had been taught at art school, minding the proportions but also doing my own thing. "New love?" I asked.

"Viejo," *old*, she said, looking around to see if her sister was around. She leaned in and lowered her voice. "But we're allowed keepsakes, right?" She laughed, although I was sure this wasn't a joke. "Y Rafa?"

Y Rafa. Great question. I wondered if my eyes, looking over to the door of the patio every two minutes, didn't give me away.

"I think I screwed up," I said, looking at her sister, García, approaching from the back. Walking slowly, every curve of her body being hugged by the maroon silk dress she was wearing. She put a hand on her sister's bony shoulder and pushed her long black hair back.

"I want one too." García pointed at the drawing of her sister, although hers would be exactly the same, the only difference being the color of the dress. The García sisters were like that: if one wanted something, the other immediately craved it. "What are you talking about?" She pulled up a chair. Sabina barely looked up at her. They were so used to following each other's footsteps that they didn't need to say hello to each other anymore. They knew the other one was always behind.

"Rafa." Sabina looked at her sister.

"Cómo está de bueno," García said, lifting her thin eyebrows and putting her elegant hand on her cheek. She was remarking on how hot

Rafa was. I rolled my eyes, and Sabina did too. "Are you guys getting back together? Ufff, mija." She exaggerated a yawn. "It's time."

I shrugged, doing the finishing touches on Sabina's midnight-blue dress.

"No," I said. "I'm focusing on Caminito right now."

"Ay, mija." García took a pocket mirror out of her sequined purse and started applying lipstick. "Right, it's always like that with you two. Eventually you'll come back to each other."

I wasn't so sure. Despite everything that had happened, my steps didn't feel any lighter. I still felt heavy and grounded to the floor. I was torn between wanting to respect what we agreed on and wanting to shout my love for Rafa from the rooftops. To say his name to the wind as much as possible so Barrio Prado would return him to me.

I felt a familiar hand on my back. It couldn't be. I turned slowly, my heart beating to the drum of the salsa.

It wasn't.

"Ven." Anton pulled me by the arm. I imagined the kitchen in flames or the bank at the door ready to claim the restaurant in front of all the guests. The gossip spreading around Caminito like a fire.

"Momento," I told las mellas, leaving the unfinished drawing on the table. "I'll be right back."

I went to the kitchen with Anton, where all the new cooks we hired for the event were pacing around the room with the rhythm of a Swiss clock. The room smelled like basil and tomatoes, a fragrant base of well-spiced soup.

"Qué pasa?" I asked, claiming my arm. "I thought something was burning por lo menos."

"Ay, Vi," Anton said, putting a hand on his mouth and one his hips. "I think the food won't be enough, come," he said and walked to the exit. I followed him into the street, and we watched together the long line of people waiting to get in. I grabbed Anton's hand. "Wow," I said, overjoyed and baffled by the response. People had rallied around Caminito.

"Vi, no time for crying," Anton said. I sniffled, quickly drying my tears. "What are we going to do?"

Mamá stood at the door, going over a list. The food wasn't going to be enough. The place wouldn't be big enough for all these people.

"Mamá." I went over to touch her arm.

She turned to me, as calm as ever, and smiled as widely as if she were starring in a commercial. "There are some open tables in the dining room. As soon as people start to leave—"

"And the food?" I asked, too loudly. Two women from the queue lifted their eyes from their phones. My sign to lower my voice again. I turned to them and put a hand over my mouth. "What are we going to serve all these people?"

"Go to the kitchen, see what you have. Come up with something." She was digging her long nails into my skin. "I'll stay here."

I went over to Anton, who stood by the exit, looking at me as if he expected me to come back with the answer. I shook my head so he would know that Mamá hadn't given us much direction. "She told us to deal."

Anton and I stood in front of the bodega, looking at what we had. Tomatoes, onions, and vegetables but not that much meat. La paella was already gone, and people had devoured the tapas and the bisque. We were out of dough for the pizzas, and it would take too long to make more.

"What cuts of meat do we have?" I asked Anton, who went into the big fridge with his shoulders hunched back and walking as if he were a fantasma—already defeated. "Only costilla." We only had ribs.

I went through the catalog of plates that Abuela used to make.

"Bolli," I said, thinking about the velvety rib soup Abuela made with thin noodles and lots of cilantro. She would serve the soup with a side plate of cabbage and soft potatoes to drench in olive oil. The soup was comforting and light but with the power to make people awake and alert. Everyone who ate that soup always had trouble going to sleep.

"Start chopping cilantro, Vi," Anton said, rushing into the kitchen, his hands carrying all the ribs that he could.

~

In Barranquilla, for parties, people made big pots of soup and sancocho. It was a tradition that was as old as the city, to close down the block and to make a big olla de sopa that would feed the entire barrio and everyone who was hungry. It didn't matter if you didn't know them. Abuela had her own version of sancocho: bolli, a costilla broth with noodles, olive oil, potatoes, and herbs.

The noodles in the sopa were perfectly cooked, and people raved about the sopa—how it had the power to make everyone sober again. People ordered more and more drinks, and Mami smiled, thinking about the long bills people would have to pay at the end of the night.

I stood with Anton by the door of the kitchen as we watched the customers at their tables sipping their soups quietly. Las mellas were lifting their soups and drinking the soup as if they were drinking cups of tea. Doña Rocío was waving her hands, telling them to lower the bowls—but las mellas didn't care. They kept sipping and slurping their noodles.

I looked at Anton, who was exhausted, and it wasn't even 10:00 p.m. Outside, there were still people waiting to come in. I wondered if we had made any progress. Anything that would get us closer to the $6,000 we needed.

"Mamá," I said as I watched the woman who had birthed me stand in the middle of the room with a microphone. I closed my eyes, mortified. The last time she had done something like this, she had almost ended up buried with Abuela.

Anton looked at me. His brown face had lost all color. "Ay Dios," he uttered.

"No se preocupen," she said. "I'll keep it quick."

As if it was part of an enchantment, the guests stopped sipping their soup. Las mellas lowered their plates, and the restaurant became quiet, ready to listen to Mamá. She spoke about Abuela, how she had created this place from nothing. A way of survival for women like her—who had often been ignored. But she was so capable of building anything she wanted, and tonight we were honoring her memory.

"Doña Emilia," Mamá said, lifting a glass of wine, "was the soul of Caminito. Her soul lives in the walls, in the spices of every plate, and in all the efforts we will continue doing so this restaurant lives on." Mamá locked eyes with me and Anton, who got a glass from a serving tray Berto was holding. "Vi, Anton, come here."

Anton and I looked at each other, surprised that she would share the spotlight with us.

"Here they are, the team that makes it all possible." I put an arm around Mamá and one around Anton. We looked at the crowd, some from Barrio Prado, and some unfamiliar faces. The lights, the music, and the smells of Abuela's foods. I wanted to take it all in, tonight. This second chance.

"Por Doña Emilia," she said, "and for las Sanoguera." The whole restaurant lifted their glasses, and we lifted our glasses with them. Abuela usually manifested herself in the house, but that night I could feel her in the restaurant, seeing Caminito full once again.

"This is all because of you because you came back," Anton said.

"This is all of us," I told him, feeling her close.

"Do you think we're going to make it?" he asked, his eyes still on the crowd that had now started eating and drinking again. The infinite conversations filled the restaurant. The salsa came back on full blast.

"We've made it so far," I said, walking to the kitchen to check on the food.

"Nena." I heard Mamá's voice call me. She was with her new lover, the mysterious man from the funeral. So different from Mamá's usual taste, and yet, I hadn't seen her so happy in so long. He was short, with short-cropped hair and a kind expression. Nothing like Mamá's old lovers, who were handsome and with full heads of pepper-and-salt hair. Mamá looked at him with tenderness, like I had never seen her look at anyone else before: with trust.

Mamá looked happy; for once she didn't seem anxious or overeager. She was serene.

"This is Vi, mi hija," Mamá said proudly to Dario.

"She looks just like you!" he said. "Dario, pleased to meet you."

I wondered if he was lying to us; no one said that about Mamá and me. She was tall, and I was short; she had wavy black hair, and mine was brown and curly; her face had dramatic cheekbones, while my face was rounder with high cheeks. Her brown skin was a couple of shades lighter. And when she walked, her hips moved to a secret melody, while mine often hung awkwardly with every step, like an ill-fitting piece of clothing.

Dario had green eyes with brown spots in them and a soft, kind expression.

"Vi, encantada. No one ever says we look alike," I said, looking at Mamá, whose arm was wrapped around Dario's. "She's so much lighter."

"I guess I'm starting to see the resemblance," Mamá said, pointing at Anton with her lips. He had brought me a plate of food with pan con tomate, Rocío's quibes with Anton's touch of mint, and pimientos rellenos.

"Let's eat," Anton said. "I'll grab a plate for myself too."

"Permiso." I smiled at Dario, who never let go of Mamá's hand. She looked enamored with the safeness he emanated. Mamá, who would never give up love, had found someone who was willing to give her that all-consuming love that she needed. The reassurance that it would never leave. The kind of love that you would fight for even if no one had ever taught you how.

Mamá deserved that kind of love—we all did.

Anton and I ate quietly, standing around a corner of the patio while we saw the couples dance around the restaurant. The pimientos were fresh and vibrant with a touch of spiciness.

"What do you think?" I asked Anton, who looked tired but satisfied, his straight black hair falling heavily across his forehead. Abuela wasn't around to tell him to get haircuts.

"This is my dream," he said, gazing at his empty plate. He looked at me from across the table and gave me a smile that showed a row of perfect white teeth. "Let's dance," he said and stood up, offering me his hand.

The song playing was one of my abuela's favorites, "Piel canela." As Anton twirled me around, his melodic voice resounded in my ears. Every word that came out of his lips was coated with honey. I danced along with him, laughing nervously at how quickly he twirled me around. Despite the food I'd just eaten, my stomach felt empty, like I was floating in the restaurant, my feet above the ground. The reinauguración felt real. If it didn't work out, we still had this. We had customers at every table for the first night in years. Abuela's dreams were coming true—our dreams.

Las mellas, who were witnessing the scene, shouted at the same time: "Ajoooo!" Surprised at Anton's light feet and the way he twirled me around on the dance floor like I was weightless.

"Are you not going to finish the drawing?" García said, lifting a champagne glass.

I lifted my index finger, indicating that I needed one more minute. I wrapped my arms around Anton and hugged him like there was no tomorrow. I closed my eyes and moved instinctively to the sound of the music.

"Baby, who taught you how to dance?" I asked him.

"Doña Emilia," Anton said without hesitating. "She was an incredible dancer, tú sabes, no?"

"No, I didn't know," I said, feeling his feet slow down. I imagined Abuela dancing with Gabriel, in some bar far away from her house and holding him close while she could. With every turn feeling like he was about to slip away from her.

"When I had my first crush and I started going to parties, she taught me how to dance after she heard me tell another cook I was too scared to ask girls to dance at parties."

I smiled, moved by the image of this Abuela I didn't recognize.

"Of course, girls." He paused, half smiling and lifting a brow. "I felt like I couldn't tell her back then."

I wasn't sure Anton had told the truth to Abuela about who he was. This city was flexible and forgiving, yet at the same time as oppressive and punishing as the force of a hurricane. "Did you ever tell her?" I said, thinking about how Anton had also had to sneak out and see people in the late hours when he was young.

"Oh, ella sabía, she knew," he said while we danced to a slower bolero. He gave me a soft twirl. "She never said anything to my face, but she knew. Of course she did, Vi."

"Do you think she minded?"

"I think she thought it was my business. Pero no, no creo. I think she loved me just as I was." Anton's eyes were watery, and I knew that he didn't like expressing emotion like this. Not in front of so many people. I cupped his face in my hands and kissed his cheek.

"She did," I said, thinking about all that Abuela had trusted Anton with. How fiercely she had loved him. How protective of him she had always been.

"You're a good dancer too," Anton said, as he held me close and put his head on my shoulder. "Lo que se hereda no se hurta."

What you inherit you can't steal. Even if she hadn't taught me, my feet seemed to move to the rhythm of a remembered beat.

~

I sat down to finish Sabina's portrait and then started García's, who told me to paint her with shorter hair so the drawings would be different. It was 1:00 a.m., and the party kept going. Anton kept serving soup, and Mamá took care of the door and the checks, with her hostess smile that was bright as the sequins that many of the women were wearing.

That night I did Doña Rocío's portrait, followed by people from the neighborhood I hadn't even met. I painted long noses, eyes that were almondlike and mysterious, and green eyes that were as wide and open as Bisabuela's eyes had been. I painted blue eyes like the sea that tugged at my heart and reminded me of Liam. I drew and drew, waiting to come across a strong chin, the brown eyes that always knew things about me, and his thick brows that I loved so much, but Rafa never sat in my chair.

As I was rubbing my eyes to scare the tiredness away, a man with a full head of white hair sat down. I couldn't tell his age; his face was wide and clear despite his snowy hair. He had a kind smile. He reminded me of someone, but I didn't know who.

"Do we know each other?" I said, taking a new white page for the drawing.

"No, mija," he said. "I don't want a drawing. I'm too old for that. Me and your abuela were good friends."

It couldn't be.

"What's your name?" I asked, the cold breeze lifting every hair of my arms.

He half smiled and shook his head. "It doesn't matter. I'm here to give you something."

I stared at him, wide eyed, mad at myself already for not knowing what to say. He took an envelope out of the pocket of his shirt.

"I came to give you this—for your abuela."

"Ah." I searched for the words I seemed to have forgotten. "Abuela—she . . ."

"Oh, I know," he said, standing up. He was a tall man, elegant, and as he turned to leave, he said, "But that's still for her. I owe her that." Despite his somber expression, there was a softness to him. "Perhaps you could take the letter to her grave next time you visit. Or you can open it and read it if you want. I guess it doesn't matter anymore."

I closed my mouth. "Ah, no, I won't. I—"

"Goodbye, Vi," he said, leaving me to wonder how he knew my name.

"What's your name?" I asked as he walked away, his dark suit blending with the dark night.

"Gabriel." He turned, his smile as perfect as I had imagined it.

A sadness took over my body for what life had chosen for them. He waved adiós again, and I lifted my hand. Wanting to capture this moment for Abuela, this goodbye that didn't belong to me but to her.

The eternal return we were always making.

~

A party always kept going until the food and the alcohol were gone, and this one kept going long enough for Anton to get tipsy, which he never did when he was working. There was plenty of food still, and people kept paying for drinks and opening bottles of wine that they paired with the food that the cooks kept producing. Trays kept going in and out of the kitchen, and I thought Anton was about to cry from joy when Mamá put an arm around his shoulders and told him, "Buen trabajo, mijo."

The musicians who had been hired to play for three hours kept playing for way longer than expected. Rocío and las mellas kept bringing them drinks and picadas that they kept eating as they sang and played salsa mixed in with bolero. They had just finished a version of

"El día que me quieras" when I wondered if Rafa was coming at all. He wouldn't be coming, I told myself. He couldn't.

"Vi, why do you keep looking at the door?" Anton asked.

"Rafa," I uttered, and Anton and las mellas nodded, as if they already knew without my having to tell them. "He's not going to come," I said out loud, hearing the sadness in my voice. I understood: we had made a choice. And yet when it came to him, there was always this reckless part of me that held on to hope.

It started raining, which meant we were all stuck here. Anton went to the back to make sure the generator was running in case there was wind and we stayed without lights.

Barranquilla was well known for the arroyos, the strong currents that could take entire cars with their force and spit them into another part of the city, the currents that had drowned people and entire families. Kids who would never return to their houses. I knew no one could possibly come in. Barranquilleros had a respect for the rain: when there was water in the city, the place became paralyzed until the last drop was on the asphalt.

"I think this is a lovely sign," Doña Rocío said, lifting her whiskey. I could hear the tangling in her voice and in her tongue. Las mellas rolled their eyes, perhaps thinking that a speech was what was coming next. "Aguacero, rain, means abundance and healing. On a night of a reinauguración, this could only mean blessings, Queridas.

"Ashe," she said, lifting her whiskey glass higher. Las mellas, Mamá, and I raised our glasses. "To Violeta and Paula. Salud. And for the memory of Doña Emilia."

~

I crossed the little path from the restaurant to the house. Mamá, Anton and I went there to count the money. We were giggling, not from the wine but from the success of the night. Anton had a bottle of wine tucked under his arm, ready to celebrate.

I opened the door, expecting Abuela to be there, waiting for us.

The bank had been very clear—in order to qualify for a payment plan, we had to deliver a payment of $6,000 more by the end of the week. Twenty-five millones de pesos.

Abuela, when it came to money, used to say, "Cuentas claras, chocolate espeso." Which translated to something like *clear agreements and thick chocolate*. I never understood that saying, but as we sat there, all three of us, I felt how true those words had been. If you had clear numbers, then you knew how much you owed.

Mamá was standing by the kitchen counter, pencil in her hand, deep in calculations. Anton stood by the counter, pouring us all big glasses of wine. I glanced over the living room table. Gabriel's letter sat there, unopened.

"Y?" I asked, glancing over to Mamá, who had just added a couple of scribbles to her notepad.

She looked over to us. The lines around her mouth pointing downward. She put the notepad on the table.

"Vi, call the bank," she said, directing her eyes to Anton, who turned off the stove although the coffee wasn't ready.

"Qué?" he asked. "Dime ya."

"With the money from the last round of champagne, we have twelve millones."

We were missing around $3,000. I stood up and put my hands on my head. Who could I call? No bank would lend me money—not when I was the one who owned the majority of this sinking ship. I thought about Gabriel—the initial investor. But Abuela wouldn't have wanted that—the story was closed, as she said. The cycle was over. I took a deep breath, knowing that our pride had hurt us so deeply, for generations. My cheeks felt warm, and I needed to sit down. The pressure in my chest returned. "No," I uttered. "Who do we know that could give us a leg up?"

Mamá shook her head and chewed on her pencil. "Espera," she whispered, only to herself.

Anton served himself a cup of coffee. "I've spent the last bit of my savings completing the money for buying the oven. And then the day of the apagón—"

"Anton!" I yelled at him from across the kitchen. "Why wouldn't you tell me? Why did you spend your own money?"

Anton shrugged. "Because it's my restaurant too." He lifted a brow, and I knew not to say anything else. He was right: Caminito belonged to all of us.

"Bueno, ya," Mamá interjected. "Stop, you're both distracting me."

Anton crossed his arms and turned his eyes to the kitchen window. "Are you sure you're counting right?" he said, examining his nails. They were short and shiny, as always, but he was focusing on anything to avoid looking at me.

Mamá nodded without responding, punching numbers into a calculator.

"Mami, give me that—you're not good at numbers."

I checked her calculations, every number from the champagne to the soups to the appetizers and all the food everyone had consumed, but her numbers held true. The realization that we were about to lose the restaurant hit me. We were so close, and yet it didn't matter. The bank didn't care that you'd tried—they only cared that you had the money. Mamá's phone rang, and she jumped from the surprise—she stared at the screen and then went into the other room without saying a word.

"I'm sorry." I looked over to Anton, who was still not looking at me. "You're right, it's your restaurant too."

He shrugged and took a sip of coffee. If we were short, it wouldn't matter who it belonged to.

Mamá came back to the room a moment later, shoeless and without saying a word. It was almost as if we weren't even there. Anton and I looked at each other, wondering what now. Mamá leaned on the counter and started running the numbers again.

"Mami?" I hesitated, wondering if I even wanted to know.

She looked up.

"I forgot about the crowdsourcing—I just checked the website." Mami's eyes were wide and bright.

Mamá showed us her screen. We had a little over $1,000. But that still didn't put us in the clear. I had nothing; with all the plane tickets, my bank account was in the ceros. In fact, I owed credit card bills that I wasn't sure how I was going to pay.

My first thought was that Abuela would have been even more mortified—not only were the Sanogueras asking for money; they were asking for money on the internet, where there would be a record of it. And despite the shame, it had not been enough.

Mamá and Anton were frozen, not saying a word. We were so close.

"Anton, what do you think?" I asked, desperate for an answer, anything that could help us.

He shook his head slowly. "I got nothing, Vi."

Anton had given it his all, and it wasn't enough. I wanted to make right for him, for us, for Abuela. Mamá started biting her nails again.

"Maybe Rocío?"

"No," Mamá said. "She's not working right now, and she was talking about not having enough for the house payments."

I thought about that mystery investor she had mentioned and had never brought up again. It had probably fallen through. I paced around the room, feeling fire on the tips of my fingers. I couldn't fail Abuela, and yet here I was doing exactly that.

What would she have done? She wouldn't have given up. I searched inside me for that fight that Abuela always had in her. She would think about her team, what they needed in order to keep going.

"Let's go to sleep," I announced. "I know this feels like defeat, but it isn't yet." I grabbed Anton's hand; he was on the verge of tears. "It isn't yet. Like Abuela used to say, tomorrow will be another day. Let's sleep on it, see where we can get the rest of the money."

Anton and Mamá looked at each other, not ready yet.

"I insist, we're no good this way." Every bone in my body hurt—from worrying, from being on my feet. I was exhausted, and I knew they were too.

Anton said goodbye with kisses on the cheek. We didn't have a chance to drink the bottle of wine. Mamá shortly after went upstairs, going up slowly as if she was waiting for me to get a call, or a text, any type of good news that would get us closer. I could tell she had been ready to celebrate.

~

Abuela was nowhere to be seen. I worried she was still mad at me because of the crowdsourcing, but I needed her right now. I needed her advice. I sat in the living room. I hadn't read the last page of the notebook because I'd wanted to make it last longer, but I knew it was time. I put the envelope that Gabriel had given me on the living room table. This letter was not for me but for Abuela to take on her journey.

"Aquí está," I told her. "It's for you."

"Hmm," I heard Abuela complain. "You don't listen. Qué terca, mija. So stubborn."

She was insulting me, and yet I exhaled a sigh of relief when I heard her voice.

"We don't have money, Abuela," I said, sitting in the darkness. Shame traveling from my throat to my belly, traveling through my veins, wanting to swallow me whole. "You trusted me, and I failed you."

"Mija, you don't know yet. I left you the restaurant because I trust you. I don't want you to live with regrets," she said. "I don't want you to live with fear like I did. Trust."

"Abuela." I let out a sigh; I didn't deserve her compassion. "Aren't you curious about the letter?" I asked. After all this time, Gabriel had returned. He must have known that she had passed, but maybe he'd wanted to see Caminito, what it had become. I wondered how he felt. If he, while walking through the restaurant, also felt her.

"You told me you don't want me to live with fear. But what about you?"

I heard her words: "Open it."

I closed my eyes, wondering if her spirit would be there when I opened the letter, if she was eager to hear what it said. I dreamed about everything that was possible—I had left for the States thinking I would find a life I could make my own, and instead, I had realized my life was here all along. In the familiar streets, in the rhythms of the restaurant.

The envelope wasn't tightly sealed, and when I opened it, I saw there was just a note. I read it out loud, hoping that she was listening:

"To my only love."

Hidden behind the note, there was a check for eight millones and five hundred thousand pesos: $2,000.

My hand started shaking; I couldn't believe what I was seeing. How deep and how vast his love for her still ran. This would make it so we had enough to give to the bank.

"Abuela? Abuela?" I called, but nothing. I hoped she was there, that she could see that even after her death, her only love still believed in her—in the place they had dreamed of once together.

CHAPTER NINETEEN: LA TROJA

I was so overjoyed I couldn't sleep. I walked up the stairs slowly, looking over my shoulder to see if she was following me, but the only sound was the crik crik of the stairs. It was too late to call Mami and Anton; it would have to wait until tomorrow. I anticipated their happiness and their relief.

I sat on my bed, ready to be washed away by her words. Despite every prediction, we had managed to make it work.

Barranquilla 1970

> *Yesterday was the day where, with the help of Mamá, we put the red sign outside that said "Caminito." The restaurant didn't have a name before, and it was mostly Mamá's recipes that occurred to her and the ones that Abuela had taught her in a mix of Spanish and Mallorquí. Pero ahora, after the haze of the first years of marriage had passed and Paula spent most days at school, I realized that the restaurant, like all things, needed a name.*

I paused, taking the notebook to my chest. How fitting that this was the entry I was reading now, about the start of it all.

Mamá and I thought long and hard about what would be a good name. Mamá mentioned that perhaps we could call it "Carmen." Or "Palma," to honor the land of our ancestors, and all the names sounded perfect when we first thought of them but didn't stick.

Then one day, Mamá started cleaning the house as she did every day after she finished giving Paula her breakfast and turned the radio on. "Caminito," her favorite song, was playing, and she said with the broom in her hand: "This is going to be a good day."

And that was that. The name of the restaurant was decided. Caminito after Carlos Gardel's song, Mamá's favorite interpretation, and after his soft voice, which Mamá said resembled angelitos cantando.

The restaurant was named after a love lost, and the restaurant was a reminder, too, of what I had lost, so although we never spoke about it, Mamá and I, we knew the name fit the place perfectly. An old song that played on loop.

Mamá said when she saw the sign that perhaps it was too red. The color was bright, and it resembled more the color of cherries than it did the color of brick, which is what we initially wanted, but it didn't really bother me. I paid more attention to the beautiful Argentine lettering and the flowers that were woven into the calligraphy, which we hadn't asked for but the artist gave to us anyway. A restaurant that was always filled with flowers with their essences and different smells lingering in the air.

Mamá and I directed the whole operation from afar. A little higher! Lower . . . a la derecha, a la izquierda! Until it was perfectly aligned to both our tastes. Mamá said that she thought the name was after the long path this restaurant would have, that Paula could inherit and perhaps one day her children. I don't like to think that far ahead, but maybe she's right.

Quizás a path that one day would take Paula and her children to Argentina or even to Spain to see the lands that we never visited and that took Abuela all the way here. The parts of us that we carry with us from a memory that doesn't belong to us but that we are destined to shelter here, day after day, until the only thing that is left in the earth is our legacy.

I thought about Anton, Mamá, and how we worked tirelessly to defend this place, which was ours. I could see their faces the next morning when I told them, "Let's go to the bank. We have everything."

~

"Six thousand dollars," Mamá said to the bank manager. "In cash."

Mamá turned to us and smiled. I wondered if she had dreamed of being able to say those exact words.

The manager counted the money and recounted it. She raised an eyebrow and took a piece of paper to give us.

"This is a payment contract. There's still money that you owe, but certainly know we can put you on a payment plan."

I released a breath, the tightness in my chest I had been carrying all these months finally dissolving. Anton put a hand on my knee and squeezed it.

"Don't be late."

"We won't," I said, taking the pen to sign.

~

We left the bank. Anton and Mamá hugged each other like old friends. I couldn't wait to go home and tell Abuela.

"Ahhh." I hugged them both. "We did it," I said, not able to let go. I could have screamed out my joy, but after all, I was Emilia Sanoguera's granddaughter. I expressed my joy on the inside.

Mamá and Anton kept laughing and hugging. I stood there, looking at the distance, feeling the warmth on my cheeks and the sun in my eyes. This was a return to beat the other false returns; for the first time, I was carving a space for myself, for my family, in the city to carry old traditions and to start anew. The cars, the restaurants spreading out in front of me, the bicycles and buses. Abuela's beloved Barrio Prado. I closed my eyes and hoped that we would always continue to honor her.

~

My life in Barranquilla, months after arriving, started feeling more calm. Owning Caminito as a team made it feel easier. For so long I was chasing something that I wanted to be mine and mine alone. But I had never anticipated how good it felt to fight for something with others.

I started getting used to the heat, and waking up in the house no longer felt strange. My life was slower and smaller here; I didn't get lost like I did on the New York City streets, and there was not as much space to wander in my old Barrio Prado, but there were other things. Heavy naps after lunch with the heat of the afternoon, on the balcones, and the food and the people I grew up with. Although she didn't live in the house, Mamá spent time in it often, gossiping with Anton and me and eating his arepas with queso and chocolate. She would come on Sundays and sleep the siesta with us, and then she would stay with us for pizza and a movie. Sometimes Dario would join us too. Mamá would rest her head on his shoulder, and I would realize that part of why it was worth it for me to come back was so I could see Mami finally get everything she wanted.

On Fridays and sometimes on weekends, I would have a couple of drinks with Anton or las mellas. Most of the time they had to drag me out and beg me not to go home after a beer. Barranquilla, with all its comfort, only made me want to sleep. It wasn't like New York, where there were always possibilities and the chance of something exciting around the corner. No, my hometown made me feel like everything was slow going and familiar like an old sweater that's ill-fitting but that you were still excited to wear.

The restaurant was recovering slowly—we were steadily on a payment plan, and although we were making more money, the payments still had us feeling very tight, but I couldn't deny it was a path forward. Neighbors and people in Barranquilla started to go to Caminito again, and it was as if they suddenly remembered it for what it was. It had been a group effort: Mami's Instagram magic, Anton's efforts to make the restaurant more affordable and with influences from Colombian and Lebanese food, and the sleepless nights of running the books, crafting plans, and trying new things. And also help from the comunidad, and Gabriel.

The heart of Barrio Prado, where people could have a drink and read a book or eat the best paella of their life, just a couple of blocks from their homes. Abuela's memory was as present as ever—even if the house was quiet.

Life passed in the city and in Barrio Prado without a word from Rafa. I often tried to remind myself that it was okay; I hadn't come home to be with him. I had come home to save Caminito, to claim a life that now I realized had always felt right. And yet when I couldn't sleep at night, or when the house felt cold and sepulchral without Abuela, I would think about him. The way we always understood each other, the deepness of his voice, the way that when his skin would touch mine, even by accident, my whole body would warm up.

Las mellas told me they saw him in La Troja.

"Was he dancing with someone else?"

They looked at each other and shrugged.

"No, I don't remember," said Sabina.

"Me neither," said García.

Which meant yes. I had gone to bed many days with the question in my head. I was back. I was here. Barranquilla without Rafa felt wrong.

Should I look for him? Should I say something? I contemplated asking las mellas, but I knew that this was a decision I needed to make on my own.

He had been very clear, and I didn't want to mess up his relationship. What would I even tell him? That after all these years, I was still in love with him? That I had never been able to forget him?

"Why does it matter?" asked Sabina.

"Because I still love him." The words got unstuck, and they slipped out of my mouth. I put a hand on my mouth, amazed by what I had said out loud.

Las mellas looked at each other.

"Then you should tell him," García said.

"Ujum," Sabina said. "Don't let it get too late."

I thought about Abuela and Gabriel—how they would never meet each other again. Where does all that longing go? At that moment, I wished that people meeting in the afterlife was a thing that happened. That Abuela would wait for him, and he knew exactly where to look. That when they were finally together, they were able to say everything that had been quiet in them for years.

~

I was nervous as I put on a shade of red lipstick. I looked at myself in the mirror; I looked the same. My curly hair was still a mess. I shook it to give it more volume. "Tu puedes, Vi." I told myself I could do it, I needed to do it. Las mellas knew that Rafa would be there. It was a

Friday, and on Fridays Rafa loved to go to La Troja to drink a couple of beers.

The place was a corner salsa club illuminated with bright white and red lights. It had an open layout with plastic chairs and was always packed to the brim. "That place doesn't even have AC," I said, looking down at my jean shorts and tennis shoes. I was wearing an old rock-band T-shirt and my hair up in a pin because I couldn't be bothered with the big triangle that was my hair on the Caribbean Coast.

"Y?" Sabina asked, her hair cascading down her back, wild and powerful like a stream. "Nunca sabes . . . you never know who could be there." She took another look at the mirror, her reflection shining back at her. Her lips were cherry red, and García's were a shade of maroon. Their beauty often took me by surprise. Together, they looked majestic, like a painting. Dressed in colors that gave the color of their skin a particular glow that only they had.

"Lista?" García said, taking my hair out from its bun and shaking it in vigorous movements with both her hands.

I touched my forehead. It was damp, and I hadn't left the house yet. The back of my neck was tingling. I was so nervous, scared I wouldn't even know what to say. Was I ready? No, but I wanted to be. I needed to be if I was ever going to break this chain of cowardice and fear over love. I stood up straight.

"Lista," I nodded. Sabina looked at me and put a curl behind my ear. She smiled, her face as radiant as if it were illuminated by the sun.

"I know." She beamed.

"Taxi is here." García looked at her phone, missing the whole scene.

I looked at myself in the mirror, despelucada, already sweating, and with bags under my eyes from working nights. I was ready.

~

Anton and some friends of las mellas were already waiting for us there. They were drinking Aguilas, Costeñitas, and shots of aguardiente. Anton, as soon as he saw me, stood up, brought two beers, and started dancing with me. He tried to move as far away as possible from them and gave me one of the Costeñitas. I took a sip and asked him what was going on.

"Ay, Vi, I can't stand them," he said as he gave me a twirl. "They're driving me insane talking about negocios and trips to Miami." I looked over at them with slick hair pulled back and shirts with huge logos on them, tight bermuda shorts, and moccasin shoes they had probably bought on a trip to the States.

"I think las mellas are dating two of them."

"Uy!" he said, putting his hand on his forehead. "No, no, no. Las mellas están locas."

I laughed, looking at the group of boys who talked as if they had potatoes stuck in their mouths. Now, they were talking about yachts. I put my arms around Anton's neck and looked up, anxious about seeing Rafa, anxious about not seeing him. Would he show up?

I had never dated or kissed anyone in this city, besides Liam, who wasn't Rafael. The city felt so empty without him, such that if I said his name, the wind would carry it and make it reverberate in the air.

"Vi, Vi."

Anton moved his shoulder to make me look up.

"Mira."

I looked and saw Rafael kissing las mellas on the cheeks. My heart started beating fast; the bass of the salsa vibrated in my ears. I got dizzy and had to close my eyes just to escape the sounds of my head and La Troja.

"He's here," I said, stating the obvious, not believing my eyes. Rafa, sharp bones, dark eyes, and passing a hand through his wavy hair. He was here, and he was by himself. I sighed, relieved that he was alone so I could talk to him freely. Rafa was smiling at las mellas and telling them something and making them laugh. He looked happy and well.

I touched my hair; it had expanded with the fury of a thousand suns. This damned humidity. I could feel sweat starting to accumulate on my hairline. "Do you think those two invited him?"

Las mellas told me that for sure we would run into him. But I hadn't realized that it was because they had told him. Típico? I could hear my heart beating. I took a deep breath and tried to organize the thoughts in my head. Maybe when I was face to face with him, the words would come out, rushing, ten years of accumulated words free flowing like a cascade.

"Probably," Anton said, shrugging. We had stopped dancing, and I wished we hadn't, just to make the encounter more natural. "You know those locas. But he came. That's something, verdad?"

"Tal vez." I said *maybe*, wondering if him being here meant that he was no longer with the person he had been seeing, Marta. But maybe he was here just to say hello. I didn't need to get ahead of myself.

"Vi," Anton said softly. "I know you want to talk to him. Ve," *go*.

I stood straight and gathered myself. One foot in front of the other, I told myself as I walked to him.

"Vi," Rafa said, with his grave voice. He seemed surprised to see me. Had las mellas not told him? Perhaps they hadn't, and Rafa would have never come if he'd known I was going to be here.

I took a deep breath. My feet were already in position to turn around and leave. But no, I had made it here. We had made it here.

"Rafa."

I smiled. We had both said each other's names as if we were discovering them for the first time.

"How are things?" I put my hand on my forehead. I needed to say something better if I wanted to keep him here.

Rafa lifted a brow and smiled too.

"Bien," he said, laughing. "The same." Under the white lights of La Troja, I noticed the new freckles on his right cheek. I wondered when he had been in the sun and with whom.

"How's the restaurant?" Rafa asked, retreating to keep his distance. His stance was wide, and he was moving from side to side. He couldn't stand still; he was as nervous as I was.

"Bien, súper bien," I said quickly, not wanting to get into it right now. This was our time. It was finally our time, if he was up for it. I had decided to tell him how I felt. Okay, I told myself. Tell him.

Rafa nodded and took a sip of his beer. His eyes were expectant; he was waiting for me to say something.

"Rafa."

"Vi."

We laughed. We'd both spoken at the same time.

The people and the party on the streets were getting louder and louder while I stood there, with a million words stuck in my throat. At my feet were a multitude of plastic caps and used lemons. Rafa looked as if he wanted to say something, too, but wanted me to speak first. I couldn't blame him.

"I need a shot," I said, thinking that after the aguardiente burned my throat, I would be able to say what I needed. "Do you want to come with me?"

Rafa followed me to the bar, bringing along the sweaty beer in his hands.

Anton was in a corner, trying to talk to one of las mellas' friends who kept shouting over the music. I tried to make eye contact with him, but he wouldn't look my way, so I took Anton's bottle of aguardiente and poured us shots. I handed one to Rafa without asking.

We lifted our glasses in silence. Clink. The sweet and tart aguardiente burned on its way down my throat.

"Mami has been talking and asking about you nonstop. She was wondering about what happened with Caminito," Rafa said.

"What did you tell her?"

"La verdad. That we hadn't spoken in a while."

Doña Magdalena could probably see through me and my confusion—she probably knew that I'd wanted to be with Rafa from the moment I first saw him after all those years. Magdalena had always rooted for our love.

A song played in the background. A familiar song we used to love. The beat was a fast tempo; my feet started moving, too, from memory.

"Quieres bailar?" I offered him my hand, uttering a prayer in my head. He nodded, taking my hand in between his and leading me to the dance floor, pulling me close. I closed my eyes, taking in his scent of pines and lemons. The closeness I wasn't sure I deserved.

I was having trouble following his feet. He kept twirling me around, making me guess his next move. If he moved right, he then gave me an unexpected spin. I tried to keep up, my legs feeling weak. Exhausted. Hadn't we danced before many times? Shouldn't I be used to dancing with him by now? Perhaps we hadn't. Couples danced in public spaces where they could be seen and admired, and we really hadn't been in the light much. If we got another chance—if he gave me another chance—I thought to myself, in between rapid twirls, I would make a point of having us dance in front of everyone in this city. Every dingy bar and every salon would see me and Rafa dance cheek to cheek.

Rafa moved me across the beat in a rush. No stopping or waiting for me to catch my breath. I waited for the song to catch a break in the middle, and I stopped for a second; during the piano solo, I gripped his hands, wanting to just hold on to him. Rafa moved his hands away, as if he was not ready to give them to me.

I decided to take advantage of the slower tempo to take control of my feet, and I started stomping with force, letting him know I was here, with him. Rafa brought me close again and twirled me again like he wasn't ready to let me lead. Like he didn't trust me. When the bridge of the song ended, and the faster salsa started again, Rafa pulled me close and swayed me side to side, his arm on my back.

We spun again and again, making it difficult for me to see his expression. He kept going, and I wondered if we would ever stop.

Another song started, a bolero with a slower piano melody. I started to lead the way, and I felt Rafa's feet and body relax. His movements open and flexible, his feet a little bit lighter, slower. Rafa twirled me across his body, my hips moving to a serene beat. We were moving more in unison now, and although the song was all about fire, we started to slow down, our feet connecting to our hips and our shoulders until we were able to put our heads closer together. When I felt Rafa's forehead pressing on mine, I could sense something in him giving up. Like a long exhale after a big day.

I closed my eyes, taking this moment in. Was this finally our time?

"Rafa," I said softly, my heart beating fast to the dancing, the things I needed to say to him, the exhilaration of finally being here with him. "I need to tell you—"

"You're a good dancer."

Was he going to let me tell him?

"Fria?" Rafa asked, going to the bar. I nodded, and he walked away to get us ice-cold beers. Did this mean he wasn't ready? Did this mean he was still with someone else? I had to be honest, regardless. Even if he didn't reciprocate, I wanted to start trusting myself, to start listening to what I wanted.

I stood there, alone, covered in sweat, with my hair not obeying me and sticking out in all directions like it always did when I was close to the sea.

I closed my eyes and twirled alone, trying to get lost in the music as I waited for him. People were dancing in couples, and those who danced alone were singing to the lyrics of the old salsa using their bodies and hands as instruments, marveling at the change of songs and smiling whenever they got the lyrics right. When Rafa turned back and looked at me from across the room as he waited for the beers, his eyes carried a touch of sadness. I felt a pang in my chest, a rush of fear that it was too late for us.

"Vi," he said, giving me the ice-cold beer when he returned.

I put the bottle on my forehead to cool down, and then I put my hands across his neck, my beer still in my hands, the bottle dangling on his neck.

A slow song started to play. I couldn't pay attention to the lyrics or the beat, so I just moved my body from side to side.

"Vi, I'm scared that you'll leave again," Rafa said, our foreheads pressed together again, so close that I felt his warm breath on my skin.

I closed my eyes, trying to hold on to this moment. His touch. The slow music. His lips so close to mine.

"No," I said. "Let me speak first." I needed to speak first. "I know you're scared. But now I know," I said, hearing the pleading in my voice. "I know this is right. We are here for a reason." I thought about how Abuela and Gabriel had missed opportunities. How Abuela had shown me her story so I wouldn't repeat it.

"If you knew—"

Rafa looked at me without a clear expression. He swallowed and looked at the side, to the streets, and taxis, and the city not minding us. Letting us do our thing.

"Vi, I need some air."

He turned back and left a bill on the table. He started to walk away toward the street. I followed him out as he passed the stands selling hot dogs, mazorcas, and arepas. I saw him walk away, and my feet were antsy, moving up and down, wanting to chase him. Was he leaving for good? Was this it? I stood still, but my feet were eager to run.

"Rafa!" I yelled. "Rafa!" He didn't turn back. Now or never. This was the moment. The street seemed to stretch and make itself longer as I quickened my pace.

"Rafa! Rafa." I caught my breath, standing in front of him. "Rafa," I uttered his name.

He closed his eyes and took one deep breath, as if he was preparing for what was about to come.

"I know I want to be with you. It took me a while to get over the fear—but it's always been—" The sounds of the street amped up, the calls of street sellers: "Cigarillo, cerveza, bombom-bun" and the never-ending pito of the taxis. The dim lights of the never-ending via 84 our only witness.

"Rafa—" I said his name one more time.

"No, let me do this. I've been trying to be this person who is different from who I was ten years ago. I've been trying to get over my pride, to say what I'm going to do. And I told you we could be done with this, we could move on—I wanted to respect your thing."

"But Rafa, I'm not—"

"It's not right." Rafa put a hand on his head. "I want to make things different for us, but I can't force you to leave him."

"Rafa!" I yelled, wanting, needing him to hear me. "I'm not with Liam anymore." I shook my head, thinking about our breakup. How in order to be with Rafa I had to shed that past life that had meant so much to me. "I'm here with you."

A smile appeared on Rafa's face, laughing due to my yelling. I smiled, too; every word that left my mouth was coated with hope.

"Are you with Marta? Are you still . . . ? Is Marta still in the picture?"

Rafa said nothing but shook his head and took a deep breath. "After you left, I knew it was unfair to be with her and have feelings for you, so I broke things off."

My heart was beating fast. I was sick with expectation about what would happen next.

"So . . . does this mean . . . ?" Rafa asked. His hands were in his pockets, and he stood shyly away from me. After ten years of being apart, it was strange finally being able to touch and be with each other. Everything was possible, and yet it felt surreal. As if reality would crumble if we touched each other for the first time.

The sky was clear, but it felt as if clouds were parting, as if the heat was breaking, and there was no noise in the city. Just us.

"It means we're good, Rafael. It only took us ten years."

I held my breath and closed my eyes, wanting to memorize this moment forever. Rafa walked slowly toward me, the food stands in the street our only witness. He grabbed my face, pulled me close, and kissed me.

My whole body reacted to his kiss: all the hair on my arms stood up. I felt a shiver on my shoulders, the recognition that my body remembered every little thing he made me feel.

I kissed him again and again, until the night businesses started to close, and the lights in La Troja dwindled. Until our lips dried out and the caracol that had stretched and turned on itself for all these years circled around, meeting itself.

We were finally where we belonged.

CHAPTER TWENTY: CARACOL

Mamá announced that she was going to marry Dario in the restaurant. They had been together for less than six months, and Mamá, in her own way of doing things, said that this time was more than enough. She knew everything she needed to know about him and enough to know that this was different. Dario was a working-class man with three daughters he had raised a couple of blocks away from the restaurant. He loved to cook and to eat, and when Mamá was bored and restless, he stopped whatever he was doing and would tell her to hop in his old cherry-colored Chevy so they could go for a ride. Mamá would tell me excitedly that sometimes they would go to the beach and have a drink, or dance salsa in the afternoon in an empty bar, and that sometimes, they had even driven as far as Barú to see the dolphins the next morning. Mamá was her usual self, lovestruck and impulsive, but what was different was that in this new stage of her life, her love had made enough room for Dario and for me, for the house and the restaurant. She was able to lose herself in him and at the same time exist for the things that demanded her attention and that had come before him.

"I know this is right," she said when I questioned her about how little time she and Dario had been together.

Although Mamá was quick to lose her head when it came to love, I was proud of her for making a decision and trusting herself. There was an aura about her that wasn't her usual overconfident self but more assured and elegant, softer. Mamá walked the streets of Barrio Prado to the sound of her own beat.

I kept all of Abuela's things and keepsakes in my room, under a new piece of furniture I'd bought so the new wood would scare away the comejen. Abuela's diary I kept with me, often reading and rereading so I would have her with me on the nights when all I could hear was silence or the rain in April. I hadn't felt Abuela's presence in the house for quite a while, but I refused to believe her spirit was gone. She would have said goodbye. But still, sometimes I feared I would never feel her with me again.

I noticed that if I read her words, I dreamed about her often. Sometimes even about her and Gabriel, whatever would have been if they had stayed together. If we all had existed, been born, untouched and unafraid of what had happened before and in our lifetimes. Abuelo, in my dream, never crossed paths with Abuela—but when I would wake up, I would be back at home with high ceilings, the old cellar, and the sweet smell of Abuela's cakes that would never leave the house.

The house and everything in it was her spirit, our inheritance. The dark and the light. The pieces of our history that she had, with all her strength, pushed to the shore until everything was on display for us to discover.

Abuela had fought and fought—even in the afterlife, she wouldn't rest—until everything we needed to leave behind was ours to feed to the waves.

~

Anton had been introducing new dishes nonstop, and the restaurant had made room for new patrons and more nights introducing the different flavors of the various families of Barranquilla. Mamá and I were the managers, but I had grown comfortable in Abuela's role: being the host and talking to customers. I felt proud to walk behind her.

We were now more than just a family-recipe restaurant or one of the oldest restaurants in Barranquilla; we were starting to generate interest in the city, and the newspaper and the local magazines were writing about us. On Fridays, sometimes we had to turn people away, and small lines began to form after six.

"Estamos llenos," *we are at capacity*. I never expected to say we were all booked in the context of Caminito. And yet, two Fridays in a row, I told people to come back the next day. And they would, every new day a new line of people waiting to come in, wanting to eat our food.

At the house, we were preparing for Mami's wedding. Our mataratón tree that connected the house and the restaurant had blossomed pink flowers that smelled like vanilla and that crowded the floor every day for us to sweep away. The house seemed to be illuminated again, and Mamá beamed in a role that was different from the one of Abuela. She was a trusting matriarch who was way too distracted by the wedding to really do much ordering around. Mamá was an unheard-of kind of matriarch, the kind that delegated plenty to us.

Mamá wanted lirios for the wedding and flores blancas but no cilantro in the bouquet. She wanted new traditions, she explained, mixed in with the old. This was a new marriage, and with it there needed to come new things. But she also wanted a bolero band that played the songs of Carlos Gardel and Pedro Infante that she'd grown up with and that she said would teach a thing or two to us young ones about real music.

In terms of food, she wanted to make the black wedding cake that needed to be refrigerated for five days—so we needed to make sure that there was enough space in the fridge—and she needed fresh Peruvian food made by Rocío's neighbor.

Black cake was traditionally served at weddings in our family. It was a black fruitcake that needed refrigeration for five days in order for the rum to set in the cake, giving depth to the sweetness of the cake. We ordered fresh ceviches and pulpo tiraditos with enough lemon juice and cilantro to feed an army. Rocío made enough baba ghanoush and quibes with Anton to feed the whole Barrio Prado and its adjacent neighbors.

We honored Bisabuela and Tatarabuela by making the coca bread with a traditional rested dough and with pimentones, tomatoes, and onions that were crisped in the oven to perfection with plenty of olive oil.

Mamá wore flowers in her hair and a blue wedding dress, Abuela's favorite color, and we performed the ceremony in Abuela's spot, where she used to sit to rest her swollen feet and supervise everyone enjoying their food. There was only a priest and me standing next to Mamá as her maid of honor.

At the end of the ceremony, when the cura had said the words "Los pronuncio marido y mujer," Mamá kissed Dario so fast you'd think they were in a hurry to spend their lives together. I clapped, feeling Mami's joy, all that it had taken for her to finally arrive at this moment. I caught eyes with Rafa, who smiled at me from the audience. When we locked eyes, I still couldn't believe that we were together. That we had finally, finally gotten it right.

The guests started whispering. There was a smell making its rounds through the air.

"It smells like honey," Rocío said, sniffing and sniffing. Her little gold party purse dangling across her legs.

"No, Mamá," Sabina said. "It smells like vanilla. Is it your perfume, García?"

"No, it smells like roses," García said, sniffing like her mother. Sabina put an arm over her face, ashamed of her mother's and sister's loud voices.

"It does smell like something sweet, verdá?" Mamá asked, newly married and having just kissed her new groom. We all looked at the chatting guests.

"It smells like Abuela's wedding cakes," I said and caught another glance of Rafael. I couldn't stop looking at him in the audience. He looked handsome in his white shirt.

We went outside with our fists filled with rice and waited for the newlyweds, standing in a line so we could shower them in the bendiciones that the lluvia de arroz would bring. The rito was brief because we were going inside right after to eat and drink at the wedding. There were no other places to gather the guests, no other places to cut the cake. Just the restaurant that awaited us, deeply cleaned and perfumed with new flowers that covered the white walls and tables.

Mamá and Dario got married during sundown hours, when the pink and blue lights filled the sunny skies of the city and the brisa started to brush our faces as we showered them in rice.

Rafa stood on his corner. I heard the vecinas and Rocío gossiping about him: "That beautiful porte. Like an old Hollywood star," they would say. "The son of a plomero but so elegant." "He's a doctor, verdad?" I directed a glance at them to make sure they knew they were being heard. I walked to Rafa, one step in front of the other, and he had eyes only for me. Rafa was immune to gossip, and if he heard, he pretended he didn't.

Doña Rocío, who was standing in front of us, was too distracted by us to throw rice at the newlyweds. She, who perhaps lost faith in me returning and in him forgiving me, couldn't stop smiling at us and whispering with the vecinas.

We kissed on the lips, and although we had been together for a while now, his kiss felt new.

"Doña Rocío can't stop pointing at me." Rafa laughed. We were standing under a tree, and we got a good view of the whole barrio. Everyone was so happy to celebrate Mamá—to see her finally so happy and secure in a love that felt like it fitted her rather than her having to squeeze herself into something that would never give her room to breathe.

"Vi, Vi, Vi." I heard Mamá call me. I looked at Rafa and kissed him again. "Un minuto," I said, walking toward Mami. She was in the middle of the crowd, smiling like I never had seen her do before. With abandon, without fear of waiting for the other shoe to drop. I went to her and hugged her, taking refuge in her smell of cloves and vanilla, her warm touch. It felt good to embrace her, to absorb some of the joy that Mamá's happy ending was gifting her. She kissed my hair and whispered in my ear. In her voice, I could hear the voices of Abuela and Bisabuela and the women behind her who spoke Mallorquí and not a lick of Spanish. The voices of my ancestors contained in a whisper.

And she said to me, her warm breath in my ear: "I'm not scared, mija, for once I feel free."

~

The older guests left the party after eating and drinking every last crumb and last drop of alcohol we had to offer, and for the first time since the restaurant was opened, we left the place without lifting a single dirty plate or cup. The mess was going to wait for us the next day, when Mamá and Dario drove away to Cartagena to spend a lazy honeymoon by the historical fortress and the beach.

Anton, las mellas, their friends, and Rafael and I closed the restaurant and went to the beach to have a couple of drinks after the wedding and get our toes wet in the cold water. Tonight, it was a luna llena, and the moonlight bathed the beach in a white light.

"To the newlyweds," Anton said, lifting his shot glass. He was barefoot and had a couple of buttons open on his shirt. We had been cooking for an entire week for the wedding, and he'd directed the whole operation without complaining once. Now he said that his feet were swollen and his hands were red from all the minor burns he had suffered in the kitchen. He hadn't slept all week, but he looked content, lying on the chair and drinking, knowing that Mamá was the happiest she had ever been, and he had been a part of that.

We lifted our glasses, slow and heavy from a night of feasting.

I felt Anton's eyes on me. His soft smile that was telling me that in reality, he wanted to make a toast for me, for us, for our friendship, and for the restaurant. For my return.

What had begun, before we had even existed, for Abuela.

Las mellas were able to hook their phones to one of the cars of their boyfriends, and music started coming out of the speakers. At first, they insisted on putting on the radio, but Anton went to the car and changed the music to Willie Colón and started dancing alone, hugging the bottle of aguardiente and twirling on naked feet.

"What if there's glass on the beach?" I asked Rafa, who wanted me to leave Anton alone to dance without his shoes on. "Or other pieces of trash. He could cut himself, he could get sick, there's so much that could happen. I'm going to go over there," I said, making the move to stand up.

"Vi, I promise that if he cuts himself, I'll fix him." Rafa extended his arm to invite me to dance. He helped me up, and we started moving to the music. "I can always cure him if there's alcohol around."

He laughed at my face of horror and lifted one of his thick eyebrows to show me he was joking. In the next twirl, Rafa grabbed my waist tighter and brought me closer to him. I closed my eyes, taking this moment in.

Rafa whispered in my ear; his breath was hot and warm. In the background, the waves were crashing with a vengeance against the shore.

"I have a confession to make," he said in such a serious tone it made me stop dancing. My heart dropped to my stomach.

"Qué?" I asked quickly.

Rafa laughed, moving from side to side, inviting me to move with him. "No, no, nothing bad."

I breathed a little easier and put my hands on the back of his neck.

"I always knew it was you and me, even through the years, the doubts. It was us. It was always us."

I wrapped my hands in his curls, and I said his name again and again. Did I always know? I wasn't sure, and I knew now that my other life in the States was also part of me and my story. But I was also sure that the caracol had brought us here, finally.

"Rafael." His name melted on my lips like butter: Rafael, Rafael, Rafael. We kissed, our lips locked in a spell fueled by the big white moon, the breeze, and the salt.

~

We woke up at dawn to a pink-and-warm-yellow sky. My skin felt sticky from sweat. My dress was covered in sand, and my neck hurt from sleeping on top of Rafa's chest. I looked around; everyone else was sleeping, and las mellas had spent the night in the back seat of a car. The empty bottles and the butts of cigarettes were scattered on the sand.

Rafa slept heavily next to me, his breath rising up and down in his chest.

I woke him up.

"Rafa, Rafa," I said and shook his chest. Loud enough so he could hear me but low enough so I wouldn't wake up anyone else.

"Rafa?" Again.

He opened his eyes slowly, looking disoriented.

"What's happening, mi amor?" He rubbed his eyes and sat up. Mi amor, I took those words in. What he used to call me when we were teenagers.

I spoke quietly: "Everyone is going to wake up soon. It's too hot," I said, tasting the salt in my mouth and the dryness in my throat.

Rafa put a hand on my knee. His touch felt safe. This was the beach where Rafa and I had been the night of his high school graduation. The night before Abuela decided that she needed to send me away to the States. This was also the beach where Abuela and Gabriel had spent their afternoon after heavy lunches of mojarra and patacones with coconut rice and cocktails. This was the beach of stops and starts. I felt Rafa's touch and the wind caressing my face, the wind generating force so it could go back to the origin and then blow stronger.

If Abuela was right and time was a caracol, all our past mistakes were not a punishment but an opportunity—everything that had delayed our way to this beach had happened for a reason. Time comes and goes, it passes and it comes back, and then it repeats the same cycle, everything growing and connecting to a center where our ancestors are in front of us and our future stands behind us.

This was the beach we had decided to go to after Mamá had gotten her second chance.

"I needed you to see this," I said, pointing to the changing colors of the early morning sky.

Rafa said nothing; he put his hands on my back and pulled me close to him. I rested my head on his chest, and he wrapped his arms around me, kissing my wild curls.

"Estamos aquí," I said, *here we are*. I closed my eyes, trying to remember this moment when everything began again.

I felt the weight of familiar hands on my shoulders; they were as warm as I remembered them. My first instinct was to be scared, but I needed to be quiet. This beach that belonged to her and Gabriel smelled of her: of sweet cinnamon and cloves and Chanel No. 5, a hint somewhere of garlic and oil—the smell of her kitchen that would never leave her. I wanted to look back, but something kept my head looking forward.

I knew that this moment wouldn't come again, that perhaps this was the last time that I would ever feel her spirit. Rafa sat next to me, unaware of what was happening.

"Abuela," I whispered, letting myself throw her name on the wind, on what had been her beach. "You can let go."

"Qué pasa?" Rafa asked what was happening, his face turning to look at me.

I knew my cheeks were wet; my tongue was tasting the salt. And yet, I couldn't say it. I shook my head, feeling her there still.

"Nada, mi amor." I smiled, telling him it was nothing. I brushed his knee, grateful that at last I could touch him whenever. That he was here with me when I was saying goodbye to her spirit.

I buried my toes in the warm sand, and in the second wave of the breeze, as Rafa told memories of our first time on the beach, Abuela whispered in my ear.

"Amor antes que miedo," Abuela whispered in my ear: *love over fear*. The beach was silent except for the crashing of the waves; the relentless sun burned my curled toes buried in the sand.

"Sí," I told the wind, taking the whole message in. When I listened to myself, everything fell into place. Rafa turned to look at me. Confused by the way I was talking.

A deep sadness washed over me. Abuela was letting go, and I knew that this was it. I held back tears—this was exciting. She was finally able to let go.

"Qué pasa, mi amor?" Rafa said, with concern in his eyes.

"Nada," I said, whipping my tears with the back of my hand. A release of all the grief I had for Abuela, turning into joy. I grabbed his hand and kissed it, feeling the warmth of his touch. The gift of finally being here with him. In return, he looked at me with as much love and devotion as he had that first day, more than thirteen years ago.

Love over fear were Abuela's final words. Those words were the ones that finally released all the burdens of Abuela and all her ancestors. The burdens that had tied them to a city, to a restaurant that demanded so much of them—the burdens of a life that was built around survival and not desire.

Abuela said her final goodbye at the beach, and with that Doña Emilia, in the afterlife, released all her fear.

BOOK CLUB QUESTIONS

The Caribbean coast of Colombia is a place known for its heat. It's sunny all year round, and tropical flowers adorn every street. To make an homage to the eternal summer of Barranquilla, may we suggest a Caminito-inspired spread?

You can serve a tortilla española with fresh bread, Catalan coca bread (dough, pimentos, paprika, onions), and a beautiful pineapple rum inverted cake.

1. Family expectations are central to the family drama in this novel. How did you think the family expectations were holding Vi back? What about Abuela?
2. The novel starts with a marriage proposal when Vi is only eighteen. Did Vi's age at the time of the proposal surprise you? Did you want her to say yes?
3. Vi leaves home when she's only eighteen and moves to the US, starting a life with Liam. Do you think she's happy there?
4. Abuela dies without being able to say goodbye in person. Has that happened to you or anyone you know? Were you able to relate to Vi's grief?
5. Who is your favorite character in Barranquilla, and why?
6. What did you think of Abuela's decision to leave Caminito to Vi? Did you think Anton or Paula deserved it more?

7. Abuela's ghost is present in Caminito. Would you wish to be reunited with family members after they pass? What is something you wish you could tell them?
8. Vi reunites with Rafa, her first love, when she returns to Barranquilla. She says no one had ever said her name like he did. Do you think one should go with the love that is more passionate and arresting or the love that is calmer and more reliable?
9. Caminito will soon be in foreclosure if they don't pay the debt. How did you feel about this? Do you think sometimes it's better to let go?
10. Food and memory are part of Caminito and the Sanogueras' family life. What were some of your favorite recipes in the book? Is food important in your family?
11. What do you think of Vi and Paula's relationship at the end? Do you think they'll get closer?
12. What do you think of Vi ultimately leaving Liam and New York City? Do you think she's making a mistake?
13. At the end of the book, Vi finally takes in the lesson of learning to listen to herself. Have you incorporated this lesson into your life? If yes, what happened to you that made you see the importance of listening to your voice?
14. Where do you see Vi and the Sanogueras in the future? What do you think is next for them?

ACKNOWLEDGMENTS

I was mostly raised by women. Every day after school, I'd come home, and my bisabuela, Carmen Jordi, and abuela, Juana Margarita Vélez Angulo, were the ones who would receive me at home and teach me everything I know about the world.

Abuela, the most brilliant woman I know, despite not finishing school, was well versed in sciences, history, and—plot twist!—ghost stories. She was the one that always told me, when life got hard, that I needed to carve my place in the world through writing. This book is as much hers as it is mine.

It was the women in my life that gave me access to all the delicious food that lives in the pages of this book: the mouthwatering paella, the pineapple upside-down cake, the tortilla Española, and the always drama-inducing tamales (yes, it really does take a couple of days to get them right!). It was also they who taught me the power of creating lives that were different from what was expected of us—love over fear. I come from a long line of immigrant women, first-generation college graduates, and business owners. It is your fearlessness that made me realize that I should try anyway, despite being afraid.

Thank you to Mamá, who gave me the love for books and the courage to go after what I want in life. Thank you, Tía María Claudia, for your unconditional love. Tías queridas Luz Estela y Carmen, you're both examples of perseverance and the power of love. To mis primos and tío, this story also belongs to you. Thank you, Papá and Brother, for your love and support. Your strength and faith inspire me every day. Gracias, Lucy Medina, for your joy and love over the years.

Wendy, Michael, and Ben, thank you for all the board games, meals, and laughs you provided me while writing this story. Love you all. Thank you, Chris, for lending me your childhood room to write the first half of this novel. Thank you, Annabel Thomas, for the inspiration.

Thank you to everyone at Amazon Publishing for believing in and championing this book. Melissa Valentine, thank you for loving this story from the start and for your invaluable feedback and honesty. Tiffany Yates Martin: your intricate notes and your attention to detail made this story so much more powerful. Thank you. To the editorial team: Kyra Wojdyla, Stephanie Chou, Jenna Justice, thank you for your precision and care. Thank you Raxenne Maniquiz, Rachel Gul, and everyone at Amazon Publishing for making this book possible.

Amanda Orozco, truly, words are not enough. I couldn't have asked for a kinder and more supportive advocate. Working together is a joy, and I so appreciate your sharp editorial notes, your warmth and creativity. I'm truly so lucky to have you in my corner. Carolina Beltran: I'm so excited to get to work together! Thank you for taking a chance on me and my story—it means the world. Working with you and Amanda is a dream come true.

Thank you to all the organizations that have championed my writing and that helped this immigrant writer find her community when she arrived in NYC: Vermont Studio Center, Caldera Arts Center, New Orleans Writers' Residency, Kweli, and NYFA's Immigrant Artist Mentoring Program. You make the world a better place.

Thank you also to my Catapult novel cohort, and to our teacher, Ingrid Rojas Contreras. I'm so lucky that the pandemic year brought us together.

To my writing friends: Connie, Di, Kimberly, Charlene, Samira, and Victoria. Your talent inspires me every day—I hope I get to keep telling stories alongside you.

To my lifelong friends: Juliana, Lina, Adriana, Amal, Marc, Carlos, and Stan. Gracias por estar. Despite the distance, I'm so lucky for the messages, the love, and the jokes that never get old.

To Andrew, love of my life. Thank you for being there for this book since day one. You read draft after draft of this story, despite all the messy iterations, all the times I doubted what this book could be. You were always there by my side, believing in my words when I didn't have the strength. Gus, our sweet dog, and you are my home.

Finally, thank you, dear reader, for taking a chance on a debut book. It is you that keeps the magic of books alive.

ABOUT THE AUTHOR

Photo © 2023 Andrew Thomas

María Alejandra Barrios Vélez is a writer born in Barranquilla, Colombia. She has an MA in creative writing from the University of Manchester and lives in Brooklyn with her husband and scruffy dog, Gus.

She was the 2020 SmokeLong Flash Fiction Fellow, and her stories have been published in *Shenandoah Literary, Vol. 1 Brooklyn, El Malpensante, Fractured Lit, SmokeLong Quarterly, The Offing,* and more. Her work has been supported by organizations such as Vermont Studio Center, Kweli, Caldera Arts, and the New Orleans Writers' Residency.

The Waves Take You Home is María's debut, inspired by the resilience and strength of the women in her family and the Caribbean city she spent most of her life in.